The Best from
Fantasy
and
Science Fiction

23rd Series

The Best from

Fantasy

and

Science Fiction

23rd Series

Edited by

EDWARD L. FERMAN

DOUBLEDAY & COMPANY, INC.

GARDEN CITY, NEW YORK

1980

The editor hereby makes grateful acknowledgment to the following authors and authors' representatives for giving permission to reprint the material in this volume:

Damon Knight for "I See You"
Virginia Kidd for "The Detweiler Boy" by Tom Reamy
Curtis Brown Ltd. for "Zorphwar!" by Stan Dryer and "Brother Hart" by Jane Yolen
Edward Bryant for "Stone"
Scott Meredith Literary Agency for "Nina" by Robert Bloch
Joanna Russ for "In Defense of Criticism"
Isaac Asimov for "Clone, Clone of My Own"
John Varley for "In the Hall of the Martian Kings"
Steven Utley for "Upstart"
Lee Killough for "A House Divided"
Baird Searles for "Multiples"; Copyright © 1980 by Baird Searles
Thomas M. Disch for "The Man Who Had No Idea"
Robert F. Young for "Project Hi-Rise"
Samuel R. Delany for "Prismatica"

ISBN: 0-385-15225-6
Library of Congress Catalog Card Number 79-7685
Copyright © 1976, 1977, 1978, 1979, 1980 by Mercury Press, Inc.

Dedication

For my mother

CONTENTS

INTRODUCTION

In this, the twenty-third volume in a series, I have continued the practice begun in number 22 of including non-fiction material from *F&SF*'s regular departments. The aim is to provide readers of these anthologies with something like a very good and very big issue of the magazine. Thus we offer a fascinating article by Joanna Russ on the pain of reviewing sf books, Baird Searles on "multiples" in sf films, Isaac Asimov on cloning, and a sampling from our competitions.

The stories in this book cover the period from our November 1976 issue through the middle of 1979, a period of great growth in the science fiction field, at least in terms of numbers. If you're the sort who likes to sniff the air for trends, you may have detected a smell of old attics, as much sf seemed to swing back to traditional, even old-fashioned themes and forms. Compare *2001* to *Star Wars*.

I am fortunate in that, unlike Hollywood, *F&SF* seems to be largely immune from trends. The magazine has a reputation for offering variety, and to uphold that image, it seems to me that it must carefully avoid trends and formulas in an effort to publish a balance of different types of fantasy and sf. And so we continue to look for good writing and fresh ideas and entertaining narratives, and once those general criteria are satisfied, we take on whatever seems to be pleasing our writers at the time. That's the best way I know of pleasing our readers.

—*Edward L. Ferman*

The Best from
Fantasy
and
Science Fiction

23rd Series

"I See You" is the first new Damon Knight story in many years; it was the feature story in *F&SF*'s special Damon Knight issue (November 1976). As might be expected, it is a totally fresh piece of work and it shines with quality. Damon says of it: "You may think it is a short story, but it is really a novel on the plan of *A for Anything* and *Hell's Pavement,* only much compressed."

I See You

by DAMON KNIGHT

You are five, hiding in a place only you know. You are covered with bark dust, scratched by twigs, sweaty and hot. A wind sighs in the aspen leaves. A faint steady hiss comes from the viewer you hold in your hands; then a voice: "Lorie, I see you—under the barn, eating an apple!" A silence. "Lorie, come on out, I see you." Another voice. "That's right, she's in there." After a moment, sulkily: "Oh, okay."

You squirm around, raising the viewer to aim it down the hill. As you turn the knob with your thumb, the bright image races toward you, trees hurling themselves into red darkness and vanishing, then the houses in the compound, and now you see Bruce standing beside the corral, looking into his viewer, slowly turning. His back is to you; you know you are safe, and you sit up. A jay passes with a whir of wings, settles on a branch. With your own eyes now you can see Bruce, only a dot of blue beyond the gray shake walls of the houses. In the viewer, he is turning toward you, and you duck again. Another voice: "Children, come in and get washed for dinner now." "Aw, Aunt Ellie!" "Mom, we're playing hide and seek. Can't we just stay fifteen minutes more?" "Please, Aunt Ellie!" "No, come on in now—

you'll have plenty of time after dinner." And Bruce: "Aw, okay. All out's in free." And once more they have not found you; your secret place is yours alone.

Call him Smith. He was the president of a company that bore his name and which held more than a hundred patents in the scientific instrument field. He was sixty, a widower. His only daughter and her husband had been killed in a plane crash in 1978. He had a partner who handled the business operations now; Smith spent most of his time in his own lab. In the spring of 1990 he was working on an image-intensification device that was puzzling because it was too good. He had it on his bench now, aimed at a deep shadow box across the room; at the back of the box was a card ruled with black, green, red and blue lines. The only source of illumination was a single ten-watt bulb hung behind the shadow box; the light reflected from the card did not even register on his meter, and yet the image in the screen of his device was sharp and bright. When he varied the inputs to the components in a certain way, the bright image vanished and was replaced by shadows, like the ghost of another image. He had monitored every television channel, had shielded the device against radio frequencies, and the ghosts remained. Increasing the illumination did not make them clearer. They were vaguely rectilinear shapes without any coherent pattern. Occasionally a moving blur traveled slowly across them.

Smith made a disgusted sound. He opened the clamps that held the device and picked it up, reaching for the power switch with his other hand. He never touched it. As he moved the device, the ghost images had shifted; they were dancing now with the faint movements of his hand. Smith stared at them without breathing for a moment. Holding the cord, he turned slowly. The ghost images whirled, vanished, reappeared. He turned the other way; they whirled back.

Smith set the device down on the bench with care. His hands were shaking. He had had the thing clamped down on the bench all the time until now. "Christ almighty, how dumb can one man get?" he asked the empty room.

You are six, almost seven, and you are being allowed to use the big viewer for the first time. You are perched on a cushion in the leather chair at the console; your brother, who has been showing you the controls with a bored and superior air, has just left the room, saying, "All right, if you know so much, do it yourself."

In fact, the controls on this machine are unfamiliar; the little viewers you have used all your life have only one knob, for nearer or farther—to move up/down, or left/right, you just point the viewer where you want to see. This machine has dials and little windows with numbers in them, and switches and pushbuttons, most of which you don't understand, but you know they are for special purposes and don't matter. The main control is a metal rod, right in front of you, with a gray plastic knob on the top. The knob is dull from years of handling; it feels warm and a little greasy in your hand. The console has a funny electric smell, but the big screen, taller than you are, is silent and dark. You can feel your heart beating against your breastbone. You grip the knob harder, push it forward just a little. The screen lights, and you are drifting across the next room as if on huge silent wheels, chairs and end tables turning into reddish silhouettes that shrink, twist and disappear as you pass through them, and for a moment you feel dizzy because when you notice the red numbers jumping in the console to your left, it is as if the whole house were passing massively and vertiginously through itself; then you are floating out the window with the same slow and steady motion, on across the sunlit pasture where two saddle horses stand with their heads up, sniffing the wind; then a stubbled field, dropping away; and now, below you, the co-op road shines like a silver-gray stream. You press the knob down to get closer, and drop with a giddy swoop; now you are rushing along the road, overtaking and passing a yellow truck, turning the knob to steer. At first you blunder into the dark trees on either side, and once the earth surges up over you in a chaos of writhing red shapes, but now you are learning, and you soar down past the crossroads, up the farther hill, and now, now you are on the big road, flying eastward, passing all the cars, rushing toward the great world where you long to be.

It took Smith six weeks to increase the efficiency of the image intensifier enough to bring up the ghost pictures clearly. When he succeeded, the image on the screen was instantly recognizable. It was a view of Jack McCranie's office; the picture was still dim, but sharp enough that Smith could see the expression on Jack's face. He was leaning back in his chair, hands behind his head. Beside him stood

Peg Spatola in a purple dress, with her hand on an open folder. She was talking, and McCranie was listening. That was wrong, because Peg was not supposed to be back from Cleveland until next week.

Smith reached for the phone and punched McCranie's number.

"Yes, Tom?"

"Jack, is Peg in there?"

"Why, no—she's in Cleveland, Tom."

"Oh, yes."

McCranie sounded puzzled. "Is anything the matter?" In the screen, he had swiveled his chair and was talking to Peg, gesturing with short, choppy motions of his arm.

"No, nothing," said Smith. "That's all right, Jack, thank you." He broke the connection. After a moment he turned to the breadboard controls of the device and changed one setting slightly. In the screen, Peg turned and walked backward out of the office. When he turned the knob the other way, she repeated these actions in reverse. Smith tinkered with the other controls until he got a view of the calendar on Jack's desk. It was Friday, June 15—last week.

Smith locked up the device and all his notes, went home and spent the rest of the day thinking.

By the end of July he had refined and miniaturized the device and had extended its sensitivity range into the infrared. He spent most of August, when he should have been on vacation, trying various methods of detecting sound through the device. By focusing on the interior of a speaker's larynx and using infrared, he was able to convert the visible vibrations of the vocal cords into sound of fair quality, but that did not satisfy him. He worked for a while on vibrations picked up from panes of glass in windows and on framed pictures, and he experimented briefly with the diaphragms in speaker systems, intercoms and telephones. He kept on into October without stopping and finally achieved a system that would give tinny but recognizable sound from any vibrating surface—a wall, a floor, even the speaker's own cheek or forehead.

He redesigned the whole device, built a prototype and tested it, tore it down, redesigned, built another. It was Christmas before he was done. Once more he locked up the device and all his plans, drawings and notes.

At home he spent the holidays experimenting with commercial adhesives in various strengths. He applied these to coated paper, let them dry, and cut the paper into rectangles. He numbered these rectangles, pasted them onto letter envelopes, some of which he stacked loose; others he bundled together and secured with rubber bands. He opened the stacks and bundles and examined them at regular intervals. Some of the labels curled up and detached themselves after twenty-six hours without leaving any conspicuous trace. He made up another batch of these, typed his home address on six of them. On each of six envelopes he typed his office address, then covered it with one of the labels. He stamped the envelopes and dropped them into a mailbox. All six, minus their labels, were delivered to the office three days later.

Just after New Year's, he told his partner that he wanted to sell out and retire. They discussed it in general terms.

Using an assumed name and a post office box number which was not his, Smith wrote to a commission agent in Boston with whom he had never had any previous dealings. He mailed the letter, with the agent's address covered by one of his labels on which he had typed a fictitious address. The label detached itself in transit; the letter was delivered. When the agent replied, Smith was watching and read the letter as a secretary typed it. The agent followed his instruction to mail his reply in an envelope without return address. The owner of the post office box turned it in marked "not here"; it went to the dead-letter office and was returned in due time, but meanwhile Smith had acknowledged the letter and had mailed, in the same way, a large amount of cash. In subsequent letters he instructed the agent to take bids for components, plans for which he enclosed, from electronics manufacturers, for plastic casings from another, and for assembly and shipping from still another company. Through a second commission agent in New York, to whom he wrote in the same way, he contracted for ten thousand copies of an instruction booklet in four colors.

Late in February he bought a house and an electronics dealership in a small town in the Adirondacks. In March he signed over his interest in the company to his partner, cleaned out his lab and left. He sold his co-op apartment in Manhattan and his summer house in Connecticut, moved to his new home and became anonymous.

You are thirteen, chasing a fox with the big kids for the first time. They have put you in the north field, the worst place, but you know better than to leave it.

"He's in the glen."

"I see him; he's in the brook, going upstream."

You turn the viewer, racing forward through dappled shade, a brilliance of leaves: there is the glen, and now you see the fox, trotting through the shallows, blossoms of bright water at its feet.

"Ken and Nell, you come down ahead of him by the springhouse. Wanda, you and Tim and Jean stay where you are. Everybody else come upstream, but stay back till I tell you."

That's Leigh, the oldest. You turn the viewer, catch a glimpse of Bobby running downhill through the woods, his long hair flying. Then back to the glen: the fox is gone.

"He's heading up past the corncrib!"

"Okay, keep spread out on both sides, everybody. Jim, can you and Edie head him off before he gets to the woods?"

"We'll try. There he is!"

And the chase is going away from you, as you knew it would, but soon you will be older, as old as Nell and Jim; then you will be in the middle of things, and your life will begin.

By trial and error, Smith has found the settings for Dallas, November 22, 1963: Dealey Plaza, 12:25 P.M. He sees the Presidential motorcade making the turn onto Elm Street. Kennedy slumps forward, raising his hands to his throat. Smith presses a button to hold the moment in time. He scans behind the motorcade, finds the sixth floor of the Book Depository Building, finds the window. There is no one behind the barricade of cartons; the room is empty. He scans the nearby rooms, finds nothing. He tries the floor below. At an open window a man kneels, holding a high-powered rifle. Smith photographs him. He returns to the motorcade, watches as the second shot strikes the President. He freezes time again, scans the surrounding buildings, finds a second marksman on a roof, photographs him. Back to the motorcade. A third and fourth shot, the last blowing off the side of the President's head. Smith freezes the action again, finds two gunmen on the grassy knoll, one aiming across the top of a station wagon, one kneeling in the shrubbery. He photographs them. He turns off the power, sits for a moment, then goes to the washroom, kneels beside the toilet and vomits.

The viewer is your babysitter, your television, your telephone (the telephone lines are still up, but they are used only as signaling devices; when you know that somebody wants to talk to you, you focus your viewer on him), your library, your school. Before puberty you watch other people having sex, but even then your curiosity is easily satisfied; after an older cousin initiates you at fourteen, you are much more interested in doing it yourself. The co-op teacher monitors your studies, sometimes makes suggestions, but more and more, as you grow older, leaves you to your own devices. You are intensely interested in African prehistory, in the European theater, and in the ant-civilization of Epsilon Eridani IV. Soon you will have to choose.

New York Harbor, November 4, 1872—a cold, blustery day. A two-masted ship rides at anchor; on her stern is lettered: *Mary Celeste*. Smith advances the time control. A flicker of darkness, light again, and the ship is gone. He turns back again until he finds it standing out under light canvas past Sandy Hook. Manipulating time and space controls at once, he follows it eastward through a flickering of storm and sun—loses it, finds it again, counting days as he goes. The farther eastward, the more he has to tilt the device downward, while the image of the ship tilts correspondingly away from him. Because of the angle, he can no longer keep the ship in view from a distance but must track it closely. November 21 and 22, violent storms: the ship is dashed upward by waves, falls again, visible only intermittently; it takes him five hours to pass through two days of real time. The 23rd is calmer, but on the 24th another storm blows up. Smith rubs his eyes, loses the ship, finds it again after a ten-minute search.

The gale blows itself out on the morning of the 26th. The sun is bright, the sea almost dead calm. Smith is able to catch glimpses of figures on deck, tilted above dark cross-sections of the hull. A sailor is splicing a rope in the stern, two others lowering a triangular sail between the foremast and the bowsprit, and a fourth is at the helm. A little group stands leaning on the starboard rail; one of them is a woman. The next glimpse is that of a running figure who advances into the screen and disappears. Now the men are lowering a boat over the side; the rail has been removed and lies on the deck. The men drop into the boat and row away. He hears them shouting to each other but cannot make out the words.

Smith turns to the ship again: the deck is empty. He dips below to look at the hold, filled with casks, then the cabin, then the forecastle.

There is no sign of anything wrong—no explosion, no fire, no trace of violence. When he looks up again, he sees the sails flapping, then bellying out full. The sea is rising. He looks for the boat, but now too much time has passed and he cannot find it. He returns to the ship and now reverses the time control, tracks it backward until the men are again in their places on deck. He looks again at the group standing at the rail; now he sees that the woman has a child in her arms. The child struggles, drops over the rail. Smith hears the woman shriek. In a moment she too is over the rail and falling into the sea.

He watches the men running, sees them launch the boat. As they pull away, he is able to keep the focus near enough to see and hear them. One calls, "My God, who's at the helm?" Another, a bearded man with a face gone tallow-pale, replies, "Never mind—row!" They are staring down into the sea. After a moment one looks up, then another. The *Mary Celeste,* with three of the four sails on her foremast set, is gliding away, slowly, now faster; now she is gone.

Smith does not run through the scene again to watch the child and her mother drown, but others do.

The production model was ready for shipping in September. It was a simplified version of the prototype, with only two controls, one for space, one for time. The range of the device was limited to one thousand miles. Nowhere on the casing of the device or in the instruction booklet was a patent number or a pending patent mentioned. Smith had called the device Ozo, perhaps because he thought it sounded vaguely Japanese. The booklet described the device as a distant viewer and gave clear, simple instructions for its use. One sentence read cryptically: "Keep Time Control set at zero." It was like "Wet Paint—Do Not Touch."

During the week of September 23, seven thousand Ozos were shipped to domestic and Canadian addresses supplied by Smith: five hundred to electronics manufacturers and suppliers, six thousand, thirty to a carton, marked "On Consignment," to TV outlets in major cities, and the rest to private citizens chosen at random. The instruction booklets were in sealed envelopes packed with each device. Three thousand more went to Europe, South and Central America, and the Middle East.

A few of the outlets which received the cartons opened them the same day, tried the devices out, and put them on sale at prices rang-

ing from $49.95 to $125. By the following day the word was beginning to spread, and by the close of business on the third day every
store was sold out. Most people who got them, either through the
mail or by purchase, used them to spy on their neighbors and on
people in hotels.

In a house in Cleveland, a man watches his brother-in-law in the
next room, who is watching his wife getting out of a taxi. She goes
into the lobby of an apartment building. The husband watches as she
gets into the elevator, rides to the fourth floor. She rings the bell beside the door marked 410. The door opens; a dark-haired man takes
her in his arms; they kiss.

The brother-in-law meets him in the hall. "Don't do it, Charlie."

"Get out of my way."

"I'm not going to get out of your way, and I tell you, don't do it.
Not now and not later."

"Why the hell shouldn't I?"

"Because if you do I'll kill you. If you want a divorce, OK, get a
divorce. But don't lay a hand on her or I'll find you the farthest place
you can go."

Smith got his consignment of Ozos early in the week, took one
home and left it to his store manager to put a price on the rest. He
did not bother to use the production model but began at once to
build another prototype. It had controls calibrated to one-hundredth
of a second and one millimeter, and a timer that would allow him to
stop a scene, or advance or regress it at any desired rate. He ordered
some clockwork from an astronomical supply house.

A high-ranking officer in Army Intelligence, watching the first
demonstration of the Ozo in the Pentagon, exclaimed, "My God,
with this we could dismantle half the establishment—all we've got to
do is launch interceptors when we see them push the button."

"It's a good thing Senator Burkhart can't hear you say that," said
another officer. But by the next afternoon everybody had heard it.

A Baptist minister in Louisville led the first mob against an Ozo
assembly plant. A month later, while civil and criminal suits against
all the rioters were still pending, tapes showing each one of them in

compromising or ludicrous activities were widely distributed in the area.

The commission agents who had handled the orders for the first Ozos were found out and had to leave town. Factories were fire-bombed, but others took their place.

The first Ozo was smuggled into the Soviet Union from West Germany by Katerina Belov, a member of a dissident group in Moscow, who used it to document illegal government actions. The device was seized on December 13 by the KGB; Belov and two other members of the group were arrested, imprisoned and tortured. By that time over forty other Ozos were in the hands of dissidents.

You are watching an old movie, *Bob and Ted and Carol and Alice*. The humor seems infantile and unimaginative to you; you are not interested in the actresses' occasional seminudity. What strikes you as hilarious is the coyness, the sidelong glances, smiles, grimaces hinting at things that will never be shown on the screen. You realize that these people have never seen anyone but their most intimate friends without clothing, have never seen any adult shit or piss, and would be embarrassed or disgusted if they did. Why did children say "pee-pee" and "poo-poo," and then giggle? You have read scholarly books about taboos on "bodily functions," but why was shitting worse than sneezing?

Cora Zickwolfe, who lived in a remote rural area of Arizona and whose husband commuted to Tucson, arranged with her nearest neighbor, Phyllis Mell, for each of them to keep an Ozo focused on the bulletin board in the other's kitchen. On the bulletin board was a note that said "OK." If there was any trouble and she couldn't get to the phone, she would take down the note, or if she had time, write another.

In April 1992, about the time her husband usually got home, an intruder broke into the house and seized Mrs. Zickwolfe before she had time to get to the bulletin board. He dragged her into the bedroom and forced her to disrobe. The state troopers got there in fifteen minutes, and Cora never spoke to her friend Phyllis again.

Between 1992 and 2002 more than six hundred improvements and supplements to the Ozo were recorded. The most important of these

was the power system created by focusing the Ozo at a narrow aperture on the interior of the Sun. Others included the system of satellite slave units in stationary orbits and a computerized tracer device which would keep the Ozo focused on any subject.

Using the tracer, an entomologist in Mexico City is following the ancestral line of a honey bee. The images bloom and expire, ten every second: the tracer is following each queen back to the egg, then the egg to the queen that laid it, then that queen to the egg. Tens of thousands of generations have passed; in two thousand hours, beginning with a Paleocene bee, he has traveled back into the Cretaceous. He stops at intervals to follow the bee in real time, then accelerates again. The hive is growing smaller, more primitive. Now it is only a cluster of round cells, and the bee is different, more like a wasp. His year's labor is coming to fruition. He watches, forgetting to eat, almost to breathe.

In your mother's study after she dies, you find an elaborate chart of her ancestors and your father's. You retrieve the program for it, punch it in, and idly watch a random sampling, back into time, first the female line, then the male . . . a teacher of biology in Boston, a suffragette, a corn merchant, a singer, a Dutch farmer in New York, a British sailor, a German musician. Their faces glow in the screen, bright-eyed, cheeks flushed with life. Someday you too will be only a series of images in a screen.

Smith is watching the planet Mars. The clockwork which turns the Ozo to follow the planet, even when it is below the horizon, makes it possible for him to focus instantly on the surface, but he never does this. He takes up his position hundreds of thousands of miles away, then slowly approaches, in order to see the red spark grow to a disk, then to a yellow sunlit ball hanging in darkness. Now he can make out the surface features: Syrtis Major and Thoth-Nepenthes leading in a long gooseneck to Utopia and the frostcap.

The image as it swells hypnotically toward him is clear and sharp, without tremor or atmospheric distortion. It is summer in the northern hemisphere: Utopia is wide and dark. The planet fills the screen, and now he turns northward, over the cratered desert still hundreds of miles distant. A dust storm, like a yellow veil, obscures the curved neck of Thoth-Nepenthes; then he is beyond it, drifting down to the edge of the frostcap. The limb of the planet reappears; he floats like a glider over the dark surface tinted with rose and violet-gray; now he can see its nubbly texture; now he can make out individual plants. He is drifting among their gnarled gray stems, their leaves of violet horn; he sees the curious misshapen growths that may be air bladders or some grotesque analogue of blossoms. Now, at the edge of the screen, something black and spindling leaps. He follows it instantly, finds it, brings it hugely magnified into the center of the screen: a thing like a hairy beetle, its body covered with thick black hairs or spines; it stands on six jointed legs, waving its antennae, its mouth parts busy. And its four bright eyes stare into his, across forty million miles.

Smith's hair got whiter and thinner. Before the 1992 Crash, he made heavy contributions to the International Red Cross and to volunteer organizations in Europe, Asia and Africa. He got drunk periodically, but always alone. From 1993 to 1996 he stopped reading the newspapers.

He wrote down the coordinates for the plane crash in which his daughter and her husband had died, but never used them.

At intervals while dressing or looking into the bathroom mirror, he stared as if into an invisible camera and raised one finger. In his last years he wrote some poems.

We know his name. Patient researchers, using advanced scanning techniques, followed his letters back through the postal system and found him, but by that time he was safely dead.

The whole world has been at peace for more than a generation. Crime is almost unheard of. Free energy has made the world rich, but the population is stable, even though early detection has wiped out most diseases. Everyone can do whatever he likes, providing his neighbors would not disapprove, and after all, their views are the same as his own.

You are forty, a respected scholar, taking a few days out to review your life, as many people do at your age. You have watched your mother and father coupling on the night they conceived you, watched yourself growing in her womb, first a red tadpole, then a thing like an embryo chicken, then a big-headed baby kicking and squirming. You have seen yourself delivered, seen the first moment when your bloody head broke into the light. You have seen yourself staggering about the nursery in rompers, clutching a yellow plastic duck. Now you are watching yourself hiding behind the fallen tree on the hill, and you realize that there are no secret places. And beyond you in the ghostly future you know that someone is watching you as you watch; and beyond that watcher another, and beyond that another. . . . Forever.

From Competition 13:

Excerpts from myopic early sf or utopian novels

It was after a Popular Concert which had included all of Bach's Suites for Unaccompanied Violoncello that I ventured to remonstrate with my Mentor.

"Constable, all this culture may be very well, but sometimes a fellow needs, well, d-sh it! What do ordinary people nowadays do for amusement?"

He frowned slightly. "My dear sir, it is out of consideration for you that I have exposed you only to our lighter forms of entertainment. I presume you are referring to something in the nature of a Music Hall, or Vaudeville. I assure you that, since the advent of Universal Education, even the popular taste has become too refined to tolerate the foolishness of sentimental songs and lurid melodrama. Also, please do not use again the expression you have just uttered. I mean the one beginning with the letter D. Our twentieth-century society has grown unaccustomed to language of such violence."

—*David T. J. Doughan*

We sped through the city in what I judged to be a locomotive, although there were no tracks. "What new wonder shall I see?" I mused, for many were the sights shown me already. My guide, an illustrious professor, halted the machine.

"In this mill, fine white flour is made. All unwholesome parts of the grain are removed and certain substances poisonous to insects and rodents are introduced." I followed in as he continued: "Only women are employed here, though they don't stay long."

"Why not?" I shouted over the din, my eye caught by a certain face.

He replied, "They quickly become deaf and so have no need to speak. Indeed, few work more than a year. They are prized as wives, for they never nag their husbands."

I looked at the girl, an exact double of my lost love. Beautiful and quiet. What more could a man ask!

—Janet E. Pearson

Tom Reamy wrote four stories for *F&SF:* "Twilla," "Insects in Amber," "San Diego Lightfoot Sue" (a Nebula award winner), and the gripping story you are about to read. He also wrote a novel, *Blind Voices.* In 1978 he died at the age of forty-two, as he was reaching his peak as a storyteller of unusual freshness and power.

The Detweiler Boy

by TOM REAMY

The room had been cleaned with pine-oil disinfectant and smelled like a public toilet. Harry Spinner was on the floor behind the bed, scrunched down between it and the wall. The almost colorless chenille bedspread had been pulled askew exposing part of the clean, but dingy, sheet. All I could see of Harry was one leg poking over the edge of the bed. He wasn't wearing a shoe, only a faded brown-and-tan argyle sock with a hole in it. The sock, long bereft of any elasticity, was crumpled around his thin rusty ankle.

I closed the door quietly behind me and walked around the end of the bed so I could see all of him. He was huddled on his back with his elbows propped up by the wall and the bed. His throat had been cut. The blood hadn't spread very far. Most of it had been soaked up by the threadbare carpet under the bed. I looked around the grubby little room but didn't find anything. There were no signs of a struggle, no signs of forced entry—but then, my BankAmericard hadn't left any signs either. The window was open, letting in the muffled roar of traffic on the Boulevard. I stuck my head out and looked, but it was three stories straight down to the neon-lit marquee of the movie house.

It had been nearly two hours since Harry called me. "Bertram, my boy, I've run across something very peculiar. I don't really know what to make of it."

I had put away the report I was writing on Lucas McGowan's hyperactive wife. (She had a definite predilection for gas-pump jockeys, car-wash boys, and parking-lot attendants. I guess it had something to do with the Age of the Automobile.) I propped my feet on my desk and leaned back until the old swivel chair groaned a protest.

"What did you find this time, Harry? A nest of international spies or an invasion from Mars?" I guess Harry Spinner wasn't much use to anyone, not even himself, but I liked him. He'd helped me in a couple of cases, nosing around in places only the Harry Spinners of the world can nose around in unnoticed. I was beginning to get the idea he was trying to play Doctor Watson to my Sherlock Holmes.

"Don't tease me, Bertram. There's a boy here in the hotel. I saw something I don't think he wanted me to see. It's extremely odd."

Harry was also the only person in the world, except my mother, who called me Bertram. "What did you see?"

"I'd rather not talk about it over the phone. Can you come over?"

Harry saw too many old private-eye movies on the late show. "It'll be a while. I've got a client coming in in a few minutes to pick up the poop on his wandering wife."

"Bertram, you shouldn't waste your time and talent on divorce cases."

"It pays the bills, Harry. Besides, there aren't enough Maltese falcons to go around."

By the time I filled Lucas McGowan in on all the details (I got the impression he was less concerned with his wife's infidelity than with her taste; that it wouldn't have been so bad if she'd been shacking up with movie stars or international playboys), collected my fee, and grabbed a Thursday special at Colonel Sanders, almost two hours had passed. Harry hadn't answered my knock, and so I let myself in with a credit card.

Birdie Pawlowicz was a fat, slovenly old broad somewhere between forty and two hundred. She was blind in her right eye and wore a black felt patch over it. She claimed she had lost the eye in a fight with a Creole whore over a riverboat gambler. I believed her. She ran the Brewster Hotel the way Florence Nightingale must have run that stinking army hospital in the Crimea. Her tenants were the losers habitating that rotting section of the Boulevard east of the Hollywood Freeway. She bossed them, cursed them, loved them, and took care of them. And they loved her back. (Once, a couple of years ago, a young black buck thought an old fat lady with one eye would be easy pickings. The cops found him three days later, two blocks away, under some rubbish in an alley where he'd hidden. He had a broken arm, two cracked ribs, a busted nose, a few missing teeth, and was stone-dead from internal hemorrhaging.)

The Brewster ran heavily in the red, but Birdie didn't mind. She had quite a bit of property in Westwood which ran very, very heavily in the black. She gave me an obscene leer as I approached the desk, but her good eye twinkled.

"Hello, lover!" she brayed in a voice like a cracked boiler. "I've lowered my price to a quarter. Are you interested?" She saw my face and her expression shifted from lewd to wary. "What's wrong, Bert?"

"Harry Spinner. You'd better get the cops, Birdie. Somebody killed him."

She looked at me, not saying anything, her face slowly collapsing into an infinitely weary resignation. Then she turned and telephoned the police.

Because it was just Harry Spinner at the Brewster Hotel on the wrong end of Hollywood Boulevard, the cops took over half an hour to get there. While we waited I told Birdie everything I knew, about the phone call and what I'd found.

"He must have been talking about the Detweiler boy," she said, frowning. "Harry's been kinda friendly with him, felt sorry for him, I guess."

"What's his room? I'd like to talk to him."

"He checked out."

"When?"

"Just before you came down."

"Damn!"

She bit her lip. "I don't think the Detweiler boy killed him."

"Why?"

"I just don't think he could. He's such a gentle boy."

"Oh, Birdie," I groaned, "you know there's no such thing as a killer type. Almost anyone will kill with a good enough reason."

"I know," she sighed, "but I still can't believe it." She tapped her

scarlet fingernails on the dulled Formica desk top. "How long had
Harry been dead?"

He had phoned me about ten after five. I had found the body at
seven. "Awhile," I said. "The blood was mostly dry."

"Before six-thirty?"

"Probably."

She sighed again, but this time with relief. "The Detweiler boy was
down here with me until six-thirty. He'd been here since about four-
fifteen. We were playing gin. He was having one of his spells and
wanted company."

"What kind of spell? Tell me about him, Birdie. "

"But he couldn't have killed Harry," she protested.

"Okay," I said, but I wasn't entirely convinced. Why would anyone deliberately and brutally murder inoffensive, invisible Harry
Spinner right after he told me he had discovered something "peculiar" about the Detweiler boy? Except the Detweiler boy?

"Tell me anyway. If he and Harry were friendly, he might know
something. Why do you keep calling him a boy; how old is he?"

She nodded and leaned her bulk on the registration desk. "Early
twenties, twenty-two, twenty-three, maybe. Not very tall, about five
five or six. Slim, dark curly hair, a real good-looking boy. Looks like
a movie star except for his back."

"His back?"

"He has a hump. He's a hunchback."

That stopped me for a minute, but I'm not sure why. I must've had
a mental picture of Charles Laughton riding those bells or Igor stealing that brain from the laboratory. "He's good-looking and he's a
hunchback?"

"Sure." She raised her eyebrows. The one over the patch didn't go
up as high as the other. "If you see him from the front, you can't
even tell."

"What's his first name?"

"Andrew."

"How long has he been living here?"

She consulted a file card. "He checked in last Friday night. The
22nd. Six days."

"What's this spell he was having?"

"I don't know for sure. It was the second one he'd had. He would
get pale and nervous. I think he was in a lot of pain. It would get

worse and worse all day; then he'd be fine, all rosy and healthy-looking."

"Sounds to me like he was hurtin' for a fix."

"I thought so at first, but I changed my mind. I've seen enough of that and it wasn't the same. Take my word. He was real bad this evening. He came down about four-fifteen, like I said. He didn't complain, but I could tell he was wantin' company to take his mind off it. We played gin until six-thirty. Then he went back upstairs. About twenty minutes later he came down with his old suitcase and checked out. He looked fine, all over his spell."

"Did he have a doctor?"

"I'm pretty sure he didn't. I asked him about it. He said there was nothing to worry about, it would pass. And it did."

"Did he say why he was leaving or where he was going?"

"No, just said he was restless and wanted to be movin' on. Sure hated to see him leave. A real nice kid."

When the cops finally got there, I told them all I knew—except I didn't mention the Detweiler boy. I hung around until I found out that Harry almost certainly wasn't killed after six-thirty. They set the time somewhere between five-ten, when he called me, and six. It looked like Andrew Detweiler was innocent, but what "peculiar" thing had Harry noticed about him, and why had he moved out right after Harry was killed? Birdie let me take a look at his room, but I didn't find a thing, not even an abandoned paperclip.

Friday morning I sat at my desk trying to put the pieces together. Trouble was, I only had two pieces and *they* didn't fit. The sun was coming in off the Boulevard, shining through the window, projecting the chipping letters painted on the glass against the wall in front of me. BERT MALLORY Confidential Investigations. I got up and looked out. This section of the Boulevard wasn't rotting yet, but it wouldn't be long.

There's one sure gauge for judging a part of town: the movie theaters. It never fails. For instance, a new picture hadn't opened in downtown L.A. in a long, long time. The action ten years ago was on the Boulevard. Now it's in Westwood. The grand old Pantages, east of Vine and too near the freeway, used to be the site of the most glittering premieres. They even had the Oscar ceremonies there for a while. Now it shows exploitation and double-feature horror films. Only Grauman's Chinese and the once Paramount, once Loew's, now

Downtown Cinema (or something) at the west end got good openings. The Nu-View, across the street and down, was showing an X-rated double feature. It was too depressing. So I closed the blind.

Miss Tremaine looked up from her typing at the rattle and frowned. Her desk was out in the small reception area, but I had arranged both desks so we could see each other and talk in normal voices when the door was open. It stayed open most of the time except when I had a client who felt secretaries shouldn't know his troubles. She had been transcribing the Lucas McGowan report for half an hour, *humphing* and *tsk-tsking* at thirty-second intervals. She was having a marvelous time. Miss Tremaine was about forty-five, looked like a constipated librarian, and was the best secretary I'd ever had. She'd been with me seven years. I'd tried a few young and sexy ones, but it hadn't worked out. Either they wouldn't play at all, or they wanted to play all the time. Both kinds were a pain in the ass to face first thing in the morning, every morning.

"Miss Tremaine, will you get Gus Verdugo on the phone, please?"

"Yes, Mr. Mallory." She dialed the phone nimbly, sitting as if she were wearing a back brace.

Gus Verdugo worked in R&I. I had done him a favor once, and he insisted on returning it tenfold. I gave him everything I had on Andrew Detweiler and asked him if he'd mind running it through the computer. He wouldn't mind. He called back in fifteen minutes. The computer had never heard of Andrew Detweiler and had only seven hunchbacks, none of them fitting Detweiler's description.

I was sitting there, wondering how in hell I would find him, when the phone rang again. Miss Tremaine stopped typing and lifted the receiver without breaking rhythm. "Mr. Mallory's office," she said crisply, really letting the caller know he'd hooked onto an efficient organization. She put her hand over the mouthpiece and looked at me. "It's for you—an obscene phone call." She didn't bat an eyelash or twitch a muscle.

"Thanks," I said and winked at her. She dropped the receiver back on the cradle from a height of three inches and went back to typing. Grinning, I picked up my phone. "Hello, Janice," I said.

"Just a minute till my ear stops ringing." The husky voice tickled my ear.

"What are you doing up this early?" I asked. Janice Fenwick was an exotic dancer at a club on the Strip nights and was working on her master's in oceanography at UCLA in the afternoons. In the year I'd known her I'd seldom seen her stick her nose into the sunlight before eleven.

"I had to catch you before you started following that tiresome woman with the car."

"I've finished that. She's picked up her last parking-lot attendant— at least with this husband," I chuckled.

"I'm glad to hear it."

"What's up?"

"I haven't had an indecent proposition from you in days. So I thought I'd make one of my own."

"I'm all ears."

"We're doing some diving off Catalina tomorrow. Want to come along?"

"Not much we can do in a wetsuit."

"The wetsuit comes off about four; then we'll have Saturday night and all of Sunday."

"Best indecent proposition I've had all week."

Miss Tremaine *humphed*. It might have been over something in the report, but I don't think it was.

I picked up Janice at her apartment in Westwood early Saturday morning. She was waiting for me and came striding out to the car all legs and healthy golden flesh. She was wearing white shorts, sneakers, and that damned Dallas Cowboys jersey. It was authentic. The name and number on it were quite well-known—even to non-football fans. She wouldn't tell me how she got it, just smirked and looked smug. She tossed her suitcase in the back seat and slid up against me. She smelled like sunshine.

We flew over and spent most of the day *glubbing* around in the Pacific with a bunch of kids fifteen years younger than I and five years younger than Janice. I'd been on these jaunts with Janice before and enjoyed them so much I'd bought my own wetsuit. But I didn't enjoy it nearly as much as I did Saturday night and all of Sunday.

I got back to my apartment on Beachwood fairly late Sunday night and barely had time to get something to eat at the Mexican restaurant around the corner on Melrose. They have marvelous carne asada. I live right across the street from Paramount, right across from the door people go in to see them tape *The Odd Couple*. Every

Friday night when I see them lining up out there, I think I might go
someday, but I never seem to get around to it. (You might think I'd
see a few movie stars living where I do, but I haven't. I did see
Seymour occasionally when he worked at Channel 9, before he went
to work for Gene Autry at Channel 5.)

I was so pleasantly pooped I completely forgot about Andrew
Detweiler. Until Monday morning when I was sitting at my desk
reading the *Times*.

It was a small story on page three, not very exciting or news-
worthy. Last night a man named Maurice Milian, age 51, had fallen
through the plate-glass doors leading onto the terrace of the high-rise
where he lived. He had been discovered about midnight when the
people living below him had noticed dried blood on *their* terrace.
The only thing to connect the deaths of Harry Spinner and Maurice
Milian was a lot of blood flowing around. If Milian had been mur-
dered, there *might* be a link, however tenuous. But Milian's death
was accidental—a dumb, stupid accident. It niggled around in my
brain for an hour before I gave in. There was only one way to get it
out of my head.

"Miss Tremaine, I'll be back in an hour or so. If any slinky
blondes come in wanting me to find their kid sisters, tell 'em to wait."

She *humphed* again and ignored me.

The Almsbury was half a dozen blocks away on Yucca. So I
walked. It was a rectangular monolith about eight stories tall, not
real new, not too old, but expensive-looking. The small terraces protruded in neat, orderly rows. The long, narrow grounds were immac-
ulate with a lot of succulents that looked like they might have been
imported from Mars. There were also the inevitable palm trees
and clumps of bird of paradise. A small, discrete, polished placard
dangled in a wrought-iron frame proclaiming, ever so softly, NO
VACANCY.

Two willowy young men gave me appraising glances in the carpeted lobby as they exited into the sunlight like exotic jungle birds.
It's one of those, I thought. My suspicions were confirmed when I
looked over the tenant directory. All the names seemed to be male,
but none of them was Andrew Detweiler.

Maurice Milian was still listed as 407. I took the elevator to four
and rang the bell of 409. The bell played a few notes of Bach, or
maybe Vivaldi or Telemann. All those old Baroques sound alike to

me. The vision of loveliness who opened the door was about forty, almost as slim as Twiggy, but as tall as I. He wore a flowered silk shirt open to the waist, exposing his bony hairless chest, and tight white pants that might as well have been made of Saran Wrap. He didn't say anything, just let his eyebrows rise inquiringly as his eyes flicked down, then up.

"Good morning," I said and showed him my ID. He blanched. His eyes became marbles brimming with terror. He was about to panic, tensing to slam the door. I smiled my friendly, disarming smile and went on as if I hadn't noticed. "I'm inquiring about a man named Andrew Detweiler." The terror trickled from his eyes, and I could see his thin chest throbbing. He gave me a blank look that meant he'd never heard the name.

"He's about twenty-two," I continued, "dark, curly hair, very good-looking."

He grinned wryly, calming down, trying to cover his panic. "Aren't they all?" he said.

"Detweiler is a hunchback."

His smile contracted suddenly. His eyebrows shot up. "Oh," he said. "Him."

Bingo!

Mallory, you've led a clean, wholesome life and it's paying off.

"Does he live in the building?" I swallowed to get my heart back in place and blinked a couple of times to clear away the skyrockets.

"No. He was . . . visiting."

"May I come in and talk to you about him?"

He was holding the door three quarters shut, and so I couldn't see anything in the room but an expensive-looking color TV. He glanced over his shoulder nervously at something behind him. The inner ends of his eyebrows drooped in a frown. He looked back at me and started to say something, then, with a small defiance, shrugged his eyebrows. "Sure, but there's not much I can tell you."

He pushed the door all the way open and stepped back. It was a good-sized living room come to life from the pages of a decorator magazine. A kitchen behind a half wall was on my right. A hallway led somewhere on my left. Directly in front of me were double sliding glass doors leading to the terrace. On the terrace was a bronzed hunk of beef stretched out nude trying to get bronzer. The hunk opened his eyes and looked at me. He apparently decided I wasn't

competition and closed them again. Tall and lanky indicated one of
two identical orange-and-brown-striped couches facing each other
across a football-field-size marble-and-glass cocktail table. He sat on
the other one, took a cigarette from an alabaster box and lit it with
an alabaster lighter. As an afterthought, he offered me one.

"Who was Detweiler visiting?" I asked as I lit the cigarette. The
lighter felt cool and expensive in my hand.

"Maurice—next door." He inclined his head slightly toward 407.

"Isn't he the one who was killed in an accident last night?"

He blew a stream of smoke from pursed lips and tapped his cigarette on an alabaster ashtray. "Yes," he said.

"How long had Maurice and Detweiler known each other?"

"Not long."

"How long?"

He snuffed his cigarette out on pure-white alabaster and sat so
prim and pristine I would have bet his feces came out wrapped in
cellophane. He shrugged his eyebrows again. "Maurice picked him
up somewhere the other night."

"Which night?"

He thought a moment. "Thursday, I think. Yes, Thursday."

"Was Detweiler a hustler?"

He crossed his legs like a Forties pin-up and dangled his Roman
sandal. His lips twitched scornfully. "If he was, he would've starved.
He was de-*formed!*"

"Maurice didn't seem to mind." He sniffed and lit another cigarette. "When did Detweiler leave?"

He shrugged. "I saw him yesterday afternoon. I was out last night
. . . until quite late."

"How did they get along? Did they quarrel or fight?"

"I have no idea. I only saw them in the hall a couple of times.
Maurice and I were . . . not close." He stood, fidgety. "There's really not anything I can tell you. Why don't you ask David and Murray. They and Maurice are . . . were thick as thieves."

"David and Murray?"

"Across the hall. 408."

I stood up. "I'll do that. Thank you very much." I looked at the
plate-glass doors. I guess it would be pretty easy to walk through one
of them if you thought it was open. "Are all the apartments alike?
Those terrace doors?"

He nodded. "Ticky-tacky."

"Thanks again."

"Don't mention it." He opened the door for me and then closed it behind me. I sighed and walked across to 408. I rang the bell. It didn't play anything, just went *bing-bong*.

David (or Murray) was about twenty-five, redheaded, and freckled. He had a slim, muscular body which was also freckled. I could tell because he was wearing only a pair of jeans, cut off very short, and split up the sides to the waistband. He was barefooted and had a smudge of green paint on his nose. He had an open, friendly face and gave me a neutral smile-for-a-stranger. "Yes?" he asked.

I showed him my ID. Instead of going pale, he only looked interested. "I was told by the man in 409 you might be able to tell me something about Andrew Detweiler."

"Andy?" He frowned slightly. "Come on in. I'm David Fowler." He held out his hand.

I shook it. "Bert Mallory." The apartment couldn't have been more different from the one across the hall. It was comfortable and cluttered, and dominated by a drafting table surrounded by jars of brushes and boxes of paint tubes. Architecturally, however, it was almost identical. The terrace was covered with potted plants rather than naked muscles. David Fowler sat on the stool at the drafting table and began cleaning brushes. When he sat, the split in his shorts opened and exposed half his butt, which was also freckled. But I got the impression he wasn't exhibiting himself; he was just completely indifferent.

"What do you want to know about Andy?"

"Everything."

He laughed. "That lets me out. Sit down. Move the stuff."

I cleared a space on the couch and sat. "How did Detweiler and Maurice get along?"

He gave me a knowing look. "Fine. As far as I know. Maurice liked to pick up stray puppies. Andy was a stray puppy."

"Was Detweiler a hustler?"

He laughed again. "No. I doubt if he knew what the word means."

"Was he gay?"

"No."

"How do you know?"

He grinned. "Haven't you heard? We can spot each other a mile away. Would you like some coffee?"

"Yes, I would. Thank you."

He went to the half wall separating the kitchen and poured two cups from a pot that looked like it was kept hot and full all the time. "It's hard to describe Andy. There was something very little-boyish about him. A real innocent. Delighted with everything new. It's sad about his back. Real sad." He handed me the cup and returned to the stool. "There was something very secretive about him. Not about his feelings; he was very open about things like that."

"Did he and Maurice have sex together?"

"No. I told you it was a stray-puppy relationship. I wish Murray were here. He's much better with words than I am. I'm visually oriented."

"Where is he?"

"At work. He's a lawyer."

"Do you think Detweiler could have killed Maurice?"

"No."

"Why?"

"He was here with us all evening. We had dinner and played Scrabble. I think he was real sick, but he tried to pretend he wasn't. Even if he hadn't been here, I would not think so."

"When was the last time you saw him?"

"He left about half an hour before they found Maurice. I imagine he went over there, saw Maurice dead, and decided to disappear. Can't say as I blame him. The police might've gotten some funny ideas. We didn't mention him."

"Why not?"

"There was no point in getting him involved. It was just an accident."

"He couldn't have killed Maurice after he left here?"

"No. They said he'd been dead over an hour. What did Desmond tell you?"

"Desmond?"

"Across the hall. The one who looks like he smells something bad."

"How did you know I talked to him and not the side of beef?"

He laughed and almost dropped his coffee cup. "I don't think Roy *can* talk."

"He didn't know nothin' about nothin'." I found myself laughing also. I got up and walked to the glass doors. I slid them open and then shut again. "Did you ever think one of these was open when it was really shut?"

"No. But I've heard of it happening."

I sighed. "So have I." I turned and looked at what he was working on at the drafting table. It was a small painting of a boy and girl, she in a soft white dress, and he in jeans and tee shirt. They looked about fifteen. They were embracing, about to kiss. It was quite obviously the first time for both of them. It was good. I told him so.

He grinned with pleasure. "Thanks. It's for a paperback cover."

"Whose idea was it that Detweiler have dinner and spend the evening with you?"

He thought for a moment. "Maurice." He looked up at me and grinned. "Do you know stamps?"

It took me a second to realize what he meant. "You mean stamp collecting? Not much."

"Maurice was a philatelist. He specialized in postwar Germany—locals and zones, things like that. He'd gotten a kilo of buildings and wanted to sort them undisturbed."

I shook my head. "You've lost me. A kilo of buildings?"

He laughed. "It's a set of twenty-eight stamps issued in the American Zone in 1948 showing famous German buildings. Conditions in Germany were still pretty chaotic at the time, and the stamps were printed under fairly makeshift circumstances. Consequently, there's an enormous variety of different perforations, watermarks, and engravings. Hundreds as a matter of fact. Maurice could spend hours and hours poring over them."

"Are they valuable?"

"No. Very common. Some of the varieties are hard to find, but they're not valuable." He gave me a knowing look. "Nothing was missing from Maurice's apartment."

I shrugged. "It had occurred to me to wonder where Detweiler got his money."

"I don't know. The subject never came up." He wasn't being defensive.

"You liked him, didn't you?"

There was a weary sadness in his eyes. "Yes," he said.

That afternoon I picked up Birdie Pawlowicz at the Brewster

Hotel and took her to Harry Spinner's funeral. I told her about
Maurice Milian and Andrew Detweiler. We talked it around and
around. The Detweiler boy obviously couldn't have killed Harry *or*
Milian, but it was stretching coincidence a little bit far.

After the funeral I went to the Los Angeles Public Library and
started checking back issues of the *Times*. I'd only made it back
three weeks when the library closed. The L.A. *Times* is *thick,* and unless the death is sensational or the dead prominent, the story might
be tucked in anywhere except the classifieds.

Last Tuesday, the 26th, a girl had cut her wrists with a razor blade
in North Hollywood.

The day before, Monday, the 25th, a girl had miscarried and hem-
orrhaged. She had bled to death because she and her boy friend were
stoned out of their heads. They lived a block off Western—very near
the Brewster—and Detweiler was at the Brewster Monday.

Sunday, the 24th, a wino had been knifed in MacArthur Park.

Saturday, the 23rd, I had three. A knifing in a bar on Pico, a
shooting in a rooming house on Irolo, and a rape and knifing in an
alley off La Brea. Only the gunshot victim had bled to death, but
there had been a lot of blood in all three.

Friday, the 22nd, the same day Detweiler checked in the Brewster,
a two-year-old boy had fallen on an upturned rake in his backyard
on Larchemont—only eight or ten blocks from where I lived on
Beachwood. And a couple of Chicano kids had had a knife fight
behind Hollywood High. One was dead and the other was in jail. Ah,
machismo!

The list went on and on, all the way back to Thursday, the 7th.
On that day was another slashed-wrist suicide near Western and
Wilshire.

The next morning, Tuesday, the 3rd, I called Miss Tremaine and
told her I'd be late getting in but would check in every couple of
hours to find out if the slinky blonde looking for her kid sister had
shown up. She *humphed.*

Larchemont is a middle-class neighborhood huddled in between
the old wealth around the country club and the blight spreading
down Melrose from Western Avenue. It tries to give the impression
of suburbia—and does a pretty good job of it—rather than just another nearly downtown shopping center. The area isn't big on apartments or rooming houses, but there are a few. I found the Detweiler

boy at the third one I checked. It was a block and a half from where the little kid fell on the rake.

According to the landlord, at the time of the kid's death Detweiler was playing bridge with him and a couple of elderly old-maid sisters in number twelve. He hadn't been feeling well and had moved out later that evening—to catch a bus to San Diego, to visit his ailing mother. The landlord had felt sorry for him, so sorry he'd broken a steadfast rule and refunded most of the month's rent Detweiler had paid in advance. After all, he'd only been there three days. So sad about his back. Such a nice, gentle boy—a writer, you know.

No, I didn't know, but it explained how he could move around so much without seeming to work.

I called David Fowler: "Yes, Andy had a portable typewriter, but he hadn't mentioned being a writer."

And Birdie Pawlowicz: "Yeah, he typed a lot in his room."

I found the Detweiler boy again on the 16th and the 19th. He'd moved into a rooming house near Silver Lake Park on the night of the 13th and moved out again on the 19th. The landlady hadn't refunded his money, but she gave him an alibi for the knifing of an old man in the park on the 16th and the suicide of a girl in the same rooming house on the 19th. He'd been in the pink of health when he moved in, sick on the 16th, healthy the 17th, and sick again the 19th.

It was like a rerun. He lived a block away from where a man was mugged, knifed, and robbed in an alley on the 13th—though the details of the murder didn't seem to fit the pattern. But he was sick, had an alibi, and moved to Silver Lake.

Rerun it on the 10th: a woman slipped in the bathtub and fell through the glass shower doors, cutting herself to ribbons. Sick, alibi, moved.

It may be because I was always rotten in math, but it wasn't until right then that I figured out Detweiler's timetable. Milian died the 1st, Harry Spinner the 28th, the miscarriage was on the 25th, the little kid on the 22nd, Silver Lake on the 19th and 16th, etc., etc., etc.

A bloody death occurred in Detweiler's general vicinity every third day.

But I couldn't figure out a pattern for the victims: male, female, little kids, old aunties, married, unmarried, rich, poor, young, old. No pattern of any kind, and there's *always* a pattern. I even checked to see if the names were in alphabetical order.

I got back to my office at six. Miss Tremaine sat primly at her desk, cleared of everything but her purse and a notepad. She reminded me quite a lot of Desmond. "What are you still doing here, Miss Tremaine? You should've left an hour ago." I sat at my desk, leaned back until the swivel chair groaned twice, and propped my feet up.

She picked up the pad. "I wanted to give you your calls."

"Can't they wait? I've been sleuthing all day and I'm bushed."

"No one is paying you to find this Detweiler person, are they?"

"No."

"Your bank statement came today."

"What's that supposed to mean?"

"Nothing. A good secretary keeps her employer informed. I was informing you."

"Okay. Who called?"

She consulted the pad, but I'd bet my last gumshoe she knew every word on it by heart. "A Mrs. Carmichael called. Her French poodle has been kidnaped. She wants you to find her."

"Ye Gods! Why doesn't she go to the police?"

"Because she's positive her ex-husband is the kidnaper. She doesn't want to get him in any trouble; she just wants Gwendolyn back."

"Gwendolyn?"

"Gwendolyn. A Mrs. Bushyager came by. She wants you to find her little sister."

I sat up so fast I almost fell out of the chair. I gave her a long, hard stare, but her neutral expression didn't flicker. "You're kidding." Her eyebrows rose a millimeter. "Was she a slinky blonde?"

"No. She was a dumpy brunette."

I settled back in the chair, trying not to laugh. "Why does Mrs. Bushyager want me to find her little sister?" I sputtered.

"Because Mrs. Bushyager thinks she's shacked up somewhere with *Mr.* Bushyager. She'd like you to call her tonight."

"Tomorrow. I've got a date with Janice tonight." She reached in her desk drawer and pulled out my bank statement. She dropped it on the desk with a papery plop. "Don't worry," I assured her, "I won't spend much money. Just a little spaghetti and wine tonight and ham and eggs in the morning." She *humphed*. My point. "Anything else?"

"A Mr. Bloomfeld called. He wants you to get the goods on Mrs. Bloomfeld so he can sue for divorce."

I sighed. Miss Tremaine closed the pad. "Okay. No to Mrs. Carmichael and make appointments for Bushyager and Bloomfeld." She lowered her eyelids at me. I spread my hands. "Would Sam Spade go looking for a French poodle named Gwendolyn?"

"He might if he had your bank statement. Mr. Bloomfeld will be in at two, Mrs. Bushyager at three."

"Miss Tremaine, you'd make somebody a wonderful mother." She didn't even *humph;* she just picked up her purse and stalked out. I swiveled the chair around and looked at the calendar. Tomorrow was the 4th.

Somebody would die tomorrow and Andrew Detweiler would be close-by.

I scooted up in bed and leaned against the headboard. Janice snorted into the pillow and opened one eye, pinning me with it. "I didn't mean to wake you," I said.

"What's the matter," she muttered, "too much spaghetti?"

"No. Too much Andrew Detweiler."

She scooted up beside me, keeping the sheet over her breasts, and turned on the light. She rummaged around on the nightstand for a cigarette. "Who wants to divorce him?"

"That's mean, Janice," I groaned.

"You want a cigarette?"

"Yeah."

She put two cigarettes in her mouth and lit them both. She handed me one. "You don't look a bit like Paul Henreid," I said.

She grinned. "That's funny. You look like Bette Davis. Who's Andrew Detweiler?"

So I told her.

"It's elementary, my dear Sherlock," she said. "Andrew Detweiler is a vampire." I frowned at her. "Of course, he's a *clever* vampire. Vampires are usually stupid. They always give themselves away by leaving those two little teeth marks on people's jugulars."

"Darling, even vampires have to be at the scene of the crime."

"He always has an alibi, huh?"

I got out of bed and headed for the bathroom. "That's suspicious in itself."

When I came out she said, "Why?"

"Innocent people usually don't have alibis, especially not one every three days."

"Which is probably why innocent people get put in jail so often." I chuckled and sat on the edge of the bed. "You may be right."

"Bert, do that again."

I looked at her over my shoulder. "Do what?"

"Go to the bathroom."

"I don't think I can. My bladder holds only so much."

"I don't mean that. Walk over to the bathroom door."

I gave her a suspicious frown, got up, and walked over to the bathroom door. I turned around, crossed my arms, and leaned against the doorframe. "Well?"

She grinned. "You've got a cute rear end. Almost as cute as Burt Reynolds'. Maybe he's twins."

"What?" I practically screamed.

"Maybe Andrew Detweiler is twins. One of them commits the murders and the other establishes the alibis."

"Twin vampires?"

She frowned. "That is a bit much, isn't it? Had they discovered blood groups in Bram Stoker's day?"

I got back in bed and pulled the sheet up to my waist, leaning beside her against the headboard. "I haven't the foggiest idea."

"That's another way vampires are stupid. They never check the victim's blood group. The wrong blood group can kill you."

"Vampires don't exactly get transfusions."

"It all amounts to the same thing, doesn't it?" I shrugged. "Oh, well," she sighed, "vampires are stupid." She reached over and plucked at the hair on my chest. "I haven't had an indecent proposition in hours," she grinned.

So I made one.

Wednesday morning I made a dozen phone calls. Of the nine victims I knew about, I was able to find the information on six.

All six had the same blood group.

I lit a cigarette and leaned back in the swivel chair. The whole thing was spinning around in my head. I'd found *a* pattern for the victims, but I didn't know if it was *the* pattern. It just didn't make sense. Maybe Detweiler *was* a vampire.

"Mallory," I said out loud, "you're cracking up."

Miss Tremaine glanced up. "If I were you, I'd listen to you," she said poker-faced.

The next morning I staggered out of bed at 6 A.M. I took a cold shower, shaved, dressed, and put Murine in my eyes. They still felt like I'd washed them in rubber cement. Mrs. Bloomfeld had kept me up until two the night before, doing all the night spots in Santa Monica with some dude I hadn't identified yet. When they checked into a motel, I went home and went to bed.

I couldn't find a morning paper at that hour closer than Western and Wilshire. The story was on page seven. Fortunately they found the body in time for the early edition. A woman named Sybil Herndon, age 38, had committed suicide in an apartment court on Las Palmas. (Detweiler hadn't gone very far. The address was just around the corner from the Almsbury.) She had cut her wrists on a piece of broken mirror. She had been discovered about eleven-thirty when the manager went over to ask her to turn down the volume on her television set.

It was too early to drop around, and so I ate breakfast, hoping this was one of the times Detweiler stuck around for more than three days. Not for a minute did I doubt he would be living at the apartment court on Las Palmas, or not far away.

The owner-manager of the court was one of those creatures peculiar to Hollywood. She must have been a starlet in the Twenties or Thirties, but success had eluded her. So she had tried to freeze herself in time. She still expected, at any moment, a call from The Studio. But her flesh hadn't cooperated. Her hair was the color of tarnished copper, and the fire-engine-red lipstick was painted far past her thin lips. Her watery eyes peered at me through a Lone Ranger mask of Maybelline on a plaster-white face. Her dress had obviously been copied from the wardrobe of Norma Shearer.

"Yes?" She had a breathless voice. Her eyes quickly traveled the length of my body. That happened often enough to keep me feeling good, but this time it gave me a queasy sensation, like I was being measured for a mummy case. I showed her my ID, and asked if I could speak to her about one of the tenants.

"Of course. Come on in. I'm Lorraine Nesbitt." Was there a flicker of disappointment that I hadn't recognized the name? She stepped back, holding the door for me. I could tell that detectives, private or otherwise, asking about her tenants wasn't a new thing. I walked into the doilied room, and she looked at me from a hundred directions. The faded photographs covered every level surface and clung to the walls like leeches. She had been quite a dish—forty years ago. She saw me looking at the photos and smiled. The make-up around her mouth cracked.

"Which one do you want to ask me about?" The smile vanished and the cracks closed.

"Andrew Detweiler." She looked blank. "Young, good-looking, with a hunchback."

The cracks opened. "Oh, yes. He's only been here a few days. The name had slipped my mind."

"He's still here?"

"Oh, yes." She sighed. "It's so unfair for such a beautiful young man to have a physical impairment."

"What can you tell me about him?"

"Not much. He's only been here since Sunday night. He's very handsome, like an angel, a dark angel. But it wasn't his handsomeness that attracted me." She smiled. "I've seen many handsome men in my day, you know. It's difficult to verbalize. He has such an incredible innocence. A lost, doomed look that Byron must have had. A vulnerability that makes you want to shield and protect him. I don't know for sure what it is, but it struck a chord in my soul. Soul," she mused. "Maybe that's it. He wears his soul on his face." She nodded, as if to herself. "A dangerous thing to do." She looked back up at me. "If that quality, whatever it is, would photograph, he would become a star overnight, whether he could act or not. Except —of course—for his infirmity."

Lorraine Nesbitt, I decided, was as nutty as a fruitcake.

Someone entered the room. He stood leaning against the door-frame, looking at me with sleepy eyes. He was about twenty-five, wearing tight chinos without underwear and a tee shirt. His hair was tousled and cut unfashionably short. He had a good-looking Kansas face. The haircut made me think he was new in town, but the eyes said he wasn't. I guess the old broad liked his hair that way.

She simpered. "Oh, Johnny! Come on in. This detective was asking about Andrew Detweiler in number seven." She turned back to me. "This is my protege, Johnny Peacock—a very talented young man. I'm arranging for a screen test as soon as Mr. Goldwyn returns

my calls." She lowered her eyelids demurely. "I was a Goldwyn Girl,
you know."

Funny, I thought Goldwyn was dead. Maybe he wasn't.

Johnny took the news of his impending stardom with total uncon-
cern. He moved to the couch and sat down, yawning. "Detweiler?
Don't think I ever laid eyes on the man. What'd he do?"

"Nothing. Just routine." Obviously he thought I was a police detective. No point in changing his mind. "Where was he last night
when the Herndon woman died?"

"In his room, I think. I heard his typewriter. He wasn't feeling
well," Lorraine Nesbitt said. Then she sucked air through her teeth
and clamped her fingers to her scarlet lips. "Do you think he had
something to do with *that?*"

Detweiler had broken his pattern. He didn't have an alibi. I
couldn't believe it.

"Oh, Lorraine," Johnny grumbled.

I turned to him. "Do you know where Detweiler was?"

He shrugged. "No idea."

"Then why are you so sure he had nothing to do with it?"

"She committed suicide."

"How do you know for sure?"

"The door was bolted from the inside. They had to break it down
to get in."

"What about the window? Was it locked too?"

"No. The window was open. But it has bars on it. No way anybody could get in."

"When I couldn't get her to answer my knock last night, I went
around to the window and looked in. She was lying there with blood
all over." She began to sniffle. Johnny got up and put his arms
around her. He looked at me, grinned, and shrugged.

"Do you have a vacancy?" I asked, getting a whiz-bang idea.

"Yes," she said, the sniffles disappearing instantly. "I have two.
Actually three, but I can't rent Miss Herndon's room for a few days—
until someone claims her things."

"I'd like to rent the one closest to number seven," I said.

I wasn't lucky enough to get number six or eight, but I did get
five. Lorraine Nesbitt's nameless, dingy apartment court was a
fleabag. Number five was one room with a closet, a tiny kitchen, and
a tiny bath—identical with the other nine units she assured me. With

a good deal of tugging and grunting, the couch turned into a lumpy bed. The refrigerator looked as if someone had spilled a bottle of Br'er Rabbit back in 1938 and hadn't cleaned it up yet. The stove looked like a lube rack. Well, I sighed, it was only for three days. I had to pay a month's rent in advance anyway, but I put it down as a bribe to keep Lorraine's and Johnny's mouths shut about my being a detective.

I moved in enough clothes for three days, some sheets and pillows, took another look at the kitchen and decided to eat out. I took a jug of Lysol to the bathroom and crossed my fingers. Miss Tremaine brought up the bank statement and *humphed* a few times.

Number five had one door and four windows—identical to the other nine Lorraine assured me. The door had a heavy-duty bolt that couldn't be fastened or unfastened from the outside. The window beside the door didn't open at all and wasn't intended to. The bathroom and kitchen windows cranked out and were tall and skinny, about twenty-four by six. The other living room window, opposite the door, slid upward. The iron bars bolted to the frame were so rusted I doubted if they could be removed without ripping out the whole window. It appeared Andrew Detweiler had another perfect alibi after all—along with the rest of the world.

I stood outside number seven suddenly feeling like a teen-ager about to pick up his first date. I could hear Detweiler's typewriter *tickety-ticking* away inside. Okay, Mallory, this is what you've been breaking your neck on for a week.

I knocked on the door.

I heard the typewriter stop ticking and the scrape of a chair being scooted back. I didn't hear anything else for fifteen or twenty seconds, and I wondered what he was doing. Then the bolt was drawn and the door opened.

He was buttoning his shirt. That must have been the delay: he wouldn't want anyone to see him with his shirt off. Everything I'd been told about him was true. He wasn't very tall; the top of his head came to my nose. He was dark, though not as dark as I'd expected. I couldn't place his ancestry. It certainly wasn't Latin-American and I didn't think it was Slavic. His features were soft without the angularity usually found in the Mediterranean races. His hair wasn't quite black. It wasn't exactly long and it wasn't exactly short. His clothes were nondescript. Everything about him was neutral—except

his face. It was just about the way Lorraine Nesbitt had described it.
If you called central casting and asked for a male angel, you'd get
Andrew Detweiler in a blond wig. His body was slim and well-
formed—from where I was standing I couldn't see the hump and
you'd never know there was one. I had a glimpse of his bare chest as
he buttoned the shirt. It wasn't muscular but it was very well made.
He was very healthy-looking—pink and flushed with health, though
slightly pale as if he didn't get out in the sun much. His dark eyes
were astounding. If you blocked out the rest of the face, leaving
nothing but the eyes, you'd swear he was no more than four years
old. You've seen little kids with those big, guileless, unguarded, inquiring eyes, haven't you?

"Yes?" he asked.

I smiled. "Hello, I'm Bert Mallory. I just moved in to number five.
Miss Nesbitt tells me you like to play gin."

"Yes," he grinned. "Come on in."

He turned to move out of my way and I saw the hump. I don't
know how to describe what I felt. I suddenly had a hurting in my gut.
I felt the same unfairness and sadness the others had, the way you
would feel about any beautiful thing with one overwhelming flaw.

"I'm not disturbing you, am I? I heard the typewriter." The room
was indeed identical to mine, though it looked a hundred per cent
more livable. I couldn't put my finger on what he had done to it to
make it that way. Maybe it was just the semidarkness. He had the
curtains tightly closed and one lamp lit beside the typewriter.

"Yeah, I was working on a story, but I'd rather play gin." He
grinned, open and artless. "If I could make money playing gin, I
wouldn't write."

"Lots of people make money playing gin."

"Oh, I couldn't. I'm too unlucky."

He certainly had a right to say that, but there was no self-pity, just
an observation. Then he looked at me with slightly distressed eyes.
"You . . . ah . . . didn't want to play for money, did you?"

"Not at all," I said and his eyes cleared. "What kind of stories do
you write?"

"Oh, all kinds." He shrugged. "Fantasy mostly."

"Do you sell them?"

"Most of 'em."

"I don't recall seeing your name anywhere. Miss Nesbitt said it was Andrew Detweiler?"

He nodded. "I use another name. You probably wouldn't know it either. It's not exactly a household word." His eyes said he'd really rather not tell me what it was. He had a slight accent, a sort of soft slowness, not exactly a drawl and not exactly Deep South. He shoved the typewriter over and pulled out a deck of cards.

"Where're you from?" I asked. "I don't place the accent."

He grinned and shuffled the cards. "North Carolina. Back in the Blue Ridge."

We cut and I dealt. "How long have you been in Hollywood?"

"About two months."

"How do you like it?"

He grinned his beguiling grin and picked up my discard. "It's very . . . unusual. Have you lived here long, Mr. Mallory?"

"Bert. All my life. I was born in Inglewood. My mother still lives there."

"It must be . . . unusual . . . to live in the same place all your life."

"You move around a lot?"

"Yeah. Gin."

I laughed. "I thought you were unlucky."

"If we were playing for money, I wouldn't be able to do anything right."

We played gin the rest of the afternoon and talked—talked a lot. Detweiler seemed eager to talk or, at least, eager to have someone to talk with. He never told me anything that would connect him to nine deaths, mostly about where he'd been, things he'd read. He read a lot, just about anything he could get his hands on. I got the impression he hadn't really *lived* life so much as he'd *read* it, that all the things he knew about had never physically affected him. He was like an insulated island. Life flowed around him but never touched him. I wondered if the hump on his back made that much difference, if it made him such a green monkey he'd had to retreat into his insular existence. Practically everyone I had talked to liked him, mixed with varying portions of pity, to be sure, but liking nevertheless. Harry Spinner liked him, but had discovered something "peculiar" about him. Birdie Pawlowicz, Maurice Milian, David Fowler, Lorraine Nesbitt, they all liked him.

And, God damn it, I liked him too.

At midnight I was still awake, sitting in number five in my jockey shorts with the light out and the door open. I listened to the ticking of the Detweiler boy's typewriter and the muffled roar of Los Angeles. And thought and thought and thought. And got nowhere.

Someone walked by the door, quietly and carefully. I leaned my head out. It was Johnny Peacock. He moved down the line of bungalows silent as a shadow. He turned south when he reached the sidewalk. Going to Selma or the Boulevard to turn a trick and make a few extra bucks. Lorraine must keep tight purse strings. Better watch it, kid. If she finds out, you'll be back on the streets again. And you haven't got too many years left where you can make good money by just gettin' it up.

I dropped in at the office for a while Friday morning and checked the first-of-the-month bills. Miss Tremaine had a list of new prospective clients. "Tell everyone I can't get to anything till Monday."

She nodded in disapproval. "Mr. Bloomfeld called."

"Did he get my report?"

"Yes. He was very pleased, but he wants the man's name."

"Tell him I'll get back on it Monday."

"Mrs. Bushyager called. Her sister and Mr. Bushyager are still missing."

"Tell her I'll get on it Monday." She opened her mouth. "If you say anything about my bank account, I'll put Spanish fly in your Ovaltine." She didn't *humph,* she giggled. I wonder how many points *that* is?

That afternoon I played gin with the Detweiler boy. He was genuinely glad to see me, like a friendly puppy. I was beginning to feel like a son of a bitch.

He hadn't mentioned North Carolina except that once the day before, and I was extremely interested in all subjects he wanted to avoid. "What's it like in the Blue Ridge? Coon huntin' and moonshine?"

He grinned and blitzed me. "Yeah, I guess. Most of the things you read about it are pretty nearly true. It's really a different world back in there, with almost no contact with the outside."

"How far in did you live?"

"About as far as you can get without comin' out the other side. Did you know most of the people never heard of television or movies

and some of 'em don't even know the name of the President? Most of
'em never been more than thirty miles from the place they were born,
never saw an electric light? You wouldn't believe it. But it's more
than just *things* that're different. People are different, think different—
like a foreign country." He shrugged. "I guess it'll all be gone before
too long though. Things keep creepin' closer and closer. Did you
know I never went to school?" he said, grinning. "Not a day of my
life. I didn't wear shoes till I was ten. You wouldn't believe it." He
shook his head, remembering. "Always kinda wished I coulda gone
to school," he murmured softly.

"Why did you leave?"

"No reason to stay. When I was eight, my parents were killed in a
fire. Our house burned down. I was taken in by a balmy old woman
who lived not far away. I had some kin, but they didn't want me."
He looked at me, trusting me. "They're pretty superstitious back in
there, you know. Thought I was . . . marked. Anyway, the old
woman took me in. She was a midwife, but she fancied herself a
witch or something. Always making me drink some mess she'd
brewed up. She fed me, clothed me, educated me, after a fashion,
tried to teach me all her conjures, but I never could take 'em
seriously." He grinned sheepishly. "I did chores for her and eventually became a sort of assistant, I guess. I helped her birth babies . . .
I mean, deliver babies a couple of times, but that didn't last long.
The parents were afraid me bein' around might mark the baby. She
taught me to read and I couldn't stop. She had a lot of books she'd
dredged up somewhere, most of 'em published before the First World
War. I read a complete set of encyclopedias—published in 1911."

I laughed.

His eyes clouded. "Then she . . . died. I was fifteen, so I left. I
did odd jobs and kept reading. Then I wrote a story and sent it to a
magazine. They bought it; paid me fifty dollars. Thought I was rich,
so I wrote another one. Since then I've been traveling around and
writing. I've got an agent who takes care of everything, and so all I
do is just write."

Detweiler's flush of health was wearing off that afternoon. He
wasn't ill, just beginning to feel like the rest of us mortals. And I was
feeling my resolve begin to crumble. It was hard to believe this beguiling kid could possibly be involved in a string of bloody deaths.
Maybe it was just a series of unbelievable coincidences. Yeah, "un-

believable" was the key word. He *had* to be involved unless the laws of probability had broken down completely. Yet I could swear Detweiler wasn't putting on an act. His guileless innocence was real, damn it, *real*.

Saturday morning, the third day since Miss Herndon died, I had a talk with Lorraine and Johnny. If Detweiler wanted to play cards or something that night, I wanted them to agree and suggest I be a fourth. If he didn't bring it up, I would, but I had a feeling he would want his usual alibi this time.

Detweiler left his room that afternoon for the first time since I'd been there. He went north on Las Palmas, dropped a large Manila envelope in the mailbox (the story he'd been working on, I guess), and bought groceries at the supermarket on Highland. Did that mean he wasn't planning to move? I had a sudden pang in my belly. What if he was staying because of his friendship with *me?* I felt more like a son of a bitch every minute.

Johnny Peacock came by an hour later acting very conspiratorial. Detweiler had suggested a bridge game that night, but Johnny didn't play bridge, and so they settled on Scrabble.

I dropped by number seven. The typewriter had been put away, but the cards and score pad were still on the table. His suitcase was on the floor by the couch. It was riveted cowhide of a vintage I hadn't seen since I was a kid. Though it wore a mellow patina of age, it had been preserved with neat's-foot oil and loving care. I may have been mistaken about his not moving.

Detweiler wasn't feeling well at all. He was pale and drawn and fidgety. His eyelids were heavy and his speech was faintly blurred. I'm sure he was in pain, but he tried to act as if nothing were wrong.

"Are you sure you feel like playing Scrabble tonight?" I asked.

He gave me a cheerful, if slightly strained, smile. "Oh, sure. I'm all right. I'll be fine in the morning."

"Do you think you ought to play?"

"Yeah, it . . . takes my mind off my . . . ah . . . headache. Don't worry about it. I have these spells all the time. They always go away."

"How long have you had them?"

"Since . . . I was a kid." He grinned. "You think it was one of those brews the old witch-woman gave me caused it? Maybe I could sue for malpractice."

"Have you seen a doctor? A real one?"

"Once."

"What did he tell you?"

He shrugged. "Oh, nothing much. Take two aspirin, drink lots of liquids, get plenty of rest, that sort of thing." He didn't want to talk about it. "It always goes away."

"What if one time it doesn't?"

He looked at me with an expression I'd never seen before, and I knew why Lorraine said he had a lost, doomed look. "Well, we can't live forever, can we? Are you ready to go?"

The game started out like a Marx Brothers routine. Lorraine and Johnny acted like two canaries playing Scrabble with the cat, but Detweiler was so normal and unconcerned they soon settled down. Conversation was tense and ragged at first until Lorraine got off on her "career" and kept us entertained and laughing. She had known a lot of famous people and was a fountain of anecdotes, most of them funny and libelous. Detweiler proved quickly to be the best player, but Johnny, to my surprise, was no slouch. Lorraine played dismally but she didn't seem to mind.

I would have enjoyed the evening thoroughly if I hadn't known someone nearby was dead or dying.

After about two hours, in which Detweiler grew progressively more ill, I excused myself to go to the bathroom. While I was away from the table, I palmed Lorraine's master key.

In another half hour I said I had to call it a night. I had to get up early the next morning. I always spent Sunday with my mother in Inglewood. My mother was touring Yucatan at the time, but that was neither here nor there. I looked at Johnny. He nodded. He was to make sure Detweiler stayed at least another twenty minutes and then follow him when he did leave. If he went anywhere but his apartment, he was to come and let me know, quick.

I let myself into number seven with the master key. The drapes were closed, and so I took a chance and turned on the bathroom light. Detweiler's possessions were meager. Eight shirts, six pairs of pants, and a light jacket hung in the closet. The shirts and jacket had been altered to allow for the hump. Except for that, the closet was bare. The bathroom contained nothing out of the ordinary—just about the same as mine. The kitchen had one plastic plate, one plastic cup, one plastic glass, one plastic bowl, one small folding skillet, one small folding sauce pan, one metal spoon, one metal fork, and a medium-sized kitchen knife. All of it together would barely fill a shoebox.

The suitcase, still beside the couch, hadn't been unpacked—except for the clothes hanging in the closet and the kitchen utensils. There was underwear, socks, an extra pair of shoes, an unopened ream of paper, a bunch of other stuff necessary for his writing, and a dozen or so paperbacks. The books were rubber-stamped with the name of a used-book store on Santa Monica Boulevard. They were a mixture: science fiction, mysteries, biographies, philosophy, several by Colin Wilson.

There was also a carbon copy of the story he'd just finished. The return address on the first page was a box number at the Hollywood post office. The title of the story was "Deathsong." I wished I'd had time to read it.

All in all, I didn't find anything. Except for the books and the deck of cards, there was nothing of Andrew Detweiler personally in the whole apartment. I hadn't thought it possible for anyone to lead such a turnip existence.

I looked around to make sure I hadn't disturbed anything, turned off the bathroom light, and got in the closet, leaving the door open a crack. It was the only possible place to hide. I sincerely hoped Detweiler wouldn't need anything out of it before I found out what was going on. If he did, the only thing I could do was confront him with what I'd found out. And then what, Mallory, a big guilty confession? With what you've found out, he could laugh in your face and have you arrested for illegal entry.

And what about this, Mallory? What if someone died nearby tonight while you were with Detweiler; what if he comes straight to his apartment and goes to bed; what if he wakes up in the morning feeling fine; what if nothing is going on, you son of a bitch?

It was so dark in there with the curtains drawn that I couldn't see a thing. I left the closet and opened them a little on the front window. It didn't let in a lot of light, but it was enough. Maybe Detweiler wouldn't notice. I went back to the closet and waited.

Half an hour later the curtains over the barred open window moved. I had squatted down in the closet and wasn't looking in that direction, but the movement caught my eye. Something hopped in the window and scooted across the floor and went behind the couch. I only got a glimpse of it, but it might have been a cat. It was probably a stray looking for food or hiding from a dog. Okay, cat, you don't bother me and I won't bother you. I kept my eye on the couch, but it didn't show itself again.

Detweiler didn't show for another hour. By that time I was sitting flat on the floor trying to keep my legs from cramping. My position wasn't too graceful if he happened to look in the closet, but it was too late to get up.

He came in quickly and bolted the door behind him. He didn't notice the open curtain. He glanced around, clicking his tongue softly. His eyes caught on something at the end of the couch. He smiled. At the *cat?* He began unfastening his shirt, fumbling at the buttons in his haste. He slipped off the shirt and tossed it on the back of a chair.

There were straps across his chest.

He turned toward the suitcase, his back to me. The hump was artificial, made of something like foam rubber. He unhooked the straps, opened the suitcase, and tossed the hump in. He said something, too soft for me to catch, and lay face down on the couch with his feet toward me. The light from the opened curtain fell on him. His back was scarred, little white lines like scratches grouped around a hole.

He had a hole in his back, between his shoulder blades, an unhealed wound big enough to stick your finger in.

Something came around the end of the couch. It wasn't a cat. I thought it was a monkey, and then a frog, but it was neither. It was human. It waddled on all fours like an enormous toad.

Then it stood erect. It was about the size of a cat. It was pink and moist and hairless and naked. Its very human hands and feet and male genitals were too large for its tiny body. Its belly was swollen, turgid and distended like an obscene tick. Its head was flat. Its jaw protruded like an ape's. It too had a scar, a big, white, puckered scar between its shoulder blades, at the top of its jutting backbone.

It reached its too-large hand up and caught hold of Detweiler's belt. It pulled its bloated body up with the nimbleness of a monkey and crawled onto the boy's back. Detweiler was breathing heavily, clasping and unclasping his fingers on the arm of the couch.

The thing crouched on Detweiler's back and placed its lips against the wound.

I felt my throat burning and my stomach turning over, but I watched in petrified fascination.

Detweiler's breathing grew slower and quieter, more relaxed. He lay with his eyes closed and an expression of almost sexual pleasure on his face. The thing's body got smaller and smaller, the skin on its belly growing wrinkled and flaccid. A trickle of blood crawled from the wound, making an erratic line across the Detweiler boy's back. The thing reached out its hand and wiped the drop back with a finger.

It took about ten minutes. The thing raised its mouth and crawled over beside the boy's face. It sat on the arm of the couch like a little gnome and smiled. It ran its fingers down the side of Detweiler's cheek and pushed his damp hair back out of his eyes. Detweiler's expression was euphoric. He sighed softly and opened his eyes sleepily. After a while he sat up.

He was flushed with health, rosy and clear and shining.

He stood up and went in the bathroom. The light came on and I heard water running. The thing sat in the same place watching him. Detweiler came out of the bathroom and sat back on the couch. The thing climbed onto his back, huddling between his shoulder blades, its hands on his shoulders. Detweiler stood up, the thing hanging onto him, retrieved the shirt, and put it on. He wrapped the straps neatly around the artificial hump and stowed it in the suitcase. He closed the lid and locked it.

I had seen enough, more than enough. I opened the door and stepped out of the closet.

Detweiler whirled, his eyes bulging. A groan rattled in his throat. He raised his hands as if fending me off. The groan rose in pitch, becoming an hysterical keening. The expression on his face was too horrible to watch. He stepped backward and tripped over the suitcase.

He lost his balance and toppled over. His arms flailed for equilibrium, but never found it. He struck the edge of the table. It caught him square across the hump on his back. He bounced and fell forward on his hands. He stood up agonizingly, like a slow motion movie, arching his spine backward, his face contorted in pain.

There were shrill, staccato shrieks of mindless torment, but they didn't come from Detweiler.

He fell again, forward onto the couch, blacking out from pain.

The back of his shirt was churning. The scream continued, hurting my ears. Rips appeared in the shirt and a small misshapen arm poked out briefly. I could only stare, frozen. The shirt was ripped to shreds. Two arms, a head, a torso came through. The whole thing ripped its way out and fell onto the couch beside the boy. Its face was twisted, tortured, and its mouth kept opening and closing with the screams. Its eyes looked uncomprehendingly about. It pulled itself along with its arms, dragging its useless legs, its spine obviously broken. It fell off the couch and flailed about on the floor.

Detweiler moaned and came to. He rose from the couch, still groggy. He saw the thing, and a look of absolute grief appeared on his face.

The thing's eyes focused for a moment on Detweiler. It looked at him, beseeching, held out one hand, pleading. Its screams continued, that one monotonous, hopeless note repeated over and over. It lowered its arm and kept crawling about mindlessly, growing weaker.

Detweiler stepped toward it, ignoring me, tears pouring down his face. The thing's struggles grew weaker, the scream became a breathless rasping. I couldn't stand it any longer. I picked up a chair and smashed it down on the thing. I dropped the chair and leaned against the wall and heaved.

I heard the door open. I turned and saw Detweiler run out.

I charged after him. My legs felt rubbery but I caught him at the street. He didn't struggle. He just stood there, his eyes vacant, trembling. I saw people sticking their heads out of doors and Johnny Peacock coming toward me. My car was right there. I pushed Detweiler into it and drove away. He sat hunched in the seat, his hands hanging limply, staring into space. He was trembling uncontrollably and his teeth chattered.

I drove, not paying any attention to where I was going, almost as deeply in shock as he was. I finally started looking at the street signs. I was on Mullholland. I kept going west for a long time, crossed the San Diego Freeway, into the Santa Monica Mountains. The pavement ends a couple of miles past the freeway, and there's ten or fifteen miles of dirt road before the pavement picks up again nearly to Topanga. The road isn't traveled much, there are no houses on it, and people don't like to get their cars dusty. I was about in the middle of the unpaved section when Detweiler seemed to calm down. I pulled over to the side of the road and cut the engine. The San Fernando Valley was spread like a carpet of lights below us. The ocean was on the other side of the mountains.

I sat and watched Detweiler. The trembling had stopped. He was asleep or unconscious. I reached over and touched his arm. He stirred and clutched at my hand. I looked at his sleeping face and didn't have the heart to pull my hand away.

The sun was poking over the mountains when he woke up. He roused and was momentarily unaware of where he was; then memory flooded back. He turned to me. The pain and hysteria were gone from his eyes. They were oddly peaceful.

"Did you hear him?" he said softly. "Did you hear him die?"

"Are you feeling better?"

"Yes. It's all over."

"Do you want to talk about it?"

His eyes dropped and he was silent for a moment. "I want to tell you. But I don't know how without you thinking I'm a monster."

I didn't say anything.

"He . . . was my brother. We were twins. Siamese twins. All those people died so I could stay alive." There was no emotion in his voice. He was detached, talking about someone else. "He kept me alive. I'll die without him." His eyes met mine again. "He was insane, I think. I thought at first I'd go mad too, but I didn't. I think I didn't. I never knew what he was going to do, who he would kill. I didn't want to know. He was very clever. He always made it look like an accident or suicide when he could. I didn't interfere. I didn't want to die. We had to have blood. He always did it so there was lots of blood, so no one would miss what he took." His eyes were going empty again.

"Why did you need the blood?"

"We were never suspected before."

"Why did you need the blood?" I repeated.

"When we were born," he said, and his eyes focused again, "we were joined at the back. But I grew and he didn't. He stayed little bitty, like a baby riding around on my back. People didn't like me . . . us, they were afraid. My father and mother too. The old witch-woman I told you about, she birthed us. She seemed always to be hanging around. When I was eight, my parents died in a fire. I think the witch-woman did it. After that I lived with her. She was demented, but she knew medicine and healing. When we were fifteen

she decided to separate us. I don't know why. I think she wanted him
without me. I'm sure she thought he was an imp from hell. I almost
died. I'm not sure what was wrong. Apart, we weren't whole. I
wasn't whole. He had something I didn't have, something we'd been
sharing. She would've let me die, but he knew and got blood for me.
Hers." He sat staring at me blankly, his mind living the past.

"Why didn't you go to a hospital or something?" I asked, feeling
enormous pity for the wretched boy.

He smiled faintly. "I didn't know much about anything then. Too
many people were already dead. If I'd gone to a hospital, they'd have
wanted to know how I'd stayed alive so far. Sometimes I'm glad it's
over, and, then, the next minute I'm terrified of dying."

"How long?"

"I'm not sure. I've never been more than three days. I can't stand
it any longer than that. He knew. He always knew when I had to
have it. And he got it for me. I never helped him."

"Can you stay alive if you get regular transfusions?"

He looked at me sharply, fear creeping back. "Please. No!"

"But you'll stay alive."

"In a cage! Like a freak! I don't want to be a freak anymore. It's
over. I want it to be over. Please."

"What do you want me to do?"

"I don't know. I don't want you to get in trouble."

I looked at him, at his face, at his eyes, at his soul. "There's a gun
in the glove compartment," I said.

He sat for a moment, then solemnly held out his hand. I took it.
He shook my hand, then opened the glove compartment. He removed the gun and slipped out of the car. He went down the hill into
the brush.

I waited and waited and never did hear a shot.

Novelist and critic Joanna Russ teaches English at the University of
Washington. When our starting book reviewer, Algis Budrys, tires,
our favorite relief reviewer is Ms. Russ. Here she offers a fascinating
article (in response to some critical letters) which tells why critics
are such snobs and are so vitriolic, among many other things.

Books: *In Defense*
of Criticism

by JOANNA RUSS

Critics seem to find it necessary, at least once in a career, to write a
statement defending criticism per se. Shaw, Pauline Kael, Eric Bent-
ley, and James Blish have all done it. That I'm doing it, too, doesn't
prove I'm in the same league, but it does indicate the persistence of
the issues involved and that they occur outside, as well as inside, science fiction.

I have tried to speak to general issues rather than "defend" my
own criticism. Issues are, in any case, more important than personalities, although there is a (small) section of fandom which sees in
aesthetic or political disagreement nothing but personal squabbling
motivated by envy. It's not for me to judge how good my criticism is;
if enough readers think it's bad, and the editor thinks so too, presum-
ably he'll stop printing it, although writing book reviews (except
for places like the New York *Times*) is underpaid, overworked, and
a labor of love. The problem is usually to recruit reviewers, not discourage them.

Here are some of the complaints that keep coming up.

1. *Don't shove your politics into your reviews. Just review the books.*

I will—when the authors keep politics out of their stories. But they never do; in fact, it seems absolutely impossible to write anything without immediately making all sorts of assumptions about what human nature is, what good and bad behavior consists of, what men ought to be, what women ought to be, which states of mind and character are valuable, which are the opposite, and so on. Once fiction gets beyond the level of minimal technical competence, a reviewer must address these judgments of value. Generally, readers don't notice the presence of familiar value judgments in stories, but do notice (and object to) unfamiliar ones as "political." Hence arises the insistence (in itself a very vehement, political judgment) that art and politics have nothing to do with one another, that artists ought to be "above" politics, and that a critic making political comments about fiction is importing something foreign into an essentially neutral area. But if "politics" means the relations of power that obtain between groups of people, and the way these are concretely embodied in personal relations, social institutions, and received ideas (among which is the idea that art ought not to be political), then such neutrality simply doesn't exist. Fiction which isn't openly polemical or didactic is nonetheless chock-full of politics. If beauty in fiction bears any relation to truth (as Matthew Arnold thought), then the human (including social and political) truth of a piece of fiction matters, for aesthetic reasons. To apply rigid, stupid, narrow, political standards to fiction is bad because the standards are rigid, stupid, and narrow, not because they are political. For an example of (to my mind) profound, searching, brilliant, political criticism, see Jean-Paul Sartre's *Saint Genet.*

2. *You don't prove what you say; you just assert it.*

This statement is, I think, based on a cognitive error inculcated (probably) by American high school education. The error is that all proofs must be of the "hard" kind, i.e., cut-and-dried and susceptible of presentation in syllogistic form. An acquaintance with the modern philosophy of science would disabuse people of this notion; even a surprising amount of scientific proof is not of this kind. As philosophers since Plato have been pointing out, aesthetic and moral matters are usually not susceptible of such "hard" proof.

3. *Then your opinion is purely subjective.*

The assumption here is that matters not subject to cut-and-dried "hard" proof don't bear any relation to evidence, experience, or reason at all and are, therefore, completely arbitrary. There is considerable indirect evidence one can bring against this view. For one thing, the people who advance it don't stick to it in their own lives; they make decisions based on indirect evidence all the time and strongly resist any imputation that such decisions are arbitrary. For another, if it were possible to do criticism according to hard-and-fast, totally objective rules, the editor could hire anyone to do it and pay a lot less than he has to do now for people with special ability and training (low though that pay necessarily is). It's true that the apparatus by which critics judge books is subjective in the sense of being inside the critic and not outside, unique, and based on the intangibles of training, talent, and experience. But that doesn't per se make it arbitrary. What can make it seem arbitrary is that the whole preliminary process of judgment, if you trace it through all its stages, is coextensive with the critic's entire education. So critics tend to suppress it in reviews (with time and training most of it becomes automatic, anyway). Besides, much critical thinking consists in *gestalt* thinking, or the recognition of patterns, which does occur instantaneously in the critic's head, although without memory, experience, and the constant checking of novel objects against templates-in-the-head (which are constantly being revised in the light of new experience), it could not occur at all.* Hence angry readers can make the objection above, or add:

4. *Everyone's entitled to his own opinion.*

Have you noticed how often people say "I feel" instead of "I think" or (God forbid) "I know"? Kids who discover "It's a free country!" at seven graduate to "Everyone's entitled to his own opinion" by fourteen. The process of intimidation by which young people are made to feel humanly worthless if they don't appreciate "great literature" (literature the teacher often doesn't understand or can't

---

* I used to inform people of the endings of television plays (before the endings happened) until my acquaintances gently but firmly informed me they would rather the endings came as a surprise. When asked how I knew what was coming, by friends who enjoyed such an odd talent (and some do), I could explain only part of the time. The cues people respond to in fiction or drama are complex and people are not always fully conscious of them.

explain)† is one of the ghastly facts of American education. Some defenses against this experience take the form of asserting there's no such thing as great art; some, that whatever moves one intensely *is* great art. Both are ways of asserting the primacy and authenticity of one's own experience, and that's fine. But whatever you (or I) like intensely isn't, just because of that, great anything, and the literary canon, although incomplete and biased, is not merely an insider's snobbish conspiracy to make outsiders feel rotten. (Although it is certainly used that way far too often.)

The problem with literature and literary criticism is that there is no obvious craft involved—so people who wouldn't dream of challenging a dance critic's comments on an *assoluta's* line or a *prima donna's* musicianship are conscious of no reason not to dismiss mine on J. R. R. Tolkien. We're all dealing with language, after all, aren't we? But there is a very substantial craft involved here, although its material isn't toes or larynxes. And some opinions are worth a good deal more than others.

5. *I knew it. You're a snob.*

Science fiction is a small country which for years has maintained a protective standards-tariff to encourage native manufactures. Many readers are, in fact, unacquainted with the general canon of English literature or the standards of criticism outside our own small field. Add to this the defensiveness so many people feel about high culture and you get the wholesale inflation of reputations James Blish lambasts in *The Issue at Hand*. Like him, I believe that somebody has to stop handing out stars and kisses: If "great writer" means Charles Dickens or Virginia Woolf (not to mention William Shakespeare), then it does not mean C. S. Lewis or J. R. R. Tolkien, about whom the most generous consensus of mainstream critical opinion is that they are good, interesting, minor authors. And so on.

6. *You're vitriolic, too.*

It's true. Critics tend to be an irritable lot. Here are some examples:

"That light-hearted body, the Bach Choir, has had what I may befittingly call another shy at the Mass in B minor." (George Ber-

---

† Or oddities that entered the curriculum decades before and refuse to be dislodged, like "To a Waterfowl." For some reason students often end up with the most sophisticated, flawed, or least-accessible works of great writers: twelve-year-olds reading *Romeo and Juliet*, for example, or *Silas Marner*.

nard Shaw, *Music in London,* v. ii, Constable & Co., Ltd., London, 1956, p. 55.)

" 'This eloquent novel,' says the jacket of Taylor Caldwell's *The Devil's Advocate,* making two errors in three words. . . ." (Damon Knight, *In Search of Wonder,* Advent, Chicago, 1967, p. 29.)

". . . Mr. Zirul has committed so many other failures of technique that a whole course in fiction writing could be erected above his hapless corpse." (William Atheling, Jr. [James Blish], *The Issue at Hand,* Advent, Chicago, 1964, p. 83.)

Why do we do it?

First, there is the reactive pain. Only those who have reviewed, year in and year out, know how truly abominable most fiction is. And we can't remove ourselves from the pain. Ordinary readers can skip, or read every third word, or quit in the middle. We can't. We must read carefully, with our sensitivities at full operation and our critical-historical apparatus always in high gear—or we may miss that subtle satire which disguises itself as cliché, that first novel whose beginning, alas, was never revised, that gem of a quiet story obscured in a loud, flashy collection, that experiment in form which could be mistaken for sloppiness, that appealing tale partly marred by (but also made possible by) naiveté, that complicated situation that only pays off near the end of the book. Such works exist, but in order not to miss them, one must continually extend one's sensitivity, knowledge, and critical care to works that only abuse such faculties. The mental sensation is that of eating garbage, I assure you, and if critics' accumulated suffering did not find an outlet in the vigor of our language, I don't know what we would do. And it's the critics who care the most who suffer the most; irritation is a sign of betrayed love. As Shaw puts it:

> ". . . criticism written without personal feeling is not worth reading. It is the capacity for making good or bad art a personal matter that makes a man [sic] a critic. . . . when people do less than their best, and do that less at once badly and self-complacently, I hate them, loathe them, detest them, long to tear them limb from limb and strew them in gobbets about the stage or platform. . . . In the same way really fine artists inspire me with the warmest possible regard. . . . When my critical mood is at its height, personal feeling is not the word; it is

passion. . . ." (*Music in London,* v. i, Constable & Co., London, 1956, pp. 51–52)

But there are other reasons. Critical judgments are so complex (and take place in such a complicated context), the vocabulary of praise and blame available in English is so vague, so fluid, and so constantly shifting, and the physical space allowed is so small that critics welcome any way of expressing judgments that will be both *precise* and *compact.* If *vivid* be added thereunto, fine—what else is good style? Hence critics, whenever possible, express their judgments in figurative language. Wit is a form of condensation (see Freud if you think this is my arbitrary fiat) just as parody is a form of criticism (see Dwight McDonald's Modern Library collection thereof).

Dramatization is another. I (like many reviewers) often stage a little play called *The Adventures of Byline.* Byline (or "I") is the same species of creature as the Kindly Editor or the Good Doctor, who appear from time to time in these pages. That is, she is a form of shorthand. When Byline rewrites story X, that doesn't mean that I—the real, historical personage—actually did or will or wish to rewrite story X, or that I expect its real, historical author to rewrite it to Byline's prescription, any more than my saying that "my" copy of *Bug Jack Barron* tried to punch "me" in the nose means that such an event really happened. Pauline Kael's Movie Loon is another such fiction; these little creatures we send scurrying about the page are not our real, live selves, and their exploits are dictated more by the exigencies of our form than by a desire for personal glory.

7. *Never mind all that stuff. Just tell me what I'd enjoy reading.*

Bless you, what makes you think I know? (See, there goes Byline.) Actually, critics can make educated guesses from time to time about the tastes of some groups of readers. Editors must, such judgments being their bread and butter—and look how often *they* fail. If judgments of beauty and truth are difficult, imagine what happens when the issue is escape reading, i.e., something as idiosyncratic as guided daydreams. Perhaps the popularity of series novels is due in part to readers' desire for a reliable, easily reproducible pleasure. But the simplest good-bad scales (like the *Daily News* system of stars) is always colliding with readers' tastes. Some writers and publishers, in order to be sure of appealing to at least a stable fraction of the market, standardize their product. This can be done, but it tends to eliminate from fiction these idiosyncratic qualities other readers find valuable, art being of an order of complexity nearer to that of human beings (high) than that of facial tissues (low).

Now back to the topic of heroic fantasy, which occasioned the foregoing.

I know it's painful to be told that something in which one has invested intense emotion is not only bad art but bad for you, not only bad for you but ridiculous. I didn't do it to be mean, honest. Nor did I do it because the promise held out by heroic fantasy—the promise of escape into a wonderful Other world—is one I find temperamentally unappealing. On the contrary. It's because I understand the intensity of the demand so well (having spent my twenties reading Eddison and Tolkien; I even adapted *The Hobbit* for the stage) that I also understand the absolute impossibility of ever fulfilling that demand. The current popularity of heroic fantasy scares me; I believe it to be a symptom of political and cultural reaction due to economic depression. So does Robin Scott Wilson (who electrified a Modern Language Association seminar by calling *Dune* a fascist book), and Michael Moorcock (see his jacket copy for Norman Spinrad's *The Iron Dream,* a novel which vehemently denounces the genre in the same terms Wilson does‡), and the writers of *Bored of the Rings,* the Lampoon parody, from which came "Arrowroot, son of Arrowshirt."

Briefly, to answer other statements in the letters: I apologize for implying that Tolkien's hobbits and Ents (or his other bucolic-comic creations) are as empty-sublime as the Big People's heroics. But I agree (see question 5) that Tolkien is a good, interesting, minor writer whose strong point is his *paysages moralisés*. Ditto C. S. Lewis, in his Narnya books. As for other writers mentioned, only strong, selective blindness could miss the Vancian cynicism or the massive Dunsanian irony (sometimes spilling over into despair) which make their heroism far from simple or unquestioned-by-the-authors-themselves. As for the others, I find them ghastly when uncorrected by comedy, or satire (Morris, sometimes), or (in Beagle's case) the nostalgic wistfulness which belongs to fantasy per se rather than the

‡ Though *Dune* is, strictly speaking, science fiction. Wilson was talking about the-great-leader syndrome, and the heroic atmosphere *Dune* shares with heroic fantasy.

publisher's category (that, historically, is what it is) of heroic fantasy. I don't need to bad-mouth Poul Anderson, James Blish having already adequately done so, calling him (in his heroic phase) "the Thane of Minneapolis. . . . Anderson can write well, but this is seldom evident while he is in his Scand avatar, when he seems invariably to be writing in his sleep." (*The Issue at Hand,* p. 72.) That our literary heritage began with feudal epics and *märchen* is no reason to keep on writing them forever. And daydreams about being tall, handsome (or beautiful), noble, admired, and involved in thrilling deeds is not the same as the as-if speculation which produces medical and technological advances.

It isn't the realists who find life dreadful. It's the romancers. After all, which group is trying to escape from life? Reality is horrible *and* wonderful, disappointing *and* ecstatic, beautiful *and* ugly. Reality is everything. Reality is what there is. Only the hopelessly insensitive find reality so pleasant as to never want to get away from it. But pain-killers can be bad for the health, and even if they were not, I am damned if anyone will make me say that the newest fad in analgesics is equivalent to the illumination, which is the other thing (besides pleasure) art ought to provide. Bravery, nobility, sublimity, and beauty that have no connection with the real world are simply fake, and once readers realize that escape *does not work,* the glamor fades, the sublime aristocrats turn silly, the profundities become simplifications, and one enters (if one is lucky) into the dreadful discipline of reality and art, like "In the Penal Colony." But George Bernard Shaw said all this almost a century ago; interested readers may look up his preface to *Arms and the Man* or that little book, *The Quintessence of Ibsenism.*

It's disheartening to see how little has changed. On the other hand, there is no pleasure like finding out the realities of human life, in which joy and misery, effort and release, dread and happiness, walk hand in hand.

We had better enjoy it. It's what there is.

—Joanna Russ

"It is the year 2783. Suddenly the galaxy is invaded by a horde of alien beings, the Zorphs. They enslave all planets in their path. You, as Captain of the Avenger, the great Terran warship, will range interstellar space, seeking out and destroying the forces of Zorph." This is but a bare outline of the ultimate in computer games . . .

Zorphwar!

by STAN DRYER

Megalo Network Message:
   June 10, 1977
Source: P. T. Warrington, Headquarters, Los Gringos, California
Destination: W. S. Halson, Programming Services, Wrapping
   Falls, New York
Subject: Schedule Compliance in Programming Services
Bill, Old Buddy, I think you have problems. J.L. was down this morning bitching about your performance. The PERT printout indicates you have slipped schedule on Accounting Project 8723 by two months. In addition, your usage of central computer facilities is running 42 percent over budget. Remember that the Megalo Corporation is not in business for its health. Accounting is depending on Program 8723 to keep track of profitability in the entire Computer Products Division.

Megalo Network Message:
   June 10, 1977
Source: W. S. Halson
Destination: P. T. Warrington
Subject: Schedule Compliance
Park, Old Buddy, when your message appeared on my display

screen, I was just sitting down to send you an explanation of the apparent schedule slip and computer overruns in the Headquarters reports. What you see are computer-generated summaries of our progress, mere pieces of paper that do not represent the full situation. For example, nowhere in those reports is the well-being of our programmers evaluated. Now I can say without equivocation that our morale down here has never been higher. Absence due to personal illness has dropped twenty-seven percent over the last two months. There have been no "Bitch to the Top" submissions from my department in the last four months.

The cause of this high morale rests with one programmer in our department, Morris Hazeldorf, the inventor of Zorphwar. While I admit that his shaggy hair and unkempt personal attire might turn you off on first encounter, Morris is an extremely bright and able young man. Single-handed, he programmed the entire HAFAS (Hierarchical Accounting File Access System). And in his spare time over the past year, Morris has been creating Zorphwar, an exciting game that operates on our system.

To give you an idea of the creativity of this young man, I have arranged for Zorphwar to be made available to you on the Executive Interactive Display Terminal in your office. After you dial into the Computer Center, simply type "ZORPH" to gain access to the game.

Let me give you a quick rundown of this exciting interactive game. It is the year 2783. Man has reached out to settle thousands of planets scattered across the galaxy. Then, suddenly, the galaxy is invaded by a horde of alien beings, the Zorphs. They enslave all planets in their path. Those that resist are destroyed without mercy. You, as Captain of the Avenger, the great Terran warship, will range interstellar space, seeking out and destroying the forces of Zorph.

On your screen you will be given a display of your current sector of the galaxy and the stars in that sector. You may fire off laser probes to determine the location of Zorph warships. You have a number of weapons at your disposal including quantum rays, antimatter missiles and, for desperate situations, doomsday torpedoes. Your ship is protected by shields against any attack, but you must be careful to maintain your energy supply. Any Zorphs in your sector will attack you and each attack will use up some of your reserve energy. If your energy is depleted, your shields fail and the next Zorph attack destroys you. You can replenish your energy reserve by returning to a friendly base. You can hop sectors using hyperspace, although void storms may toss you about a bit in space and time. In addition, you will have to handle a variety of problems with your ship such as invasion by mind-warping beings, power-system failure, and occasional crew mutinies. The console commands that control your warship are simple and are given in the attached instructions being transmitted to your local printout facility.

Now do not get the idea that everyone here is simply sitting around playing Zorphwar. That is far from the case. While our schedules have slipped a bit in the last couple of months, morale is at an all-time high. With a crew of satisfied programmers, I feel there is nothing we cannot accomplish.

Finally, before you make any snap judgments, I ask that you log in on your console and try Zorphwar. Good hunting!

Megalo Network Message:
   June 30, 1977
Source: P. T. Warrington
Destination: W. S. Halson
Subject: Promotion to Fleet Captain

Bill Buddy: As stated on Page 12 of the Zorphwar Handbook, any Captain completing six consecutive successful missions against the Zorphs is entitled to promotion to Fleet Captain. If you will check my War Record File, you will discover that I destroyed all Zorphs in the galaxy in the six games I played yesterday afternoon. Please send along whatever certificate you have to indicate my Fleet Captain status.

As for schedules, I have discussed the matter with J.L. and demonstrated Zorphwar to him. Both of us are in entire agreement with your analysis. Maintaining morale *is* one of our primary goals, and we are sure you have things under control. J.L. is, by the way, interested in access to Zorphwar on his own executive terminal. I trust that you will see to the necessary arrangements.

As for the exception reports triggered by your schedule slippage, J.L. has signed off on the necessary forms to justify a new schedule. We have doubled the expected times required to complete phases four through seven. While this stretches out the predicted completion for Project 8723 by two years, we feel that you people are doing important work in other areas and should not be forced to produce a program of use only to those uptight jokers in Accounting.

Now I must get back to Zorphwar. Twenty more successful missions, and I move up to Sector Commandant!

Megalo Network Message:
   July 6, 1977
Source: W. S. Halson
Destination: P. T. Warrington
Subject: Enclosed Certificate
Congratulations, Fleet Captain! I am pleased to transmit to the facsimile printer in your area a copy of your certificate suitable for framing and wall display. Note that it is a fine example of computer-generated art, a project that a couple of my people have been working on for the last six months.

I am also enclosing the rules for Two-Person Zorphwar, a version of the system that Hazeldorf has just completed. Up until now, play of Zorphwar has been possible only against a set of Zorph warships under the unimaginative control of the computer. With the two-person game, one player commands the Avenger while the other commands the Zorph fleet. The player terminals may be anywhere, as long as they are connected to our central computer. Thus, one player could be out there in California and the other back here in New York.

Megalo Network Message:
   July 13, 1977
Source: P. T. Warrington
Destination: W. S. Halson
Subject: Doom of Warship Avenger
Earthling Swine! I, Parker, Emperor and Commander and Chief of the Hordes of Zorph, do here give warning. Tomorrow afternoon at 14:00 hours I shall commence the obliteration of all decadent humanoid pigs in my galaxy. Be at your console at the appointed hour! You are forewarned but foredoomed.

Megalo Network Message:
   July 15, 1977
Source: W. S. Halson
Destination: P. T. Warrington
Subject: Zorphwar Exposure
Park Baby, I think we have a problem. That was a great game of

Zorphwar we had yesterday, and I must commend you on how well you handled the forces of Zorph. It was a challenge all the way, and if I had not been on my toes, your final desperate tactic of launching all twelve thousand of your doomsday torpedoes would have destroyed me. However, when you made your attack, I was safely docked at a base star and thus protected by its powerful energy screens. Your attack succeeded only in wiping out the remnants of your own forces.

Unfortunately, launching twelve thousand torpedoes simultaneously put a serious overload on our computer system. Zorphwar runs at A-1 priority on our machine, which means that any other use of the machine is halted while Zorphwar computations are completed. As you may have noticed, it took approximately forty minutes for the machine to compute the paths through the galaxy of those torpedoes, to determine their impact points, and to calculate the radius of destruction of each burst. Normally such overloads are handled by adjusting the work load in the Computer Center. However, at three thirty yesterday, the Center was in the midst of printing the paychecks for the entire Computer Products Division. The little delay our game occasioned upset the very tight schedule for that operation. As a result, all checks from R through Z were not printed on time and failed to make the courier flight to the West Coast. That is the reason your paycheck was not delivered to you today. Regrettably, it is also the reason that Division President Talling and Corporation Comptroller Westland were not paid this week. While you are more familiar than I am with the personalities at Headquarters, I suspect that both of these gentlemen like to receive their paychecks. I trust that, if any investigations come out of this little incident, you will do your best to emphasize the fact that the Zorphwar program has already been modified to permit the launching of no more than ten doomsday torpedoes in one attack. Thus, this particular problem can never occur again.

Megalo Network Message:
 July 18, 1977
 Source: P. T. Warrington
 Destination: W. S. Halson
 Subject: Zorphwar Development Schedule
Bill, Old Man: You were right as to the reaction of our President and Comptroller. The old stuff really hit the fan with about a dozen

ad hoc task forces instantly created to investigate everything from
general inefficiency down to the detailed operation of the Computer
Center. Someone immediately spilled the beans about Zorphwar. (I
suspect it was J.L., covering his ass.) Friday afternoon Westland
came slamming into my office to ask about a thousand questions
about our schedules and the cost of running Zorphwar. I tried to get
him to try using the program, but he was too upset to listen to
reason. He gave me one hour to produce a full report justifying the
project and went storming back up to the executive wing. I'm afraid
that your ass and mine would have been in the sling but for a stroke
of incredible luck.

When Westland left, I headed for the men's room to down a couple of aspirin to steady my nerves. And who should I meet coming
out of the door but Admiral Venerate. Venerate and I are old bud-
dies, having been together on the Potlatch Investigation Team some
eight years ago. At that time I proved there were no irregularities in
the award of the Potlatch missile contract to Megalo. Venerate
proved that the Navy had done nothing wrong. I was promoted to
this staff position. Venerate moved up to Admiral.

"What brings you to the Megalo Corporation?" I asked him, trying to affect the nonchalance of a happy executive.

"I have just been given the ultimate garbage presentation," he
said. "Your boys should know better than to try to snow me about
naval-training games."

I smiled and spoke some platitudes about the vast technical expertise available at the Megalo Corporation and their ability to respond
quickly to any technical challenge.

"Damn it," said the Admiral, "I don't want technical expertise. I
want a working system."

The old light bulb went on inside my head. "You want a working
system?" I said. "You follow me."

I led the Admiral into my office and fired up Zorphwar on the
tube.

"Now before you play," I said, "you must understand that we did
not wish it known we were working on a proposed naval system.
Thus, we have pretended that we are fighting a space war of the future against the mythical race of Zorphs. The weapons you will be
using will not have the standard Navy nomenclature, but you'll have
no trouble recognizing what they really are."

"Smart thinking," said Venerate. "Now how do I get this game started?"

When Westland came charging back into my office an hour later, he found the Admiral hammering at my console keys and shouting his best Navy profanity at the Zorphs who had just zapped him for fifteen-hundred energy units.

"You are witnessing a demonstration of the Zorphwar Naval Battle Simulation System," I said to Westland. "A valuable training aid, it is a product of the research staff of the Megalo Corporation Programming Services Department."

Westland stood there with his lower jaw down around his ankles watching Venerate polish off the last of the Zorph fleet. The Admiral turned around grinning like a child of ten who has found a pony under the Christmas tree. "That is what I call action!" he cried.

He turned to Westland. "How come you dunderheads didn't show me this right off?" he demanded.

By now, I am sure, the Naval Support Bid Team has descended upon Programming Services to begin costing out the proposal for a production version of Zorphwar. They are talking about a system with one hundred terminals running on two Megalo 861's for starters. Eventually they may order a dozen 861's. Everyone here in Headquarters is too excited about the prospect of selling that kind of hardware to worry about why the program was written in the first place.

Megalo Network Message:
    August 26, 1977
    Source: W. S. Halson
    Destination: P. T. Warrington
    Subject: Zorphwar Contract

Park, Old Friend: I just want to bring you up to date on the Zorphwar contract. The team of programmers and technical writers is in place. The schedule for putting together a production package is a bit tight, considering that the only documentation available from Hazeldorf was a picture of a Zorph he had sketched on the back of an envelope.

Speaking of Hazeldorf, I was a little disappointed in his reaction to the project. When I explained to him what this contract would mean to the Megalo Corporation and how I expected him to assume a leadership role in the production of the final package, he simply shook his head and said, "The Zorphs aren't going to like this." I hope the kid isn't going flaky on us.

Megalo Network Message:
    September 21, 1977
Source: P. T. Warrington
Destination: W. S. Halson
Subject: Zorphwar Contract
Bill, Old Buddy: I hate to bring this up, but J.L. was down this morning to say that there have been no reports on the progress of the Zorphwar project from you people. Please get the necessary input into the computer as quickly as possible so we can start tracking this vital project. I hope that this omission on your part does not mean that schedules are slipping down there.

Zorph Commonwealth Network
    Message: Celestial Date 7654-55
Source: Central Computing Message Processing
Destination: P. T. Warrington Tribute Station 756
Subject: Admission to Commonwealth of Zorph
His Imperial Majesty, Ruler of Zorphdom and the Greater Galaxy, The Middle Claw of Justice in the Universe, Benefactor of all Sentient Beings, does hereby proclaim that your planet, Solus III, has been admitted to the Commonwealth of Zorph as a Status V member. As a member in this privileged class, you will be expected to pay tribute in measure of your standing. The requisite payment for your Corporation is twelve ingots of gold of 100-kilogram weight per week. These should be placed on the roof of the Megalo Corporation Headquarters for pickup by Zorph shuttle craft. Failure to comply with this order will result in immediate penalties, including criminal trials of your leaders. Address all subsequent messages to Message Central for relay to the Zorph commandship assigned to your sector.

Megalo Network Message:
    September 22, 1977
Source: P. T. Warrington
Destination: W. S. Halson
Subject: Attempts at Humor
Bill, this is definitely not the time for jokes. Something has gone

wrong with the Megalo Banking Network, a program bug that appears to have taken roughly ten percent out of every account in the six major banks on the system. The funds have been transferred to some unknown account. This place is, needless to say, Panic City, with vice-presidents screaming for action all over the place.

Fortunately, I intercepted your little jest before anyone else saw it. Now forget the fun and games and get that data into the computer pronto.

Zorph Commonwealth Network
  Message: Celestial Date 7654-57
Source: Central Computing Message Processing
Destination: P. T. Warrington
Message sent represents an invalid communication and has not been dispatched to addressee. Please respond immediately to Central Processing with date and time of initial tribute delivery.

Date: September 23, 1977
From: P. T. Warrington
To: W. S. Halson
Subject: Problems with Communications Network
I am sending this message by mail as there seems to be something wrong with the Megalo telephone system and the message network is all fouled up. Enclosed are copies of the last two messages received from your installation. I shall assume that your screwball friend Hazeldorf has gotten into the guts of the message-switching system and reprogrammed it to produce these messages as a practical joke. If this is the case, correct the situation immediately and dismiss Hazeldorf. Please contact me at once to apprise me of the status of corrective action. I assume that you are still in charge down there and that all of this is merely some kind of poor-taste humor.

It *is* all a joke, isn't it?

From Competition 14:
Science fiction "What's the question?" jokes.

A: Heinlein
Q: What's the shortest distance between two heinpoints?
A: Three Hearts and Three Lions
Q: In Sword & Sorcery Poker, what beats a full castle?
A: Hellstrom's Hive
Q: What is Hellstrom always scratching? (Similarly from others)
A: Piers Anthony's "Orn."
Q: Say, Guv, what's the author of "Chthon" 'ave in 'is car that he loves to 'onk?
A: Simak, Sohl, Spinrad and Sturgeon
Q: Name three sci-fi authors and something that goes great on a bagel with onion.

—*Steve Steinberg*

A: When Harlie Was One
Q: When was this picture taken?
A: The Sands of Mars
Q: What's this red, gritty stuff in my egg salad sandwich?
A: Dune
Q: Whad's da pard of a song dad isn'd da woids?

—*J. G. Sattler*

A: The Man Who Folded Himself
Q: Who is that peeking out of a manila envelope in the slush pile?
A: The Mote in God's Eye
Q: What did it take nine million heavy-duty cranes and sixteen billion gallons of Visine to remove?

A: Dune/Dhalgren/Froomb
Q: How did little June Darlene Fromm pronounce her name when she had the mumps?

—Bruce Berges

A: The Demolished Man
Q: What is the state of the Competition Editor after each contest?
A: Buy Jupiter!
Q: What did the man who sold the moon do next?
A: The Sheep Look Up
Q: What happens when there's No Blade of Grass?
A: The Lathe of Heaven
Q: Where can you watch As the World Turns?

—Chris Leithiser

A: The Day the Sun Stood Still
Q: When did you get that awful sunburn?
A: Friends Come in Boxes
Q: How can you tell your friends from your enemies?
A: Postmarked the Stars
Q: Why has this letter taken 1732 years to be delivered?
A: Against the Fall of Night
Q: Why are you wearing that enormous hard hat?

—Mary H. Schaub

Ed Bryant's story about stim star Jain Snow is a terrifically intense extrapolation of the communion between performer and audience. It received a Nebula nomination from the Science Fiction Writers of America for best short story of the year.

Stone

by EDWARD BRYANT

Up above the burning city, a woman wails the blues. How she cries out, how she moans. Flames fed by tears rake fingers across the sky.
   It is an old, old song:

> *Fill me like the mountains*
> *Fill me like the sea*

Writhing in the heat, she stands where there is no support. The fire licks her body.

> *All of me*

So finely drawn, and with the glitter of ice, the manipulating wires radiate outward. Taut bonds between her body and the flickering darkness, all wires lead to the intangible overshadowing figure behind her. Without expression, Atropos gazes down at the woman.
   Face contorting, she looks into the hearts of a million fires and cries out.

> *All of me*

—As Atropos raises the terrible, cold-shining blades of the Norn-shears and with only the barest hesitation cuts the wires. Limbs spread-eagled to the compass points, the woman plunges into the flames. She is instantly and utterly consumed.

The face of Atropos remains shrouded in shadows.

II

the poster

alpertron presents

IN CONCERT

JAIN SNOW

with

MOOG INDIGO

sixty-track stim by RobCal
June 23, 24 -
One show nightly at 2100

Tickets $30, $26, $22.
Available from all Alpertron
outlets or at the door.

ROCKY MOUNTAIN
CENTRAL ARENA -
DENVER

III

My name is Robert Dennis Clary and I was born twenty-three years ago in Oil City, Pennsylvania, which is also where I was raised. I've got a degree in electrical engineering from MIT and some grad credit at Cal Tech in electronics. *"Not suitable, Mr. Clary,"* said the dean. *"You lack the proper team spirit. Frankly speaking, you are selfish. And a cheat."*

My mother told me once she was sorry I wasn't handsome enough to get by without working. *Listen, Ma, I'm all right. There's nothing wrong with working the concert circuit.* I'm working damned hard now. I was never genius enough that I could have got a really good job with, say, Bell Futures or one of the big space firms. But I've got one marketable talent—what the interviewer called a peculiarly coordinative affinity for multiplex circuitry. *He looked a little stunned after I finished with the stim console. "Christ, kid, you really get into it, don't you?"*

That's what got me the job with Alpertron, Ltd., the big promotion and booking agency. I'm on the concert tour and work their stim board, me and my console over there on the side of the stage. It isn't that much different in principle from playing one of the instruments in the backup band, though it's a hell of a lot more complex than even Nagami's synthesizer. It all sounds simple enough: my console is the critical link between performer and audience. Just one glorified feedback transceiver: pick up the empathic load from Jain, pipe it into the audience, they react and add their own load, and I feed it all back to the star. And then around again as I use the sixty stim tracks, each with separate controls to balance and augment and intensify. It can get pretty hairy, which is why not just anyone can do the job. It helps that I seem to have a natural resistance to the sideband slopover radiation from the empathic transmissions. *"Ever think of teaching?" said the school voc counselor. "No," I said. "I want the action."*

And that's why I'm on the concert circuit with Jain Snow; as far as I'm concerned, the only real blues singer and stim star.

Jain Snow, my intermittent unrequited love. *Her voice is shagreen-rough; you hear it smooth until it tears you to shreds.*

She's older than I am, four, maybe five years; but she looks like she's in her middle teens. Jain's tall, with a tumbleweed bush of red hair; her face isn't so much pretty as it is intense. I've never known anyone who didn't want to make love to her. *"When you're a star," she said once, half drunk, "you're not hung up about taking the last cookie on the plate."*

That includes me, and sometimes she's let me come into her bed. But not often. *"You like it?" she said. I answered sleepily, "You're really good." "Not me," she said. "I mean being in a star's bed." I told her she was a bitch and she laughed.* Not often enough.

I know I don't dare force the issue; even if I did, there would still be Stella.

Stella Vanilla—I've never learned exactly what her real last name is—is Jain's bodyguard. Other stim stars have whole platoons of karate-trained killers for protection. Jain needs only Stella. *"Stella, pick me up a fifth? Yeah, Irish. Scotch if they don't."*

She's shorter than I am, tiny and dark with curly chestnut hair. She's also proficient in any martial art I can think of. And if all else fails, in her handbag she carries a .357 Colt Python with a four-inch barrel. When I first saw that bastard, I didn't believe she could even lift it.

But she can. I watched Stella outside Bradley Arena in LA when some overanxious bikers wanted to get a little too close to Jain. *"Back off, creeps." "So who's tellin' us?"* She had to hold the Python with both hands, but the muzzle didn't waver. Stella fired once; the slug tore the guts out of a parked Harley-Wankel. The bikers backed off very quickly.

Stella enfolds Jain in her protection like a raincape. It sometimes amuses Jain; I can see that. *Stella, get Alpertron on the phone for me. Stella? Can you score a couple grams? Stella, check out the dudes in the hall. Stella—* It never stops.

When I first met her, I thought that Stella was the coldest person I'd ever encountered. *And in Des Moines I saw her crying alone in a darkened phone booth—Jain had awakened her and told her to take a walk for a couple hours while she screwed some rube she'd picked up in the hotel bar. I tapped on the glass; Stella ignored me.*

Stella, do you want her as much as I?

So there we are—a nice symbolic obtuse triangle. And yet— We're all just one happy show-biz family.

IV

This is Alpertron, Ltd.'s, own chartered jet, flying at 37,000 feet above western Kansas. Stella and Jain are sitting across the aisle from me. It's a long flight and there's been a lull in the usually boisterous flight conversation. Jain flips through a current Neiman-Marcus catalogue; exclusive mail-order listings are her present passion.

I look up as she bursts into raucous laughter. "I'll be goddamned. Will you look at this?" She points at the open catalogue on her lap.

Hollis, Moog Indigo's color operator, is seated behind her. She leans forward and cranes her neck over Jain's shoulder. "Which?"

"That," she says. "The VTP."

"What's VTP?" says Stella.

Hollis says, "Video tape playback."

"Hey, everybody!" Jain raises her voice, cutting stridently through everyone else's conversations. "Get this. For a small fee, these folks'll put a video tape gadget in my tombstone. It's got everything— stereo sound and color. All I've got to do is go in before I die and cut the tape."

"Terrific!" Hollis says. "You could leave an album of greatest hits. You know, for posterity. Free concerts on the grass every Sunday."

"That's really sick," Stella says.

"Free, hell." Jain grins. "Anybody who wants to catch the show can put a dollar in the slot."

Stella stares disgustedly out the window.

Hollis says, "Do you want one of those units for your birthday?"

"Nope." Jain shakes her head. "I'm not going to need one."

"Never?"

"Well . . . not for a long time." But I think her words sound unsure.

Then I only half listen as I look out from the plane across the scattered cloud banks and the Rockies looming to the west of us. Tomorrow night we play Denver. *"It's about as close to home as I'm gonna get," Jain had said in New Orleans when we found out Denver was booked.*

"A what?" Jain's voice is puzzled.

"A cenotaph," says Hollis.

"Shut up," Stella says. "Damn it."

V

We're in the Central Arena, the architectural pride of Denver District. This is the largest gathering place in all of Rocky Mountain, that heterogeneous, anachronistic strip-city clinging to the front ranges of the continental divide all the way from Billings down to the southern suburb of El Paso.

The dome stretches up beyond the range of the house lights. If it were rigid, there could never be a Rocky Mountain Central Arena. But it's made of a flexible plastic-variant and blowers funnel up heated air to keep it buoyant. We're on the inner skin of a giant balloon. When the arena's full, the body heat from the audience keeps the dome aloft, and the arena crew turns off the blowers.

I killed time earlier tonight reading the promo pamphlet on this place. As the designer says, the combination of arena and spectators turns the dome into one sustaining organism. At first I misread it as "orgasm."

I monitor crossflow conversations through plugs inserted in both ears as set-up people check out the lights, sound, color, and all the rest of the systems. Finally some nameless tech comes on circuit to give my stim console a run-through.

"Okay, Rob, I'm up in the booth above the east aisle. Give me just a tickle." *My nipples were sensitized to her tongue, rough as a cat's.*

I'm wired to a test set fully as powerful as the costume Jain'll wear later—just not as exotic. I slide a track control forward until it reaches the five-position on a scale calibrated to one hundred.

"Five?" the tech says.

"Right."

"Reading's dead-on. Give me a few more tracks."

I comply. *She kisses me with lips and tongue, working down across my belly.*

"A little higher, please."

I push the tracks to fifteen.

"You're really in a mood, Rob."

"So what do you want me to think?" I say.

"Jesus," says the tech. "You ought to be performing. The crowd would love it."

"They pay Jain. She's the star." *I tried to get on top; she wouldn't let me. A moment later it didn't matter.*

"Did you just push the board to thirty?" The tech's voice sounds strange.

"No. Did you read that?"

"Negative, but for a moment it felt like it." He pauses. "You're not allowing your emotional life to get in the way of your work, are you?"

"Screw off," I answer. "None of your business."

"No threats," says the tech. "Just a suggestion."

"Stick it."

"Okay, okay. She's a lovely girl, Rob. And like you say, she's the star."

"I know."

"Fine. Feed me another five tracks, Rob; broad spectrum this time."

I do so and the tech is satisfied with the results. "That ought to do it," he says. "I'll get back to you later." He breaks off the circuit. All checks are done; there's nothing now on the circuits but a background scratch like insects climbing over old newspapers. *She will not allow me to be exhausted for long.*

Noisily, the crowd is starting to file into the arena.

I wait for the concert.

VI

There's never before been a stim star the magnitude of Jain Snow. Yet somehow the concert tonight fails. Somewhere the chemistry goes wrong. The faces out there are as always—yet somehow they are not *involved*. They care, but not enough.

I don't think the fault's in Jain. I detect no significant difference from other concerts. Her skin still tantalizes the audience as nakedly, only occasionally obscured by the cloudy metal mesh that transforms her entire body into a single antenna. I've been there when she's performed a hell of a lot better, maybe, but I've also seen her perform worse and still come off the stage happy.

It isn't Moog Indigo; they're laying down the sound and light patterns behind Jain as expertly as always.

Maybe it's me, but I don't think I'm handling the stim console badly. If I were, the nameless tech would be on my ass over the com circuit.

Jain goes into her final number. It does not work. The audience is enthusiastic and they want an encore, but that's just it: they shouldn't want one. They shouldn't *need* one.

She comes off the stage crying. I touch her arm as she walks past my console. Jain stops and rubs her eyes and asks me if I'll go back to the hotel with her.

VII

It seems like the first time I was in Jain Snow's bed. Jain keeps the room dark and says nothing as we go through the positions. Her breathing grows a little ragged; that is all. And yet she is more demanding of me than ever before.

When it's done, she holds me close and very tightly. Her rate of breathing slows and becomes regular. I wonder if she is asleep.

"Hey," I say.

"What?" She slurs the word sleepily.

"I'm sorry about tonight."

". . . Not your fault."

"I love you very much."

She rolls to face me. "Huh?"

"I love you."

"No, babe. Don't say that."

"It's true," I say.

"Won't work."

"Doesn't matter," I say.

"It can't work."

I know I don't have any right to feel this, but I'm pissed, and so I move away in the bed. "I don't care." *The first time: "Such a goddamned adolescent, Rob."*

After a while, she says, "Robbie, I'm cold," and so I move back to her and hold her and say nothing. I realize, rubbing against her hip, that I'm again hard; she doesn't object as I pour back into her all the frustration she unloaded in me earlier.

Neither of us sleeps much the rest of the night. Sometime before dawn I doze briefly and awaken from a nightmare. I am disoriented and can't remember the entirety of the dream, but I do remember hard wires and soft flows of electrons. My eyes suddenly focus and I see her face inches away from mine. Somehow she knows what I am thinking. "Whose turn is it?" she says. *The antenna.*

VIII

At least a thousand hired kids are there setting up chairs in the arena this morning, but it's still hard to feel I'm not alone. The dome is that big. Voices get lost here. Even thoughts echo.

"It's gonna be a hell of a concert tonight. I know it." Jain had said that and smiled at me when she came through here about ten. She'd swept down the center aisle in a flurry of feathers and shimmering red strips, leaving all the civilians stunned and quivering.

God only knows why she was up this early; over the last eight

months, I've never seen her get up before noon on a concert day.
That kind of sleep-in routine would kill me. I was out of bed by eight
this morning, partly because I've got to get this console modified by
showtime, and partly because I didn't feel like being in the star's bed
when she woke up.

"The gate's going to be a lot bigger than last night," Jain had said.
"Can you handle it?"

"Sure. Can you?"

Jain had flashed me another brilliant smile and left. And so I sit
here substituting circuit chips.

A couple kids climb on stage and pull breakfasts out of their back-
packs. "You ever read this?" says one, pulling a tattered paperback
from his hip pocket. His friend shakes her head. "You?" He turns
the book in my direction; I recognize the cover.

It was two, maybe three months ago in Memphis, in a studio just
before rehearsal. Jain had been sitting and reading. She reads quite a
lot, though the promotional people downplay it—Alpertron, Ltd.,
likes to suck the country-girl image for all it's worth.

"What's that?" Stella says.

"A book." Jain holds up the book so she can see.

"I know that." Stella reads the title: *Receptacle.* "Isn't that the—"

"Yeah," says Jain.

Everybody knows about *Receptacle*—the best seller of the year.
It's all fact, about the guy who went to Prague to have a dozen
artificial vaginas implanted all over his body. Nerve grafts, neural
rerouting, the works. I'd seen him interviewed on some talk show
where he'd worn a jumpsuit zipped to the neck.

"It's grotesque," Stella says.

Jain takes back the book and shrugs.

"Would you try something like this?"

"Maybe I'm way beyond it." *A receptacle works only one-way.*

Stella goes white and bites off whatever it is she was about to say.

"Oh, baby, I'm sorry." Jain smiles and looks fourteen again. Then
she stands and gives Stella a quick hug. She glances over at me and
winks, and my face starts to flush. *One-way.*

Now, months later, I remember it and my skin again goes warm.
"Get out of here," I say to the kids. "I'm trying to concentrate."
They look irritated, but they leave.

I'm done with the circuit chips. Now the easy stuff. I wryly note the male and female plugs I'm connecting. *Jain . . .*

The com circuit buzzes peremptorily and Jain's voice says, "Robbie? Can you meet me outside?"

I hesitate, then say, "Sure, I'm almost done with the board."

"I've got a car; we're going away."

"What?"

"Just for the afternoon."

"Listen, Jain—"

She says, "Hurry," and cuts off.

It's gonna be a hell of a concert.

                                    IX

Tonight's crowd strains even the capacity of the Rocky Mountain Central Arena. The gate people say there are more than nine hundred thousand people packed into the smoky recesses of the dome. It's not just hard to believe; it's scary. But computer ticket-totes don't lie.

I look out at the crowd and it's like staring at the Pacific after dark; the gray waves march out to the horizon until you can't tell one from the other. Here on the stage, the crowd-mutter even sounds like the sea, exactly as though I was on the beach trying to hear in an eighteen-foot surf. It all washes around me and I'm grateful for the twin earpieces, reassured to hear the usual check-down lists on the in-house com circuit.

I notice that the blowers have cut off. It's earlier than usual, but obviously there's enough body heat to keep the dome buoyed aloft. I imagine the Central Arena drifting away like that floating city they want to make out of Venice, California. There is something appealing about the thought of this dome floating away like dandelion fluff. But now the massive air-conditioning units hum on and the fantasy dies.

The house lights momentarily dim and the crowd noise raises a few decibels. I realize I can't see features or faces or even separate bodies. There are simply too many people to comprehend. The crowd has fused into one huge tectonic slab of flesh.

"Rob, are you ready?" The tech's soft voice in my earpiece.

"Ready."

"It's a big gate tonight. Can you do it?"

Sixty overlay tracks and one com board between Jain and maybe a cool million horny, sweating spectators? "Sure," I say. "Easy." But momentarily I'm not sure and I realize how tightly I'm gripping the ends of the console. I consciously will my fingers to loosen.

"Okay," the tech says. "But if anything goes wrong, cut it. Right? Damp it completely."

"Got it."

"Fine," he says. "About a minute, stand by. Ms. Snow wants to say hello."

"Hello, Robbie?"

"Yeah," I say. "Good luck."

Interference crackles and what she says is too soft to hear.

I tell her, "Repeat, please."

"Stone don't break. At least not easy." She cuts off the circuit.

I've got ten seconds to stare out at that vast crowd. Where, I wonder, did the arena logistics people scrape up almost a million in/out headbands? I know I'm hallucinating, but for just a moment I see the scarlet webwork of broadcast power reaching out from my console to those million skulls. I don't know why; I find myself reaching for the shield that covers the emergency total cutoff. I stop my hand.

The house lights go all the way down; the only illumination comes from a thousand exit signs and the equipment lights. Then Moog Indigo troops onstage as the crowd begins to scream in anticipation. The group finds their instruments in the familiar darkness. The crowd is already going crazy.

Hollis strokes her color board and shoots concentric spheres of hard primaries expanding through the arena; Red, yellow, blue. Start with the basics. Red.

Nagami's synthesizer spews a volcanic flow of notes like burning magma.

And then Jain is there. Center stage.

"Damn it," says the tech in my ear. "Level's too low. Bring it up in back." I must have been dreaming. I am performing stupidly, like an amateur. Gently I bring up two stim balance slides.

"—love you. Every single one of you."

The crowd roars back. The filling begins. I cut in four more low-level tracks.

"—ready. How about you?"

They're ready. I cut in another dozen tracks, then mute two. Things are building just a little too fast. The fine mesh around Jain's body seems to glitter with more than reflected light. Her skin already gleams with moisture.

"—get started easy. And then things'll get hard. Yeah?"

"YEAH!" from thousands of throats simultaneously.

I see her stagger slightly. I don't think I am feeding her too much too fast, but mute another pair of tracks anyway. Moog Indigo takes their cue and begins to play. Hollis gives the dome the smoky pallor of slow-burning leaves. Then Jain Snow sings.

And I fill her with them. And give her back to them.

> *space and time*
> *measured in my heart*

X

In the afternoon:

Jain gestures in an expansive circle. "This is where I grew up."

The mountains awe me. "Right here?"

She shakes her head. "It was a lot like this. My pa ran sheep. Maybe a hundred miles north."

"But in the mountains?"

"Yeah. Really isolated. My pa convinced himself he was one of the original settlers. He was actually a laid-off aerospace engineer out of Seattle."

The wind flays us for a moment; Jain's hair whips and she shakes it back from her eyes. I pull her into the shelter of my arms, wrapping my coat around us both. "Do you want to go back down to the car?"

"Hell, no," she says. "A mountain zephyr can't scare me off."

I'm not used to this much open space; it scares me a little, though I'm not going to admit that to Jain. We're above timberline, and the mountainside is too stark for my taste. I suddenly miss the rounded, wooded hills of Pennsylvania. Jain surveys the rocky fields rubbed raw by wind and snow, and I have a quick feeling she's scared too. "Something wrong?"

"Nope. Just remembering."

"What's it like on a ranch?"

"Okay, if you don't like people," she says slowly, obviously recalling details. "My pa didn't."

"No neighbors?"

"Not a one in twenty miles."

"Brothers?" I say. "Sisters?"

She shakes her head. "Just my pa." I guess I look curious because she looks away and adds, "My mother died of tetanus right after I was born. It was a freak thing."

I try to change the subject. "Your father didn't come down to the first concert, did he? Is he coming tonight?"

"No way," she says. "He didn't and he won't. He doesn't like what I do." I can't think of anything to say now. After a while Jain rescues me. "It isn't your hassle, and it isn't mine anymore."

Something perverse doesn't let me drop it now. "So you grew up alone."

"You noticed," she says softly. "You've got a hell of a way with understatement."

I persist. "Then I don't understand why you still come up here. You must hate this."

"Ever see a claustrophobe deliberately walk into a closet and shut the door? If I don't fight it this way—" Her fingers dig into my arms. Her face is fierce. "This has got to be better than what I do on stage." She swings away from me. "Shit!" she says. "Damn it all to hell." She stands immovable, staring down the mountain for several minutes. When she turns back toward me, her eyes are softer and there's a fey tone in her voice. "If I die—" She laughs. "When I die. I want my ashes here."

"Ashes?" I say, unsure how to respond. *Humor her.* "Sure."

"You." She points at me. "Here." She indicates the rock face. The words are simple commands given to a child.

"Me." I manage a weak smile.

Her laugh is easy and unstrained now. "Kid games. Did you do the usual things when you were a kid, babe?"

"Most of them." *I hardly ever won, but then I liked to play games with outrageous risks.*

"Hammer, rock and scissors?"

"Sure, when I was really young." I repeat by long-remembered rote: "Rock breaks scissors, scissors cut paper, paper covers rock."

"Okay," she says. "Let's play." I must look doubtful. "Rob," she says warningly.

"Okay." I hold out my right hand.

Jain says, "One, two, three." On "three," we each bring up our right hand. Hers is a clenched fist: stone. My first two fingers form the snipping blades of a pair of scissors. "I win!" she crows, delighted.

"What do you win?"

"You. Just for a little while." She pulls my hands close and lays them on her body.

"Right here on the mountain?" I say.

"I'm from pioneer stock. But you—" She shrugs. "Too delicate?" I laugh and pull her close.

"Just—" She hesitates. "Not like the other times? Don't take this seriously, okay?"

In my want I forget the other occasions. "Okay."

Each of us adds to the other's pleasure, and it's better than the other times. But even when she comes, she stares through me, and I wonder whose face she's seeing—no, not even that: how many faces she's seeing. *Babe, no man can fill me like* they *do.*

And then I come also and—briefly—it doesn't matter.

My long coat is wrapped around the two of us, and we watch each other inches apart. "So much passion, Rob. . . . It seems to build."

I remember the stricture and say, "You know why."

"You really like me so much?" *The little-girl persona.*

"I really do."

"What would you do for me, if I asked you?"

"Anything."

"Would you kill for me?"

I say, "Sure."

"Really?"

"Of course." I smile. I know how to play.

"This is no game."

My face must betray my confusion. I don't know how I should react.

Her expression mercurially alters to sadness. "You're scissors, Robbie. All shiny cold metal. How can you ever hope to cut stone?"

Would I want to?

XI

Things get worse.

Is it simply that I'm screwing up on my own hook, or is it because we're exploring a place no performance has ever been? I don't have

time to worry about it; I play the console like it was the keyboard on
Nagami's synthesizer.

> *Take it*
> *When you can get it*
> *Where you can get it*

Jain sways and the crowd sways; she thrusts and the crowd
thrusts. It is one gigantic act. It as as though a temblor shakes the
Front Range.

Insect chittering in my earpiece: "What the hell's going on, Rob?
I'm monitoring the stim feed. You're oscillating from hell to fade-
out."

"I'm trying to balance." I juggle slides. "Any better?"

"At least it's no worse," says the tech. He pauses. "Can you manage the payoff?"

The payoff. The precision-engineered and carefully timed upslope
leading to climax. The Big Number. I've kept the stim tracks pla-
teaued for the past three sets. "Coming," I say. "It's coming. There's
time."

"You're in bad trouble with New York if there isn't," says the
tech. "I want to register a jag. Now."

"Okay," I say.

> *Love me*
> *Eat me*
> *All of me*

"Better," the tech says. "But keep it rising. I'm still only register-
ing a sixty per cent."

*Sure, bastard. It isn't your brain burning with the output of these
million strangers.* My violence surprises me. But I push the stim up
to seventy. Then Nagami goes into a synthesizer riff, and Jain sags
back against a vertical rank of amps.

"Robbie?" It comes into my left ear, on the in-house com circuit
reserved for performer and me alone.

"I'm here, Jain."

"You're not trying, babe."

I stare across the stage and she's looking back at me. Her eyes
flash emerald in the wave from Hollis' color generator. She sub-
vocalizes so her lips don't move.

"I mean it."

"This is new territory," I answer. "We never had a million before." I know she thinks it's an excuse.

"This is it, babe," she says. "It's tonight. Will you help me?"

I've known the question would come, though I hadn't known who'd articulate it—her or me. My hesitation stretches much longer in my head than it does in realtime. *So much passion, Rob. . . . It seems to build. Would you kill for me?* "Yes," I say.

"Then I love you," and breaks off as the riff ends and she struts back out into the light. I reluctantly touch the console and push the stim to seventy-five. Fifty tracks are in. *Jain, will you love me if I don't?*

A bitter look

Eighty. I engage five more tracks. Five to go. The crowd's getting damn near all of her. And, of course, the opposite's true.

A flattering word

Since I first heard her in Washington, I've loved this song the best. I push more keys. Eighty-two. Eighty-five. I know the tech's happily watching the meters.

A kiss

The last tracks cut in. *Okay, you're getting everything from the decaying food in her gut to her deepest buried childhood fears of an empty echoing house.*

Ninety.

A sword

And the song ends, one last diminishing chord, but her body continues to move. For her there is still music.

On the com circuit the tech yells: "Idiot! I'm already reading ninety. Ninety, damn it. There's still one number to go."

"Yeah," I say. "Sorry. Just . . . trying to make up for previous lag-time."

He continues to shout and I don't answer. On the stage Nagami and Hollis look at each other and at the rest of the group, and then Moog Indigo slides into the last number with scarcely a pause. Jain turns toward my side of the stage and gives me a soft smile. And then it's back to the audience and into the song she always tops her concerts with, the number that really made her.

Fill me like the mountains

Ninety-five. There's only a little travel left in the console slides.

The tech's voice is aghast. "Are you out of your mind, Rob? I've got a ninety-five here—damned needle's about to peg. Back off to ninety."

"Say again?" I say. "Interference. Repeat, please."

"I said back off! We don't want her higher than ninety."

Fill me like the sea

Jain soars to the climax. I shove the slides all the way forward. The crowd is on its feet; I have never been so frightened in my life.

"Rob! I swear to God you're canned, you—"

Somehow Stella's on the com line too: "You son of a bitch! You hurt her—"

Jain flings her arms wide. Her back impossibly arches.

All of me

One hundred.

I cannot rationalize electronically what happens. I cannot imagine the affection and hate and lust and fear cascading into her and pouring back out. But I see the antenna mesh around her naked body glowing suddenly whiter until it flares in an actinic flash and I shut my eyes.

When I open them again, Jain is a blackened husk tottering toward the front of the stage. Her body falls over the edge into the first rows of spectators.

The crowd still thinks this is part of the set, and they love it.

XII

No good-bys. I know I'm canned. When I go into the Denver Alpertron office in another day and a half to pick up my final check, some subordinate I've never seen before gives me the envelope.

"Thanks," I say. He stares at me and says nothing.

I turn to leave and meet Stella in the hall. The top of her head comes only to my shoulders, and so she has to tilt her face up to glare at me. She says, "You're not going to be working for any promoter in the business. New York says so."

"Fine," I say. I walk past her.

Before I reach the door, she stops me by saying, "The initial report is in already."

I turn. "And?"

"The verdict will probably end up accidental death. Everybody's bonded. Jain was insured for millions. Everything will turn out all right for everyone." She stares at me for several seconds. "Except · Jain. You bastard."

We have our congruencies.

The package comes later, along with a stiff legal letter from a firm of attorneys. The substance of the message is this: "Jain Snow wished you to have possession of this. She informed you prior to her demise of her desires; please carry them out accordingly." The packet contains a chrome cylinder with a screw cap. The cylinder contains ashes; ashes and a few bone fragments. I check. Jain's ashes, unclaimed by father, friends, or employer.

I drive west, away from the soiled towers of the strip-city. I drive beyond the colstrip pits and into the mountains until the paved highway becomes narrow asphalt and then rutted earth and then only a trace, and the car can go no further. With the metal cylinder in one hand I flee on foot until I no longer hear sounds of city or human beings.

At last the trees end and I climb over bare mountain grades. I rest briefly when the pain in my lungs is too sharp to ignore. At last I reach the summit.

I scatter Jain's ashes on the wind.

Then I hurl the empty cylinder down toward the timberline; it rolls and clatters and finally is only a distant glitter on the talus slope.

"Jain!" I scream at the sky until my voice is gone and vertigo destroys my balance. The echoes die. *As Jain died.*

I lie down unpeacefully—exhausted—and sleep, and my dreams are of weathered stone. And I awake empty.

From Competition 15:

Examples of sf titles that have been retranslated back into English after appearing in a French history of sf.

I Am Crying, Said the Policeman, PHILIP K. DICK
He Has a Hole in His Head and His Teeth Glow in the Dark, ROGER ZELAZNY
Nocturnal and Diurnal Animals, ROGER ZELAZNY
R Is for Spaceship, RAY BRADBURY
The Tin Men Go to Sleep, ISAAC ASIMOV
All Animals Are Vegetables, CLIFFORD SIMAK

—*Cambridge University Science Fiction Society*

A Box of Scruples, JAMES BLISH
Dendrites, LESTER DEL REY
Get Out of My Way! Get Out of My Way!, HARRY HARRISON
A For Whatever, DAMON KNIGHT
Humaner, THEODORE STURGEON
A Serious Undertaking, HAL CLEMENT

—*Chris Riesbeck*

Towards Here Is Coming An Evil Thing, RAY BRADBURY
Rascal Moon, ALGIS BUDRYS
To Your Broadcast Bodies, Get Yourselves, PHILIP JOSE FARMER
Tales of A Moribund Bird, HARLAN ELLISON
Farther Than Apollo, BARRY MALZBERG

—*Michael Bishop*

Sturgeon Lives Comfortably, THEODORE STURGEON
Mr. Robot, That's Me, ISAAC ASIMOV
Guts, LESTER DEL REY
We Sold Space, POHL & KORNBLUTH
Shove Over! Shove Over!, HARRY HARRISON

—Daniel P. Dern

Don't Ask, Dragoon, GORDON DICKSON
A Bit Unclear, H. BEAM PIPER
Not That One, TOM TRYON

—John Billingsley

Here is yet another treat from the master of the contemporary chiller. And speaking of chills, Robert Bloch's latest book is a collection of scary stories published by Doubleday and titled *Cold Chills*.

Nina

by ROBERT BLOCH

After the love-making Nolan needed another drink.

He fumbled for the bottle beside the bed, gripping it with a sweaty hand. His entire body was wet and clammy, and his fingers shook as they unscrewed the cap. For a moment Nolan wondered if he was coming down with another bout of fever. Then, as the harsh heat of the rum scalded his stomach, he realized the truth.

Nina had done this to him.

Nolan turned and glanced at the girl who lay beside him. She stared up through the shadows with slitted eyes unblinking above high cheekbones, her thin brown body relaxed and immobile. Hard to believe that only moments ago this same body had been a writhing, wriggling coil of insatiable appetite, gripping and enfolding him until he was drained and spent.

He held the bottle out to her. "Have a drink?"

She shook her head, eyes hooded and expressionless, and then Nolan remembered that she didn't speak English. He raised the bottle and drank again, cursing himself for his mistake.

It had been a mistake, he realized that now, but Darlene would never understand. Sitting there safe and snug in the apartment in Trenton, she couldn't begin to know what he'd gone through for her sake—hers and little Robbie's. Robert Emmett Nolan II, nine weeks old now, his son, whom he'd never seen. That's why he'd taken the job, signed on with the company for a year. The money was good, enough to keep Darlene in comfort and tide them over after he got back. She couldn't have come with him, not while she was carrying the kid, so he came alone, figuring no sweat.

No sweat. That was a laugh. All he'd done since he got here was sweat. Patrolling the plantation at sunup, loading cargo all day for the boats that went downriver, squinting over paperwork while night closed down on the bungalow to imprison him behind a wall of jungle darkness. And at night the noises came—the hum of insect hordes, the bellow of caimans, the snorting snuffle of peccary, the ceaseless chatter of monkeys intermingled with the screeching of a million mindless birds.

So he'd started to drink. First the good bourbon from the company's stock, then the halfway-decent trade gin, and now the cheap rum.

As Nolan set the empty bottle down he heard the noise he'd come to dread worst of all—the endless echo of drums from the huts huddled beside the riverbank below. Miserable wretches were at it again. No wonder he had to drive them daily to fulfil the company's quota. The wonder was that they did anything at all after spending every night wailing to those damned drums.

Of course it was Moises who did the actual driving; Nolan couldn't even chew them out properly because they were too damned dumb to understand plain English.

Like Nina, here.

Again Nolan looked down at the girl who lay curled beside him on the bed, silent and sated. She wasn't sweating; her skin was curiously cool to the touch, and in her eyes was a mystery.

It was the mystery that Nolan had sensed the first time he saw her staring at him across the village compound three days ago. At first he thought she was one of the company people—somebody's wife, daughter, sister. That afternoon, when he returned to the bungalow, he caught her staring at him again at the edge of the clearing. So he asked Moises who she was, and Moises didn't know. Apparently she'd just arrived a day or two before, paddling a crude catamaran downriver from somewhere out of the denser jungle stretching a thousand miles beyond. She had no English, and according to Moises, she didn't speak Spanish or Portuguese either. Not that she'd made any attempts to communicate; she kept to herself, sleeping in the catamaran moored beside the bank across the river and not even venturing into the company store by day to purchase food.

"Indio," Moises said, pronouncing the word with all the contempt of one in whose veins ran a ten per-cent admixture of the proud blood of the *conquistadores.* "Who are we to know the way of savages?" He shrugged.

Nolan had shrugged, too, and dismissed her from his mind. But that night as he lay on his bed, listening to the pounding of the drums, he thought of her again and felt a stirring in his loins.

She came to him then, almost as though the stirring had been a silent summons, came like a brown shadow gliding out of the night. Soundlessly she entered, and swiftly she shed her single garment as she moved across the room to stand staring down at him on the bed. Then, as she sank upon his nakedness and encircled his thighs, the stirring in his loins became a throbbing and the pounding in his head drowned out the drums.

In the morning she was gone, but on the following night she returned. It was then that he'd called her Nina—it wasn't her name, but he felt a need to somehow identify this wide-mouthed, pink-tongued stranger who slaked herself upon him, slaked his own urgency again and again as her hissing breath rasped in his ears.

Once more she vanished while he slept, and he hadn't seen her all day. But at times he'd been conscious of her secret stare, a coldness falling upon him like an unglimpsed shadow, and he'd known that tonight she'd come again.

Now, as the drums sounded in the distance, Nina slept. Unmindful of the din, heedless of his presence, her eyes hooded and she lay somnolent in animal repletion.

Nolan shuddered. That's what she was; an animal. In repose, the lithe brown body was grotesquely elongated, the wide mouth accentuating the ugliness of her face. How could he have coupled with this creature? Nolan grimaced in self-disgust as he turned away.

Well, no matter—it was ended now, over once and for all. Today the message had arrived from Belem: Darlene and Robbie were on the ship, ready for the flight to Manaos. Tomorrow morning he'd start downriver to meet them, escort them here. He'd had his qualms about their coming; they'd have to face three months in this hellhole before the year was up, but Darlene had insisted.

And she was right. Nolan knew it now. At least they'd be together and that would help see him through. He wouldn't need the bottle any more, and he wouldn't need Nina.

Nolan lay back and waited for sleep to come, shutting out the sound of the drums, the sight of the shadowy shape beside him. Only a few hours until morning, he told himself. And in the morning, the nightmare would be over.

The trip to Manaos was an ordeal, but it ended in Darlene's arms. She was blonder and more beautiful than he'd remembered, more loving and tender than he'd ever known her to be, and in the union that was their reunion Nolan found fulfillment. Of course there was none of the avid hunger of Nina's coiling caresses, none of the mindless thrashing to final frenzy. But it didn't matter; the two of them were together at last. The two of them, and Robbie.

Robbie was a revelation.

Nolan hadn't anticipated the intensity of his own reaction. But now, after the long trip back in the wheezing launch, he stood beside the crib in the spare bedroom and gazed down at his son with an overwhelming surge of pride.

"Isn't he adorable?" Darlene said. "He looks just like you."

"You're prejudiced." Nolan grinned, but he was flattered. And when the tiny pink starshell of a hand reached forth to meet his fingers, he tingled at the touch.

Then Darlene gasped.

Nolan glanced up quickly. "What's the matter?" he said.

"Nothing." Darlene was staring past him. "I thought I saw someone outside the window."

Nolan followed her gaze. "No one out there." He moved to the window, peered at the clearing beyond. "Not a soul."

Darlene passed a hand before her eyes. "I guess I'm just over-tired," she said. "The long trip—"

Nolan put his arm around her. "Why don't you go lie down? Mama Dolores can look after Robbie."

Darlene hesitated. "Are you sure she knows what to do?"

"Look who's talking!" Nolan laughed. "They don't call her Mama for nothing—she's had ten kids of her own. She's in the kitchen right now, fixing Robbie's formula. I'll go get her."

So Darlene went down the hall to their bedroom for a siesta, and

Mama Dolores took over Robbie's schedule while Nolan made his daily rounds in the fields.

The heat was stifling, worse than anything he could remember. Even Moises was gasping for air as he gunned the jeep over the rutted roadway, peering into the shimmering haze.

Nolan wiped his forehead. Maybe he'd been too hasty, bringing Darlene and the baby here. But a man was entitled to see his own son, and in a few months they'd be out of this miserable sweatbox forever. No sense getting uptight; everything was going to be all right.

But at dusk, when he returned to the bungalow, Mama Dolores greeted him at the door with a troubled face.

"What is it?" Nolan said. "Something wrong with Robbie?"

Mama shook her head. "He sleeps like an angel," she murmured. "But the *senora*—"

In their room, Darlene lay shivering on the bed, eyes closed. Her head moved ceaselessly on the pillows even when Nolan pressed his palm against her brow.

"Fever." Nolan gestured to Mama Dolores, and the old woman held Darlene still while he forced the thermometer between her lips.

The red column inched upwards. "One hundred and four." Nolan straightened quickly. "Go fetch Moises. Tell him I want the launch ready, *pronto*. We'll have to get her to the doctor at Manaos."

Darlene's eyes fluttered open; she'd heard.

"No, you can't! The baby—"

"Do not trouble yourself. I will look after the little one." Mama's voice was soothing. "Now you must rest."

"No, please—"

Darlene's voice trailed off into an incoherent babbling, and she sank back. Nolan kept his hand on her forehead; the heat was like an oven. "Now just relax, darling. It's all right. I'm going with you."

And he did.

If the first trip had been an ordeal, this one was an agony: a frantic thrust through the sultry night on the steaming river, Moises sweating over the throttle as Nolan held Darlene's shuddering shoulders against the straw mattress in the stern of the vibrating launch. They made Manaos by dawn and roused Dr. Robales from slumber at his house near the plaza.

Then came the examination, the removal to the hospital, the tests and the verdict. A simple matter, Dr. Robales said, and no need for alarm. With proper treatment and rest she would recover. A week here in the hospital—

"A week?" .Nolan's voice rose. "I've got to get back for the loading. I can't stay here that long!"

"There is no need for you to stay, *senor*. She shall have my personal attention, I assure you."

It was small comfort, but Nolan had no choice. And he was too tired to protest, too tired to worry. Once aboard the launch and heading back, he stretched out on the straw mattress in a sleep that was like death itself.

Nolan awakened to the sound of drums. He jerked upright with a startled cry, then realized that night had come and they were once again at anchor beside the dock. Moises grinned at him in weary triumph.

"Almost we do not make it," he said. "The motor is bad. No matter, it is good to be home again."

Nolan nodded, flexing his cramped limbs. He stepped out onto the dock, then hurried up the path across the clearing. The darkness boomed.

Home? This corner of hell; where the drums dinned and the shadows leaped and capered before flickering fires?

All but one, that is. For as Nolan moved forward, another shadow glided out from the deeper darkness beside the bungalow.

It was Nina.

Nolan blinked as he recognized her standing there and staring up at him. There was no mistaking the look on her face or its urgency, but he had no time to waste in words. Brushing past her, he hastened to the doorway and she melted back into the night.

Mama Dolores was waiting for him inside, nodding her greeting. "Robbie—is he all right?"

"*Si, senor*. I take good care. *Por favor,* I sleep in his room."

"Good." Nolan turned and started for the hall, then hesitated as Mama Dolores frowned. "What is it?" he said.

The old woman hesitated. "You will not be offended if I speak?"

"Of course not."

Mama's voice sank to a murmur. "It concerns the one outside."

"Nina?"

"That is not her name, but no matter." Mama shook her head.

"For two days she has waited there. I see you with her now when you return. And I see you with her before—"

"That's none of your business!" Nolan reddened. "Besides, it's all over now."

"Does she believe that?" Mama's gaze was grave. "You must tell her to go."

"I've tried. But the girl comes from the mountains; she doesn't speak English—"

"I know." Mama nodded. "She is one of the snake-people."

Nolan stared at her. "They worship snakes up there?"

"No, not worship."

"Then what do you mean?"

"These people—they *are* snakes."

Nolan scowled. "What is this?"

"The truth, *senor*. This one you call Nina—this girl—is not a girl. She is of the ancient race from the high peaks, where the great serpents dwell. Your workers here, even Moises, know only the jungle, but I come from the great valley beneath the mountains, and as a child I learned to fear those who lurk above. We do not go there, but sometimes the snake-people come to us. In the spring when they awaken, they shed their skins, and for a time they are fresh and clean before the scales grow again. It is then that they come, to mate with men."

She went on like that, whispering about creatures half-serpent and half-human, with bodies cold to the touch, limbs that could writhe in boneless contortion to squeeze the breath from a man and crush him like the coils of a giant constrictor. She spoke of forked tongues, of voices hissing forth from mouths yawning incredibly wide on movable jawbones. And she might have gone on, but Nolan stopped her now; his head was throbbing with weariness.

"That's enough," he said. "I thank you for your concern."

"But you do not believe me."

"I didn't say that." Tired as he was, Nolan still remembered the basic rule—never contradict these people or make fun of their superstitions. And he couldn't afford to alienate Mama now. "I shall take precautions," he told her, gravely. "Right now I've got to rest. And I want to see Robbie."

Mama Dolores put her hand to her mouth. "I forget—the little one, he is alone—"

She turned and padded hastily down the hallway, Nolan behind her. Together they entered the nursery.

"Ah!" Mama exhaled a sigh of relief. "The *pobrecito* sleeps."

Robbie lay in his crib, a shaft of moonlight from the window bathing his tiny face. From his rosebud mouth issued a gentle snore.

Nolan smiled at the sound, then nodded at Mama. "I'm going to turn in now. You take good care of him."

"I will not leave." Mama settled herself in a rocker beside the crib. As Nolan turned to go, she called after him softly. "Remember what I have told you, *senor*. If she comes again—"

Nolan moved down the hall to his bedroom at the far end. He hadn't trusted himself to answer her. After all, she meant well; it was just that he was too damned tired to put up with any more nonsense from the old woman.

In his bedroom something rustled.

Nolan flinched, then halted as the shadow-shape glided forth from the darkened corner beside the open window.

Nina stood before him and she was stark naked. Stark naked, her arms opening in invitation.

He retreated a step. "No," he said.

She came forward, smiling.

"Go away—get out of here."

He gestured her back. Nina's smile faded and she made a sound in her throat, a little gasp of entreaty. Her hands reached out—

"Damn it, leave me alone!"

Nolan struck her on the cheek. It wasn't more than a slap, and she couldn't have been hurt. But suddenly Nina's face contorted as she launched herself at him, her fingers splayed and aiming at his eyes. This time he hit her hard—hard enough to send her reeling back.

"Out!" he said. He forced her to the open window, raising his hand threateningly as she spewed and spit her rage, then snatched her garment and clambered over the sill into the darkness beyond.

Nolan stood by the window watching as Nina moved away across the clearing. For a moment she turned in a path of moonlight and looked back at him—only a moment, but long enough for Nolan to see the livid fury blazing in her eyes.

Then she was gone, gliding off into the night where the drums thudded in distant darkness.

She was gone, but the hate remained. Nolan felt its force as he stretched out upon the bed. Ought to undress, but he was too tired. The throbbing in his head was worse, pulsing to the beat of the drums. And the hate was in his head, too. God, that ugly face! Like the thing in mythology—what was it?—the Medusa. One look turned men to stone. Her locks of hair were live serpents.

But that was legend, like Mama Dolores' stories about the snake-people. Strange—did every race have its belief in such creatures? Could there be some grotesque, distorted element of truth behind all these old wives' tales?

He didn't want to think about it now; he didn't want to think of anything. Not Nina, not Darlene, not even Robbie. Darlene would be all right, Robbie was fine, and Nina was gone. That left him, alone here with the drums. Damned pounding. Had to stop, had to stop so he could sleep—

It was the silence that awakened him. He sat up with a start, realizing he must have slept for hours, because the shadows outside the window were dappled with the grayish pink of dawn.

Nolan rose, stretching, then stepped out into the hall. The shadows were darker here and everything was still.

He went down the hallway to the other bedroom. The door was ajar and he moved past it, calling softly. "Mama Dolores—"

Nolan's tongue froze to the roof of his mouth. Time itself was frozen as he stared down at the crushed and pulpy thing sprawled shapelessly beside the rocker, its sightless eyes bulging from the swollen purple face.

No use calling her name again; she'd never hear it. And Robbie—

Nolan turned in the frozen silence, his eyes searching the shadows at the far side of the room.

The crib was empty.

Then he found his voice and cried out; cried out again as he saw the open window and the gray vacancy of the clearing beyond.

Suddenly he was at the window, climbing out and dropping to the matted sward below. He ran across the clearing, through the trees and into the open space before the riverbank.

Moises was in the launch, working on the engine. He looked up as Nolan ran towards him, shouting.

"What are you doing here?"

"There is the problem of the motor. It requires attention. I come early, before the heat of the day—"

"Did you see her?"

"Who, *senor?*"

"The girl—Nina—"

"Ah, yes. The *Indio*." Moises nodded. "She is gone, in her cata-maran, up the river. Two, maybe three hours ago, just as I arrive."

"Why didn't you stop her?"

"For what reason?"

Nolan gestured quickly. "Get that engine started—we're going after her."

Moises frowned. "As I told you, there is the matter of the repairs. Perhaps this afternoon—"

"We'll never catch her then!" Nolan gripped Moises' shoulder. "Don't you understand? She's taken Robbie!"

"Calm yourself, *senor*. With my own eyes I saw her go to the boat and she was alone, I swear it. She does not have the little one."

Nolan thought of the hatred in Nina's eyes, and he shuddered. "Then what did she do with him?"

Moises shook his head. "This I do not know. But I am sure she has no need of another infant."

"What are you talking about?"

"I notice her condition when she walked to the boat." Moises shrugged, but even before the words came, Nolan knew.

"Why do you look at me like that, *senor?* Is it not natural for a woman to bulge when she carries a baby in her belly?"

Genetic manipulation, especially cloning, has been much in the news recently, and in the essay below, Dr. Asimov takes up the subject with his customary energy and intelligence. Imagine, if you will, one hundred Isaac Asimov clones!

Science: *Clone, Clone of My Own*

by ISAAC ASIMOV

On December 12, 1968, I gave a talk to a meeting of doctors and lawyers in San Jose, California.* Naturally, I was asked to speak on some subject that would interest both groups. Some instinct told me that medical malpractice suits might interest both but would nevertheless not be a useful topic. I spoke on genetic engineering instead, therefore, and, toward the end, discussed the matter of cloning.

In the audience was my good friend of three decades—the well-known science fiction writer, bon vivant, and wit, Randall Garrett. Out of the corner of my eye, I noticed a piece of paper placed on the podium as I talked about cloning. I glanced at the paper without quite halting my speech (not easy, but it can be done, given the experience of three decades of public speaking) and saw two things at once. First, it was one of Randall's superlative pieces of satiric verse,

* Those of my Gentle Readers who know that under no circumstances will I take a plane need not register shock. I traveled to California and back by train. —Yes, they still run.

and second, it was clearly intended to be sung to the tune of "Home on the Range."

Needed to understand the verse is merely the fact that, genetically, the distinction between human male and female is that every male cell has an X and a Y chromosome and that every female cell has two X chromosomes.† Therefore, if, at the moment of conception or shortly thereafter, a Y chromosome can somehow be changed to an X chromosome, a male will *ipso facto* be changed into a female.

Here, then, is "Randall's Song," to which I took the liberty of adding a verse myself:

> (1st verse) *O, give me a clone*
> *Of my own flesh and bone*
> *With its Y chromosome changed to X;*
> *And when it is grown*
> *Then my own little clone*
> *Will be of the opposite sex.*
>
> (chorus) *Clone, clone of my own,*
> *With its Y chromosome changed to X;*
> *And when I'm alone*
> *With my own little clone*
> *We will both think of nothing but sex.*
>
> (2nd verse) *O, give me a clone,*
> *Hear my sorrowful moan,*
> *Just a clone that is wholly my own;*
> *And if it's an X*
> *Of the feminine sex*
> *O, what fun we will have when we're prone.*

When I was through with my talk and with the question-and-answer session, I sang "Randall's Song" in my most resonant baritone and absolutely brought the house down.

Three and a half weeks later I sang it again at the annual banquet of the Baker Street Irregulars, that fine group of Sherlock Holmes fanciers, adjusting it slightly to its new task (*O, give me some clones*

† See "Counting Chromosomes," *F&SF*, June 1968.

/ *Of the great Sherlock Holmes* / *With their Y chromosomes*—),
and brought the house down again.

But you may, by now, be asking yourself, "What's a clone?"

It's been in the news a great deal lately, but recognizing a word
and knowing what it represents can be two different things. So let's
go into the matter—

The word "clone" is Greek, exactly as it stands, provided you
spell it in Greek letters, and it means "twig."

A clone is any organism (or group of organisms) that arises out of
a cell (or group of cells) by means other than sexual reproduction.
Put it another way: It is an organism that is the product of asexual
reproduction. Put it still another way: It is an organism with a single
parent, whereas an organism that arises from sexual reproduction
(except where self-fertilization is possible) has two parents.

Asexual reproduction is a matter of course among one-celled organisms (though sexual reproduction can also take place), and it is
also very common in the plant world.

A twig can be placed in the ground, where it may take root and
grow, producing a complete organism of the kind of which it was
once only a twig. Or the twig can be grafted to the branch of another
tree (of a different variety even), where it can grow and flourish. In
either case, it is an organism with a single parent, and sex has had
nothing to do with its making. It is because human beings first encountered this asexual form of reproduction, in connection with fruit
trees probably, that such a one-parent organism of non-sexual origin is called a "twig"; that is, "clone."

And what of multicellular animals?

Asexual reproduction can take place among them as well. The
more primitive the animal—that is, the less diversified and specialized
its cells are—the more likely it is that asexual reproduction can take
place.

A sponge, or a freshwater hydra, or a flatworm, or a starfish can,
any of them, be torn into parts and these parts, if kept in their usual
environment, will each grow into a complete organism. The new organisms are clones.

Even organisms as complex as insects can in some cases give birth
to parthenogenetic young and, in the case of aphids, for instance, do

so as a matter of course. In these cases, an egg cell, containing only a half set of chromosomes, does not require union with a sperm cell to supply the other half set. Instead, the egg cell's half set merely duplicates itself, producing a full set, all from the female parent, and the egg then proceeds to divide and become an independent organism, again a kind of clone.

In general, though, complex animals and, in particular, vertebrates do not clone but engage in sexual reproduction exclusively.

Why?—Two reasons.

In the first place, as an organism becomes more complex and specialized, its organs, tissues, and cells become more complex and specialized as well. The cells are so well adapted to perform their highly specialized functions, that they can no longer divide and differentiate as the original egg cells did.‡

This seems a terrible disadvantage. Organisms that can clone, reproducing themselves asexually, would seem to be much better off than other organisms—who must go to the trouble of finding partners and who must engage in all the complex phenomena, both physical and chemical, involved in sexual reproduction. Think of all the human beings who, for one slight flaw or another, can't have children —a problem that would be unknown if we could just release a toe and have it grow into another individual while we grew another toe.

Here comes the second reason, then. There's an evolutionary advantage to sexual reproduction that more than makes up for all the inconveniences.* In cloning, the genetic contents of new organisms remain identical with those of the original organisms, except for occasional mutations. If the organism is very efficiently adapted to its surroundings, this is useful, but it is an extremely conservative mechanism that reduces the chance of change. Any alteration in the environment could quickly lead to the extinction of a species.

In the case of sexual reproduction, every new organism has a

‡ This is not mysterious. We see an analogy on the social plane. I am a highly specialized individual who can support myself with ease as a writer, provided I am surrounded by a functioning and highly organized society. Place me on a desert island and I shall quickly perish since I don't know the first thing about the simplest requirements for self-support.

* Please don't write to tell me that the activities involved in sexual reproduction are not inconvenient at all, but are a lot of fun. I know that better than you do, whoever you are. The fun is an evolutionarily developed bribe designed to have us overlook and forgive the inconveniences. If you are a woman, you will see the point more quickly, perhaps, than a man will.

brand-new mix of genes, half from one parent, half from another. Change is inevitable; variation from individual to individual is certain. A species in which sexual reproduction is the norm has the capacity to adapt readily to slight alterations in environment since some of its variants are then favored over others. Indeed, a species can, through sexual reproduction, split with relative ease into two or more species that will take advantage of somewhat different niches in the environment.

In short, a sexually reproducing species evolves much more quickly than a cloning species, and such difficult-to-evolve specializations as intelligence are not likely to arise in the entire lifetime of a habitable planet, without sexual reproduction.

Yet in one specialized way cloning can take place in even the most advanced animals—even in the human being.

Consider a human egg cell, fertilized by a human sperm cell. We now have a fertilized egg cell which contains a half set of genes from its mother and a half set from its father.

This fertilized egg cell cannot become an independently living organism for some nine months, for it must divide and redivide within its mother's womb and be nourished by way of its mother's bloodstream. It must develop, specialize, and grow larger until it has developed the necessary ability to live independently. Even after it emerges from its mother's womb, it requires constant and unremitting care for a period of time before it can be trusted to care for itself.

Nevertheless, the matter of necessary care is genetically irrelevant. The fertilized egg is already a separate organism with its genetic characteristics fixed and unique.

The first step in the development of the fertilized egg is that it divides into two cells that cling together. Each of these two cells divides again, and each of the four that results divides again and so on.

If, after the first cell division, the two offspring cells, for any reason, should happen to fall apart, each offspring cell may then go on to develop into a complete organism of its own. The result is a pair of identical twins, each with the same genetic equipment and each of the same sex, of course. In a sense, each twin is a clone of the other.

There is no reason to suppose that this separation of offspring cells can't happen over and over, so that three or four or any number of organisms might not develop from the original fertilized egg. As a matter of practical fact, however, a mother's womb can only hold so much, and if there are multiple organisms developing, each is sure to be smaller than a single organism. The more organisms that develop, the smaller each one and, in the end, they will be too small to survive after delivery.

There are such things as identical triplets and quadruplets, but I doubt that any higher number of infants would survive long after birth without the advantages of modern medical technique. Even then it is hard enough.

Identical twins are very like each other and often display mirror-image characteristics. (I once had a chemistry professor with his nose canted to the left. His identical-twin brother had his nose canted to the right, I was told.)

It is also possible, however, though not usual, for a woman to bring two different egg cells to fruition at the same time. If both are fertilized, two children will be born who are each possessed of genetic equipment different from the other. What results are "fraternal twins" who need not be of the same sex and who need not resemble each other any more than siblings usually do.

Consider the fertilized egg again. Every time it divides and redivides, the new cells that form inherit the same genetic equipment possessed by the original fertilized egg.

Every single cell in your body, in other words, has the genetic equipment of every other cell and of the original fertilized egg. Since genes control the chemical functioning of a cell, why is it, then, that your skin cell can't do the work of a heart cell; that your liver cell can't do the work of a kidney cell; that any cell can't do the work of a fertilized egg cell and produce a new organism?

The answer is that though all the genes are there in every cell of your body, they aren't all working alike. The cell is an intricate assemblage of chemical reactions, chemical building blocks, chemical products, and physical structures, all of which influence one another. Some genes are inhibited and some are stimulated, in a variety of ways depending on subtle factors, with the result that different cells in your body have genetic equipment in which only characteristic parts are working at characteristic rates.

Such specialized development begins in the earliest embryo, as some cells come into being on the outside of the embryo, some on the inside; some with more of the original yolk, some with less; some with first chance at absorbing nutrients from the maternal bloodstream, some with only a later chance. The details are clearly of the greatest importance to human biology, and biologists just don't yet know them.

Naturally, the ordinary "somatic cells" of an adult human body, with their genetic equipment working only in highly specialized ways, cannot divide into a whole organism if left to themselves. Many body cells, such as those of the muscles or nerves, have become so specialized they can't divide at all. Only the sex cells, eggs and sperm, retain the lack of genetic specialization required to produce a new organism under the proper circumstances.

Is there any way of unspecializing the genetic structure of somatic cells so as to allow them to develop into a new organism?

Well, the genes are contained in the nucleus of the cell, which makes up a small portion of the total and is marked off by a membrane of its own. Outside the nucleus is the cytoplasm of a cell, and it is the material in the cytoplasm that provides the various chemicals that help serve to inhibit or stimulate the action of the genes.

Suppose, then, the nucleus of a somatic cell were surrounded with the cytoplasm of an egg cell. Would the genetic equipment in the nucleus unblock, and would the egg cell then proceed to divide and redivide? Would it go on to form an individual with the genetic equipment of the original somatic cell and, therefore, of the person from whom the somatic cell was taken? If so, the new organism would be a clone of the person who donated the somatic cell.

The technique has been tried on different animals. You begin with an unfertilized egg cell and treat it in such a way as to remove its nucleus, either by delicately cutting it out or by using some chemical process. In the place of the removed egg cell nucleus, you insert the nucleus of a somatic cell of the same (or, possibly, an allied) species, and then let nature take its course.

This has been successfully tried with animals as complex as a tadpole.

It stops being easy after the frog, though. Frog eggs are naked and can be manipulated easily. They develop in water and can just lie there after the micro-operation.

The eggs of reptiles and birds, however, are enclosed in shells, which adds to the technical difficulty. The eggs of mammals are very small, very delicate, very easily damaged. Furthermore, even if a mammalian egg has had its nucleus replaced, it would then have to be implanted into the womb of a female and allowed to come to term there.

The practical problems of mammalian cloning are such that there is no chance of its happening for some time yet. Yet biologists are anxious to perform the feat and are trying hard. Eventually, they will no doubt succeed. What purpose will it serve?

If clones can be produced wholesale, a biologist can have a whole group of animals with identical genetic equipment; a set of ten thousand identical-twin mice, let us say. There are many animal experiments that can be conducted with the hope of more useful results if the question of genetic variation could be eliminated.

By the addition of other genetic-engineering techniques, it might be possible to produce a whole series of animals with identical genetic equipment, except that in each case, one gene is removed or altered—a different gene in each individual perhaps. The science of genetics would then advance in seven-league strides.

There would be practical uses, too. A prize bull or a champion egg-laying hen could be cloned, and the genetic characteristics that make the record-breaking aspects of the animal possible would be preserved without the chance of diminution by the interplay of genes obtained from a second parent.

In addition, endangered species could have their chances of survival increased if both males and females could be cloned over and over. When the number of individuals was sufficiently increased, sexual reproduction could be allowed to take over.

We might even dream of finding a frozen mammoth with some cell nuclei not entirely dead. We might then clone one by way of an elephant's womb. If we could find a male and a female mammoth—

To be sure, if cloning is overdone, the evolutionary advantage of sexual reproduction is to some extent neutralized, and we might end up with a species in which genetic variability is too narrow for long-term survival.

It is important to remember that the most important genetic possession of any species is not this gene or that, *but the whole mixed bag.* The greater the variety of genes available to a species, the more secure it is against the vicissitudes of fortune. The existence of congenital disorders and gene deficiencies is the price paid for the advantage of variety and versatility.

And what about cloned human beings, which is, after all, the subject matter of "Randall's Song"?

These may never be as important as you think. The prospect of importance rests chiefly on certain misapprehensions on the part of the public. Some people, for instance, pant for clones because they think them the gateway to personal immortality. That is quite wrong.

Your clone is not *you*. Your clone is your twin brother (or sister) and is no more you than your ordinary identical twin would be. Your clone does not have your consciousness, and if *you* die, you are *dead*. You do not live on in your clone. Once that is understood, I suspect that much of the interest in clones will disappear.

Some people fear clones, on the other hand, because they imagine that morons will be cloned in order to make it possible to build up a great army of cannon fodder that despots will use for world conquest.

Why bother? There has never been any difficulty in finding cannon fodder anywhere in the world, even without cloning, and the ordinary process of supplying new soldiers for despots is infinitely cheaper than cloning.

More reasonably, it could be argued that the clone of a great human being would retain his genetic equipment and, therefore, would be another great human being of the same kind. In that case, the chief use of cloning would be to reproduce genius.

That, I think, would be a waste of time. We are not necessarily going to breed thousands of transcendent geniuses out of an Einstein or thousands of diabolical villains out of a Hitler.

After all, a human being is more than his genes. Your clone is the result of your nucleus being placed into a foreign egg cell and the foreign cytoplasm in that egg cell will surely have an effect on the development of the clone. The egg will have to be implanted into a foreign womb and that, too, will have an influence on the development of the organism.

Even if a woman were to have one of her somatic nuclei implanted into one of her own egg cells and if she were then to have the egg cell implanted into the womb of her own mother (who, we will assume, is still capable of bearing a child), the new organism will be born into different circumstances and that would have an effect on its personality, too.

For instance, suppose you wanted one hundred Isaac Asimovs so that the supply of *F&SF* essays would never run out. You would then have to ask what it was that made me the kind of writer I am—or a writer at all. Was it only my genes?

I was brought up in a candy store under a father of the old school who, although he was Jewish, was the living embodiment of the Protestant ethic. My nose was kept to the grindstone until I could no longer remove it. Furthermore, I was brought up during the Great Depression and had to find a way of making a living—or I would inherit the candy store, which I desperately didn't want to do. Furthermore, I lived in a time when science fiction magazines, and pulp magazines generally, were going strong, and when a young man could sell clumsily written stories because the demand was greater than the supply.

Put it all together, they spell M-E.

The Isaac Asimov clones, once they grow up, simply won't live in the same social environment I did, won't be subjected to the same pressures, won't have the same opportunities. What's more, when I wrote, I just wrote—no one expected anything particular from me. When my clones write, their products will always be compared to the Grand Original and that would discourage and wipe out anyone.

The end result will be that though my clones, or some of them, might turn out to be valuable citizens of one kind or another, it would be very unlikely that any one of them would be another Isaac Asimov, and their production would not be worthwhile. Whatever good they might do would not be worth the reduction they would represent in the total gene variability of humanity.

Yet cloning would not be totally useless, either. There would be the purely theoretical advantage of studying the development of embryos with known variations in their genes which, except for those variations, would have identical genetic equipment. (This would raise serious ethical questions, as all human experimentation does, but that is not the issue at the moment.)

Then, too, suppose it were possible to learn enough about human embryonic development to guide embryos into all sorts of specialized bypaths that would produce a kind of monster that had a full-sized heart, with all else vestigial, or a full-sized kidney or lung or liver or leg. With just one organ developing, techniques of forced growth (in the laboratory, of course, and not in a human womb) might make development to full size a matter of months only.

We can therefore imagine that at birth, every human individual will have scrapings taken from his little toe, thus attaining a few hundred living cells that can be at once frozen for possible eventual use. (This is done at birth, because the younger the cell, the more efficiently it is likely to clone.)

These cells could serve as potential organ banks for the future. If the time were to come when an adult found he had a limping heart or fading pancreas or whatever, or if a leg had been lost in an accident or had had to be amputated, then those long-frozen cells would be defrosted and put into action.

An organ replacement would be grown and since it would have precisely the same genetic equipment as the old, the body would not reject it. —Surely that is the best possible application of cloning.

John Varley's first story for *F&SF* was "Picnic on Nearside" in 1974. Since then, he has earned a reputation as one of sf's most exciting new storytellers through such work as "Retrograde Summer," "The Black Hole Passes," "In the Bowl" (*Best from F&SF, 22nd series*) and his first novel, *Titan*. This story was another Nebula award nominee.

In the Hall of the Martian Kings

by JOHN VARLEY

It took perseverance, alertness, and a willingness to break the rules to watch the sunrise in Tharsis Canyon. Matthew Crawford shivered in the dark, his suit heater turned to emergency setting, his eyes trained toward the east. He knew he had to be watchful. Yesterday he had missed it entirely, snatched away from him in the middle of a long, unavoidable yawn. His jaw muscles stretched, but he controlled it and kept his eyes firmly open.

And there it was. Like the lights in a theater after the show is over: just a quick brightening, a splash of localized bluish-purple over the canyon rim, and he was surrounded by footlights. Day had come, the truncated Martian day that would never touch the blackness over his head.

This day, like the nine before it, illuminated a Tharsis radically changed from what it had been over the last sleepy ten thousand years. Wind erosion of rocks can create an infinity of shapes, but it never gets around to carving out a straight line or a perfect arc. The human encampment below him broke up the jagged lines of the rocks with regular angles and curves.

The camp was anything but orderly. No one would get the impression that any care had been taken in the haphazard arrangement of dome, lander, crawlers, crawler tracks, and scattered equipment. It had grown, as all human base camps seem to grow, without pattern. He was reminded of the footprints around Tranquillity Base, though on a much larger scale.

Tharsis Base sat on a wide ledge about halfway up from the uneven bottom of the Tharsis arm of the Great Rift Valley. The site had been chosen because it was a smooth area, allowing easy access up a gentle slope to the flat plains of the Tharsis Plateau, while at the same time only a kilometer from the valley floor. No one could agree which area was most worthy of study: plains or canyon. So this site had been chosen as a compromise. What it meant was that the exploring parties had to either climb up or go down, because there wasn't a damn thing worth seeing near the camp. Even the exposed layering and its areological records could not be seen without a half-kilometer crawler ride up to the point where Crawford had climbed to watch the sunrise.

He examined the dome as he walked back to camp. There was a figure hazily visible through the plastic. At this distance he would have been unable to tell who it was if it weren't for the black face. He saw her step up to the dome wall and wipe a clear circle to look through. She spotted his bright red suit and pointed at him. She was suited except for her helmet, which contained her radio. He knew he was in trouble. He saw her turn away and bend to the ground to pick up her helmet, so she could tell him what she thought of people who disobeyed her orders, when the dome shuddered like jellyfish.

An alarm started in his helmet, flat and strangely soothing coming from the tiny speaker. He stood there for a moment as a perfect smoke ring of dust billowed up around the rim of the dome. Then he was running.

He watched the disaster unfold before his eyes, silent except for the rhythmic beat of the alarm bell in his ears. The dome was dancing and straining, trying to fly. The floor heaved up in the center, throwing the black woman to her knees. In another second the interior was a whirling snowstorm. He skidded on the sand and fell forward, got up in time to see the fiberglass ropes on the side nearest him snap free from the steel spikes anchoring the dome to the rock.

The dome now looked like some fantastic Christmas ornament, filled with snowflakes and the flashing red and blue lights of the emergency alarms. The top of the dome heaved over away from him, and the floor raised itself high in the air, held down by the unbroken anchors on the side farthest from him. There was a gush of snow and dust; then the floor settled slowly back to the ground. There was no motion now but the leisurely folding of the depressurized dome roof as it settled over the structures inside.

The crawler skidded to a stop, nearly rolling over, beside the deflated dome. Two pressure-suited figures got out. They started for the dome, hesitantly, in fits and starts. One grabbed the other's arm and pointed to the lander. The two of them changed course and scrambled up the rope ladder hanging over the side.

Crawford was the only one to look up when the lock started cycling. The two people almost tumbled over each other coming out of the lock. They wanted to *do* something, and quickly, but didn't know what. In the end, they just stood there silently twisting their hands and looking at the floor. One of them took off her helmet. She was a large woman, in her thirties, with red hair shorn off close to the scalp.

"Matt, we got here as . . ." She stopped, realizing how obvious it was. "How's Lou?"

"Lou's not going to make it." He gestured to the bunk where a heavyset man lay breathing raggedly into a clear plastic mask. He was on pure oxygen. There was blood seeping from his ears and nose.

"Brain damage?"

Crawford nodded. He looked around at the other occupants of the room. There was the Surface Mission Commander, Mary Lang, the black woman he had seen inside the dome just before the blowout. She was sitting on the edge of Lou Prager's cot, her head cradled in her hands. In a way, she was a more shocking sight than Lou. No one who knew her would have thought she could be brought to this limp state of apathy. She had not moved for the last hour.

Sitting on the floor huddled in a blanket was Martin Ralston, the chemist. His shirt was bloody, and there was dried blood all over his face and hands from the nosebleed he'd only recently gotten under control, but his eyes were alert. He shivered, looking from Lang, his titular leader, to Crawford, the only one who seemed calm enough to deal with anything. He was a follower, reliable but unimaginative.

Crawford looked back to the newest arrivals. They were Lucy Stone McKillian, the red-headed ecologist, and Song Sue Lee, the exobiologist. They still stood numbly by the airlock, unable as yet to come to grips with the fact of fifteen dead men and women beneath the dome outside.

"What do they say on the *Burroughs?*" McKillian asked, tossing her helmet on the floor and squatting tiredly against the wall. The lander was not the most comfortable place to hold a meeting; all the couches were mounted horizontally since their purpose was cushioning the acceleration of landing and takeoff. With the ship sitting on its tail, this made ninety per cent of the space in the lander useless. They were all gathered on the circular bulkhead at the rear of the lifesystem, just forward of the fuel tank.

"We're waiting for a reply," Crawford said. "But I can sum up what they're going to say: not good. Unless one of you two has some experience in Mars-lander handling that you've been concealing from us."

Neither of them bothered to answer that. The radio in the nose sputtered, then clanged for their attention. Crawford looked over at Lang, who made no move to go answer it. He stood up and swarmed up the ladder to sit in the copilot's chair. He switched on the receiver.

"Commander Lang?"

"No, this is Crawford again. Commander Lang is . . . indisposed. She's busy with Lou, trying to do something."

"That's no use. The doctor says it's a miracle he's still breathing. If he wakes up at all, he won't be anything like you knew him. The telemetry shows nothing like the normal brain wave. Now I've got to talk to Commander Lang. Have her come up." The voice of Mission Commander Weinstein was accustomed to command, and about as emotional as a weather report.

"Sir, I'll ask her, but I don't think she'll come. This is still her operation, you know." He didn't give Weinstein time to reply to that. Weinstein had been trapped by his own seniority into commanding the *Edgar Rice Burroughs,* the orbital ship that got them to Mars and had been intended to get them back. Command of the *Podkayne,* the disposable lander that would make the lion's share of the headlines, had gone to Lang. There was little friendship between the two, especially when Weinstein fell to brooding about the very real financial benefits Lang stood to reap by being the first woman on Mars, rather than the lowly mission commander. He saw himself as another Michael Collins.

Crawford called down to Lang, who raised her head enough to mumble something.

"What'd she say?"

"She said take a message." McKillian had been crawling up the ladder as she said this. Now she reached him and said in a lower voice, "Matt, she's pretty broken up. You'd better take over for now."

"Right, I know." He turned back to the radio, and McKillian listened over his shoulder as Weinstein briefed them on the situation as he saw it. It pretty much jibed with Crawford's estimation, except at one crucial point. He signed off and they joined the other survivors.

He looked around at the faces of the others and decided it wasn't the time to speak of rescue possibilities. He didn't relish being a leader. He was hoping Lang would recover soon and take the burden from him. In the meantime he had to get them started on something. He touched McKillian gently on the shoulder and motioned her to the lock.

"Let's go get them buried," he said. She squeezed her eyes shut tight, forcing out tears, then nodded.

It wasn't a pretty job. Halfway through it, Song came down the ladder with the body of Lou Prager.

"Let's go over what we've learned. First, now that Lou's dead there's very little chance of ever lifting off. That is, unless Mary thinks she can absorb everything she needs to know about piloting the *Podkayne* from those printouts Weinstein sent down. How about it, Mary?"

Mary Lang was laying sideways across the improvised cot that had recently held the *Podkayne* pilot, Lou Prager. Her head was nodding listlessly against the aluminum hull plate behind her, her chin was on her chest. Her eyes were half-open.

Song had given her a sedative from the dead doctor's supplies on the advice of the medic aboard the *E.R.B.* It had enabled her to stop fighting so hard against the screaming panic she wanted to unleash. It hadn't improved her disposition. She had quit; she wasn't going to do anything for anybody.

When the blowout started, Lang had snapped on her helmet quickly. Then she had struggled against the blizzard and the undulating dome bottom, heading for the roofless framework where the other members of the expedition were sleeping. The blowout was over in ten seconds, and she then had the problem of coping with the collapsing roof, which promptly buried her in folds of clear plastic. It was far too much like one of those nightmares of running knee-deep in quicksand. She had to fight for every meter, but she made it.

She made it in time to see her shipmates of the last six months gasping soundlessly and spouting blood from all over their faces as they fought to get into their pressure suits. It was a hopeless task to choose which two or three to save in the time she had. She might have done better but for the freakish nature of her struggle to reach them; she was in shock and half believed it was only a nightmare. So she grabbed the nearest, who happened to be Doctor Ralston. He had nearly finished donning his suit; so she slapped his helmet on him and moved to the next one. It was Luther Nakamura, and he was not moving. Worse, he was only half suited. Pragmatically she should have left him and moved on to save the ones who still had a chance. She knew it now, but didn't like it any better than she had liked it then.

While she was stuffing Nakamura into his suit, Crawford arrived. He had walked over the folds of plastic until he reached the dormitory, then sliced through it with his laser normally used to vaporize rock samples.

And he had had time to think about the problem of whom to save. He went straight to Lou Prager and finished suiting him up. But it was already too late. He didn't know if it would have made any difference if Mary Lang had tried to save him first.

Now she lay on the bunk, her feet sprawled carelessly in front of her. She slowly shook her head back and forth.

"You sure?" Crawford prodded her, hoping to get a rise, a show of temper, *anything*.

"I'm sure," she mumbled. "You people know how long they

trained Lou to fly this thing? And he almost cracked it up as it was. I
. . . ah, nuts. It isn't possible."

"I refuse to accept that as a final answer," he said. "But in the
meantime we should explore the possibilities if what Mary says is
true."

Ralston laughed. It wasn't a bitter laugh; he sounded genuinely
amused. Crawford plowed on.

"Here's what we know for sure. The *E.R.B.* is useless to us. Oh,
they'll help us out with plenty of advice, maybe more than we want,
but any rescue is out of the question."

"We know that," McKillian said. She was tired and sick from the
sight of the faces of her dead friends. "What's the use of all this
talk?"

"Wait a moment," Song broke in. "Why can't they . . . I mean
they have plenty of time, don't they? They have to leave in six
months, as I understand it, because of the orbital elements, but in
that time . . . "

"Don't you know anything about spaceships?" McKillian shouted.
Song went on, unperturbed.

"I do know enough to know the *Edgar* is not equipped for an atmosphere entry. My idea was, not to bring down the whole ship but
only what's aboard the ship that we need. Which is a pilot. Might
that be possible?"

Crawford ran his hands through his hair, wondering what to say.
That possibility had been discussed, and was being studied. But it
had to be classed as extremely remote.

"You're right," he said. "What we need is a pilot, and that pilot is
Commander Weinstein. Which presents problems legally, if nothing
else. He's the captain of a ship and should not leave it. That's what
kept him on the *Edgar* in the first place. But he did have a lot of
training on the lander simulator back when he was so sure he'd be
picked for the ground team. You know Winey, always the instinct to
be the one-man show. So if he thought he could do it, he'd be down
here in a minute to bail us out and grab the publicity. I understand
they're trying to work out a heat-shield parachute system from one of
the drop capsules that were supposed to ferry down supplies to us
during the stay here. But it's very risky. You don't modify an aero-
dynamic design lightly, not one that's supposed to hit the atmosphere
at ten thousand-plus kilometers. So I think we can rule that out.

They'll keep working on it, but when it's done, Winey won't step into the damn thing. He wants to be a hero, but he wants to live to enjoy it, too."

There had been a brief lifting of spirits among Song, Ralston, and McKillian at the thought of a possible rescue. The more they thought about it, the less happy they looked. They all seemed to agree with Crawford's assessment.

"So we'll put that one in the Fairy Godmother file and forget about it. If it happens, fine. But we'd better plan on the assumption that it won't. As you may know, the *E.R.B.*-*Podkayne* are the only ships in existence that can reach Mars and land on it. One other pair is in the congressional funding stage. Winey talked to Earth and thinks there'll be a speedup in the preliminary paperwork and the thing'll start building in a year. The launch was scheduled for five years from now, but it might get as much as a year boost. It's a rescue mission now, easier to sell. But the design will need modification, if only to include five more seats to bring us all back. You can bet on there being more modifications when we send in our report on the blowout. So we'd better add another six months to the schedule."

McKillian had had enough. "Matt, what the hell are you talking about? Rescue mission? Damn it, you know as well as I that if they find us here, we'll be long dead. We'll probably be dead in another year."

"That's where you're wrong. We'll survive."

"How?"

"I don't have the faintest idea." He looked her straight in the eye as he said this. She almost didn't bother to answer, but curiosity got the best of her.

"Is this just a morale session? Thanks, but I don't need it. I'd rather face the situation as it is. Or do you really have something?"

"Both. I don't have anything concrete except to say that we'll survive the same way humans have always survived: by staying warm, by eating, by drinking. To that list we have to add 'by breathing.' That's a hard one, but other than that we're no different than any other group of survivors in a tough spot. I don't know what we'll have to do, specifically, but I know we'll find the answers."

"Or die trying," Song said.

"Or die trying." He grinned at her. She at least had grasped the essence of the situation. Whether survival was possible or not, it was necessary to maintain the illusion that it was. Otherwise, you might as well cut your throat. You might as well not even be born, because life is an inevitably fatal struggle to survive.

"What about air?" McKillian asked, still unconvinced.

"I don't know," he told her cheerfully. "It's a tough problem, isn't it?"

"What about water?"

"Well, down in that valley there's a layer of permafrost about twenty meters down."

She laughed. "Wonderful. So that's what you want us to do? Dig down there and warm the ice with our pink little hands? It won't work, I tell you."

Crawford waited until she had run through a long list of reasons why they were doomed. Most of them made a great deal of sense. When she was through, he spoke softly.

"Lucy, listen to yourself."

"I'm just—"

"You're arguing on the side of death. Do you want to die? Are you so determined that you won't listen to someone who says you can live?"

She was quiet for a long time, then shuffled her feet awkwardly. She glanced at him, then at Song and Ralston. They were waiting, and she had to blush and smile slowly at them.

"You're right. What do we do first?"

"Just what we were doing. Taking stock of our situation. We need to make a list of what's available to us. We'll write it down on paper, but I can give you a general rundown." He counted off the points on his fingers.

"One, we have food for twenty people for three months. That comes to about a year for the five of us. With rationing, maybe a year and a half. That's assuming all the supply capsules reach us all right. In addition, the *Edgar* is going to clean the pantry to the bone and give us everything they can possibly spare and send it to us in the three spare capsules. That might come to two years or even three.

"Two, we have enough water to last us forever if the recyclers keep going. That'll be a problem, because our reactor will run out of power in two years. We'll need another power source, and maybe another water source.

"The oxygen problem is about the same. Two years at the outside.

We'll have to find a way to conserve it a lot more than we're doing. Offhand, I don't know how. Song, do you have any ideas?"

She looked thoughtful, which produced two vertical punctuation marks between her slanted eyes.

"Possibly a culture of plants from the *Edgar*. If we could rig some way to grow plants in Martian sunlight and not have them killed by the ultraviolet. . . ."

McKillian looked horrified, as any good ecologist would.

"What about contamination?" she asked. "What do you think that sterilization was for before we landed? Do you want to louse up the entire ecological balance of Mars? No one would ever be sure if samples in the future were real Martian plants or mutated Earth stock."

"What ecological balance?" Song shot back. "You know as well as I do that this trip has been nearly a zero. A few anaerobic bacteria, a patch of lichen, both barely distinguishable from Earth forms—"

"That's just what I mean. You import Earth forms now, and we'll never tell the difference."

"But it could be done, right? With the proper shielding so the plants won't be wiped out before they ever sprout, we could have a hydroponics plant functioning—"

"Oh, yes, it could be done. I can see three or four dodges right now. But you're not addressing the main question, which is—"

"Hold it," Crawford said. "I just wanted to know if you had any ideas." He was secretly pleased at the argument; it got them both thinking along the right lines, moved them from the deadly apathy they must guard against.

"I think this discussion has served its purpose, which was to convince everyone here that survival is possible." He glanced uneasily at Lang, still nodding, her eyes glassy as she saw her teammates die before her eyes.

"I just want to point out that instead of an expedition, we are now a colony. Not in the usual sense of planning to stay here forever, but all our planning will have to be geared to that fiction. What we're faced with is not a simple matter of stretching supplies until rescue comes. Stopgap measures are not likely to do us much good. The answers that will save us are the long-term ones, the sort of answers a colony would be looking for. About two years from now we're going to have to be in a position to survive with some sort of lifestyle that could support us forever. We'll have to fit into this environment where we can and adapt it to us where we can. For that, we're better off than most of the colonists of the past, at least for the short term. We have a large supply of everything a colony needs: food, water, tools, raw materials, energy, brains, and women. Without these things, no colony has much of a chance. All we lack is a regular resupply from the home country, but a really good group of colonists can get along without that. What do you say? Are you all with me?"

Something had caused Mary Lang's eyes to look up. It was a reflex by now, a survival reflex conditioned by a lifetime of fighting her way to the top. It took root in her again and pulled her erect on the bed, then to her feet. She fought off the effects of the drug and stood there, eyes bleary but aware.

"What makes you think that women are a natural resource, Crawford?" she said, slowly and deliberately.

"Why, what I meant was that without the morale uplift provided by members of the opposite sex, a colony will lack the push needed to make it."

"That's what you meant, all right. And you meant women, available to the *real* colonists as a reason to live. I've heard it before. That's a male-oriented way to look at it, Crawford." She was regaining her stature as they watched, seeming to grow until she dominated the group with the intangible power that marks a leader. She took a deep breath and came fully awake for the first time that day.

"We'll stop that sort of thinking right now. I'm the mission commander. I appreciate you taking over while I was . . . how did you say it? Indisposed. But you should pay more attention to the social aspects of our situation. If anyone is a commodity here, it's you and Ralston, by virtue of your scarcity. There will be some thorny questions to resolve there, but for the meantime we will function as a unit, under my command. We'll do all we can to minimize social competition among the women for the men. That's the way it must be. Clear?"

She was answered by quiet assent and nods of the head. She did not acknowledge it but plowed right on.

"I wondered from the start why you were along, Crawford." She was pacing slowly back and forth in the crowded space. The others got out of her way almost without thinking, except for Ralston who still huddled under his blanket. "A historian? Sure, it's a fine idea, but pretty impractical. I have to admit that I've been thinking of you as a luxury, and about as useful as the nipples on a man's chest. But I was wrong. All the NASA people were wrong. The Astronaut Corps fought like crazy to keep you off this trip. Time enough for that on later flights. We were blinded by our loyalty to the test-pilot philosophy of space flight. We wanted as few scientists as possible and as many astronauts as we could manage. We don't like to think of ourselves as ferry-boat pilots. I think we demonstrated during Apollo that we could handle science jobs as well as anyone. We saw you as a kind of insult, a slap in the face by the scientists in Houston to show us how low our stock has fallen."

"If I might be able to—"

"Shut up. But we were wrong. I read in your resume that you were quite a student of survival. What's your honest assessment of our chances?"

Crawford shrugged, uneasy at the question. He didn't know if it was the right time to even postulate that they might fail.

"Tell me the truth."

"Pretty slim. Mostly the air problem. The people I've read about never sank so low that they had to worry about where their next breath was coming from."

"Have you ever heard of Apollo 13?"

He smiled at her. "Special circumstances. Short-term problems."

"You're right, of course. And in the only two other real space emergencies since that time, all hands were lost." She turned and scowled at each of them in turn.

"But we're *not* going to lose." She dared any of them to disagree, and no one was about to. She relaxed and resumed her stroll around the room. She turned to Crawford again.

"I can see I'll be drawing on your knowledge a lot in the years to come. What do you see as the next order of business?"

Crawford relaxed. The awful burden of responsibility, which he had never wanted, was gone. He was content to follow her lead.

"To tell you the truth, I was wondering what to say next. We have to make a thorough inventory. I guess we should start on that."

"That's fine, but there is an even more important order of business. We have to go out to the dome and find out what the hell caused the blowout. The damn thing should *not* have blown; it's the first of its type to do so. And from the *bottom*. But it did blow, and we should know why, or we're ignoring a fact about Mars that might still kill us. Let's do that first. Ralston, can you walk?"

When he nodded, she sealed her helmet and started into the lock. She turned and looked speculatively at Crawford.

"I swear, man, if you had touched me with a cattle prod you couldn't have got a bigger rise out of me than you did with what you said a few minutes ago. Do I dare ask?"

Crawford was not about to answer. He said, with a perfectly straight face, "Me? Maybe you should just assume I'm a chauvinist."

"We'll see, won't we?"

"What is that stuff?"

Song Sue Lee was on her knees, examining one of the hundreds of short, stiff spikes extruding from the ground. She tried to scratch her head but was frustrated by her helmet.

"It looks like plastic. But I have a strong feeling it's the higher life-form Lucy and I were looking for yesterday."

"And you're telling me those little spikes are what poked holes in the dome bottom? I'm not buying that."

Song straightened up, moving stiffly. They had all worked hard to empty out the collapsed dome and peel back the whole, bulky mess to reveal the ground it had covered. She was tired and stepped out of character for a moment to snap at Mary Lang.

"I didn't tell you that. We pulled the dome back and found spikes. It was your inference that they poked holes in the bottom."

"I'm sorry," Lang said quietly. "Go on with what you were saying."

"Well," Song admitted, "it wasn't a bad inference, at that. But the holes I saw were not punched through. They were eaten away." She waited for Lang to protest that the dome bottom was about as chemically inert as any plastic yet devised. But Lang had learned her lesson. And she had a talent for facing facts.

"So. We have a thing here that eats plastic. And seems to be made of plastic, into the bargain. Any ideas why it picked this particular spot to grow, and no other?"

"I have an idea on that," McKillian said. "I've had it in mind to do some studies around the dome to see if the altered moisture content we've been creating here had any effect on the spores in the soil. See, we've been here nine days, spouting out water vapor, carbon dioxide, and quite a bit of oxygen into the atmosphere. Not much, but maybe more than it seems, considering the low concentrations that are naturally available. We've altered the biome. Does anyone know where the exhaust air from the dome was expelled?"

Lang raised her eyebrows. "Yes, it was under the dome. The air we exhausted was warm, you see, and it was thought it could be put to use one last time before we let it go, to warm the floor of the dome and decrease heat loss."

"And the water vapor collected on the underside of the dome when it hit the cold air. Right. Do you get the picture?"

"I think so," Lang said. "It was so little water, though. You know we didn't want to waste it; we condensed it out until the air we exhausted was dry as a bone."

"For Earth, maybe. Here it was a torrential rainfall. It reached seeds or spores in the ground and triggered them to start growing. We're going to have to watch it when we use anything containing plastic. What does that include?"

Lang groaned. "All the air-lock seals, for one thing." There were grimaces from all of them at the thought of that. "For another, a good part of our suits. Song, watch it, don't step on that thing. We don't know how powerful it is or if it'll eat the plastic in your boots, but we'd better play it safe. How about it, Ralston? Think you can find out how bad it is?"

"You mean identify the solvent these things use? Probably, if we can get some sort of work space and I can get to my equipment."

"Mary," McKillian said, "it occurs to me that I'd better start looking for airborne spores. If there are some, it could mean that the airlock on the *Podkayne* is vulnerable. Even thirty meters off the ground."

"Right. Get on that. Since we're sleeping in it until we can find out what we can do on the ground, we'd best be sure it's safe. Meantime, we'll all sleep in our suits." There were helpless groans at this, but no protests. McKillian and Ralston headed for the pile of salvaged equipment, hoping to rescue enough to get started on their analyses. Song knelt again and started digging around one of the ten-centimeter spikes.

Crawford followed Lang back toward the *Podkayne*.

"Mary, I wanted . . . is it all right if I call you Mary?"

"I guess so. I don't think 'Commander Lang' would wear well over five years. But you'd better still *think* commander."

He considered it. "All right, Commander Mary." She punched him playfully. She had barely known him before the disaster. He had been a name on a roster and a sore spot in the estimation of the Astronaut Corps. But she had borne him no personal malice, and now found herself beginning to like him.

"What's on your mind?"

"Ah, several things. But maybe it isn't my place to bring them up now. First, I want to say that if you're . . . ah, concerned, or doubtful of my support or loyalty because I took over command for a while . . . earlier today, well . . ."

"Well?"

"I just wanted to tell you that I have no ambitions in that direction," he finished lamely.

She patted him on the back. "Sure, I know. You forget, I read your dossier. It mentioned several interesting episodes that I'd like you to tell me about someday, from your 'soldier-of-fortune' days—"

"Hell, those were grossly overblown. I just happened to get into some scrapes and managed to get out of them."

"Still, it got you picked for this mission out of hundreds of applicants. The thinking was that you'd be a wild card, a man of action with proven survivability. Maybe it worked out. But the other thing I remember on your card was that you're not a leader. No, that you're a loner who'll cooperate with a group and be no discipline problem, but you work better alone. Want to strike out on your own?"

He smiled at her. "No, thanks. But what you said is right. I have no hankering to take charge of anything. But I do have some knowledge that might prove useful."

"And we'll use it. You just speak up, I'll be listening." She started to say something, then thought of something else. "Say, what are your ideas on a woman bossing this project? I've had to fight that all the way from my Air Force days. So if you have any objections you might as well tell me up front."

He was genuinely surprised. "You didn't take that crack seriously, did you? I might as well admit it. It was intentional, like that cattle prod you mentioned. You looked like you needed a kick in the ass."

"And thank you. But you didn't answer my question."

"Those who lead, lead," he said, simply. "I'll follow you as long as you keep leading."

"As long as it's in the direction you want?" She laughed, and poked him in the ribs. "I see you as my Grand Vizier, the man who holds the arcane knowledge and advises the regent. I think I'll have to watch out for you. I know a little history, myself."

Crawford couldn't tell how serious she was. He shrugged it off.

"What I really wanted to talk to you about is this: You said you couldn't fly this ship. But you were not yourself, you were depressed and feeling hopeless. Does that still stand?"

"It stands. Come on up and I'll show you why."

In the pilot's cabin, Crawford was ready to believe her. Like all flying machines since the days of the windsock and open cockpit, this one was a mad confusion of dials, switches, and lights designed to awe anyone who knew nothing about it. He sat in the copilot's chair and listened to her.

"We had a back-up pilot, of course. You may be surprised to learn that it wasn't me. It was Dorothy Cantrell, and she's dead. Now I know what everything does on this board, and I can cope with most of it easily. What I don't know, I could learn. Some of the systems are computer-driven; give it the right program and it'll fly itself, in space." She looked longingly at the controls, and Crawford realized that, like Weinstein, she didn't relish giving up the fun of flying to boss a gang of explorers. She was a former test pilot, and above all things she loved flying. She patted an array of hand controls on her right side. There were more like them on the left.

"This is what would kill us, Crawford. What's your first name? Matt. Matt, this baby is a flyer for the first forty thousand meters. It doesn't have the juice to orbit on the jets alone. The wings are folded up now. You probably didn't see them on the way in, but you saw the models. They're very light, supercritical, and designed for this atmosphere. Lou said it was like flying a bathtub, but it flew. And it's a *skill,* almost an art. Lou practiced for three years on the best simulators we could build and still had to rely on things you can't learn in a simulator. And he barely got us down in one piece. We didn't noise it around, but it was a *damn* close thing. Lou was young; so was Cantrell. They were both fresh from flying. They flew every day, they had the *feel* for it. They were tops." She slumped back into her chair. "I haven't flown anything but trainers for eight years."

Crawford didn't know if he should let it drop.

"But you were one of the best, everyone knows that. You still don't think you could do it?"

She threw up her hands. "How can I make you understand? This is nothing like anything I've ever flown. You might as well . . ." She groped for a comparison, trying to coax it out with gestures in the air. "Listen. Does the fact that someone can fly a biplane, maybe even be the best goddamn biplane pilot that ever was, does that mean they're qualified to fly a helicopter?"

"I don't know."

"It doesn't. Believe me."

"All right. But the fact remains that you're the closest thing on Mars to a pilot for the *Podkayne*. I think you should consider that when you're deciding what we should do." He shut up, afraid to sound like he was pushing her.

She narrowed her eyes and gazed at nothing.

"I have thought about it." She waited for a long time. "I think the chances are about a thousand to one against us if I try to fly it. But I'll do it, if we come to that. And that's *your* job. Showing me some better odds. If you can't, let me know."

Three weeks later, the Tharsis Canyon had been transformed into a child's garden of toys. Crawford had thought of no better way to describe it. Each of the plastic spikes had blossomed into a fanciful windmill, no two of them just alike. There were tiny ones, with the vanes parallel to the ground and no more than ten centimeters tall. There were derricks of spidery plastic struts that would not have looked too out of place on a Kansas farm. Some of them were five meters high. They came in all colors and many configurations, but all had vanes covered with a transparent film like cellophane, and all were spinning into colorful blurs in the stiff Martian breeze. Crawford thought of an industrial park built by gnomes. He could almost see them trudging through the spinning wheels.

Song had taken one apart as well as she could. She was still shaking her head in disbelief. She had not been able to excavate the long insulated taproot, but she could infer how deep it went. It extended all the way down to the layer of permafrost, twenty meters down.

The ground between the windmills was coated in shimmering plastic. This was the second part of the plants' ingenious solution to survival on Mars. The windmills utilized the energy in the wind, and the plastic coating on the ground was in reality two thin sheets of plastic with a space between for water to circulate. The water was heated by the sun then pumped down to the permafrost, melting a little more of it each time.

"There's still something missing from our picture," Song had told them the night before, when she delivered her summary of what she had learned. "Marty hasn't been able to find a mechanism that would permit these things to grow by ingesting sand and rock and turning it into plasticlike materials. So we assume there is a reservoir of something like crude oil down there, maybe frozen in with the water."

"Where would that have come from?" Lang had asked.

"You've heard of the long-period Martian seasonal theories? Well, part of it is more than a theory. The combination of the Martian polar inclination, the precessional cycle, and the eccentricity of the orbit produces seasons that are about twelve thousand years long. We're in the middle of winter, though we landed in the nominal 'summer.' It's been theorized that if there were any Martian life it would have adapted to these longer cycles. It hibernates in spores during the cold cycle, when the water and carbon dioxide freeze out at the poles, then comes out when enough ice melts to permit biological processes. We seem to have fooled these plants; they thought summer was here when the water vapor content went up around the camp."

"So what about the crude?" Ralston asked. He didn't completely believe that part of the model they had evolved. He was a laboratory chemist, specializing in inorganic compounds. The way these plants produced plastics without high heat, through purely catalytic interactions, had him confused and defensive. He wished the crazy windmills would go away.

"I think I can answer that," McKillian said. "These organisms barely scrape by in the best of times. The ones that have made it waste nothing. It stands to reason that any really ancient deposits of crude oil would have been exhausted in only a few of these cycles. So it must be that what we're thinking of as crude oil must be something a little different. It has to be the remains of the last generation."

"But how did the remains get so far below ground?" Ralston asked. "You'd expect them to be high up. The winds couldn't bury them that deep in only twelve thousand years."

"You're right," said McKillian. "I don't really know. But I have a theory. Since these plants waste nothing, why not conserve their bodies when they die? They sprouted from the ground; isn't it possible they could withdraw when things start to get tough again? They'd leave spores behind them as they retreated, distributing them all through the soil. That way, if the upper ones blew away or were sterilized by the ultraviolet, the ones just below them would still thrive when the right conditions returned. When they reached the permafrost, they'd decompose into this organic slush we've postulated, and . . . well, it does get a little involved, doesn't it?"

"Sounds all right to me," Lang assured her. "It'll do for a working theory. Now what about airborne spores?"

It turned out that they were safe from that imagined danger. There were spores in the air now, but they were not dangerous to the colonists. The plants attacked only certain kinds of plastics, and then only in certain stages of their lives. Since they were still changing, it bore watching, but the airlocks and suits were secure. The crew was enjoying the luxury of sleeping without their suits.

And there was much work to do. Most of the physical sort devolved on Crawford and, to some extent, on Lang. It threw them together a lot. The other three had to be free to pursue their researches, as it had been decided that only in knowing their environment would they stand a chance.

The two of them had managed to salvage most of the dome. Working with patching kits and lasers to cut the tough material, they had constructed a much smaller dome. They erected it on an outcropping of bare rock, rearranged the exhaust to prevent more condensation on the underside, and added more safety features. They now slept in a pressurized building inside the dome, and one of them stayed awake on watch at all times. In drills, they had come from a deep sleep to full pressure-integrity in thirty seconds. They were not going to get caught again.

Crawford looked away from the madly whirling rotors of the windmill farm. He was with the rest of the crew, sitting in the dome with his helmet off. That was as far as Lang would permit anyone to go except in the cramped sleeping quarters. Song Sue Lee was at the radio giving her report to the *Edgar Rice Burroughs*. In her hand was one of the pump modules she had dissected out of one of the plants. It consisted of a half-meter set of eight blades that turned freely on teflon bearings. Below it were various tiny gears and the pump itself. She twirled it idly as she spoke.

"I don't really get it," Crawford admitted, talking quietly to Lucy McKillian. "What's so revolutionary about little windmills?"

"It's just a whole new area," McKillian whispered back. "Think about it. Back on Earth, nature never got around to inventing the wheel. I've sometimes wondered why not. There are limitations, of course, but it's such a good idea. Just look what *we've* done with it. But all motion in nature is confined to up and down, back and forth, in and out, or squeeze and relax. Nothing on Earth goes round and round, unless we built it. Think about it."

Crawford did, and began to see the novelty of it. He tried in vain to think of some mechanism in an animal or plant of Earthly origin that turned and kept on turning forever. He could not.

Song finished her report and handed the mike to Lang. Before she could start, Weinstein came on the line.

"We've had a change in plan up here," he said, with no preface. "I hope this doesn't come as a shock. If you think about it, you'll see the logic in it. We're going back to Earth in seven days."

It didn't surprise them too much. The *Burroughs* had given them just about everything it could in the form of data and supplies. There was one more capsule load due; after that, its presence would only be a frustration to both groups. There was a great deal of irony in having two such powerful ships so close to each other and being so helpless to do anything concrete. It was telling on the crew of the *Burroughs*.

"We've recalculated everything based on the lower mass without the twenty of you and the six tons of samples we were allowing for. By using the fuel we would have ferried down to you for takeoff, we can make a faster orbit down toward Venus. The departure date for that orbit is seven days away. We'll rendezvous with a drone capsule full of supplies we hadn't counted on." And besides, Lang thought to herself, it's much more dramatic. *Plunging sunward on the chancy cometary orbit, their pantries stripped bare, heading for the fateful rendezvous* . . .

"I'd like your comments," he went on. "This isn't absolutely final as yet."

They all looked at Lang. They were reassured to find her calm and unshaken.

"I think it's the best idea. One thing: you've given up on any thoughts of me flying the *Podkayne?*"

"No insult intended, Mary," Weinstein said gently. "But, yes, we have. It's the opinion of the people Earthside that you couldn't do it. They've tried some experiments, coaching some very good pilots and putting them into the simulators. They can't do it, and we don't think you could, either."

"No need to sugar-coat it. I know it as well as anyone. But even a billion to one shot is better than nothing. I take it they think Crawford is right, that survival is at least theoretically possible?"

There was a long hesitation. "I guess that's correct. Mary, I'll be frank. I don't think it's possible. I hope I'm wrong, but I don't expect . . ."

"Thank you, Winey, for the encouraging words. You always did know what it takes to buck a person up. By the way, that other mission, the one where you were going to ride a meteorite down here to save our asses, that's scrubbed, too?"

The assembled crew smiled, and Song gave a high-pitched cheer. Weinstein was not the most popular man on Mars.

"Mary, I told you about that already," he complained. It was a gentle complaint, and, even more significant, he had not objected to the use of his nickname. He was being gentle with the condemned. "We worked on it around the clock. I even managed to get permission to turn over command temporarily. But the mock-ups they made Earthside didn't survive the re-entry. It was the best we could do. I couldn't risk the entire mission on a configuration the people back on Earth wouldn't certify."

"I know. I'll call you back tomorrow." She switched the set off and sat back on her heels. "I swear, if the Earthside tests on a roll of toilet paper didn't . . . he wouldn't . . ." She cut the air with her hands. "What am I saying? That's petty. I don't like him, but he's right." She stood up, puffing out her cheeks as she exhaled a pent-up breath.

"Come on, crew, we've got a lot of work."

They named their colony New Amsterdam, because of the windmills. The name of whirligig was the one that stuck on the Martian plants, though Crawford held out for a long time in favor of spinnakers.

They worked all day and tried their best to ignore the *Burroughs* overhead. The messages back and forth were short and to the point. Helpless as the mother ship was to render them more aid, they knew they would miss it when it was gone. So the day of departure was a stiff, determinedly nonchalant affair. They all made a big show of going to bed hours before the scheduled breakaway.

When he was sure the others were asleep, Crawford opened his eyes and looked around the darkened barracks. It wasn't much in the way of a home; they were crowded against each other on rough pads made of insulating material. The toilet facilities were behind a flimsy barrier against one wall, and smelled. But none of them would have wanted to sleep outside in the dome, even if Lang had allowed it.

The only light came from the illuminated dials that the guard was supposed to watch all night. There was no one sitting in front of them. Crawford assumed the guard had gone to sleep. He would have been upset, but there was no time. He had to suit up, and he welcomed the chance to sneak out. He began to furtively don his pressure suit.

As a historian, he felt he could not let such a moment slip by unobserved. Silly, but there it was. He had to be out there, watch it with his own eyes. It didn't matter if he never lived to tell about it, he must record it.

Someone sat up beside him. He froze, but it was too late. She rubbed her eyes and peered into the darkness.

"Matt?" she yawned. "What's . . . what is it? Is something—"

"Shh. I'm going out. Go back to sleep. Song?"

"Um hmmm." She stretched, dug her knuckles fiercely into her eyes, and smoothed her hair back from her face. She was dressed in a loose-fitting bottoms of a ship suit, a gray piece of dirty cloth that badly needed washing, as did all their clothes. For a moment, as he watched her shadow stretch and stand up, he wasn't interested in the *Burroughs*. He forced his mind away from her.

"I'm going with you," she whispered.

"All right. Don't wake the others."

Standing just outside the airlock was Mary Lang. She turned as they came out, and did not seem surprised.

"Were you the one on duty?" Crawford asked her.

"Yeah. I broke my own rule. But so did you two. Consider yourselves on report." She laughed and beckoned them over to her. They linked arms and stood staring up at the sky.

"How much longer?" Song asked, after some time had passed.

"Just a few minutes. Hold tight." Crawford looked over to Lang and thought he saw tears, but he couldn't be sure in the dark.

There was a tiny new star, brighter than all the rest, brighter than Phobos. It hurt to look at it but none of them looked away. It was the fusion drive of the *Edgar Rice Burroughs*, heading sunward, away from the long winter on Mars. It stayed on for long minutes, then sputtered and was lost. Though it was warm in the dome, Crawford was shivering. It was ten minutes before any of them felt like facing the barracks.

They crowded into the airlock, carefully not looking at each other's faces as they waited for the automatic machinery. The inner door opened and Lang pushed forward—and right back into the airlock. Crawford had a glimpse of Ralston and Lucy McKillian; then Mary shut the door.

"Some people have no poetry in their souls," Mary said.

"Or too much," Song giggled.

"You people want to take a walk around the dome with me? Maybe we could discuss ways of giving people a little privacy."

The inner lock door was pulled open, and there was McKillian, squinting into the bare bulb that lighted the lock while she held her shirt in front of her with one hand.

"Come on in," she said, stepping back. "We might as well talk about this." They entered, and McKillian turned on the light and sat down on her mattress. Ralston was blinking, nervously tucked into his pile of blankets. Since the day of the blowout he never seemed to be warm enough.

Having called for a discussion, McKillian proceeded to clam up. Song and Crawford sat on their bunks, and eventually as the silence stretched tighter, they all found themselves looking to Lang.

She started stripping out of her suit. "Well, I guess that takes care of that. So glad to hear all your comments. Lucy, if you were expecting some sort of reprimand, forget it. We'll take steps first thing in the morning to provide some sort of privacy for that, but, no matter what, we'll all be pretty close in the years to come. I think we should all relax. Any objections?" She was half out of her suit when she paused to scan them for comments. There were none. She stripped to her skin and reached for the light.

"In a way it's about time," she said, tossing her clothes in a corner. "The only thing to do with these clothes is burn them. We'll all smell better for it. Song, you take the watch." She flicked out the lights and reclined heavily on her mattress.

There was much rustling and squirming for the next few minutes as they got out of their clothes. Song brushed against Crawford in the dark and they murmured apologies. Then they all bedded down in their own bunks. It was several tense, miserable hours before anyone got to sleep.

The week following the departure of the *Burroughs* was one of hysterical overreaction by the New Amsterdamites. The atmosphere was forced and false; an eat-drink-and-be-merry feeling pervaded everything they did.

They built a separate shelter inside the dome, not really talking aloud about what it was for. But it did not lack for use. Productive work suffered as the five of them frantically ran through all the possible permutations of three women and two men. Animosities developed, flourished for a few hours, and dissolved in tearful reconciliations. Three ganged up on two, two on one, one declared war on all the other four. Ralston and Song announced an engagement, which lasted ten hours. Crawford nearly came to blows with Lang, aided by McKillian. McKillain renounced men forever and had a brief, tempestuous affair with Song. Then Song discovered McKillian with Ralston, and Crawford caught her on the rebound, only to be thrown over for Ralston.

Mary Lang let it work itself out, only interfering when it got violent. She herself was not immune to the frenzy but managed to stay aloof from most of it. She went to the shelter with whoever asked her, trying not to play favorites, and gently tried to prod them back to work. As she told McKillian toward the first of the week, "At least we're getting to know one another."

Things did settle down, as Lang had known they would. They entered their second week alone in virtually the same position they had started: no romantic entanglements firmly established. But they knew each other a lot better, were relaxed in the close company of each other, and were supported by a new framework of interlocking friendships. They were much closer to being a team. Rivalries never died out completely, but they no longer dominated the colony. Lang worked them harder than ever, making up for the lost time.

Crawford missed most of the interesting work, being more suited for the semiskilled manual labor that never seemed to be finished. So he and Lang had to learn about the new discoveries at the nightly briefings in the shelter. He remembered nothing about any animal life being discovered, and so when he saw something crawling through the whirligig garden, he dropped everything and started over to it.

At the edge of the garden he stopped, remembering the order from Lang to stay out unless collecting samples. He watched the thing— bug? turtle?—for a moment, satisfied himself that it wouldn't get too far away at its creeping pace, and hurried off to find Song.

"You've got to name it after me," he said as they hurried back to the garden. "That's my right, isn't it, as the discoverer?"

"Sure," Song said, peering along his pointed finger. "Just show me the damn thing and I'll immortalize you."

The thing was twenty centimeters long, almost round, and dome-shaped. It had a hard shell on top.

"I don't know quite what to do with it," Song admitted. "If it's the only one, I don't dare dissect it, and maybe I shouldn't even touch it."

"Don't worry, there's another over behind you." Now that they were looking for them, they quickly spied four of the creatures. Song took a sample bag from her pouch and held it open in front of the beast. It crawled halfway into the bag, then seemed to think something was wrong. It stopped, but Song nudged it in and picked it up. She peered at the underside and laughed in wonder.

"Wheels," she said. "The thing runs on wheels."

"I don't know where it came from," Song told the group that night. "I don't even quite believe in it. It'd make a nice educational toy for a child, though. I took it apart into twenty or thirty pieces, put it back together, and it still runs. It has a high-impact polystyrene carapace, nontoxic paint on the outside—"

"Not really polystyrene," Ralston interjected.

". . . and I guess if you kept changing the batteries it would run forever. And it's *nearly* polystyrene, that's what you said."

"Were you serious about the batteries?" Lang asked.

"I'm not sure. Marty thinks there's a chemical metabolism in the upper part of the shell, which I haven't explored yet. But I can't really say if it's alive in the sense we use. I mean, it runs on *wheels!* It has three wheels, suited for sand, and something that's a cross between a rubber-band drive and a mainspring. Energy is stored in a coiled muscle and released slowly. I don't think it could travel more than a hundred meters. Unless it can recoil the muscle, and I can't tell how that might be done."

"It sounds very specialized," McKillian said thoughtfully. "Maybe we should be looking for the niche it occupies. The way you describe it, it couldn't function without help from a symbiote. Maybe it fertilizes the plants, like bees, and the plants either donate or are robbed of the power to wind the spring. Did you look for some mechanism the bug could use to steal energy from the rotating gears in the whirligigs?"

"That's what I want to do in the morning," Song said. "Unless Mary will let us take a look tonight?" She said it hopefully, but without real expectation. Mary Lang shook her head decisively.

"It'll keep. It's *cold* out there, baby."

A new exploration of the whirligig garden the next day revealed several new species, including one more thing that might be an animal. It was a flying creature, the size of a fruit fly, that managed to glide from plant to plant when the wind was down by means of a freely rotating set of blades, like an autogiro.

Crawford and Lang hung around as the scientists looked things over. They were not anxious to get back to the task that had occupied them for the last two weeks: that of bringing the *Podkayne* to a horizontal position without wrecking her. The ship had been rigged with stabilizing cables soon after landing, and provision had been made in the plans to lay the ship on its side in the event of a really big windstorm. But the plans had envisioned a work force of twenty, working all day with a maze of pulleys and gears. It was slow work and could not be rushed. If the ship were to tumble and lose pressure, they didn't have a prayer.

So they welcomed an opportunity to tour fairyland. The place was even more bountiful than the last time Crawford had taken a look. There were thick vines that Song assured him were running with water, both hot and cold, and various other fluids. There were more of the tall variety of derrick, making the place look like a pastel oilfield.

They had little trouble finding where the matthews came from. They found dozens of twenty-centimeter lumps on the sides of the large derricks. They evidently grew from them like tumors and were released when they were ripe. What they were for was another matter. As well as they could discover, the matthews simply crawled in a straight line until their power ran out. If they were wound up again, they would crawl farther. There were dozens of them lying motionless in the sand within a hundred-meter radius of the garden.

Two weeks of research left them knowing no more. They had to abandon the matthews for the time, as another enigma had cropped up which demanded their attention.

This time Crawford was the last to know. He was called on the radio and found the group all squatted in a circle around a growth in the graveyard.

The graveyard, where they had buried their fifteen dead crewmates on the first day of the disaster, had sprouted with life during the week after the departure of the *Burroughs*. It was separated from the original site of the dome by three hundred meters of blowing sand. So McKillian assumed this second bloom was caused by the water in the bodies of the dead. What they couldn't figure out was why this patch should differ so radically from the first one.

There were whirligigs in the second patch, but they lacked the variety and disorder of the originals. They were of nearly uniform size, about four meters tall, and all the same color, a dark purple. They had pumped water for two weeks, then stopped. When Song examined them, she reported the bearings were frozen, dried out. They seemed to have lost the plasticizer that kept the structures fluid and living. The water in the pipes was frozen. Though she would not commit herself in the matter, she felt they were dead. In their place was a second network of pipes which wound around the derricks and spread transparent sheets of film to the sunlight, heating the water which circulated through them. The water was being pumped, but not by the now-familiar system of windmills. Spaced along each of the pipes were expansion-contraction pumps with valves very like those in a human heart.

The new marvel was a simple affair in the middle of that living petrochemical complex. It was a short plant that sprouted up half a meter, then extruded two stalks parallel to the ground. At the end of each stalk was a perfect globe, one gray, one blue. The blue one was much larger than the gray one.

Crawford looked at it briefly, then squatted down beside the rest, wondering what all the fuss was about. Everyone looked very solemn, almost scared.

"You called me over to see this?"

Lang looked over at him, and something in her face made him nervous.

"Look at it, Matt. Really look at it." So he did, feeling foolish, wondering what the joke was. He noticed a white patch near the top of the largest globe. It was streaked, like a glass marble with swirls of opaque material in it. It looked *very* familiar, he realized, with the hair on the back of his neck starting to stand up.

"It turns," Lang said quietly. "That's why Song noticed it. She came by here one day and it was in a different position than it had been."

"Let me guess," he said, much more calmly than he felt. "The little one goes around the big one, right?"

"Right. And the little one keeps one face turned to the big one. The big one rotates once in twenty-four hours. It has an axial tilt of twenty-three degrees."

"It's a . . . what's the word? Orrery. It's an orrery." Crawford had to stand up and shake his head to clear it.

"It's funny," Lang said, quietly. "I always thought it would be something flashy, or at least obvious. An alien artifact mixed in with caveman bones, or a spaceship entering the system. I guess I was thinking in terms of pottery shards and atom bombs."

"Well, that all sounds pretty ho-hum to me up against *this*," Song said. "Do you . . . do you *realize* . . . what are we talking about here? Evolution, or . . . or engineering? Is it the plants themselves that did this, or were they made to do it by whatever built them? Do you see what I'm talking about? I've felt funny about those wheels for a long time. I just won't believe they'd evolve naturally."

"What do you mean?"

"I mean I think these plants we've been seeing were designed to be the way they are. They're *too* perfectly adapted, *too* ingenious to have just sprung up in response to the environment." Her eyes seemed to wander, and she stood up and gazed into the valley below them. It was as barren as anything that could be imagined: red and yellow and brown rock outcroppings and tumbled boulders. And in the foreground, the twirling colors of the whirligigs.

"But why this thing?" Crawford asked, pointing to the impossible artifact-plant. "Why a model of the Earth and Moon? And why right here, in the graveyard?"

"Because we were expected," Song said, still looking away from them. "They must have watched the Earth, during the last summer season. I don't know; maybe they even went there. If they did, they would have found men and women like us, hunting and living in caves. Building fires, using clubs, chipping arrowheads. You know more about it than I do, Matt."

"Who are *they?*" Ralston asked. "You think we're going to be meeting some Martians? People? I don't see how. I don't believe it."

"I'm afraid I'm skeptical, too," Lang said. "Surely there must be some other way to explain it."

"No! There's no other way. Oh, not people like us, maybe. Maybe we're seeing them right now, spinning like crazy." They all looked uneasily at the whirligigs. "But I think they're not here yet. I think we're going to see, over the next few years, increasing complexity in these plants and animals as they build up a biome here and get ready for the builders. Think about it. When summer comes, the conditions will be very different. The atmosphere will be almost as dense as ours, with about the same partial pressure of oxygen. By then, thousands of years from now, these early forms will have vanished. These things are adapted for low pressure, no oxygen, scarce water. The later ones will be adapted to an environment much like ours. And *that's* when we'll see the makers, when the stage is properly set." She sounded almost religious when she said it.

Lang stood up and shook Song's shoulder. Song came slowly back to them and sat down, still blinded by a private vision. Crawford had a glimpse of it himself, and it scared him. And a glimpse of something else, something that could be important but kept eluding him.

"Don't you see?" she went on, calmer now. "It's too pat, too much of a coincidence. This thing is like a . . . a headstone, a monument. It's growing right here in the graveyard, from the bodies of our friends. Can you believe in that as just a coincidence?"

Evidently no one could. But likewise, Crawford could see no reason why it should have happened the way it did.

It was painful to leave the mystery for later, but there was nothing to be done about it. They could not bring themselves to uproot the thing, even when five more like it sprouted in the graveyard. There was a new consensus among them to leave the Martian plants and animals alone. Like nervous atheists, most of them didn't believe Song's theories but had an uneasy feeling of trespassing when they went through the gardens. They felt subconsciously that it might be better to leave them alone in case they turned out to be private property.

And for six months, nothing really new cropped up among the whirligigs. Song was not surprised. She said it supported her theory that these plants were there only as caretakers to prepare the way for the less hardy, air-breathing varities to come. They would warm the soil and bring the water closer to the surface, then disappear when their function was over.

The three scientists allowed their studies to slide as it became more important to provide for the needs of the moment. The dome material was weakening as the temporary patches lost strength, and so a new home was badly needed. They were dealing daily with slow leaks, any of which could become a major blowout.

The *Podkayne* was lowered to the ground, and sadly decommissioned. It was a bad day for Mary Lang, the worst since the day of the blowout. She saw it as a necessary but infamous thing to do to a proud flying machine. She brooded about it for a week, becoming short-tempered and almost unapproachable. Then she asked Crawford to join her in the private shelter. It was the first time she had asked any of the other four. They lay in each other's arms for an hour, and Lang quietly sobbed on his chest. Crawford was proud that she had chosen him for her companion when she could no longer maintain her tough, competent show of strength. In a way, it was a strong thing to do, to expose weakness to the one person among the four who might possibly be her rival for leadership. He did not betray the trust. In the end, she was comforting him.

After that day Lang was ruthless in gutting the old *Podkayne*. She supervised the ripping out of the motors to provide more living space, and only Crawford saw what it was costing her. They drained the fuel tanks and stored the fuel in every available container they could scrounge. It would be useful later for heating, and for recharging batteries. They managed to convert plastic packing crates into fuel containers by lining them with sheets of the double-walled material the whirligigs used to heat water. They were nervous at this vandalism, but had no other choice. They kept looking nervously at the graveyard as they ripped up meter-square sheets of it.

They ended up with a long cylindrical home, divided into two small sleeping rooms, a community room, and a laboratory-storehouse-workshop in the old fuel tank. Crawford and Lang spent the first night together in the "penthouse," the former cockpit, the only room with windows.

Lying there wide awake on the rough mattress, side by side in the warm air with Mary Lang, whose black leg was a crooked line of shadow laying across his body, looking up through the port at the sharp, unwinking stars—with nothing done yct about the problems of oxygen, food, and water for the years ahead and no assurance he would live out the night on a planet determined to kill him—Crawford realized he had never been happier in his life.

On a day exactly eight months after the disaster, two discoveries were made. One was in the whirligig garden and concerned a new plant that was bearing what might be fruit. They were clusters of grape-sized white balls, very hard and fairly heavy. The second discovery was made by Lucy McKillian and concerned the absence of an event that up to that time had been as regular as the full moon.

"I'm pregnant," she announced to them that night, causing Song to delay her examination of the white fruit.

It was not unexpected; Lang had been waiting for it to happen since the night the *Burroughs* left. But she had not worried about it. Now she must decide what to do.

"I was afraid that might happen," Crawford said. "What do we do, Mary?"

"Why don't you tell me what you think? You're the survival expert. Are babies a plus or a minus in our situation?"

"I'm afraid I have to say they're a liability. Lucy will be needing extra food during her pregnancy, and afterward, and it will be an extra mouth to feed. We can't afford the strain on our resources." Lang said nothing, waiting to hear from McKillian.

"Now wait a minute. What about all this line about 'colonists' you've been feeding us ever since we got stranded here? Who ever heard of a colony without babies? If we don't grow, we stagnate, right? We *have* to have children." She looked back and forth from Lang to Crawford, her face expressing formless doubts.

"We're in special circumstances, Lucy," Crawford explained. "Sure, I'd be all for it if we were better off. But we can't be sure we can even provide for ourselves, much less a child. I say we can't afford children until we're established."

"Do you want the child, Lucy?" Lang asked quietly.

McKillian didn't seem to know what she wanted. "No. I . . . but, yes. Yes, I guess I do." She looked at them, pleading for them to understand.

"Look, I've never had one, and never planned to. I'm thirty-four years old and never, never felt the lack. I've always wanted to go places, and you can't with a baby. But I never planned to become a colonist on Mars, either. I . . . things have changed, don't you see? I've been depressed." She looked around, and Song and Ralston were nodding sympathetically. Relieved to see that she was not the only one feeling the oppression, she went on, more strongly. "I think if I go another day like yesterday and the day before—and today—I'll end up screaming. It seems so pointless, collecting all that information, for what?"

"I agree with Lucy," Ralston said, surprisingly. Crawford had thought he would be the only one immune to the inevitable despair of the castaway. Ralston in his laboratory was the picture of carefree detachment, existing only to observe.

"So do I," Lang said, ending the discussion. But she explained her reasons to them.

"Look at it this way, Matt. No matter how we stretch our supplies, they won't take us through the next four years. We either find a way of getting what we need from what's around us, or we all die. And if we find a way to do it, then what does it matter how many of us there are? At the most, this will push our deadline a few weeks or a month closer, the day we have to be self-supporting."

"I hadn't thought of it that way," Crawford admitted.

"But that's not important. The important thing is what you said from the first, and I'm surprised you didn't see it. If we're a colony, we expand. By definition. Historian, what happened to colonies that failed to expand?"

"Don't rub it in."

"They died out. I know that much. People, we're not intrepid space explorers anymore. We're not the career men and women we set out to be. Like it or not, and I suggest we start liking it, we're pioneers trying to live in a hostile environment. The odds are very much against us, and we're not going to be here forever, but like Matt said, we'd better plan as if we were. Comment?"

There was none, until Song spoke up thoughtfully.

"I think a baby around here would be fun. Two should be twice as much fun. I think I'll start. Come on, Marty."

"Hold on, honey," Lang said dryly. "If you conceive now, I'll be forced to order you to abort. We have the chemicals for it, you know."

"That's discrimination."

"Maybe so. But just because we're colonists doesn't mean we have to behave like rabbits. A pregnant woman will have to be removed from the work force at the end of her term, and we can only afford one at a time. After Lucy has hers, then come ask me again. But watch Lucy carefully, dear. Have you really thought what it's going to take? Have you tried to visualize her getting into her pressure suit in six or seven months?"

From their expressions, it was plain that neither Song nor McKillian had thought of it.

"Right," Lang went on. "It'll be literal confinement for her, right here in the *Poddy*. Unless we can rig something for her, which I seriously doubt. Still want to go through with it, Lucy?"

"Can I have a while to think it over?"

"Sure. You have about two months. After that, the chemicals aren't safe."

"I'd advise you to do it," Crawford said. "I know my opinion means nothing after shooting my mouth off. I know I'm a fine one to talk; I won't be cooped up in here. But the colony needs it. We've all felt it: the lack of a direction or a drive to keep going. I think we'd get it back if you went through with this."

McKillian tapped her teeth thoughtfully with the tip of a finger.

"You're right," she said. "Your opinion *doesn't* mean anything." She slapped his knee delightedly when she saw him blush. "I think it's yours, by the way. And I think I'll go ahead and have it."

The penthouse seemed to have gone to Lang and Crawford as an unasked-for prerogative. It just became a habit, since they seemed to have developed a bond between them and none of the other three complained. Neither of the other women seemed to be suffering in any way. So Lang left it at that. What went on between the three of them was of no concern to her as long as it stayed happy.

Lang was leaning back in Crawford's arms, trying to decide if she wanted to make love again, when a gunshot rang out in the *Podkayne*.

She had given a lot of thought to the last emergency, which she still saw as partly a result of her lag in responding. This time she was through the door almost before the reverberations had died down, leaving Crawford to nurse the leg she had stepped on in her haste.

She was in time to see McKillian and Ralston hurrying into the lab at the back of the ship. There was a red light flashing, but she quickly saw it was not the worst it could be; the pressure light still glowed green. It was the smoke detector. The smoke was coming from the lab.

She took a deep breath and plunged in, only to collide with Ralston as he came out, dragging Song. Except for a dazed expression and a few cuts, Song seemed to be all right. Crawford and McKillian joined them as they lay her on the bunk.

"It was one of the fruit," she said, gasping for breath and coughing. "I was heating it in a beaker, turned away, and it blew. I guess it sort of stunned me. The next thing I knew, Marty was carrying me out here. Hey, I have to get back in there! There's another one . . . it could be dangerous, and the damage, I have to check on that—" She struggled to get up but Lang held her down.

"You take it easy. What's this about another one?"

"I had it clamped down, and the drill—did I turn it on, or not? I can't remember. I was after a core sample. You'd better take a look. If the drill hits whatever made the other one explode, it might go off."

"I'll get it," McKillian said, turning toward the lab.

"You'll stay right here," Lang barked. "We know there's not enough power in them to hurt the ship, but it could kill you if it hit you right. We stay right here until it goes off. The hell with the damage. And shut that door, quick!"

Before they could shut it they heard a whistling, like a teakettle coming to boil, then a rapid series of clangs. A tiny white ball came through the doorway and bounced off three walls. It moved almost faster than they could follow. It hit Crawford on the arm, then fell to the floor where it gradually skittered to a stop. The hissing died away, and Crawford picked it up. It was lighter than it had been. There was a pinhole drilled in one side. The pinhole was cold when he touched it with his fingers. Startled, thinking he was burned, he stuck his finger in his mouth, then sucked on it absently long after he knew the truth.

"These 'fruit' are full of compressed gas," he told them. "We have to open up another, carefully this time. I'm almost afraid to say what gas I think it is, but I have a hunch that our problems are solved."

By the time the rescue expedition arrived, no one was calling it that. There had been the little matter of a long, brutal war with the Palestinian Empire, and a growing conviction that the survivors of the First Expedition had not had any chance in the first place. There had been no time for luxuries like space travel beyond the Moon and no billions of dollars to invest while the world's energy policies were being debated in the Arabian Desert with tactical nuclear weapons.

When the ship finally did show up, it was no longer a NASA ship. It was sponsored by the fledgling International Space Agency. Its crew came from all over Earth. Its drive was new, too, and a lot better than the old one. As usual, war had given research a kick in the pants. Its mission was to take up the Martian exploration where the first expedition had left off and, incidentally, to recover the remains of the twenty Americans for return to Earth.

The ship came down with an impressive show of flame and billowing sand, three kilometers from Tharsis Base.

The captain, an Indian named Singh, got his crew started on erecting the permanent buildings, then climbed into a crawler with three officers for the trip to Tharsis. It was almost exactly twelve Earth-years since the departure of the *Edgar Rice Burroughs*.

The *Podkayne* was barely visible behind a network of multicolored vines. The vines were tough enough to frustrate their efforts to push through and enter the old ship. But both lock doors were open, and sand had drifted in rippled waves through the opening. The stern of the ship was nearly buried.

Singh told his people to stop, and he stood back admiring the complexity of the life in such a barren place. There were whirligigs twenty meters tall scattered around him, with vanes broad as the wings of a cargo aircraft.

"We'll have to get cutting tools from the ship," he told his crew. "They're probably in there. What a place this is! I can see we're going to be busy." He walked along the edge of the dense growth, which now covered several acres. He came to a section where the predominant color was purple. It was strangely different from the rest of the garden. There were tall whirligig derricks but they were frozen, unmoving. And covering all the derricks was a translucent network of ten-centimeter-wide strips of plastic, which was thick enough to make an impenetrable barrier. It was like a cobweb made of flat, thin material instead of fibrous spider-silk. It bulged outward between all the crossbraces of the whirligigs.

"Hello, can you hear me now?"

Singh jumped, then turned around, looked at the three officers. They were looking as surprised as he was.

"Hello, hello, hello? No good on this one, Mary. Want me to try another channel?"

"Wait a moment. I can hear you. Where are you?"

"Hey, he hears me! Uh, that is, this is Song Sue Lee, and I'm right in front of you. If you look real hard into the webbing, you can just make me out. I'll wave my arms. See?"

Singh thought he saw some movement when he pressed his face to the translucent web. The web resisted his hands, pushing back like an inflated balloon.

"I think I see you." The enormity of it was just striking him. He kept his voice under tight control, as his officers rushed up around him, and managed not to stammer. "Are you well? Is there anything we can do?"

There was a pause. "Well, now that you mention it, you might have come on time. But that's water through the pipes, I guess. If you have some toys or something, it might be nice. The stories I've told little Billy of all the nice things you people were going to bring! There's going to be no living with him, let me tell you."

This was getting out of hand for Captain Singh.

"Ms. Song, how can we get in there with you?"

"Sorry. Go to your right about ten meters, where you see the steam coming from the web. There, see it?" They did, and as they looked, a section of the webbing was pulled open and a rush of warm air almost blew them over. Water condensed out of it in their face-plates, and suddenly they couldn't see very well.

"Hurry, hurry, step in! We can't keep it open too long." They groped their way in, scraping frost away with their hands. The web closed behind them, and they were standing in the center of a very complicated network made of single strands of the webbing material. Singh's pressure gauge read 30 millibars.

Another section opened up and they stepped through it. After three more gates were passed, the temperature and pressure were nearly Earth-normal. And they were standing beside a small oriental woman with skin tanned almost black. She had no clothes on, but seemed adequately dressed in a brilliant smile that dimpled her mouth and eyes. Her hair was streaked with gray. She would be—Singh stopped to consider—forty-one years old.

"This way," she said, beckoning them into a tunnel formed from more strips of plastic. They twisted around through a random maze, going through more gates that opened when they neared them, some-times getting on their knees when the clearance lowered. They heard the sound of children's voices.

They reached what must have been the center of the maze and found the people everyone had given up on. Eighteen of them. The children became very quiet and stared solemnly at the new arrivals, while the other four adults . . .

The adults were standing separately around the space while tiny helicopters flew around them, wrapping them from head to toe in strips of webbing like human maypoles.

"Of course we don't know if we would have made it without the assist from the Martians," Mary Lang was saying, from her perch on an orange thing that might have been a toadstool. "Once we figured out what was happening here in the graveyard, there was no need to explore alternative ways of getting food, water, and oxygen. The need just never arose. We were provided for."

She raised her feet so a group of three gawking women from the ship could get by. They were letting them come through in groups of five every hour. They didn't dare open the outer egress more often than that, and Lang was wondering if it was too often. The place was crowded, and the kids were nervous. But better to have the crew satisfy their curiosity in here where we can watch them, she reasoned, than have them messing things up outside.

The inner nest was free-form. The New Amsterdamites had allowed it to stay pretty much the way the whirlibirds had built it, only taking down an obstruction here and there to allow humans to move around. It was a maze of gauzy walls and plastic struts, with clear plastic pipes running all over and carrying fluids of pale blue, pink, gold, and wine. Metal spigots from the *Podkayne* had been inserted in some of the pipes. McKillian was kept busy refilling glasses for the visitors who wanted to sample the antifreeze solution that was fifty per cent ethanol. It was good stuff, Captain Singh reflected as he drained his third glass, and that was what he still couldn't understand.

He was having trouble framing the questions he wanted to ask, and he realized he'd had too much to drink. The spirit of celebration, the rejoicing at finding these people here past any hope; one could hardly stay aloof from it. But he refused a fourth drink regretfully.

"I can understand the drink," he said, carefully. "Ethanol is a simple compound and could fit into many different chemistries. But it's hard to believe that you've survived eating the food these plants produced for you."

"Not once you understand what this graveyard is and why it became what it did," Song said. She was sitting cross-legged on the floor nursing her youngest, Ethan.

"First you have to understand that all this you see"—she waved around at the meters of hanging soft-sculpture, causing Ethan to nearly lose the nipple—"was designed to contain beings who are no more adapted to *this* Mars than we are. They need warmth, oxygen at fairly high pressures, and free water. It isn't here now, but it can be created by properly designed plants. They engineered these plants to be triggered by the first signs of free water and to start building places for them to live while they waited for full summer to come. When it does, this whole planet will bloom. Then we can step outside without wearing suits or carrying airberries."

"Yes, I see," Singh said. "And it's all very wonderful, almost too much to believe." He was distracted for a moment, looking up to the ceiling where the airberries—white spheres about the size of bowling balls—hung in clusters from the pipes that supplied them with high-pressure oxygen.

"I'd like to see that process from the start," he said. "Where you suit up for the outside, I mean."

"We were suiting up when you got here. It takes about half an hour; so we couldn't get out in time to meet you."

"How long are those . . . suits good for?"

"About a day," Crawford said. "You have to destroy them to get out of them. The plastic strips don't cut well, but there's another specialized animal that eats that type of plastic. It's recycled into the system. If you want to suit up, you just grab a whirlibird and hold onto its tail and throw it. It starts spinning as it flies, and wraps the end product around you. It takes some practice, but it works. The stuff sticks to itself, but not to us. So you spin several layers, letting each one dry, then hook up an airberry, and you're inflated and insulated."

"Marvelous," Singh said, truly impressed. He had seen the tiny whirlibirds weaving the suits, and the other ones, like small slugs, eating them away when the colonists saw they wouldn't need them. "But without some sort of exhaust, you wouldn't last long. How is that accomplished?"

"We use the breather valves from our old suits," McKillian said. "Either the plants that grow valves haven't come up yet, or we haven't been smart enough to recognize them. And the insulation isn't perfect. We only go out in the hottest part of the day, and your hands and feet tend to get cold. But we manage."

Singh realized he had strayed from his original question.

"But what about the food? Surely it's too much to expect for these Martians to eat the same things we do. Wouldn't you think so?"

"We sure did, and we were lucky to have Marty Ralston along. He kept telling us the fruits in the graveyard were edible by humans. Fats, starches, proteins; all identical to the ones we brought along. The clue was in the orrery, of course."

Lang pointed to the twin globes in the middle of the room, still keeping perfect Earth time.

"It was a beacon. We figured that out when we saw they grew only in the graveyard. But what was it telling us? We felt it meant that we were expected. Song felt that from the start, and we all came to agree with her. But we didn't realize just how much they had prepared for us until Marty started analyzing the fruits and nutrients here.

"Listen, these Martians—and I can see from your look that you still don't really believe in them, but you will if you stay here long enough—they know genetics. They really know it. We have a thousand theories about what they may be like, and I won't bore you with them yet, but this is one thing we do know. They can build anything they need, make a blueprint in DNA, encapsulate it in a spore and bury it, knowing exactly what will come up in forty thousand years. When it starts to get cold here and they know the cycle's drawing to an end, they seed the planet with the spores and . . . do something. Maybe they die, or maybe they have some other way of passing the time. But they know they'll return.

"We can't say how long they've been prepared for a visit from us. Maybe only this cycle; maybe twenty cycles ago. Anyway, at the last cycle they buried the kind of spores that would produce these little gismos." She tapped the blue ball representing the Earth with one foot.

"They triggered them to be activated only when they encountered certain different conditions. Maybe they knew exactly what it would be; maybe they only provided for a likely range of possibilities. Song thinks they've visited us, back in the Stone Age. In some ways it's easier to believe than the alternative. That way they'd know our genetic structure and what kinds of food we'd eat, and could prepare.

" 'Cause if they didn't visit us, they must have prepared other spores. Spores that would analyze new proteins and be able to duplicate them. Further than that, some of the plants might have been able to copy certain genetic material if they encountered any. Take a look at that pipe behind you." Singh turned and saw a pipe about as thick as his arm. It was flexible, and had a swelling in it that continuously pulsed in expansion and contraction.

"Take that bulge apart and you'd be amazed at the resemblance to a human heart. So there's another significant fact; this place started out with whirligigs, but later modified itself to use human heart pumps from the genetic information *taken from the bodies of the men and women we buried.*" She paused to let that sink in, then went on with a slightly bemused smile.

"The same thing for what we eat and drink. That liquor you drank, for instance. It's half alcohol, and that's probably what it would have been without the corpses. But the rest of it is very similar to hemoglobin. It's sort of like fermented blood. Human blood."

Singh was glad he had refused the fourth drink. One of his crew members quietly put his glass down.

"I've never eaten human flesh," Lang went on, "but I think I know what it must taste like. Those vines to your right; we strip off the outer part and eat the meat underneath. It tastes good. I wish we could cook it, but we have nothing to burn and couldn't risk it with the high oxygen count, anyway."

Singh and everyone else was silent for a while. He found he really was beginning to believe in the Martians. The theory seemed to cover a lot of otherwise inexplicable facts.

Mary Lang sighed, slapped her thighs, and stood up. Like all the others, she was nude and seemed totally at home with it. None of them had worn anything but a Martian pressure suit for eight years. She ran her hand lovingly over the gossamer wall, the wall that had provided her and her fellow colonists and their children protection from the cold and the thin air for so long. He was struck by her easy familiarity with what seemed to him outlandish surroundings. She looked at home. He couldn't imagine her anywhere else.

He looked at the children. One wide-eyed little girl of eight years was kneeling at his feet. As his eyes fell on her, she smiled tentatively and took his hand.

"Did you bring any bubblegum?" the girl asked.

He smiled at her. "No, honey, but maybe there's some in the ship." She seemed satisfied. She would wait to experience the wonders of Earthly science.

"We were provided for," Mary Lang said quietly. "They knew we were coming and they altered their plans to fit us in." She looked back to Singh. "It would have happened even without the blowout and the burials. The same sort of thing was happening around the *Podkayne,* too, triggered by our waste; urine and feces and such. I don't know if it would have tasted quite as good in the food department, but it would have sustained life."

Singh stood up. He was moved, but did not trust himself to show it adequately. So he sounded rather abrupt, though polite.

"I suppose you'll be anxious to go to the ship," he said. "You're going to be a tremendous help. You know so much of what we were sent here to find out. And you'll be quite famous when you get back to Earth. Your back pay should add up to quite a sum."

There was a silence, then it was ripped apart by Lang's huge laugh. She was joined by the others, and the children, who didn't know what they were laughing about but enjoyed the break in the tension.

"Sorry, Captain. That was rude. But we're not going back."

Singh looked at each of the adults and saw no trace of doubt. And he was mildly surprised to find that the statement did not startle him.

"I won't take that as your final decision," he said. "As you know, we'll be here six months. If at the end of that time any of you want to go, you're still citizens of Earth."

"We are? You'll have to brief us on the political situation back there. We were United States citizens when we left. But it doesn't matter. You won't get any takers, though we appreciate the fact that you came. It's nice to know we weren't forgotten." She said it with total assurance, and the others were nodding. Singh was uncomfortably aware that the idea of a rescue mission had died out only a few years after the initial tragedy. He and his ship were here now only to explore.

Lang sat back down and patted the ground around her, ground that was covered in a multiple layer of the Martian pressure-tight web, the kind of web that would have been made only by warm-blooded, oxygen-breathing, water-economy beings who needed protection for their bodies until the full bloom of summer.

"We *like* it here. It's a good place to raise a family, not like Earth the last time I was there. And it couldn't be much better now, right after another war. And we can't leave, even if we wanted to." She flashed him a dazzling smile and patted the ground again.

"The Martians should be showing up any time now. And we aim to thank them."

From Competition 18:

SF titles in which two or more words are transposed

CAMPBELL'S *There Goes Who?*
STURGEON'S *Well Sturgeon Is Alive and . . .*
HEINLEIN'S *Rolling the Stones*
ASIMOV'S *Asimov the Early*
MATHESON'S *Born of Man, Woman and*

—*Marc Russell*

CLARKE'S *Tales White From the Hart*
BURROUGH'S *Ant Tarzan and the Men*
HENDERSON'S *The Different People: No Flesh*
LUNDWALL'S *What About Science: It's All Fiction*

—*Wes and Lynn Pederson*

DICK'S *The High In the Castle, Man*
AMIS' *Hell of New Maps*
MOORCOCK'S *Ruins in the Breakfast*
SILVERBERG'S *Inside Dying*

—*Harvey Abramson*

The Sturgeon of Theodore Best
ASIMOV'S *The Trilogy Foundation*
ANDERSON'S *Me Call Joe*

—*Al Sarrantonio*

156

CAPEK'S *URR*
RUSS'S *It Changed? When?*
MOORE'S *Eye the Girl With Rapid Movements*

—Jeremy Hole

DICK'S *We Can Wholesale It For You, Remember?*
SILVERBERG'S *Dead With The Born*

—Barry N. Malzberg

HERBERT'S *The Frank Worlds of Herbert*
ELLISON'S *Gentleman and Other Junkie Stories of the Hung-up Generation*

—David Lubar

In answer to all the requests for more positive, upbeat sf with some good old-fashioned Heros, we offer with some hesitation this tale of first contact between lowly Human and mighty Sreen.

Upstart

by STEVEN UTLEY

"You must obey the edict of the Sreen," the Intermediaries have told us repeatedly, "there is no appeal," but the captain won't hear of it, not for a moment. He draws himself up to his full height of two meters and looms threateningly over the four or five Intermediaries, who are, after all, small and not particularly substantial-looking beings, mere wisps of translucent flesh through which their bluish skeletal structures and pulsing organs can be seen.

"You take us in to talk to the Sreen," the captain tells them, "you take us in right *now*, do you hear me?" His voice is like a sword coming out of its scabbard, an angry, menacing, deadly metal-on-metal rasp. "You take us to these God-damned Sreen of yours and let us talk to them."

The Intermediaries shrink before him, fluttering their pallid appendages in obvious dismay, and bleat in unison, "No, no, what you request is impossible. The decision of the Sreen is final, and, anyway, they're very busy right now, they can't be bothered."

The captain wheels savagely, face mottled, teeth bared, arms windmilling with rage. I have never seen him this furious before, and it frightens me. Not that I cannot appreciate and even share his anger toward the Sreen, of course. The Sreen have been very arbitrary and high-handed from the start, snatching our vessel out of normal space, scooping it up and stuffing it into the maw of their own craft, establishing communication with us through their Intermediaries, then issuing their incredible edict. They do not appear to care that they have interfered with Humankind's grandest endeavor. Our vessel is Terra's first bona fide starship, in which the captain and I were to have accelerated through normal space to light-velocity, activated the tardyon-tachyon conversion system and popped back into normal space in the neighborhood of Alpha Centauri. I can understand how the captain feels.

At the same time, I'm afraid that his rage will get us into extremely serious trouble. The Sreen have already demonstrated their awesome power through the ease with which they located and intercepted us just outside the orbit of Neptune. Their vessel is incomprehensible, a drupelet-cluster of a construct which seems to move in casual defiance of every law of physics, half in normal space, half in elsewherespace. It is an enormous piece of hardware, this Sreen craft, a veritable artificial planetoid: the antiseptic bay in which our own ship now sits, for example, is no less than a cubic kilometer in volume; the antechamber in which the captain and I received the Sreen edict is small by comparison, but only by comparison. Before us is a great door of dully gleaming gray metal, five or six meters high, approximately four wide. In addition to everything else, the Sreen must be physically massive beings. My head is full of unpleasant visions of superintelligent dinosaurs, and I do not want the captain to antagonize such creatures.

"Sir," I say, "there's nothing we can do here. We're just going to have to return home and let Earth figure a way out of this thing. Let them handle it." Absurd, absurd, I know how absurd the suggestion is even as I voice it, no one on Earth is going to be able to defy the edict. "We haven't any choice, sir, they want us to go now, and I think we'd better do it."

The captain glares at me and balls his meaty hands into fists. I tense in expectation of blows which do not fall. Instead, he shakes his head emphatically and turns to the Intermediaries. "This is ridiculous. Thoroughly ridiculous."

"Captain—"

He silences me with an imperious gesture. "Who do these Sreen think they *are?*"

"The true and indisputable masters of the universe," the Intermediaries pipe in one high but full-toned voice, "the lords of Creation."

"I want to see them," the captain insists.

"You must return to your ship," they insist, "and obey the will of the Sreen."

"Like hell! Like bloody God-damned hell! Where are they? What makes them think they have the right, the *right,* to claim the whole damned *universe* for themselves?" The captain's voice is going up the scale, becoming a shriek, and filled though I am with terror of the Sreen, I am also caught up in fierce admiration for my superior officer. He may be a suicidal fool to refuse to accept the situation, but there is passion in his foolishness, and it is an infectious passion. "How *dare* they treat us this way? What do they *mean,* ordering us to go home and stay there because *they* own the universe?"

He takes a step toward the door. The Intermediaries move to block his path. With an inarticulate screech, he ploughs through them, swatting them aside with the backs of his hands, kicking them out of his way with his heavy-booted feet. The Intermediaries break easily, and it occurs to me then that they are probably as disposable a commodity among the Sreen as tissue paper is among human beings. One Intermediary is left limping along after the captain. Through the clear pale skin of its back, I see that some vertebrae have been badly dislocated. The thing nevertheless succeeds in over-taking the captain and wrapping its appendages around his calf, bleating all the while, "No, no, you must abide by the edict, even as every other inferior species has, you must abide. . . ." The captain is having trouble disentangling himself, and so I go to him. Together, we tear the Intermediary loose. The captain flings it aside, and it bounces off the great portal, spins across the polished floor, lies crushed and unmoving.

Side by side, we pause directly before the door. My teeth, I suddenly realize, are chattering with fear. "Captain," I say as my resolve begins to disintegrate, "why are we doing this?"

"The nature of the beast," he mutters, almost sadly, and smacks the palm of his gloved hand against the portal. "Sreen!" he yells. "Come out, Sreen!"

And we wait.

"If we don't make it home from this," I say at length, "if they never hear from us back on Earth, never know what became of their starship—"

"They'll just keep tossing men and women at the stars until some-one does come back. Sreen or no Sreen." The captain strikes the door again, with the edge of his fist this time. "Sreen!" A bellow which, curiously, does not echo in the vast antechamber. *"Sreen!* SREEN!"

The door starts to swing back on noiseless hinges, and a breath of cold, unbelievably cold air touches our faces. The door swings open. The door swings open. The door swings open forever before we finally see into the next chamber.

"Oh my God," I whisper to the captain, "oh, oh my God."

They are titans, they are the true and indisputable masters of the universe, the lords of Creation, and they are unhappy with us. They speak, and theirs is a voice that shatters mountains. "WHO. ARE. YOU?"

The captain's lips draw back over his teeth in a mirthless grin as he plants his fists on his hips, throws back his head, thrusts out his jaw. "Who wants to know?"

Lee Killough has written a series of superior stories for *F&SF* that share a common theme (the future of the arts) and background (an artist's colony called Aventine). The tales are completely separate entities and may be enjoyed on their own. This one concerns the visit to Aventine of Selene and Amanda, two different personalities that share the body of one beautiful young woman.

A House Divided

by LEE KILLOUGH

Amanda Gail and Selene Randall came to Aventine during the autumn hiatus, when the last of the summer residents had gone back to jobs in the city or followed the sun south, and the winter influx of skiers and skaters was still some weeks away. Aventine scarcely noticed them, and if my current cohab had not gone off through the Diana Mountain Stargate on some interstellar artists' junket, they might never have been more than clients to me, either. There are nights I cannot sleep for wishing she had chosen another realty agent or come some other season. I was alone, though, in the boredom of autumn when Amanda walked into my office with her seeds of tragedy and elected me gardener.

"Matthew Gordon?" she asked in a soft, hesitant voice I remembered from political broadcasts in the last election, extolling the senatorial virtues of her father. "I'm Amanda Gail. I wired you about renting a cabin?"

I nodded. "I have your wire."

Her pictures, though, did not do her justice. Not only was I surprised to find her taller than I expected, fully as tall as I was, but no media camera had ever captured the glow that shone out through her otherwise rather plain face, giving her the look of a Renaissance Madonna and adding nostalgic charm to her loose topknot of copper hair and high-waisted Regency-style dress.

"How many will be in your party?" I asked.

Eyes with the warm brilliance of goldstone looked at me through her lashes. "I'm alone."

I nodded again, at the same time wondering how Amanda Gail could ever, really, consider herself alone. The acrimonious divorce of former Olympic runner Margot Randall and Senator Charles Christopher Gail had traumatically divided not only Amanda's childhood but her very psyche. Five years ago, when Margot Randall died in a hovercraft accident and Amanda moved to Washington full-time, it emerged that for most of her childhood, Amanda Selene Gail had been two personalities, Amanda Gail and another calling herself Selene Randall. The revelation, and their decision to remain dissociated, had made them the darlings of the gossip columns.

"Senator Moran told me I could live here in privacy. Is that true?" Amanda asked.

"Yes. Aventine has too many rich and famous residents to care about another celebrity, and as we have no hotels or public transportation and the cabletrain from Gateside is the only way in, aside from private aircraft on private landing fields, we manage to discourage most reporters and curiosity seekers."

She smiled. "Wonderful."

That smile was remarkable. It turned the light in her to dazzling incandescence.

"My runabout is outside. I'll show you what I have available."

I was carrying a long list of rentals, owned by summer people who authorized winter leasing to pay for the upkeep on their property. They were all over Aventine, from a few apartments down near the shopping square to cabins in the woods and along the shores of both the Lunamere and Heliomere. I explained the choices to Amanda as I handed her into the runabout and unplugged the car from its charger. The Lunamere's main attraction in winter was that it froze over, making sixteen kilometers of ice for skating. The Heliomere was fed by hot springs and, at thirty-five degrees C, was suitable for year-round swimming.

"I'm no swimmer but I prefer hot water to ice," Amanda said.

I drove her up to a little A-frame at No. 43 Apollo on the lower shore of the Heliomere. It was a good size for a single person, with a deck all around and steps down to the beach in back. Amanda admired the white expanse of the beach, which would have gratified the city council. They had once spent a good deal importing all those tons of sand from some distant world on the stargate system to cover the razor flint nature originally laid there.

What brought another of those incredible smiles was the interior. Not only did the carpeting continue up the walls, but as she walked from the kitchen, across the lounge area to the fireplace, and turned to look up at the sleeping loft, each place her feet touched a patch changed color to a pale, clear yellow. She stared, then laughed and ran her hands along the back of a chair. It, too, changed color, to a pattern of pastel greens and yellows.

"PolySensitives," she said. "I haven't seen any of these since I was a little girl." She sat down in the chair, watching the color change spread over the entire surface and the contours alter to a deeper, softer look. "How fun."

Unfortunately the polys were not always fun. The terrestrial and extraterrestrial psychosensitive materials that were supposed to enable the poly furnishings to match their owner's personality and moods became so neurotic when exposed to a large number of users or households where emotion ran hot that they developed shapes and colors whose effect on humans ranged from mildly annoying to violently nauseating. Polys were appropriate for Amanda, though. They could suit both her and her alter ego and eliminate any conflict over taste in furniture.

Amanda said, "I think this will be fine. Where do I sign the lease?"

That brought her alter to mind. "Will Selene be signing, too?"

The light in her dimmed, leaving her only a lanky girl in an anachronistic dress. She pulled at a copper lock dangling down over her temple. "There's no need. The courts won't recognize us as separate people. What one does is legally binding on the other."

I was dismayed by the effect the question had on her. I forced heartiness into my voice. "Then let's drive back to the office and sign. You can move in today."

Driving down the mountain, I pointed out the villas and estates of some of our celebrity citizens: actress Lillith Mannors, novelist Forrest Jakovich, and our extraterrestrial, Gepbhal Gepbhanna. I was finally rewarded by seeing the light come back on in her. At the office I explained that the owner of No. 43 would only let the cabin until May. Was that all right with her?

"I hope I'll be gone before then. I'm just on holiday until I decide what to do with my life."

I raised my brows. "You've given up being hostess for your father?"

She lowered her eyes. "My father remarried last month. He doesn't need me any longer. But a woman of twenty-six ought to be leaving home anyway."

"I'm surprised there's any problem what to do. Your dancing has already won critical acclaim."

The light in her dimmed. "Selene is the dancer. I don't know anything about it."

"But if *she* knows—" I began, then, as her light went out entirely, said, "I'm sorry; I didn't mean to upset you. I was just curious. . . ."

"Everyone is." Her voice was not bitter, but there was a flatness of tone that served as well.

I brought the subject back to business. "If you come to May and aren't ready to leave, I'll find you another cabin."

She tugged at the lock of hair over her temple again. "By that time, it will be Selene's decision."

My curiosity reared up again. The gossip columnists speculated a great deal about how Amanda and Selene managed their dual existence, but because neither personality gave interviews on the subject, it had to remain only speculation. The custody decision, however, was public knowledge. January to June had gone to Margot Randall, July to December to the Senator. It sounded like the alters might still divide their year that way. But rather than distress Amanda further by asking about it, I bit my tongue and hurried out to get the lease from my secretary.

While Caro typed in the blanks, I wondered at the difference between Amanda Gail's attitude toward Selene and that portrayed by the columnists. They made it sound like kinky fun. Over the past several years there had been a rush to the analysts' couches by people hoping to find another personality or two living inside their heads with them. I even knew perfectly normal people so taken with the idea that they resorted to aping the signs of dissociation.

Amanda was still very quiet when I took the lease in to her. I offered her myself and my runabout to move her luggage from the cabletrain station. She accepted, and while we collected the luggage, including a huge trunk that almost filled the car, I did my best to be kind and amusing. Finally, she started glowing again. I left her with the key, my telephone number, and a warning that, since the cabins on either side of her for some distance were empty, she should keep her doors locked. I also promised to call her the next day to see if she needed anything.

"Not too early, please?" she said. "I like to sleep late."

"Why don't I come over at noon? We'll have lunch somewhere and I can show you the sights."

She smiled. "That sounds lovely."

I lived on the Heliomere myself, just a kilometer away from Amanda's cabin. I don't sleep late, and the next morning while I was taking my wake-up walk along the beach, I saw no reason not to pass her cabin. I could take a brief look to make sure everything was all right, then come back for her at noon as agreed. I was enjoying the frosty bite of the air in my nose and throat and the surreal effect of the steam rising off the dawn-pink Heliomere when I saw Amanda running up the beach toward me, her hair flying long and loose around her.

My initial spasm of panic passed as I realized she was wearing an exercise jacket and shorts and only jogging, not running. She saw me about the same moment. She spun around as though to run away, then shrugged and waited for me to catch up.

"I thought you like to sleep late," I said.

She started walking. "Mandy does."

I almost missed the next step turning to stare at her. "You're Selene?"

She did look different. She held her chin high, making her seem even taller than she had yesterday. Her eye contact was direct rather than through her lashes, and the color of her eyes themselves was less goldstone than the feral warmth of topaz. Too, despite her slow walk beside me, she radiated energy so electric it fairly raised the hair on my arm nearest her. Even her voice was changed—higher, firm, rapid.

"Are you in command today, then?" I asked.

"No." She shook her hair back over her shoulders. "I don't take over officially until January. I just come early to exercise."

I raised my brows. "That's dedication."

"That's necessity. Without daily practice I'll tighten up and my elevations will fall."

"Elevations?"

Without breaking stride, she kicked high over her head and grinned at me. "Elevations." Then she stopped and turned to face me. "I'll have to ask you for a favor. Mandy doesn't know about my practice sessions. Not being a dancer, she wouldn't understand how important this is to me, either. She'd just be upset knowing I was here out of my time. So when you take her to lunch today, please don't mention you saw me."

I frowned. "If you know I'm taking her to lunch, how is it she doesn't know what you're doing?"

"I'm continuously aware; she's only conscious when she's out."

That hardly seemed fair to me. As though she read my mind, Selene said, "I didn't plan it; it just works out that way."

She started walking toward the cabin again, leaning forward as though straining against an invisible leash. I could almost hear the crackle of contained energy within her.

"You won't tell her, will you?" she asked anxiously.

I thought about it a minute. There seemed to be no harm in Selene being here. "No, I won't tell her."

She sighed in relief. "Gordy, you're a friend. We'll meet again."

The leash broke. She bounded away down the sand. As though that were not release enough, she flung herself into a succession of cartwheels and forward flips. She went around a curve of the beach and out of sight, still cartwheeling. By the time I reached the curve, she had disappeared.

At noon Amanda was waiting for me out on her deck. She came down the steps toward the runabout with a regal grace so unlike Selene's bridled energy it was hard to believe they possessed the same body.

"Good morning, Mr. Gordon." She smiled, leaving me breathless. "Where are we going?"

"To a cafe called The Gallery."

Its main attraction, aside from being one of the two cafes open this month, was that while we waited for our order we could walk around the cafe looking at the paintings and sculpture on exhibition by local artists.

"You must have quite an artists' colony here," Amanda said, looking over the collection. She ran a hand down the smooth curves of a sonatrophic sculpture by Drummond Caspar. The trope leaned toward the sound of her voice.

"We do. Between them and our celebrity citizens, shopkeepers and simple businessmen like me are a minority group. Aventine is really a village with a large population."

"Then what are the sights you mentioned?"

"The most unique collection of architecture in the world."

Her goldstone eyes widened in disbelief. "Architecture?"

I grinned. "I, somewhat naturally, am a connoisseur of buildings, and I promise you, Miss Gail, that nowhere else will you find such a free exercise of idiosyncrasies in home design."

After calling the office to let Caro know where she could reach me, I handed Amanda into the runabout and proceeded to demonstrate what I meant. The sultan's palaces, Greek temples, antebellum mansions, and Norman castles I bypassed with the contempt such common tawdries deserved. Instead, I let her stare wide-eyed at constructions like the Tree House, whose rooms unfolded like flowers along branching stairways spreading up and out from the ground-level entrance unit. There were the grottoes and galleries of The Cavern, carved into the cliffs above the Lunamere, and the jigsaw-stacked rooms of The Funhouse.

"It's marvelous," Amanda said. "And people actually live in them?"

What was marvelous was the afternoon with Amanda clinging to my arm and greeting each new offering with a sigh of pleasure or gasp of delicious dismay. In the course of it she stopped calling me Mr. Gordon, too, and began saying Matthew. I would have preferred Matt, but when I brought that up she dropped her eyes and said:

"If you don't mind, I prefer some formality. As my father says, this modern rush to intimacy promotes sex but prevents conversation and understanding."

I did not feel ready to dispute Senator Gail. "Then I take it you don't want me to call you Mandy?"

"No!" Her vehemence startled me. She quickly lowered her voice and went on: "My friends call me Amanda."

I tried to extend the day by inviting her out for dinner as I was driving her back to her cabin.

She declined with a smile. "I really should finish unpacking."

"I can help."

She shook her head. "Thank you, anyway."

I did extract a promise that she would let me show her more houses another day; then I made myself leave. I drove home reflecting what pleasant and restful company she was. A man could do far worse than her for a companion. I wondered, too, when I might see Selene again.

There was a note from her on my door the next morning.

Gordy,
You should have insisted on dinner last night. Playing hostess for the Senator never included kitchen duty. Help Mandy get a meal subscription.

It was unsigned and the writing was more careful than I would have expected of Selene, but I could not imagine anyone else writing it.

I called Amanda at noon. Without mentioning the note, I asked about her cooking.

After a short pause she said, "I just throw things together."

I shuddered. "You need more than that. I'm going to call a food service in Gateside and take out a subscription for you; then I insist you have your meals with me, either out or cooked by me, until your first week's supply of meals is delivered."

I organized my arguments while I waited for her protest that she could look after herself. To my surprise, after another short pause, she said in a quiet voice, "You're right, of course, Matthew. Thank you for taking so much trouble for me."

Nothing was trouble which guaranteed me the chance to see her twice a day. When I met Selene on the beach several days later, I thanked her.

She shrugged, running in place while she talked to me. "Someone has to let you know when things need to be done."

She started off up the beach.

"May I run with you?" I called after her.

She looked back without stopping. "If you like. I'd like having someone besides myself to talk to. It's only fair to warn you, though. I'm harder to get along with than Mandy."

She was nothing if not honest. In the succeeding mornings, if I ran too slowly, she simply left me behind. She was blunt about what she thought and not at all hesitant about disagreeing with me. Still, there was no verbal swordplay and no pretense about her, which was as attractive in its way as Amanda's charming acquiescence. And I never ceased to be fascinated by the difference between Amanda's serenity and Selene's coiled-spring energy.

Selene also kept me informed on what needed to be done, either around the cabin or for Amanda. Morning after morning, she would hand me a note when I met her. I was always glad of an excuse to see more of Amanda, but I was puzzled by the notes.

"Why write?" I asked Selene.

That particular morning she was working through a set of torturous-looking exercises that made my muscles protest to watch. She never broke the rhythm of them and her voice came in gasps between stretches and bends. "Habit, I guess. I always left . . . notes for Mandy."

"Like these?"

"Basically. In the beginning . . . it was to tell her . . . about me, then . . . to let her know . . . who I met and what . . . I learned in school . . . my half the . . . year so people wouldn't . . . know about . . . us."

"When did you become two people?"

She rolled to her feet. Swinging up onto the deck, she began using the railing as a bar for ballet exercises. She shot me an amused glance. "Ever curious, aren't you, Gordy?" But before I could protest, she grinned. "We split when we were six. I told Mandy about it when we were seven, after we'd learned to read and write. Any more questions?"

"Yes. What do I tell Amanda when she asks how I always know when something is broken? You don't want me to say anything about you, but I don't want to lie to her."

Selene went on exercising. "She won't ask. People have been taking care of Mandy all her life. She takes it for granted we know what she needs." She straightened, pink with exertion. "Oh, I'd better warn you. Next week is the Senator's birthday. Mandy will be asking you to take her shopping for a gift." She blew me a theatrical kiss and disappeared inside.

Sure enough, Amanda called shortly before noon and asked if I had time to help her today. Caro looked disapproving but had to admit the appointment book was empty.

"Where can I reach you?" she asked as I hung up the phone.

"Somewhere in Gateside."

Caro rolled her eyes. Before she could express her opinion of running out of town on a working day, I left to pick up Amanda.

Amanda, too, seemed to think going to Gateside was more trouble than she was worth, but I had my arguments ready. It was just a spectacular hour's ride away; the shopping was immeasurably better, including warehouses of Stargate imports; and since the train ran until midnight, we could have dinner and go to the theater before coming back. That persuaded her.

By the end of the day I still thought it had been a good idea, though my feet ached from following her through what had to be every shop in Gateside before Amanda found a gift she thought worthy of her father. I requested a window table at the Beta Cygnus, where we could get some coffee and rest while we watched cafe patrons and people in the street outside.

Amanda sat back sipping her coffee with a contented smile. "I hope your business isn't suffering because of all the time you've spent on me."

"*I'd* suffer if I couldn't spend time on you."

She smiled. "You're very gallant. Oh, look."

She pointed out the window at a passing group who were sporting a rainbow of fanciful hair colors and wearing leotards and tights beneath coats thrown casually around their shoulders.

"They're probably from the Blue Orion Theatre up the street. Would you like to see the show there tonight?"

"I'd love to." She looked at me through her lashes. "I can't think when I've enjoyed another man's company as much as yours."

She was almost drowned out by a rising tide of babble at the door. I looked around to see the group from the street pouring into the cafe in loud and animated conversation with each other. One of them, a tall lithe man with hair, eye shadow, and fingernails striped fuchsia and lavender, broke off from the group and headed toward us with a grin.

"Se*leene*, love," he said. "What a delightful sur*prise.*"

Amanda recoiled.

My chair scraped back as I stood up. "Who are you?"

He stopped, blinking at me. He looked at Amanda's horrified expression and frowned uncertainly. "Teddy—ah—that is—Gerald Theodore. Selene and I were dancing partners and cohabs in London three years ago."

"I'm not Selene," Amanda whispered.

The dancer raised a brow. "Ah—I see. You're the other one." He grinned at me. "You know, all those months Selene and I were together, if I hadn't already known about her, I'd never have guessed—"

"Matthew, I'd like to leave." Amanda fumbled for her cape.

I helped her to her feet and into her cape. With a hand under her elbow, I guided her out of the Beta Cygnus, leaving the dancer staring open-mouthed after us.

I flagged a cab to take us back to the cabletrain station. Amanda said nothing for the entire ride, just sat staring at her hands clenched in her lap. I put an arm around her. She stiffened momentarily at my touch, then buried her face against my shoulder. At the station, waiting for the train to come in, she sat up and began pushing at her hair.

"I'm sorry. I know it seems an inconsequential thing to go to pieces about, but every time I meet one of Selene's friends I feel like spiders are crawling over me. They're all so . . . grotesque." Amanda shuddered. "I don't know how she can actually live with such creatures. I suppose it's her nature. I've never let a man touch me, but she—she'll have any man who strikes her fancy, just like her mother."

I felt my brows hop. Her voice was almost vicious in tone.

"My father could have been President but for Margot Randall. The woman was rapacious, vulgar, egocentric, and totally amoral. She nearly drove my father mad before he realized there was no helping her."

I was disturbed by her vehemence and the implied criticism of Selene. "You don't know Selene is like that," I said in what I intended to be a soothing voice. "You've never met her."

"I've met her friends."

That ended the subject for her. She was quiet the remaining ride home. She reached for my hand after a few minutes, though, and held it, squeezing a bit from time to time. I was content.

At the cabin she said, "I'm sorry I was poor company."

"That's all right. Do you feel better now?"

She gave me a faint smile. "Some. You're a wonderful man, Matthew. If I didn't feel like Selene is leering over my shoulder, I'd kiss you good-night. Another time I will. Please call me tomorrow."

I drove on home wishing I could have stayed. I wondered what Selene would have to say about the incident.

Selene laughed. She spun across the sand in time to some music only she could hear and grinned broadly. "Poor Vestal Virgin. How shocking to be confronted with the possibility the temple of her body has been defiled."

I had expected a more sympathetic reaction. I snapped, "You don't sound very sorry it happened."

She stopped in midstride with her leg in the air. She held the position a few moments, then slowly lowered the leg and hooked her hair behind her ears while fixing me with a speculative topaz gaze. Her voice was deliberate. "Why should I be? Nothing happened. Teddy is a dear thing and Mandy's archaic sensibilities are her problem, not mine."

I stared at her. "You don't like Amanda, do you?"

She considered the accusation. "I wouldn't choose her for a friend. I think she's insipid and gutless. She could have sent Teddy on his way with a few polite words instead of making an incident of it. Still, I think I pity rather than dislike her. Don't I let myself get sucked into looking after her like everyone else? That sweet, yielding dependency is no more than what her father trained into her. It's the Senator I dislike." She snorted. "Imagine a contemporary man with a nineteenth-century taste in women. No wonder my mother left him." She began dancing again.

I was still angry, not ready to stop the fight yet. "She left *him?* It is my understanding that her infidelities forced him to divorce her."

The jab left her untouched. With perfect calm and not even a pause in her movement, she said, "He had the press, I believe." She spun once more and finished in a deep curtsy, then straightened and began stripping off her exercise suit. "I'm going to swim. Will you come with me?"

She threw herself into the Heliomere without looking back. After a bit I undressed and followed her. Compared to the chill of the air, the water felt boiling hot. The heat drew out the last of my anger, though. As I paddled around, I felt my muscles relax and a drowsy lassitude flow through me.

Too soon, it seemed, Selene was shouting, "Don't go to sleep, Gordy. It's time to get out."

We made the cold dash across the beach to the cabin, picking up our clothes on the way. Inside we huddled together wishing for a fire and toweled ourselves dry while the polycarpet ran rainbows of browns and electric blues around our feet. In the course of it I got my arms around Selene. I pulled her against me. She met my mouth hungrily, but when I started pulling her toward the fake animal pelt in front of the fireplace, she rammed me with a sharp hipbone and wiggled loose.

"I don't have time. I have to dry my hair before I wake Mandy."

"You never have time for anything but exercising. Will you ever?"

She licked her lips. "Ask me in January."

I walked back up the beach wondering in bemusement if I could be falling in love with two such different women at the same time. If so, how fortunate they were the same woman.

I called Amanda later. I expected to find her herself, yesterday already forgotten, but she still sounded anxious. "Matthew, can you come up?"

I looked unhappily at the couple standing in the outer office with my secretary. What a time for clients to walk in. "I have some people here. Can it possibly wait?"

There was a pause while she debated. "I guess so, but, please, come when you can."

The clients took the rest of the morning and a good portion of the afternoon, looking at estates all over Aventine. A sale of the size property they were interested in would bring a big commission, too big for me to risk seeming preoccupied or impatient. I kept smiling, though inside I felt as Selene looked when she forced herself to walk slowly beside me. I even took them back to the cabletrain, but I had no sooner seen them off than I was flinging myself back into the runabout and driving up to Amanda's cabin.

"What's wrong?" I asked, walking in.

Amanda sat wrapped in a shawl and staring into the empty fireplace. The polychair had turned pale gray. "She's trying to take over, Matthew."

I pulled another chair up beside her and sat down. "What do you mean?"

She pulled the shawl tighter around her. "When I got up this morning, that chair you're sitting in was bright blue. It's always brown or yellow for you. Selene has to have been sitting in it."

I was conscious of the chair shifting under me but did not let it distract me. "Does that mean she's taking over?"

Amanda laced and unlaced her fingers in her lap. "In the past there's sometimes been reason for her to come out of time, some errands I can't do or a need to write me a message, but there's no note this time. I also found damp towels that weren't there last night. If she isn't honoring our agreement any longer, soon it won't be minutes she's taking, it will be hours, then days, until there's no time left I can count on for my own. I don't know what to do, Matthew. How can I fight her?"

"I know a psychiatrist who spends her weekends here in Aventine. Perhaps she can help."

"No!" Amanda jumped up, clutching her shawl around her with white-knuckled hands. "She'd only want to reintegrate me."

I stood, too, and cupped her face between my hands. "Would that be so terrible? Then all the time would be yours."

"But I'd have to become part of . . . what Selene is." She pulled away from me, shaking her head. "That's unthinkable. I couldn't bear it. There's no other way but to go on as I am. So promise me, Matthew, promise that if you ever see Selene, you'll tell me. I have to know when she's stealing time."

I took a deep breath and lied with a straight face. "I promise."

Amanda walked into my arms and buried her face against my neck. "Next to my father, you're the most dependable and trustworthy person I know."

If I looked as guilty as I felt, I was glad she could not see my face.

She stirred in my arms. I felt a ripple of tension in her body. She lifted her head and kissed me hard. I grabbed her shoulders and held her off at arm's length to look at her.

"Selene," I hissed. "What are you doing here?"

"I sensed you felt the two of us ought to talk." She slipped out of my hands and went to curl up in one of the chairs.

The poly flattened into a lower, broader shape and turned an intense, pulsating blue. It was odd to see Selene in Amanda's clothes, but odder yet that, despite them, she looked like herself and not Amanda. Energy ran like a restless, self-willed thing under her skin. She could not even sit without that coiled-spring tension.

"Talk, Gordy," she said.

"I'd intended to do it tomorrow. What am I supposed to tell Amanda when she comes back?"

"Tell her she fell asleep. By the way, thanks for saying nothing about me."

"Next time I'll tell her. I won't lie to her again. So I guess this will all have to stop."

She frowned. "You mean quit running together?"

"I mean quit everything: running, swimming, practicing . . ."

"Quit *practicing?*" Her face set. "I can't afford to stop practicing. Gordy, it's time she doesn't *use*. She hasn't missed it before, and if I'm careful not to let her catch me out again, she'll never miss it."

I shook my head. "You're breaking an agreement."

"I'm not taking over, though. You know that's just a paranoid fantasy. I use only enough time for practice and no more."

I sighed. "You seem to have all the best of it."

She snorted. "I wonder. Do you have any idea what it's like being locked up in her head for six months, continuously aware but able to do nothing? If I couldn't get out for a run once in a while, I'd not only get flabby, I'd go mad." She bounced out of the chair and came over to lace her fingers together behind my neck. "What about you? It's three months until January. How can I give up seeing you for three whole months?"

I did not like that idea, either, but . . . "What else can we do? Shall I lie to Amanda and hate you for making me do it?"

She winced. "No."

"We'll be able to see each other all we like in January."

"January." She groaned the word. "That's forever. Kiss me good-by, Gordy."

Kissing Selene was like grabbing a high-voltage wire. The charge in her swept through us both. I could almost smell the smoke from my sizzling nerve endings. And this time when I pushed her onto the pelt before the fireplace, she did not resist.

I came out of the post-coital lassitude to realize my nerves were not cauterized after all. They recognized that the room was chilling.

Selene was already fastening her dress. I groped halfheartedly for my clothes.

"This would be a nice night for a fire. Shall I build one?" I asked.

Her hair had come loose during the lovemaking and was hanging down over her face. She parted it to look at me. My breathing stopped. Her eyes were goldstone.

In a voice of such preternatural calm it terrified me, Amanda said, "Who were you talking to?"

It was impossible to answer with ice in my chest. I could only stare back while she hunted around for her hairpins.

"I do hope you aren't going to say it was me, not with a chair adapted to Selene right beside you."

There appeared to be nothing I could say. I crawled into my pants.

She found the pins. Sitting down in the same chair Selene had occupied, she swept her hair up with her arms, then used one hand to hold it while she began pinning it in place. The poly turned a bright mottle of yellow and orange.

"I checked the clock," she said.

Her voice faltered only a little but her hands began to shake. The orange in the chair's color went darker and the yellows bled away. Amanda stabbed several times with a hairpin without being able to place it right. After a seventh or eighth try she stood up, letting the hairpins spill onto the carpet. She walked to the far end of the fireplace, where she stood with her back to me, toying with the tops of the fire tools. "It hasn't been long at all since—since I told you I . . . trusted you."

That hurt. I climbed to my feet and reached out to touch her shoulder. "I was talking to her for your sake."

She turned. "For *my* sake? Matthew, please don't lie to me again." There were tears in her voice.

"I'm not lying. I was arguing that Selene shouldn't use any of your time."

"It was a very . . . short argument." Her voice began to catch. "And I find the . . . conclusion rather . . . inconsistent." Her control was cracking. Tears spilled out of her eyes. Her hand was white on the handle of the tool caddy.

Guilt and her pain tore at me. I chased through my head for something to comfort her. "Mandy, I—"

I bit my tongue but it was too late. She shrieked like a stricken animal and came at me swinging. There was a poker in her hand.

I backed away, throwing my arms up to protect my head. Amanda might not be athletic, but she had all her released emotion and Selene's sinewy gymnastic strength behind that swing. What probably saved my life was that she did not have Selene's conscious coordination. The poker only brushed my forearm before smashing into the stone of the fireplace.

I forgot to watch out for the rebound. Pain lanced up my arm. I went down, bouncing my head off the edge of the hearth shelf as I fell.

Amanda screamed again. I tried to roll sideways but my body would not respond and I steeled myself for the second, almost surely fatal blow. But, instead, there was the thud of something dropping on the floor. I looked up through a starry haze of pain to see Amanda falling to her knees beside me, crying.

"Matthew—Matthew, I'm sorry. I didn't meant to hurt you." Her hand stroked my forehead. "It was the name you called me. I hit out at the name. I know what happened wasn't really your fault. Selene started it."

I started to frown. It hurt hellishly. There seemed to be silver wrapped around the edges of my vision, too. "Selene isn't the evil genius you think, Amanda." My voice sounded thin.

"Don't defend her. She's just like her mother, and my father told me what *she* was. Selene's been after my time ever since her mother died. Now she wants everything that makes my time worth living, too." She clutched her hands together, lacing and unlacing the fingers.

I was appalled. This kind of thinking had been going on behind her Madonna's serenity? "You can't really believe that."

"She probably let me catch the two of you making love so I'd throw you out and she could have you to herself." Amanda sat back hugging herself as though cold. "I know what she's doing but I don't know what to do to stop her. If she were a cancer, I could cut her out. How do I cure myself of this—this parasite of the mind?"

She stood, using an arm of a chair to help push herself to her feet. From where her hand touched, livid streamers of orange and scarlet radiated out across the surface of the poly while the shape narrowed and trembled. A marbled pool of the same colors spread from her feet into the carpet. She stood with her eyes searching the cabin as though she expected to find an answer there. Her gaze fixed on the kitchen.

"Cut her out," she said.

She ran for the kitchen, her feet leaving a path like bloody stepping stones.

"Amanda," I called.

I tried to sit up but my head weighed a thousand kilos. I managed to turn over on my side and, as though down a silver tunnel, watched Amanda jerk open a drawer. She reached in. I gritted my teeth against the nausea the effort of moving brought and lurched onto my hands and knees.

Her hand came out of the drawer with a thin knife.

"Amanda!" I crawled toward the kitchen, dragging the weight of my head with me. "Amanda, what are you doing?"

The arm the poker had hit gave away, dropping my head and shoulders onto the carpet. The shock sent a new wave of nausea through me and muffled my vision and hearing in black velvet.

I could not have been out more than moments. When my sight cleared I was staring into polycarpet turned murky green. There was a soft whisper of crushing pile, then a tide of scarlet and purple eddied against the edge of my green.

"I'm going to cut her out, Matthew," Amanda's voice said from above me. It was low but trembling, a breath away from hysteria. "She only comes to dance. I read once about a horse whose tendons were cut just a little, but he never was able to race again."

"My God!" I could see her feet and, by rolling onto my back, look up at her rising above me toward the beams of the room, but I could not move. My head seemed nailed to the floor. The knife gleamed in her hand. "Selene," I called. "I can't reach her. Help me."

Amanda cried, "Matthew, don't—" Her eyes widened with horror. Her mouth moved again.

But this time it was Selene's voice, firm and brisk, that spoke. "I think we'd better have a talk, Mandy."

There was another twisting of the facial features. Amanda, her voice rising, said, "You can't do this, Selene. You're cheating."

"I can't let you ruin my dancing career."

"It's the only way I know to make you go away and leave me alone."

Amanda backed as she spoke, until she was stopped by a wall. The polycarpet extending up the surface responded to her touch with an exploding aurora of hot oranges, reds, and violets.

"I've tried living with you," Amanda said, "but it doesn't work. Now I won't have anything more to do with you!"

"You have no choice." Tendrils of green and blue wormed their way into the pattern. "I'm as much a part of this body as you are. Hamstring me and we'll just both be cripples."

Scarlet wiped out the blues and greens. Amanda cried, "Let's see."

She swooped toward her ankles with the knife. The long skirt of her dress hung in the way. Before she could pick up the hem, her left hand stiffened.

"No," she screamed. "Selene, let go of my hand!"

Behind the left shoulder the polycarpet turned bright blue. The left hand reached for the right wrist.

Amanda wrenched herself sideways, stabbing at the left hand. "Leave me alone."

The left hand dodged. "You don't seem to understand, Mandy—I can't. We're joined indissolubly, till death us do part," Selene said.

"All right!"

The knife turned toward her own chest. Selene's hand leaped to intercept, closing on Amanda's wrist. Amanda screamed inarticulately. Her whole body convulsed with the effort to tear loose. Selene held on. Slowly, Selene twisted the wrist back and down while the poly around them swirled in wave after wave of color pulsating with every labored breath of the struggling body. The maelstrom spread out across the floor and up the walls, even affected the chairs so that they, too, raged with color and pulsed to the time of Amanda's breathing.

Amanda's wrist bent back farther. Her fingers fought to hold on to the knife, but with each moment they loosed more.

Amanda sobbed. "I'm going to kill you, Selene. Sooner or later, I'll kill you."

"No." Selene's voice came through clenched teeth. "I won't allow that, Mandy. And I won't retire. You'll just have to live with me as always."

"I won't. I can't bear it." Amanda screamed once more as the knife dropped from her fingers.

Selene sent it out of reach with a swift kick of her left foot. "You'll have to learn."

"Selene," I said, "don't push too hard."

Amanda was looking wild, her eyes darting around like those of a trapped animal.

"You're stuck, Mandy," Selene said. "There's no way out."

"No, no, no, no."

I was terrified by the desperation in Amanda's wail. "Selene, stop it!"

But she went on relentlessly, deaf to me. "We have to live together all our lives, Mandy. No matter how much you hate it, you're already a part of me, and I of you."

Amanda whimpered and fell silent.

The next moment it was Selene, wholly Selene, who stood there. She hurried across the room and knelt beside me. "Are you all right? You've got blood all over your head."

I grabbed her wrist. "Never mind me. How's Amanda?"

She snapped her wrist loose and stood. "You need a doctor." She turned toward the phone.

"What about Amanda?"

Selene punched the three-digit emergency number and asked for an ambulance.

"Selene, *where is Amanda?*"

Selene hung up the phone. "She's gone."

"Gone?" I sat bolt upright. A wave of dizziness knocked me flat again. "How can she be gone?"

"It was an intolerable situation for her. She went catatonic to escape."

Relief flooded me. "Then she's still alive."

"But I can't reach her. She won't respond to anything I do."

"Haven't you done enough?" I sighed. "When I called you, I didn't mean for you to push her like that. Couldn't you guess what she might do? We'll call my psychiatrist friend and have her help bring Amanda back."

Selene moved around the room, touching the chairs, working her bare feet through the carpet, soothing away the bizarre reflections of the struggle. Gradually, the chairs and carpet softened to bright blue.

"Selene, did you hear me?"

She stopped moving. "I heard, Gordy."

"Then will you call my friend?"

She did not move or answer.

"Selene!"

She looked down at me with clouded topaz eyes. "I'll . . . think about it."

From Competition 19:
Limericks incorporating an sf title into the last line

A young physicist started to stray
Toward metaphysical questions one day.
  He said, "Research begins
  Not with angels and pins,
But with, 'How much does one pearly *Gateway?*'."

—*David Lubar*

We'll curry your princess-turned-frogs,
And groom your domestic balrogs,
  But for those with convention-
  al pets we should mention,
In passing, *We Also Walk Dogs*.

—*Margery Goldstein*

Though my vowels may sound a bit wuzzy,
And my consonants (hic) somewhat muzzy,
  Don't drink I am thunk—
  I mean think I am drunk;
My tongue's just a (hic) *Little Fuzzy*.

—*Doris McElfresh*

Said the red-head, while curling a tress,
"There have been (tho' I should not confess),

Three earls; a brass band;
Dukes numerous and
Nine Princes In Amber, no less."

—*Phoebe Ellis*

Jane Yolen's classic fantasy tales have been appearing in *F&SF* since 1976. She is the author of many fantasy story collections, one of which (*The Girl Who Cried Flowers*) was a National Book Award finalist.

Brother Hart

by JANE YOLEN

Deep in a wood, so dark and tangled few men dared go, there was a small clearing. And in that clearing lived a girl and her brother hart.

By day, in his deer shape, Brother Hart would go out and forage on green grass and budlings while his sister remained at home.

But whenever dusk began, the girl Hinda would go to the edge of the clearing and call out in a high, sweet voice:

> Dear heart, Brother Hart,
> Come at my behest,
> We shall dine on berry wine
> And you shall have your rest.

Then, in his deer heart, her brother would know the day's enchantment was at an end and run swiftly home. There, at the lintel over the cottage door, he would rub between his antlers till the hide on his forehead broke bloodlessly apart. He would rub and rub further still till the brown hide skinned back along both sides and he stepped out a naked man.

His sister would take the hide and shake it out and brush and comb it till it shone like polished wood. Then she hung the hide up by the antlers beside the door, with the legs dangling down. It would hang there limp and soulless till the morning when Brother Hart donned it once again and raced off to the lowland meadows to graze.

What spell had brought them there, deep in the wood, neither could recall. The woods, the meadow, the clearing, the deer hide, the cottage door were all they knew.

Now one day in late spring, Brother Hart had gone as usual to the lowland meadows leaving Hinda at home. She had washed and scrubbed the little cottage till it was neat and clean. She had put new straw in their bedding. But as she stood by the window brushing out her long dark hair, an unfamiliar sound greeted her ears: a loud, harsh calling, neither bird nor jackal nor good grey wolf.

Again and again the call came. So Hinda went to the door, for she feared nothing in the wood. And who should come winded to the cottage but Brother Hart. He had no words to tell her in his deer form, but blood beaded his head like a crown. It was the first time she had ever seen him bleed. He pushed past her and collapsed, shivering, on their bed.

Hinda ran over to him and would have bathed him with her tears, but the jangling noise called out again, close and insistent. She ran to the window to see.

There was a man outside in the clearing. At least she thought it was a man. Yet he did not look like Brother Hart, who was the only man she knew.

He was large where Brother Hart was slim. He was fair where Brother Hart was dark. He was hairy where Brother Hart was smooth. And he was dressed in animal skins that hung from his shoulders to his feet. About the man leapt fawning wolves, some spotted like jackals, some tan and some white. He pushed them from him with a rough sweep of his hand.

"I seek a deer," he called when he glimpsed Hinda's face, a pale moon, at the window.

But when Hinda came out of the door, closing it behind her to hide what lay inside, the man did not speak again. Instead he took off his fur hat and laid it upon his heart, kneeling down before her.

"Who are you?" asked Hinda. "What are you? And why do you seek the deer?" Her voice was gentle but firm.

The man neither spoke nor rose but stared at her face.

"Who are you?" Hinda asked again. "Say what it is you are."

As if she had broken a spell, the man spoke at last. "I am but a man," he said. "A man who has traveled far and seen much, but never a beauty such as yours."

"You shall not see it again, then," said Hinda. "For a man who hunts the deer can be no friend of mine."

The man rose then, and Hinda marveled at the height of him, for he was as tall as the cottage door and his hands were grained like wood.

"Then I shall hunt the deer no more," he said, "if you will give me leave to hunt that which is now all at once dearer to me."

"And what is that?"

"You, dear heart," he said, reaching for her.

Like a startled creature, Hinda moved away from him, but remembering her brother inside the cottage, she found voice to say "Tomorrow." She reached behind her and steadied herself on the door handle. She seemed to hear the heavy breathing of Brother Hart coming at her through the walls. "Come tomorrow."

"I shall surely come." He bowed, turned, and then was gone, walking swiftly, a man's stride, through the woods. His animals were at his heels.

Hinda's eyes followed him down the path until she counted even the shadows of trees as his own. When she was certain he was gone, she opened the cottage door and went in. The cottage was suddenly close and dark, filled with the musk of deer.

Brother Hart lay on their straw bed. When he looked up at her, Hinda could not bear the twin wounds of his eyes. She turned away and said, "You may go out now. It is safe. He will not hunt you again."

The deer rose heavily to his feet, nuzzled open the door, and sprang away to the meadows.

But he was home again at dark.

When he stepped out of his skin and entered the cottage, he did not greet his sister with his usual embrace. Instead he said, "You did not call me to the clearing. You did not say my name. Only when I was tired and the sun almost gone did I know it was time to come home."

Hinda could not answer. She could not even look at him. His nakedness shamed her more than his words. She put their food on the table and they ate their meal in silence. Then they slept like beasts and without dreams.

When the sun called Brother Hart to his deerskin once again, Hinda opened the door. Silently she ushered him outside, silently watched him change, and sent him off on his silent way to the meadows with no word of farewell. Her thoughts were on the hunter, the man of the wolves. She never doubted he would come.

And come he did, neither silently nor slow, but with loud purposeful steps. He stood for a moment at the clearing's edge, looking at Hinda, measuring her with his eyes. Then he laughed and crossed to her.

He stayed all the day with her and taught her words she had never known. He drew pictures in the dirt of kingdoms she had never seen. He sang songs she had never heard before, singing them softly into her ears. But he touched no more than her hand.

"You are as innocent as any creature in the woods," he said over and over in amazement.

And so passed the day.

Suddenly it was dusk, and Hinda looked up with a start. "You must go now," she said.

"Nay, I must stay."

"No, no, you must go," Hinda said again. "I cannot have you here at night. If you love me, go." Then she added softly, her dark eyes on his, "But come again in the morning."

Her fear touched him. So he stood and smoothed down the skins of his coat. "I will go. But I will return."

He whistled his animals to him and left the clearing as swiftly as he had come.

Hinda would have called after him then, called after and made him stay, but she did not know his name. So she went instead to the clearing's edge and cried:

> Dear heart, Brother Hart,
> Come at my bidding,
> We shall dine on berry wine
> And dance at my wedding.

And hearing her voice, Brother Hart raced home.

He stopped at the clearing's edge, raised his head, and sniffed. The smell of man hung on the air, heavy and threatening. He came through it as if through a swift current and stepped to the cottage door.

Rubbing his head more savagely than ever on the lintel, as if to rip off his thoughts with his hide, Brother Hart removed his skin.

"The hunter was here," he said as he crossed the door's threshold.

"He does not seek you," Hinda replied.

"You will not see him again. You will tell him to go."

"I see him for your sake," said Hinda. "If he sees me, he does not see you. If he hunts me, he does not hunt you. I do it for you, brother dear."

Satisfied, Brother Hart sat down to eat. But Hinda was not hungry. She watched her brother for a while through slotted eyes.

"You should sleep," she said at last. "Sleep and I will rub your head and sing to you."

"I *am* tired," he answered. "My head aches where yesterday he struck me. My heart aches still with the fear. I tremble all over. You are right. I should sleep."

So he lay down on the bed and Hinda sat by him. She rubbed cinquefoil on his head to soothe it and sang him many songs, and soon Brother Hart was asleep.

When the moon lit the clearing, the hunter returned. He could not wait until the morning. Hinda's fear had become his own. He dared not leave her alone. But he moved quietly as a beast in the dark. He left his dogs behind.

The cottage in the clearing was still except for a breath of song, wordless and longing, that floated on the air. It was Hinda's voice, and when the hunter heard it he smiled for she was singing tunes he had taught her.

He moved out into the clearing, more boldly now. Then suddenly he stopped. He saw a strange shape hanging by the cottage door. It was a deerskin, a fine buck's hide, hung by the antlers and the legs dangling down.

Caution, an old habit, claimed him. He circled the clearing, never once making a sound. He approached the cottage from the side, and Hinda's singing led him on. When he reached the window, he peered in.

Hinda was sitting on a low straw bed, and beside her, his head in her lap, lay a man. The man was slim and naked and dark. His hair was long and straight and came to his shoulders. The hunter could not see his face, but he lay in sleep like a man who was no stranger to the bed.

The hunter controlled the shaking of his hands, but he could not control his heart. He allowed himself one moment of fierce anger. With his knife he thrust a long gash on the left side of the deerskin that hung by the door. Then he was gone.

In the cottage Brother Hart cried out in his sleep, a swift sharp cry. His hand went to his side and, suddenly, under his heart appeared a thin red line like a knife's slash that bled for a moment. Hinda caught his hand up in hers and at the sight of the blood grew pale. It was the second time she had seen Brother Hart bleed.

She got up without disturbing him and went to the cupboard where she found a white linen towel. She washed the wound with water. The cut was long but it was not deep. Some scratch got in the woods perhaps. She knew it would heal before morning. So she lay down beside him and fitted her body to his. Brother Hart stirred slightly but did not waken. Then Hinda, too, was asleep.

In the morning Brother Hart rose, but his movements were slow. "I wish I could stay," he said to his sister. "I wish this enchantment were at an end."

But the rising sun summoned him outside. He donned the deerskin and leapt away.

Hinda stood at the door and raised her hand to shade her eyes. The last she saw of him was the flash of white tail as he sped off into the woods.

But she did not go into the cottage to clean. She stood waiting for the hunter to come. Her eyes and ears strained for the signs of his approach. There were none.

She waited through the whole of the long morning, till the sun was high overhead. Not until then did she go indoors, where she threw herself down on the straw bedding and wept.

At dusk the sun began to fade and the cottage darken. Hinda got up. She went out to the clearing's edge and called:

> Dear heart, Brother Hart,
> Come at my crying.
> We shall dine on berry wine
> And . . .

But she got no further. A loud sound in the woods stayed her. It was too heavy for a deer. And when the hunter stepped out of the woods on the very path that Brother Hart usually took, Hinda gave a gasp, part delight, part fear.

"You have come," she said, and her voice trembled.

The hunter searched her face with his eyes but could not find what he was seeking. He walked past her to the cottage door. Hinda followed behind him, uncertain.

"I have come," he said. His back was to her. "I wish to God I had not."

"What do you mean?"

"I sought the deer today," he said.

Hinda's hand went to her mouth.

"I sought the deer today. And what I seek, I find." He did not turn. "We ran him long, my dogs and I. When he was at bay, he fought hard. I gave the beast's liver and heart to my dogs. But this I saved for you."

He held up his hands then, and a deerskin unrolled from them. With a swift, savage movement, he tacked it to the door with his knife. The hooves did not quite touch the ground.

Hinda could see two slashes in the hide, one on each side, under the heart. The slash on the left was an old wound, crusted but clean. The slash on the right was new, and from it blood still dripped.

She leaned forward and touched the wound with her hand. Tears started in her eyes. "Oh, my dear Brother Hart," she cried. "It was for me you died. Now your enchantment *is* at an end."

The hunter whirled around to face her then. "He was your brother?" he asked.

She nodded. "He was my heart." Looking straight at him, she added, "What was his is mine by right." Her chin was up and her head held high. She reached past the hunter and pulled the knife from the door with an ease that surprised him. Gently she took down the skin. She shook it out once and smoothed the nap with her hand. Then, as if putting on a cloak, she wrapped the skin around her shoulders and pulled the head over her own.

As the hunter watched, she began to change. Like a rippled reflection in a pool coming slowly into focus, he saw slim brown legs, brown haunch, brown body and head. The horns shriveled and fell to the ground. Only her eyes remained the same.

The doe looked at the hunter for a moment more. A single tear started in her eye, but before it had time to fall, she turned, sprang away into the fading light, and was gone.

Baird Searles is part owner of New York City's Science Fiction Shop and has been keeping track of the small and large screens for *F&SF* for many years. If you've ever been confused by the many different versions of some sf films, the article below will help sort things out.

Films: *Multiples*

by BAIRD SEARLES

It's a cliché of the American entertainment industry that if it works (i.e., if it makes money), do it again. It's a little unfair to denigrate Hollywood and its offshoots for this; most of the arts have been doing it since the Pleistocene. Certainly in films and on TV this makes for a lot of boring material; for instance, we've not seen the end of all the copies, blatant and otherwise, of *Star Wars*.

As a lover of variations on a theme, though, I'm usually intrigued when a producer decides to use exactly the same property that has been made into a movie before. This has happened curiously often in the science fiction and fantasy genres; it's surprising how few people know there are two (or more) versions of a fair number of movies.

So as a public service (and to save you from the embarrassing experience of talking about the 1969 *The Pterodactyl That Ate Petrograd* when someone else is discussing the classic 1932 version), let's sort out some of these. (With one or two exceptions, I'll ignore silent films as being for the most part lost in the dim past.)

For instance, a while back when watching a 1944 epic called *Weird Woman,* I realized that here was a version of Fritz Leiber's *Conjure Wife* that I hadn't run into before. The story (of the use of magic by faculty wives in that most mundane of settings, the American university) totally lost its point here, since its chilling quality comes from the very ordinariness of the people involved, and the professor's wife of *Weird Woman* is given a childhood background of Caribbean voodoo. Much closer is the well-known version, *Burn Witch, Burn,* which has become a sort of minor classic.

Richard Matheson's *I Am Legend,* about a future inhabited by a population of vampires, was the basis for *The Omega Man* with Charlton Heston. In this case, an earlier film from the same source was more interesting—the 1963 *The Last Man on Earth* with Vincent Price.

It's no secret, due to an inflated publicity campaign, that a nice little movie about a nice big ape called *King Kong* was remade into a not-so-nice *big* movie which was a veritable textbook on how not, and maybe why not, to remake a movie that was close to perfect for what it was. Much of the subtler pleasure of the early *King Kong* comes from its period charm—the naiveté, the wonderfully pretentious dialogue, even the oonga-boonga black natives. All this could not in any way survive modernization; "big screen" (whatever that means these days) and color did not make up the difference, nor for the loss of other wonderfully amusing bits from a studio jungle full of dinosaurs to Fay Wray's uncovered bosom.

A similar case is that of H. G. Wells's *The Island of Dr. Moreau,* filmed with superbly demonic atmosphere as *Island of Lost Souls* in 1932. Charles Laughton, maybe the best actor yet to appear on film, gives an extraordinary performance as Dr. M., and Bela Lugosi captures the spirit of the beast men as the Speaker of the Law with the abhuman quality that characterized his Dracula. Now Burt Lancaster is one of film's most underrated actors, but his straightforward non-intellectual approach to the doctor role undermined the '70s trip to the Island; Richard Basehart didn't help matters by looking like a beneficent Old Testament prophet in the Lugosi role. But even Laughton and Lugosi would have been hard put to come across, with the later film's completely uninteresting script and camerawork.

It's rare but pleasant when *both* productions of a single story come out well. *One Million B.C.* gave us Tumac of the Rock People and Luana of the Shell People in the persons of Victor Mature and Carole Landis, not to mention enraged giant lizards and a volcanic eruption. *One Million Years B.C.* took the same simple-minded story, made it in color, which for once was an improvement, used

splendid effects by Ray Harryhausen, and
as Tumac and Raquel Welch as Luana,
spectacular special effects themselves. Æ
grim but beautiful setting of endless ro
mysteriously evocative moment in what seem
of a lower form of man, and a beautifully origina
mostly of rocks struck together. As you may gather, ı₁
favorite schlock movies.

The Thief of Bagdad may set some sort of record with th
acceptable productions, all using widely different variations on the
story of a thief who saves a princess. The silent 1924 *Thief,* with
Douglas Fairbanks, looks pretty primitive in places but also has
some special effects that can still awe. Alexander Korda's 1940 *Thief*
doubles that in spades (the giant flying genie is just one of many),
plus it has monumentally lavish sets. Even the Steve Reeves version
seems to have been made with more care and wit than the rest of Mr.
Reeves' spaghetti spectaculars, containing some good film magic of
its own and a resounding score with one of those epic romantic
themes (based, it must be said, on a theme from the Rozsa music for
Korda).

Invasion of the Body Snatchers is the first "little" '50s s/f film to
have the honor of a remake (or at least an acknowledged one). They
should have left well enough alone in this case. Color instead of
b&w, a big city for the claustrophobic small town, and six chases for
every one in the original did not make it better, just bigger.

Here Comes Mr. Jordan was a whimsical film fantasy of the 1940s
about a boxer taken to Heaven before he was due; as compensation,
he was redelivered into another man's body, with all sorts of sup-
posedly humorous complications. I didn't think it was very funny
then, and I didn't think it was very funny when it reappeared as
Heaven Can Wait, though Warren Beatty did a nice job as the dumb
athletic type (a football player now) and Dyan Cannon shrieked to
great effect a couple of times.

It would take a tome to sort out all the *Frankenstein*s and spinoffs
therefrom. Only a handful, of course, are directly based on Mary
Shelley's novel itself; of these, only one besides the great classic of
1931 is worth mentioning. That is *Frankenstein: The True Story*.
Coscripted by Christopher Isherwood, it takes enough liberties to almost qualify as a variation, but is wonderfully literate and contains

f the most beautiful photography that has ever graced a sci-
fiction film.

here are more that I haven't mentioned; two films of *She,* two of
e Lost World, innumerable versions of *Midsummer Night's
Dream.* And yet more to come: As the science fiction and fantasy
films prove to be moneymakers, old properties will be dusted off,
"modernized," and reproduced. I can see the piece I'll do for *The
Best from Fantasy and Science Fiction: 50th Series,* sorting out several versions of *The Thing,* grumbling about the musical remake of
2001: A Space Odyssey, and commenting on the new production of
Star Wars, featuring Mark Hamill as Obi-wan Kenobi.

Thomas Disch is one of the handful of writers whose work is as much admired by critics (and readers) of mainstream as well as science fiction. He wrote six fine stories for *F&SF* in the 1960s. Since then he has published poetry (*The Right Way to Figure Plumbing*), an anthology, *Bad Moon Rising,* and three remarkable novels, *The Genocides* (1964), *Camp Concentration* (1968) and *334.* He has just completed a new sf novel, *On Wings of Song.*

The Man Who Had No Idea

by THOMAS M. DISCH

At first he'd assumed that he'd failed. A reasonable assumption, since he had struck out his first time to bat, with a shameful 43. But when two weeks had gone by and there was still no word from the Board of Examiners, he wondered if maybe he'd managed to squeak through. He didn't see how he could have. The examiner, a wizened, white-haired fuddy-duddy whose name Barry instantly forgot, had been hostile and aggressive right from the word go, telling Barry that he thought his handshake was too sincere. He directed the conversation first to the possible dangers of excessive sunbathing, which was surely an oblique criticism of Barry's end-of-August tan and the leisure such a tan implied, then started in on the likelihood that dolphins were as intelligent as people. Barry, having entered the cubicle resolved to stake all his chips on a tactic of complete candor, had said, one, he was too young to worry about skin cancer and, two, he had no interest in animals except as meat. This started the examiner off on the psychic experiences of some woman he'd read about in *Reader's Digest.* Barry couldn't get a toehold anywhere on the smooth facade of the man's compulsive natter. He got the feeling, more and more, that *he* was keeping score and the old fart was being tested, an attitude that did not bode well. Finally, with ten minutes left on the clock, he'd just up and left, which was not, strictly speaking, a violation. It did imply that some kind of closure had been achieved, which definitely was not the case; he'd panicked, pure and simple. A fiasco from which he'd naturally feared the worst in the form of a letter addressed to Dear Applicant. ("We regret to inform you, etc. . . .") But possibly the old fart had been making things deliberately difficult, testing him, possibly his reactions hadn't been that entirely inappropriate. Possibly he'd passed.

When another two weeks went by without the Board of Examiners saying boo, he couldn't stand the suspense any longer and went down to Center St. to fill out a form that asked basically where did he stand. A clerk coded the form and fed it into the computer. The computer instructed Barry to fill out another form, giving more details. Fortunately he'd brought the data the computer wanted, so he was able to fill out the second form on the spot. After a wait of less than ten minutes, his number lighted up on the board and he was told to go to Window 28.

Window 28 was the window that issued licenses: he had passed!

"I passed," he announced incredulously to the clerk at the window.

The clerk had the license with his name on it, Barry Riordan, right there in her hand. She inserted it into the slot of a gray machine which responded with an authoritative *chunk*. She slid the validated license under the grille.

"Do you know—I still can't believe it. This is *my* license: that's really incredible."

The clerk tapped the shut-up button pinned on the neckband of her T-shirt.

"Oh. Sorry, I didn't notice. Well . . . thanks."

He smiled at her, a commiserating guilty smile, and she smiled back, a mechanical next-please smile.

He didn't look at the license till he was out on the street. Stapled to the back of it was a printed notice:

IMPORTANT

Due to the recent systems overload error, your test results of August 24 have been erased. Therefore, in accordance with Bylaw 9(c),

Section XII, of the Revised Federal Communications Act, you are being issued a Temporary License, valid for three months from the date of issue, subject to the restrictions set forth in Appendix II of the Federal Communications Handbook (18th edition).

You may reapply for another examination at any time. An examination score in or above the eighth percentile will secure the removal of all restrictions, and you will immediately receive your Permanent License. A score in the sixth or seventh percentile will not affect the validity of your Temporary License, though its expiration date may be extended by this means for a period of up to three months. A score in the fifth percentile or below will result in the withdrawal of your Temporary License.

Holders of a Temporary License are advised to study Chapter Nine ("The Temporary License") in the Federal Communications Handbook. Remember that direct, interactive personal communications are one of our most valuable heritages. Use your license wisely. Do not abuse the privilege of free speech.

So in fact he hadn't passed the exam. Or maybe he had. He'd never find out.

His first elation fizzled out and he was left with his usual flattened sense of personal inconsequence. Tucking the license into his ID folder, he felt like a complete charlatan, a nobody pretending to be a somebody. If he'd scored in the first percentile, he'd have been issued this license the same as if he'd scored in the tenth. And he knew with *a priori* certainty that he hadn't done that well. The most he'd hoped for was another seven points, just enough to top him over the edge, into the sixth percentile. Instead he'd had dumb luck.

Not to worry, he advised himself. The worst is over. You've got your license. How you got it doesn't matter.

Oh, yeah, another and less friendly inward voice replied. Now all you need are three endorsements. Lots of luck.

Well, I'll *get* them, he insisted, hoping to impress the other voice with the authenticity and vitality of his self-confidence. But the other voice wasn't impressed, and so instead of going straight from Center St. to the nearest speakeasy to celebrate, he took the subway home and spent the evening watching first a fascinating documentary on calcium structures and then Celebrity Circus, with Willy Marx. Willy had four guests: a famous prostitute, a tax accountant who had just published his memoirs, a comedian who did a surrealistic skit about a speakeasy for five-year-olds, and a novelist with a speech impediment who got into an argument with the comedian about whether his skit was essentially truthful or unjustifiably cruel. In the middle of their argument Barry came down with a murderous headache, took two aspirins, and went to bed. Just before he fell asleep, he thought: I could call them and tell them what *I* thought.

But what did he think?

He didn't know.

That, in a nutshell, was Barry's problem. At last he had his license and could talk to anyone he wanted to talk to, but he didn't know what to talk *about*. He had no ideas of his own. He agreed with anything anyone said. The skit had been *both* essentially truthful *and* unjustifiably cruel. Too much sunbathing probably was dangerous. Porpoises probably were as smart as people.

Fortunately for his morale, this state of funk did not continue long. Barry didn't let it. The next night he was off to Partyland, a 23rd St. speakeasy that advertised heavily on late-night TV. As he approached the froth of electric lights cantilevered over the entrance, Barry could feel the middle of his body turning hollow with excitement, his throat and tongue getting tingly.

There was only a short line, and in a moment he was standing in front of the box office window. "Ring?" the window asked. He looked at the price list. "Second," he said, and slid his Master Charge into the appropriate slot. "License, please," said the window, winking an arrow that pointed at another slot. He inserted his license into the other slot, a bell went ding, and *mira!* He was inside Partyland, ascending the big blue escalator up to his first first-hand experience of direct, interactive personal communication. Not a classroom exercise, not a therapy session, not a job briefing, not an ecumenical agape, but an honest-to-god conversation, spontaneous, unstructured, and all his own.

The usher who led him to his seat in the second ring sat down beside him and started to tell him about a Japanese department store that covered an entire sixteen and a half acres, had thirty-two restaurants, two movie theaters, and a children's playground.

"That's fascinating, isn't it?" the usher concluded, after setting forth further facts about this remarkable department store.

"I suppose it is," Barry said noncommittally. He couldn't figure out why the usher wanted to tell him about a department store in Japan.

"I forget where I read about it," the usher said. "In some magazine or other. Well, mix in, enjoy yourself, and if you want to order anything, there's a console that rolls out from this end table." He demonstrated.

The usher continued to hover, smiling, over his chair. Finally Barry realized he was waiting for a tip. Without any idea of what was customary, he gave him a dollar, which seemed to do the trick.

He sat there in his bulgy sponge of a chair, grateful to be alone and able to take in the sheer size and glamor of the place. Partyland was an endless middle-class living room, a panorama of all that was gracious, tasteful, and posh. At least from here in the second ring it *seemed* endless. It had a seating capacity, according to its ads, of 780, but tonight wasn't one of its big nights and a lot of the seats were empty.

At intervals that varied unpredictably the furniture within this living room would rearrange itself, and suddenly you would find yourself face-to-face with a new conversational partner. You could also, for a few dollars more, hire a sofa or armchair that you could drive at liberty among the other chairs, choosing your partners rather than leaving them to chance. Relatively few patrons of Partyland exercised this option, since the whole point of the place was that you could just sit back and let your chair do the driving.

The background music changed from Vivaldi's *Four Seasons* to a Sondheim medley, and all the chairs in Barry's area suddenly lifted their occupants up in the air and carried them off, legs dangling, to their next conversational destination. Barry found himself sitting next to a girl in a red velvet evening dress with a hat of paper feathers and polyhedrons. The band of the hat said, "I'm a Partyland Smarty-pants."

"Hi," said the girl in a tone intended to convey a worldly-wise satiety but achieved no more than blank anomie. "What's up?"

"Terrific, just terrific," Barry replied with authentic warmth. He'd always scored well at this preliminary stage of basic communication, which was why, at the time, he'd so much resented his examiner's remark about his handshake. There was nothing phoney about his handshake, and he knew it.

"I like your shoes," she said.

Barry looked down at his shoes. "Thanks."

"I like shoes pretty much generally," she went on. "I guess you could say I'm a kind of shoe freak." She snickered wanly.

Barry smiled, at a loss.

"But yours are particularly nice. How much did you pay for them, if you don't mind my asking?"

Though he minded, he hadn't the gumption to say so. "I don't remember. Not a lot. They're really nothing special."

"*I* like them," she insisted. Then, "My name's Cinderella. What's yours?"

"Is it really?"

"Really. You want to see my ID?"

"Mm."

She dug into her ID folder, which was made of the same velvet as her dress, and took out her license. It was blue, like his (a Temporary License), and, again like his, there was a staple in the upper left-hand corner.

"See?" she said. "Cinderella B. Johnson. It was my mother's idea. My mother had a really weird sense of humor sometimes. She's dead now, though. Do you like it?"

"Like what?"

"My name."

"Oh, yeah, sure."

"Because some people don't. They think it's affected. But I can't help the name I was born with, can I?"

"I was going to ask you—"

Her face took on the intent, yet mesmerized look of a quiz show contestant. "Ask, ask."

"The staple on your license—why is it there?"

"What staple?" she countered, becoming in an instant rigid with suspicion, like a hare that scents a predator.

"The one on your license. Was there something attached to it orignally?"

"Some notice . . . I don't know. How can I remember something like that? Why do you ask?"

"There's one like it on mine."

"So? If you ask me, this is a damned stupid topic for a conversation. Aren't you going to tell me *your* name?"

"Uh . . . Barry."

"Barry what?"

"Barry Riordan."

"An Irish name: that explains it then."

He looked at her questioningly.

"That must be where you got your gift of gab. You must have kissed the Blarney stone."

She's crazy, he thought.

But crazy in a dull, not an interesting way. He wondered how long they'd have to go on talking before the chairs switched round again. It seemed such a waste of time talking to another temp, since he could only get the endorsements he needed from people who held Permanent Licenses. Of course, the practice was probably good for him. You can't expect to like everyone you meet, as the Communications Handbook never tired of pointing out, but you can always try and make a good impression. Someday you'd meet someone it was crucial to hit it off with and your practice would pay off.

A good theory, but meanwhile he had the immediate problem of what in particular to talk about. "Have you heard about the giant department store in Japan?" he asked her. "It covers sixteen acres."

"Sixteen and a half," she corrected. "You must read *Topic* too."

"Mm."

"It's a fascinating magazine. I look at it almost every week. Sometimes I'm just too busy, but usually I skim it, at least."

"Busy doing . . . ?"

"Exactly." She squinted across the vast tasteful expanse of Partyland, then stood up and waved. "I think I've *recognized* someone," she said excitedly, preening her paper feathers with her free hand. Far away, someone waved back.

Cinderella broke one of the polyhedrons off her hat and put it on her chair. "So I'll remember which it is," she explained. Then, contritely, "I hope you don't mind."

"Not at all."

Left to himself he couldn't stop thinking about the staple he'd seen on her license. It was like the seemingly insignificant clue in a detective story from which the solution to the whole mystery gradually unfolds. For didn't it strongly suggest that she too had been given the benefit of the doubt, that she'd got her license not because her score entitled her to it, but thanks to Bylaw 9(c), Section XII? The chagrin of being classified in the same category with such a nitwit! Partyland was probably *full* of people in their situation, all hoping to connect with some bona fide Permanent License holder, instead of which they went around colliding with each other.

A highly depressing idea, but he did not on that account roll out the console to select a remedy from the menu. He knew from long experience that whatever could make him palpably happier was also liable to send him into a state of fugue in which conversation in the linear sense became next to impossible. So he passed the time till the next switchover by working out, in his head, the square roots of various five-digit numbers. Then, when he had a solution, he'd check it on his calculator. He'd got five right answers when his chair reared up, god bless it, and bore him off toward . . . Would it be the couple chained, wrist to wrist, on the blue settee? No, at the last moment, his chair veered left and settled down in front of an unoccupied bentwood rocker. A sign in the seat of the rocker said: "I feel a little sick. Back in five minutes."

Barry was just getting used to the idea of going on to six-digit figures when a woman in a green sofa wheeled up to him and asked what kind of music he liked.

"Any kind, really."

"Any or none, it amounts to much the same thing."

"No, honestly. Whatever is playing I usually like it. What are they playing here? I like that."

"Muzak," she said dismissively.

It was, in fact, still the Sondheim medley, but he let that pass. It wasn't worth an argument.

"What do you do?" she demanded.

"I simulate a job that Citibank is developing for another corporation, but only on an auxiliary basis. Next year I'm supposed to start full-time."

She grimaced. "You're new at Partyland, aren't you?"

He nodded. "First time tonight. In fact, this is my first time ever in any speakeasy. I just got my license yesterday."

"Well, welcome to the club." With a smile that might as well have been a sneer. "I suppose you're looking for endorsements?"

Not from you, he wanted to tell her. Instead he looked off into the distance at the perambulations of a suite of chairs in another ring. Only when all the chairs had settled into place did he refocus on the woman in the foreground. He realized with a little zing of elation that he had just administered his first snub!

"What did Freddy say when you came in?" she asked in a conspiratorial if not downright friendly tone. (His snub had evidently registered.)

"Who is Freddy?"

"The usher who showed you to your seat. I saw him sit down and talk with you."

"He told me about some Japanese department store."

She nodded knowingly. "Of course—I should have known. Freddy shills for *Topic* magazine and that's one of their featured stories this week. I wonder what they pay him. Last week their cover story was about Ireina Khokolovna, and all Freddy could talk about was Ireina Khokolovna."

"Who is Ireina Khokolovna?" he asked.

She hooted a single derisory hoot. "I thought you said you liked music!"

"I do," he protested. But, clearly, he had just failed a major test. With a sigh of weariness and a triumphant smile, the woman rotated her sofa around one hundred and eighty degrees and drove off in the direction of the couple chained together on the blue settee.

The couple rose in unison and greeted her with cries of "Maggie!" and "Son of a gun!" It was impossible for Barry, sitting so nearby and having no one to talk to himself, to avoid eavesdropping on their conversation, which concerned (no doubt as a rebuke to his ignorance) Ireina Khokolovna's latest *superb* release from Deutsche Grammophon. She was at her best in Schumann, her Wolf was *comme ci, comme ça.* Even so, Khokolovna's Wolf was miles ahead of Adriana Motta's, or even Gwyneth Batterham's, who, for all her real intelligence, was developing a distinct wobble in her upper register. Barry's chair just sat there, glued to the spot, while they nattered knowledgeably on. He wished he were home watching Willy Marx—or anywhere but Partyland.

"Mine's Ed," said the occupant of the bentwood rocker, a young man of Barry's own age, build, and hair style.

"Pardon?" said Barry.

"I said," he said, with woozy precision, "my name is Ed."

"Oh. Mine's Barry. How are you, Ed?"

He held out his hand. Ed shook it gravely.

"You know, Barry," Ed said, "I've been thinking about what you were saying, and I think the whole problem is *cars*. Know what I mean?"

"Elaborate," Barry suggested.

"Right. The thing about cars is . . . Well, I live in Elizabeth across the river, right? So any time I come here I've got to drive, right? Which you might think was a drag, but in fact I always feel terrific. You know?"

Barry nodded. He didn't understand what Ed was saying in any very specific way, but he knew he agreed with him.

"I feel . . . free. If that doesn't seem too ridiculous. Whenever I'm driving my car."

"What have you got?" Barry asked.

"A Toyota."

"Nice. Very nice."

"I don't think I'm unique that way," said Ed.

"No, I wouldn't say so."

"Cars *are* freedom. And so what all this talk about an energy crisis boils down to is—" He stopped short. "I think I'm having a fugue."

"I think maybe you are. But that's all right. I do too. It'll pass."

"Listen, what's your name?"

"Barry," Barry said. "Barry Riordan."

Ed held out his hand. "Mine's Ed. Say, are you trying to pick up an endorsement?"

Barry nodded. "You too?"

"No. In fact, I think I've still got one left. Would you like it?"

"Jesus," said Barry. "Yeah, sure."

Ed took out his ID folder, took his license from the folder, tickled the edge of the endorsement sticker from the back of the license with his fingernail, and offered it to Barry.

"You're sure you want me to have this?" Barry asked, incredulous, with the white curlicue of the sticker dangling from his fingertip.

Ed nodded. "You remind me of somebody."

"Well, I'm awfully grateful. I mean you scarcely know me."

"Right," said Ed, nodding more vigorously. "But I liked what you were saying about cars. That made a lot of sense."

"You know," Barry burst out in a sudden access of confessional bonhomie, "I feel confused *most* of the time."

"Right."

"But I can never express it. Everything I *say* seems to make more sense than what I can feel inside of me."

"Right, right."

The music changed from the Sondheim medley to the flip side of *The Four Seasons,* and Barry's chair lifted him up and bore him off toward the couple in the blue settee, while Ed, limp in the bentwood rocker, was carried off in the opposite direction.

"Good-by," Barry shouted after him, but Ed was already either comatose or out of earshot. "And thanks again!"

The MacKinnons introduced themselves. His name was Jason. Hers was Michelle. They lived quite nearby, on West 28th, and were interested, primarily, in the television shows they'd seen when they were growing up, about which they were very well-informed. Despite a bad first impression, due to his associating them with Maggie of the green sofa, Barry found himself liking the MacKinnons enormously, and before the next switchover he put his chair in the LOCK position. They spent the rest of the evening together, exchanging nostalgic tidbits over coffee and slices of Partyland's famous pineapple pie. At closing time he asked if they would either consider giving him an endorsement. They said they would have, having thoroughly enjoyed his company, but unfortunately they'd both used up their quota for that year. They seemed genuinely sorry, but he felt it had been a mistake to ask.

His first endorsement proved to have been beginner's luck. Though he went out almost every night to a different speakeasy and practically lived at Partyland during the weekends, when it was at its liveliest, he never again had such a plum fall in his lap. He didn't get within sniffing distance of his heart's desire. Most people he met were temps, and the few Permanent License holders inclined to be friendly to him invariably turned out, like the MacKinnons, to have already disposed of their allotted endorsements. Or so they said. As the weeks went by and anxiety mounted, he began to be of the cynical but widely held opinion that many people simply removed the stickers from their licenses so it would *seem* they'd been used. According to Jason MacKinnon, a completely selfless endorsement, like his from Ed, was a rare phenomenon. Quid pro quos were the general rule, in the form either of cash on the barrel or services rendered. Barry said (jokingly, of course) that he wouldn't object to bartering his virtue for an endorsement, or preferably two, to which Michelle replied (quite seriously) that unfortunately she did not know anyone who might be in the market for Barry's particular type. Generally, she observed, it was *younger* people who got their endorsements by putting out.

Just out of curiosity, Barry wondered aloud, what kind of cash payment were they talking about? Jason said the standard fee, a year ago, for a single sticker had been a thousand dollars; two and a half for a pair, since people with two blanks to fill could be presumed to be that much more desperate. Due however to a recent disproportion between supply and demand, the going price for a single was now seventeen hundred; a double, a round four thousand. Jason said he could arrange an introduction at that price, if Barry were interested.

"I will tell you," said Barry, "what you can do with your stickers."

"Oh, now," said Michelle placatingly. "We're still your *friends,* Mr. Riordan, but business is business. If it were our own *personal* stickers we were discussing, we wouldn't *hesitate* to give you an endorsement absolutely *gratis.* Would we, Jason?"

"Of course not, no question."

"But we're middlemen, you see. We have only limited flexibility in the terms we can offer. Say, fifteen hundred."

"And three and a half for the pair," Jason added. "And that is a rock-bottom offer. You won't do better anywhere else."

"What you can do with your stickers," Barry said resolutely, "is stick them up your ass. Your asses, rather."

"I wish you wouldn't take that attitude, Mr. Riordan," said Jason in a tone of sincere regret. "We do like you, and we have enjoyed your company. If we didn't, we would certainly not be offering this opportunity."

"Bullshit," said Barry. It was the first time he'd used an obscenity conversationally, and he brought it off with great conviction. "You knew when my license would expire, and you've just been stringing me along, hoping I'd get panicky."

"We have been *trying,*" said Michelle, "to help."

"Thanks. I'll help myself."

"How?"

"Tomorrow I'm going back to Center St. and take the exam again."

Michelle MacKinnon leaned across the coffee table that separated the blue settee from Barry's armchair and gave him a sound motherly smack on the cheek. "Wonderful! That's the way to meet a challenge —head on! You're bound to pass. After all, you've had three months of practice. You've become much more fluent these past months."

"Thanks." He got up to go.

"Hey—" Jason grabbed Barry's hand and gave it an earnest squeeze. "Don't forget, if you *do* get your Permanent License—"

"When he gets it," Michelle amended.

"Right—*when* you get it, you know where you can find us. We're always here on the same settee."

"You two are unbelievable," Barry said. "Do you honestly think I'd sell you my endorsements? Assuming"—he knocked on the varnished walnut coffee table—"I pass my exam."

"It is safer," Michelle said, "to work through a professional introduction service than to try and peddle them on your own. Even though everyone breaks it, the law is still the law. Individuals operating on their own are liable to get caught, since they don't have an arrangement with the authorities. We do. That's why, for instance, it would do you no good to report us to the Communications Control Office. Others have done so in the past, and it did *them* no good."

"None of them ever got a Permanent License, either," Jason added, with a twinkle of menace.

"That, I'm sure, was just coincidence," said Michelle. "After all, we're speaking of only two cases, and neither of the individuals in question was particularly bright. Bright people wouldn't be so quixotic, would they?" She underlined her question with a Mona Lisa smile, and Barry, for all his indignation and outrage, couldn't keep from smiling back. Anyone who could drop a word like "quixotic" into the normal flow of conversation and make it seem so natural couldn't be all wrong.

"Don't worry," he promised, tugging his hand out of Jason's. "I'm not the quixotic type."

But when he said it, it sounded false. It wasn't fair.

Barry was as good as his word and went to Center St. the very next morning to take his third exam. The computer assigned him to

Marvin Kolodny, Ph.D. in cubicle 183. The initials worried him. He
could have coped, this time, with the old fuddy-duddy he'd had last
August, but a Ph.D.? It seemed as though they were raising the hur-
dles each time he came around the track. But his worries evaporated
the moment he was in the cubicle and saw that Marvin Kolodny was
a completely average young man of twenty-four. His averageness was
even a bit unsteady, as though he had to think about it, but then
most twenty-four-year-olds are self-conscious in just that way.

It's always a shock the first time you come up against some particular kind of authority figure—a dentist, a psychiatrist, a cop—who is
younger than you are, but it needn't lead to disaster as long as you
let the authority figure know right from the start that you intend to
be deferential, and this was a quality that Barry conveyed without
trying.

"Hi," said Barry, with masterful deference. "I'm Barry Riordan."

Marvin Kolodny responded with a boyish grin and offered his
hand. An American flag had been tattooed on his right forearm. On
a scroll circling the flagpole was the following inscription:

Let's All
Overthrow
the United States
Government
by Force &
Violence

On his other forearm there was a crudely executed rose with his
name underneath: Marvin Kolodny, Ph.D.

"Do you mean it?" Barry asked, marveling over Marvin's tattoo as
they shook hands. He managed to ask the question without in the
least seeming to challenge Marvin Kolodny's authority.

"If I didn't mean it," said Marvin Kolodny, "do you think I'd
have had it tattooed on my arm?"

"I suppose not. It's just so . . . unusual."

"I'm an unusual person," said Marvin Kolodny, leaning back in
his swivel chair and taking a large pipe from the rack on his desk.

"But doesn't *that* idea"—Barry nodded at the tattoo—"conflict with
your having this particular job? Aren't you part of the U. S. Government yourself?"

"Only for the time being. I'm not suggesting that we overthrow the
government *tomorrow*. A successful revolution isn't possible until the

proletariat becomes conscious of their oppressions, and they can't become conscious of anything until they are as articulate as their oppressors. Language and consciousness aren't independent processes, after all. Talking is thinking turned inside-out. No more, no less."

"And which am I?"

"How's that?"

"Am I a proletarian or an oppressor?"

"Like most of us these days, I would say you're probably a little of each. Are you married, uh . . ." (He peeked into Barry's file.) ". . . Barry?"

Barry nodded.

"Then that's one form of oppression right there. Children?"

Barry shook his head.

"Do you live with your wife?"

"Not lately. And even when we were together, we never talked to each other, except to say practical things like 'When is your program going to be over?' Some people just aren't that interested in talking. Debra certainly isn't. That's why—" (He couldn't resist the chance to explain his earlier failures.) "—I did so poorly on my earlier exams. Assuming I *did* get a low score last time, which isn't certain since the results were erased. But assuming that I did, that's the reason. I never got any practice. The basic day-to-day conversational experiences most people have with their spouses never happened in my case."

Marvin Kolodny frowned—an ingratiating, boyish frown. "Are you sure you're being entirely honest with yourself, Barry? Few people are completely willing to talk about something. We've all got hobby-horses. What was your wife interested in? Couldn't you have talked about that?"

"In religion, mostly. But she didn't care to talk about it, unless you agreed with her."

"Have you *tried* to agree with her?"

"Well, you see, Dr. Kolodny, what she *believes* is that the end of the world is about to happen. Next February. That's where she's gone now—to Arizona, to wait for it. This is the third time she's taken off."

"Not an easy woman to discourage, by the sound of it."

"I think she really *wants* the world to end. And, also, she *does* like Arizona."

"Have you considered a divorce?" Marvin Kolodny asked.

"No, absolutely not. We're still basically in love. After all, most married couples end up not saying much to each other. Isn't that so? Even before Debra got religious, we weren't in the habit of talking to each other. To tell the truth, Dr. Kolodny, I've never been much of a talker. I think I was put off it by the compulsory talk we had to do in high school."

"That's perfectly natural. I hated compulsory talk myself, though I must admit I was good at it. What about your job, Barry? Doesn't that give you opportunities to develop communication skills?"

"I don't communicate with the public directly. Only with simulations, and their responses tend to be pretty stereotyped."

"Well, there's no doubt that you have a definite communications problem. But I think it's a problem you can lick! I'll tell you what, Barry: officially, I shouldn't tell you this myself, but I'm giving you a score of 65." He held up his hand to forestall an effusion. "Now, let me explain how that breaks down. You do very well in most categories—Affect, Awareness of Others, Relevance, Voice Production, et cetera, but where you do fall down is in Notional Content and Originality. There you could do better."

"Originality has always been my Waterloo," Barry admitted. "I just don't seem to be able to come up with my own ideas. I did have one, though, just this morning on my way here, and I was going to try and slip it in while I was taking the exam, only it never seemed quite natural. Have you ever noticed that you never see baby pigeons? All the pigeons you see out on the street are the same size—full-grown. But where do they come from? Where are the little pigeons? Are they hidden somewhere?" He stopped short, feeling ashamed of his idea. Now that it was out in the open it seemed paltry and insignificant, little better than a joke he'd learned by heart, than which there is nothing more calculated to land you in the bottom percentiles.

Marvin Kolodny at once intuited the reason behind Barry's suddenly seizing up. He was in the business, after all, of understanding unspoken meanings and evaluating them precisely. He smiled a sympathetic, mature smile.

"Ideas . . ." he said, in a slow, deliberate manner, as though each word had to be weighed on a scale before it was put into the sentence. ". . . aren't . . . things. Ideas—the most authentic ideas—are the natural, effortless result of any vital relationship. Ideas are what happen when people connect with each other creatively."

Barry nodded.

"Do you mind my giving you some honest advice, Barry?"

"Not at all, Dr. Kolodny. I'd be grateful."

"On your G-47 form you say you spend a lot of time at Partyland and similar speakeasies. I realize that's where you did get your first endorsement, but really, don't you think you're wasting your time in that sort of place? It's a tourist trap!"

"I'm aware of that," Barry said, smarting under the rebuke.

"You're not going to meet anyone there but temps and various people who are out to fleece temps. With rare exceptions."

"I know, I know. But I don't know where *else* to go."

"Why not try this place?" Marvin Kolodny handed Barry a printed card, which read:

INTENSITY FIVE

A New Experience in Interpersonal Intimacy
5 Barrow Street
New York 10014

Members Only

"I'll certainly try it," Barry promised. "But how do I get to be a member?"

"Tell them Marvin sent you."

And that was all there was to it—he had passed his exam with a score just five points short of the crucial eighth percentile. Which was a tremendous accomplishment but also rather frustrating in a way, since it meant he'd come *that* close to not having to bother scouting out two more endorsements. Still, with another three months in which to continue his quest and an introduction to Intensity Five, Barry had every reason to be optimistic.

"Thank you, Dr. Kolodny," Barry said, lingering in the doorway of the cubicle. "Thanks terrifically."

"That's all right, Barry. Just doing my job."

"You know . . . I wish . . . Of course, I know it's not permissible, you being an examiner and all . . . but I wish I knew you in a personal way. Truly. You're a very heavy individual."

"Thank you, Barry. I know you mean that, and I'm flattered. Well, then—" He took his pipe from his mouth and lifted it in a kind of salute. "So long. And Merry Christmas."

Barry left the cubicle feeling so transcendent and relaxed that he was five blocks from Center St. before he remembered that he'd neglected to have his license revalidated at Window 28. As he headed back to the Federal Communications Building, his senses seemed to register all the ordinary details of the city's streets with an unnatural, hyped clarity: the smell of sauerkraut steaming up from a hot dog cart, the glint of the noon sun on the mica mixed into the paving blocks of the sidewalk, the various shapes and colors of the pigeons, the very pigeons, perhaps, that had inspired his so-called idea earlier that day. But it was true, what he'd said. All the pigeons were the same size.

A block south of the Federal Communications Building, he looked up, and there strung out under the cornice of the building was the motto, which he had never noticed before, of the Federal Communications Agency:

> PLANNED FREEDOM IS THE
> ROAD TO LASTING
> PROGRESS.

So simple, so direct, and yet when you thought about it, almost impossible to understand.

Barrow St. being right in the middle of one of the city's worst slums, Barry had been prepared (he'd thought) for a lesser degree of stateliness and bon ton than that achieved by Partyland, but even so the dismal actuality of Intensity Five went beyond anything he could have imagined. A cavernous one-room basement apartment with bare walls, crackly linoleum over a concrete floor, and radiators that hissed and gurgled ominously without generating a great deal of heat. The furniture consisted of metal folding chairs, most of them folded and stacked, a refreshment stand that sold orange juice and coffee, and a great many freestanding, brimful metal ashtrays. Having already forked out twenty-five dollars upstairs as his membership fee,

Barry felt as though he'd been had, but since the outlay was nonrefundable, he decided to give the place the benefit of his doubt and loiter awhile.

He had been loitering, alone and melancholy, for the better part of an hour, eavesdropping to his right on a conversation about somebody's drastic need to develop a more effective persona and to his left on a discussion of the morality of our involvement in Mexico, when a black woman in a white nylon jumpsuit and a very good imitation calf-length mink swept into the room, took a quick survey of those present, and sat down, unbelievably, by him!

Quick as a light switch he could feel his throat go dry and his face tighten into a smile of rigid insincerity. He blushed, he trembled, he fainted dead away, but only metaphorically.

"I'm Columbine Brown," she said, as though that offered an explanation.

Did she expect him to recognize her? She was beautiful enough, certainly, to have been someone he ought to recognize, but if he had seen her on TV, he didn't remember. In a way she seemed almost *too* beautiful to be a noted personality, since there is usually something a little idiosyncratic about each of them, so they can be told apart. Columbine Brown was beautiful in the manner not of a celebrity but of a deluxe (but not customized) sports car.

"I'm Barry Riordan," he managed to bring out, tardily.

"Let's put our cards on the table, shall we, Mr. Riordan? I am a Permanent Card holder. What are you?"

"A temp."

"It's fair to assume then that you're here to find an endorsement."

He began to protest. She stopped him with just one omniscient and devastating glance. He nodded.

"Unfortunately, I have used up my quota. However"—she held up a single perfect finger—"it's almost the New Year. If you're not in a desperate hurry . . . ?"

"Oh, I've got till March."

"I'm not promising anything, you understand. Unless we hit it off. If we do, then fine, you have my endorsement. Fair enough?"

"It's a deal."

"You feel you can trust me?" She lowered her eyes and tried to look wicked and temptress-like, but it was not in the nature of her kind of beauty to do so.

"Anywhere," he replied. "Implicitly."

"Good." As though of its own volition her coat slipped off her shoulders onto the back of the folding chair. She turned her head sideways and addressed the old woman behind the refreshment counter. "Evelyn, how about an orange juice." She looked at him. He nodded. "Make it two."

Then, as though they'd been waiting for these preliminaries to be concluded, tears sprang to her eyes. A tremor of heartfelt emotion colored her lovely contralto voice as she said, "Oh Jesus, what am I going to do? I can't take any more! I am just so . . . so goddamned wretched! I'd like to kill myself. No, that isn't true. I'm confused, Larry. But I know one thing—I am an *angry* woman and I'm going to start fighting back!"

It would have been inconsiderate to break in upon such testimony by mentioning that his name was not, in fact, Larry. What difference does one letter make, after all?

"Have you ever been to the Miss America Pageant on 42nd St.?" she asked him, drying her eyes.

"I can't say I have. I always mean to, but you know how it is. It's the same with the Statue of Liberty. It's always there, so you never get around to it."

"I'm Miss Georgia."

"No kidding!"

"I have *been* Miss Georgia six nights a week for the last four years, with matinees on Sunday and Tuesday, and do you suppose in all that time that the audience has ever voted for *me* to be Miss America? Ever?"

"*I* would certainly vote for you."

"Never once," she went on fiercely, ignoring his supportiveness. "It's always Miss Massachusetts, or Miss Ohio, who can't do anything but play a damn jew's-harp, if you'll excuse my language, or Miss Oregon, who still can't remember the blocking for *Lovely to Look At,* which she has been dancing since before *I* graduated from high school. There's no one in the whole damn line-up who hasn't been crowned once. Except me."

"I'm sorry to hear it."

"I am a *good* singer. I can tap dance like a house on fire. My balcony scene would break your heart. And I can say objectively that I've got better legs than anyone except, possibly, Miss Wyoming."

"But you've never been Miss America," Barry said sympathetically.

"What do you think that *feels* like, here?" She grabbed a handful of white nylon in the general area of her heart.

"I honestly don't know, Miss . . ." (He'd forgotten her last name.) ". . . Georgia."

"At Intensity Five I'm just plain Columbine, honey. The same as you're just Larry. And not knowing isn't much of an answer. Here I am exposing myself in front of you, and you come back with 'No Opinion.' I don't buy that."

"Well, to be completely candid, Columbine, it's hard for me to imagine your feeling anything but terrific. To be Miss Georgia and have such a lot of talent—isn't that *enough?* I would have thought you'd be very happy."

Columbine bit her lip, furrowed her brow, and evidenced, in general, a sudden change of heart. "God, Larry—you're right! I've been kidding myself: the pageant isn't my problem—it's my excuse. My problem"—her voice dropped, her eyes avoided his—"is timeless and well-known. I fell in love with the wrong man for me. And now it's too late. Would you like to hear a long story, Larry? A long and very unhappy story?"

"Sure. That's what I'm here for, isn't it?"

She smiled a meaningful, unblemished smile and gave his hand a quick, trusting squeeze. "You know, Larry—you're an all-right guy."

Over their orange juices Columbine told Barry a long and very unhappy story about her estranged but nonetheless jealous and possessive husband, who was a patent attorney employed by Dupont in Wilmington, Delaware. Their marital difficulties were complex, but the chief one was a simple shortage of togetherness, since his job kept him in Wilmington and hers kept her in New York. Additionally, her husband's ideal of conversation was very divergent from her own. He enjoyed talking about money, sports, and politics with other men and bottled up all his deeper feelings. She was introspective, outgoing, and warmhearted.

"It would be all right for a while," she recalled. "But the pressure would build until I had to go out and find someone to talk to. It is a basic human need, after all. Perhaps *the* basic need. I had no choice."

"And then he'd find out, I suppose," said Barry.

She nodded. "And go berserk. It was awful. No one can live that way."

Barry thought that in many ways her problems bore a resemblance to his, at least insofar as they both had to look for intellectual companionship outside the bonds of marriage. But when he began to elaborate upon this insight and draw some interesting parallels between his experience and hers, Columbine became impatient. She did not come right out and tell him that he was in breach of contract, but that was definitely the message conveyed by her glazed inattention. Responsive to her needs, he resisted the impulse to make any further contributions of his own and sat back and did his level best to be a good listener and nothing more.

When Columbine had finally run the gamut of all her feelings, which included fear, anger, joy, pain, and an abiding and entirely unreasoning sense of dread, she thanked him, gave him her address and phone number, and said to get in touch in January for his endorsement.

Jubilation, he thought. Bingo. Hallelujah.

But not quite. He still had to get one more endorsement. But now it seemed possible, likely, even inevitable. A matter, merely, of making the effort and reaping the reward.

Dame Fortune had become so well-disposed to him that he got his third endorsement (though in point of hard fact, his second) the very next night. The fated encounter took place at Morone's One-Stop Shopping, a mom-and-pop mini-grocery on Sixth Ave. right next to the International Supermarket. Although Morone's charged more for most items, Barry preferred shopping there because it offered such a limited and unchallenging range of choices (cold meats, canned goods, beer, Nabisco cookies) that he never felt intimidated and ashamed of his selections at the check-out counter. He hated to cook, but was that any reason he should be made to feel inadequate? Morone's was made to order for people like Barry, of which there are great numbers.

That night, as he was hesitating between a dinner of Spam and Chef Boy-ar-dee ravioli or Spam and Green Giant corn niblets, the woman who had been standing in front of the frozen food locker suddenly started talking to herself. The Morones looked at each other in alarm. Neither of them were licensed talkers, which was a further attraction of their store, since one's exchanges with them were limited to such basic permissible amenities as "How are you," "Take care," and giving out prices.

What the woman was saying was of a character to suggest that she had just that minute gone crazy. "The pain," she explained calmly to the ice cream section of the freezer, "only comes on when I do this." She stooped closer to the ice cream and winced. "But then it's pure hell. I want to cut my leg off, have a lobotomy, anything to make it stop. Yet I know the problem isn't in my leg at all. It's in my back. Here." She touched the small of her back. "A kind of short circuit. Worse than bending over is twisting sideways. Even turning my head can set it off. Sometimes, when I'm alone, I'll start crying just at the thought of it, at knowing I've become so damned superannuated." She sighed. "Well, it happens to everyone, and I suppose it could be worse. There's no use complaining. Life goes on, as they say."

Having come round to a sensible, accepting attitude, she turned from the freezer to witness the effect of her outburst on the Morones, who looked elsewhere, and on Barry, who couldn't resist meeting her eyes head-on. Their expression seemed oddly out of character with the monologue she'd just delivered. They were piercing (as against vulnerable) steely-gray eyes that stared defiance from a face all sags and wrinkles. Without the contradiction of such eyes, her face would have seemed ruined and hopeless; with them, she looked just like an ancient centurion in a movie about the Roman Empire.

She grimaced. "No need to panic. It's not an emergency. I'm licensed."

Barry proffered his most harmless smile. "I wasn't even thinking of that."

She didn't smile back. "Then what were you thinking?"

"I guess I was feeling sorry."

To which her reaction was, alarmingly, to laugh.

Feeling betrayed and pissed-off, he grabbed the nearest can of vegetables (beets, he would later discover, and he hated beets) and handed it to Mr. Morone with the can of Spam.

"That it?" Mr. Morone asked.

"A six-pack of Schlitz," he said, quite off the top of his head.

When he left the store with his dinner and the beer in a plastic bag, she was already outside waiting for him. "I wasn't laughing at you, young man," she told him, taking the same coolly aggrieved tone she'd taken toward the ice cream. "I was laughing at myself. Obviously, I *was* asking for pity. So if I should get some, I shouldn't be surprised, should I. My name's Madeline, but my friends call me Mad. You're supposed to laugh."

"Mine's Barry," he said. "Do you drink beer?"

"Oh, I'm not drunk. I discovered long ago that one needn't actually drink in order to have the satisfaction of behaving outrageously."

"I meant, would you like some now, with me? I've got a six-pack."

"Certainly. Barry, you said? You're so *direct* it's almost devious. Let's go to my place. It's only a couple blocks away. You see—I can be direct myself."

Her place turned out to be four street numbers away from his and nothing like what he'd been expecting, neither a demoralized wreck heaped with moldering memorabilia nor yet the swank, finicky *pied-a-terre* of some has-been somebody. It was a plain, pleasant 1½-room apartment that anyone could have lived in and almost everyone did, with potted plants to emphasize the available sunlight and pictures representing various vanished luxuries on the wall, the common range of furniture from aspiring to makeshift, and enough ordinary debris to suggest a life being carried on, with normative difficulty, among these carefully cultivated neutralities.

Barry popped the tops off two beer cans and Madeline swept an accumulation of books and papers off a tabletop and onto a many-cushioned bed. They sat down at the table.

"Do you know what it's called?" he asked. "The disease you've got?"

"Sciatica. Which is more a disorder than a disease. Let's not talk about it, okay?"

"Okay, but *you'll* have to think of what we do talk about. I'm no good at coming up with topics for conversation."

"Why is that?"

"No ideas. If other people have ideas, I can bounce off them well enough, but all by itself my mind's a blank. I envy people like you who are able to start talking out of the blue."

"Mm," said Madeline, not unkindly. "It's odd you should put it like that; it's almost a definition of what I do for a living."

"Really, what's that?"

"I'm a poet."

"No kidding. You can make a living by being a poet?"

"Enough to get by."

Barry refused to believe her. Neither the woman nor her apartment corresponded with his preconceptions of poets and the necessarily indigent life they must lead. "Have you ever published a book?" he asked craftily.

"Twenty-two. More than that, if you count limited editions and pamphlets and such." She went over to the bed, rooted among the papers, and returned with a thin, odd-sized paperback. "This is the latest." The front cover said in tasteful powder-blue letters on a background of dusky cream: MADELINE IS MAD AGAIN: New Poems by Madeline Swain. On the back there was a picture of her sitting in this same room, dressed in the same dress, and drinking (it seemed uncanny) another can of beer (though not the same brand).

Barry turned the book over in his hands, examining the cover and the photo alternately, but would no more have thought of looking inside than of lifting Madeline's skirts to peek at her underclothes. "What's it about?" he asked.

"Whatever I happened to be thinking at the moment I wrote each poem."

That made sense but didn't answer his question. "When do you write them?"

"Generally, whenever people ask me to."

"Could you write a poem right now? About what you're thinking?"

"Sure, no trouble." She went to the desk in the corner of the room and quickly wrote the following poem, which she handed to Barry to read:

> A Reflection
> Sometimes the repetition of what we have
> just said will suggest a new meaning
> or possibilities of meaning
> we did not at first suppose to be there.
> We think we have understood our words,
> then learn that we have not,
> since their essential meaning
> only dawns on us the second time round.

"This is what you were thinking just now?" he asked skeptically.

"Are you disappointed?"

"I thought you'd write something about me."

"Would you like me to do that?"

"It's too late now."

"Not at all."

She went to her desk and returned a moment later with a second poem:

> Aubade
> I was sorry to hear
> That you've got to be going.
> But you're not?
> Then I'm sorry to hear that.

"What does the title mean?" he asked, hoping it might modify the unfriendly message of the four short lines that followed.

"An aubade is a traditional verse-form that a lover addresses to his (or her) beloved at dawn, when one of them is leaving for work."

He tried to think of a compliment that wouldn't be completely insincere. "Heavy," he allowed at last.

"Oh, I'm afraid it's not much good. I can usually do better. I guess I don't trust you enough. Though you're quite likable; that's another matter."

"Now I'm likable! I thought"—he dangled the poem by one corner —"you were just hinting that I should leave?"

"Nonsense. You haven't even finished your beer. You *mustn't* hold what I write against me. Poets can't be held responsible for what they say in their poems. We're all compulsive traitors, you know."

Barry said nothing, but his expression must have conveyed his disapproval.

"Now don't be like that. Treason is a necessary part of the job, the way that handling trash cans is a part of being a garbage man. Some poets go to a great deal of trouble to disguise their treacheries; my inclination is to be up-front and betray everyone right from the start."

"Do you have many friends?" he asked, needlingly.

"Virtually none. Do you think I'd go around talking to myself in grocery stores if I had friends?"

He shook his head, perplexed. "I'll tell you, Madeline, it doesn't make sense to me. Surely if you were nice to other poets, they'd be nice to you, on the basic principle of scratch-my-back."

"Oh, of course. Minor poets do nothing else. They positively swarm. I'd rather be major and lonely, thank you very much."

"Sounds arrogant to me."

"It is. I am. *C'est la vie.*" She took a long, throat-rippling sip of the Schlitz and set her can down on the table, empty. "What I like about you, Barry, is that you manage to say what you think without seeming the least homicidal. Why?"

"Why do I say what I think? It's easiest."

"No: why are you so accommodating to me, when I'm being such a bitch? Are you looking for an endorsement?"

He blushed. "Is it that obvious?"

"Well, as you don't appear to be either a mugger or a rapist, there had to be some reason you followed a dotty old woman home from her latest nervous breakdown. Let's make a deal, shall we?"

"What sort of deal?"

"You stay around and nudge some more poems out of me. I'm feeling the wind in my sails, but I need a muse. If you give me twenty good ideas for poems, I'll give you your endorsement."

Barry shook his head. "Twenty different ideas? Impossible."

"Don't think of them as ideas then, think of them as questions."

"Ten," he insisted. "Ten is a lot."

"Fifteen," she countered.

"All right, but including the two you've already written."

"Done!"

She sat down and waited for Barry to be inspired. "Well?" she inquired, after a long silence.

"I'm trying to think."

He tried to think of what most poems were about. Love seemed the likeliest subject, but he couldn't imagine Madeline, at her age and with her temperament, being in love with anybody. Still, that was her problem. He didn't have to write the poem, only propose it.

"All right," he said. "Write a poem about how much you're in love with me."

She looked miffed. "Don't flatter yourself, young man. I may have inveigled you into my apartment, but I am *not* in love with you."

"Pretend then. And don't make it anything flip like that last one. Make it sad and delicate and use some rhymes."

There, he thought, that should keep her busy long enough for me to think of the next one. He opened a second beer and took a meditative swallow. Did poets ever write poems about drinking beer? Or was that too general? Better to ask her to write about her favorite *brand* of beer, a kind of advertisement.

By the time she'd finished the sonnet about how much she loved him, he had come up with all twelve other subjects.

1. A poem about her favorite beer, written as though it were an ad.
2. A poem in the form of a Christmas-shopping list.
3. A poem embodying several important long-range economic forecasts.
4. A poem about a rabbit (there was a porcelain rabbit on one of the shelves) suitable to be sung to a baby.
5. A very short poem to be carved on the tombstone of her least favorite president, living or dead.
6. A poem apologizing to the last person she had been especially rude to.
7. A poem for a Get Well card to someone who has sciatica.
8. A poem analyzing her feelings about beets.
9. A poem that skirts all around a secret she's never told anyone and then finally decides to keep it a secret.
10. A poem giving an eyewitness account of something awful happening in Arizona, in February.
11. A poem justifying capital punishment in cases where one has been abandoned by one's lover. (This in its final, expanded form was to become the longest poem in her next collection, "The Ballad of Lucius McGonaghal Sloe," which begins:

> I fell head over heels just four evenings ago
> With a girl that I'm sure you all know,
>   But I couldn't hold her,
>   And that's why I sold her,
> To Lucius McGonaghal Sloe.

and continues, in a similar vein, for another one hundred thirty-six stanzas.)
12. A poem presenting an affirmative, detailed description of her own face.

Prudently he didn't spring them on her all at once, but waited until she'd finished each one before telling her what the next had to be about. She didn't raise any further objections until he came to Number 8, whereupon she insisted she didn't have any feelings about beets whatsoever. He refused to believe her, and to prove his point he cooked up a quick dinner on her hotplate of Spam and canned beets (it was rather late by then, and they were famished). Before she'd had three mouthfuls, the poem started coming to her, and by the time she'd got it into final shape, five years later, it was far and away the best of the lot.

For the next many days Barry didn't speak to a soul. He felt no need to communicate anything to anyone. He had his three endorsements—one from a poet who'd published twenty-two books—and he was confident he could have gone out and got three more a day if he'd needed to. He was off the hook.

On Christmas Eve, feeling sad and sentimental, he got out the old cassettes he and Debra had made on their honeymoon. He played them on the TV, one after the other, all through the night, waxing mellower and mellower and wishing she were here. Then, in February, when the world had once again refused to end, she did come home, and for several days it was just as good as anything on the cassettes. They even, for a wonder, talked to each other. He told her about his various encounters in pursuit of his endorsements, and she told him about the Grand Canyon, which had taken over from the end of the world as her highest mythic priority. She loved the Grand Canyon with a surpassing love and wanted Barry to leave his job and go with her to live right beside it. Impossible, he declared. He'd worked eight years at Citibank and accrued important benefits. He accused her of concealing something. Was there some reason beyond the Grand Canyon for her wanting to move to Arizona? She insisted it was strictly the Grand Canyon, that from the first moment she'd seen it she'd forgotten all about Armageddon, the Number of the Beast, and all the other accouterments of the Apocalypse. She couldn't explain: he would have to see it himself. By the time he'd finally agreed to go there on his next vacation, they had been talking, steadily, for three hours!

Meanwhile, Columbine Brown had been putting him off with a variety of excuses and dodges. The phone number she'd given him was her answering service, the address was an apartment building with guard dogs in the lobby and a doorman who didn't talk, or listen. Barry was obliged to wait out on the sidewalk, which wasn't possible, due to a cold wave that persisted through most of January. He left a message at the Apollo Theater, where the pageant was held, giving three different times he would be waiting for her at Intensity Five. She never showed. By mid-February, he'd begun to be alarmed. Early one morning, defying the weather, he posted himself outside her building and waited (five miserable hours) till she appeared. She was profusely apologetic, explained that she *did* have his sticker, there was no problem, he shouldn't worry, but she had an appointment she had to get to, in fact she was already late, and so if he'd come back tonight, or better yet (since she had to see somebody after the pageant and didn't know when she'd be home) at this time tomorrow? Thoughtfully, she introduced him to the doorman so he wouldn't have to wait out in the cold.

At this time tomorrow Columbine made another nonappearance, and Barry began to suspect she was deliberately avoiding him. He decided to give her one last chance. He left a message with the doorman saying he would be by to collect his you-know-what at half past twelve the next night. Alternately, she could leave it in an envelope with the doorman.

When he arrived the following evening, the doorman led him down the carpeted corridor, unlocked the elevator (the dogs growled portentously until the doorman said *"Aus!"*), and told him to ring at door 8-C.

It was not Columbine who let him in, but her understudy, Lida Mullens. Lida informed Barry that Columbine had joined her husband in Wilmington, Delaware, and there was no knowing when, if ever, she might return to her post as Miss Georgia. She had not left the promised sticker, and Lida seriously doubted whether she had any left, having heard, through the grapevine, that she'd sold all three of them to an introduction service on the day they came in the mail. With his last gasp of self-confidence Barry asked Lida Mullens whether *she* would consider giving him an endorsement. He promised to pay her back in kind the moment he was issued his own license. Lida informed him airily that she didn't have a license. Their entire conversation had been illegal.

The guilt that immediately marched into his mind and evicted every other feeling was something awful. He knew it was irrational, but he couldn't help it. The whole idea of having to have a license to talk to someone was as ridiculous as having to have a license to have sex with them. Right? Right! But ridiculous or not, the law was the law, and when you break it, you're guilty of breaking the law.

The nice thing about guilt is that it's so easy to repress. Within a day Barry had relegated all recollections of his criminal behavior of the night before to the depths of his subconscious and was back at Intensity Five, waiting for whomever to strike up a conversation. The only person who so much as glanced his way, however, was Evelyn, the woman behind the refreshment stand. He went to other speakeasies, but it was always the same story. People avoided him. Their eyes shied away. His vibrations became such an effective repellent that he had only to enter a room in order to empty it of half its custom. Or so it seemed. When one is experiencing failure, it is hard to resist the comfort of paranoia.

With only a week left till his temporary license expired, Barry abandoned all hope and all shame and went back to Partyland with fifteen hundred dollars in cash, obtained from Beneficial Finance.

The MacKinnons were not in their blue settee, and neither Freddy the usher nor Madge of the green sofa could say what had become of them. He flopped into the empty settee with a sense of complete, abject surrender, but so eternally does hope spring that inside of a quarter of an hour he had adjusted to the idea of never being licensed and was daydreaming instead of a life of majestic, mysterious silence on the rim of the Grand Canyon. He rolled out the console and ordered a slice of pineapple pie and some uppers.

The waitress who brought his order was Cinderella Johnson. She was wearing levis and a T-shirt with the word "Princess" in big, glitter-dust letters across her breasts. Her hat said: "Let Tonight Be Your Enchanted Evening at Partyland!"

"Cinderella!" he exclaimed. "Cinderella Johnson! Are you *working* here?"

She beamed. "Isn't it wonderful? I started three days ago. It's like a dream come true."

"Congratulations."

"Thanks." Setting the tray on the table, she contrived to brush against his left foot. "I see you're wearing the same shoes."

"Mm."

"Is something the matter?" she asked, handing him the uppers with a glass of water. "You look gloomy, if you'll forgive my saying so."

"Sometimes it does you good to feel gloomy." One of the pills insisted on getting stuck in his throat. Just like, he thought, a lie.

"Hey, do you mind if I sit down on your couch a minute? I am frazzled. It's a tremendous opportunity, working here, but it does take it out of you."

"Great," said Barry. "Fine. Terrific. I could use some company."

She sat down close to him and whispered into his ear, "If anyone, such as Freddy, for instance, should happen to ask what we were talking about, say it was the New Wooly Look, okay?"

"That's *Topic*'s feature story this week?"

She nodded. "I guess you heard about the MacKinnons."

"I asked, but I didn't get any answers."

"They were arrested, for trafficking, right here on this couch, while they were taking money from the agent that had set them up. There's no way they can wiggle out of it this time. People say how sorry they are and everything, but I don't know: they *were* criminals, after all. What they were doing only makes it harder for the rest of us to get our endorsements honestly."

"I suppose you're right."

"Of course I'm right."

Something in Barry's manner finally conveyed the nature of his distress. The light dawned: "You have *got* your license, haven't you?"

Reluctantly at first, then with the glad, uncloseted feeling of shaking himself loose over a dance floor, Barry told Cinderella of his ups and downs during the past six months.

"Oh, that is so terrible," she commiserated at the end of his tale. "That is so unfair."

"What can you do?" he asked, figuratively.

Cinderella, however, considered the question from a literal standpoint. "Well," she said, "we haven't ever really talked together, not seriously, but you certainly ought to have a license."

"It's good of you to say so," said Barry morosely.

"So—if you'd like an endorsement from me . . . ?" She reached into her back pocket, took out her license, and peeled off an endorsement sticker.

"Oh, no, really, Cinderella. . . ." He took the precious sticker between thumb and forefinger. "I don't deserve this. Why should you go out on a limb for someone you scarcely know?"

"That's okay," she said. "I'm sure you'd have done just the same for me."

"If there is anything I can do in return . . . ?"

She frowned, shook her head vehemently, and then said, "Well . . . maybe. . . ."

"Name it."

"Could I have one of your shoes?"

He laughed delightedly. "Have both of them!"

"Thanks, but I wouldn't have room."

He bent forward, undid the laces, pulled off his right shoe, and handed it to Cinderella.

"It's a beautiful shoe," she said, holding it up to the light. "Thank you *so* much."

And that is the end of the story.

Robert F. Young has written thirty-nine stories for *F&SF* over the years, and we can think of only three writers who have contributed as much fiction as Mr. Young (Poul Anderson, Avram Davidson, and Ron Goulart). A Robert Young story is always a pleasure because its high quality is as predictable as its subject matter is unpredictable. Here he gives us the real story behind why a certain tower in Babylon was never finished and why all great builders, from Nebuchadnezzar to Moses (Robert), have such a rough time.

Project Hi-Rise

by ROBERT F. YOUNG

As soon as we got word that the strike was on, we walked off the job. It was 10:40 A.M. Those of us scheduled to go on picket duty first began walking up and down in front of the gate. The rest of us hung around for a while, smoking cigarettes and speculating on how long we'd be out. Then we meandered on home.

The minute she saw me, Debbie's face fell. When we voted the Union in last month, she had a fit, and ever since then she's been dreading a walkout. How were we going to manage now, she asked me when I came in the door, with prices the way they were and with no money coming in? I told her not to worry, that with the Project so close to completion and the King on their backs morning, noon and night, the Company would have to come across pronto. She said she hoped so, what with another mouth to feed any day now and our savings account down to two figures, and what would I like for dinner—baked fish or fried figs? I said baked fish.

Women don't understand about strikes, about how important it is for workers to show who they're working for that they mean business when they say they want more money. Sure, I know the Project's an important undertaking, but construction workers have to live the same as anybody else, no matter how important what they're constructing is. Like the Organizer says, it's dog-eat-dog these days, and workingmen have to look out for themselves, nobody else is going to.

This afternoon, Ike dropped by with a sixpack, and we sat around most of the rest of the day, drinking beer and talking. He's up for picket duty tonight; I'm not scheduled till tomorrow morning. I'm glad, because that'll give me a chance to attend the Union meeting tonight. Ike told me to listen real good so I could tell him all about it, and I said I would.

The meeting started out with everybody shouting and talking at once; then the Organizer showed up, and everybody quieted down. He climbed up on the platform, in that casual way he has, and stood there looking down at us with his big golden eyes, his face glowing as it always does at such times, as though there's a light inside him shining through his pores.

"Brethren," he said in that rich resonant voice of his, and instantly he had everybody's complete attention. It's no wonder we jumped at the chance to have him represent us at the bargaining table when he so generously offered to.

"Brethren," he repeated. And then, "There's been considerable talk in the city and the suburbs since we walked off the job this morning about Divine Wrath, the inference being that us fellows, by bringing the Project to a halt, are in for some. Well, don't you believe it, fellow members of Local 209—don't you believe it for one minute! Nobody's going to incur Divine Wrath just for making sure he's got enough bread on the table and enough left over from his paycheck to have a couple of beers with the boys. If anybody's going to incur it, the Company is. Because I happen to have it from a pretty good source—and you can quote me on this if you like—that somebody up there doesn't *want* the Project completed."

All of us applauded. It was just what we'd wanted to hear. After the applause died away, the Organizer outlined what we were striking for, and I paid strict attention so I could tell Ike. It adds up to a pretty nice package: a fifteen-percent across-the-board hourly rate increase; full-paid hospitalization; retirement after twenty-five years service; nine paid holidays; three weeks vacation after four years on the job; and a podiatric clinic, financed and maintained by the Company, where brickmakers can receive immediate treatment for chilblains, arthritis and fallen arches.

After the meeting a bunch of us stopped in The Fig Leaf for a few beers. I was still there when Ike got off picket duty and dropped by. I told him about the package and he agreed it was a nice one. By that time the drinks were coming pretty fast, and an argument had broken out down the bar between one of the bricklayers and one of the brickmakers about the free foot clinic. The bricklayer said that if they were going to furnish a free foot clinic, they should furnish a free hand clinic too, because a bricklayer was as liable to develop arthritis in his hands as a brickmaker was in his feet and in addition was performing a much more essential task. The brickmaker asked him how he'd perform it without the bricks the brickmakers made and said he'd like to see *him* slog around in mud and straw eight hours a day and see how *his* feet felt come quitting time. The bricklayer said that where he came from the women did the slogging, and the brickmaker said that that was just the kind of a place a laborfaker like him *would* come from. Somebody broke it up just in time.

Not long afterward I left. I didn't want to be hung-over on my first spell of picket duty. It was a cool night, and the stars were thick in the sky. I caught glimpses of the Project as I made my way home through the narrow streets. It dominates the whole city. The whole Plain, for that matter. It had sort of a pale, blurred look in the starlight, the six completed stages blending together, the uncompleted seventh one softly serrated against the night sky. Working on it every day, I've kind of forgot how high it is, how much higher it's going to be when we get back on the job. The highest thing ever, they say. I won't dispute that. It makes a palm tree look like a blade of grass and a man look like an ant. Looking at it tonight, I felt proud to be one of the builders. It was as though I'd built the whole thing myself. That's the way a bricklayer feels sometimes. It's really great. I feel sorry for brickmakers. You'd never catch me slogging all day in a mud hole.

Picket duty wasn't as bad as I thought it would be. There's been some talk about the Company hiring scabs, but I guess that's all it is —talk. Anyway, nobody tried to get in. Not that they'd have succeeded if they had. The setup is ideal for picketing. You'd almost think the Company had built the wall around the Project to make it easy for strikers to picket the place, come strike time, instead of to keep people from stealing bricks. The gate's pretty wide, of course, but four pickets can guard it easily, and the wall's high enough to discourage anybody from trying to scale it.

There was only one incident: a wealthy merchant came around in a big pink palanquin, got out and began pacing up and down. He didn't say anything—just kept looking up at that half-finished seventh stage and shaking his head. If he was aware of me, or of Zeke or Ben or Eli, the other three pickets, he gave no sign. Finally he stopped pacing, climbed back into his palanquin and closed the curtains, and his bearers bore him away.

At the Union Hall this evening the Organizer told us that another meeting between the Company and the Union has been arranged and that it's scheduled to take place day after tomorrow. This time, there's going to be a Mediator present—one that the King himself appointed. Maybe now we'll get somewhere. I hope so. We've only been out a week, but it seems twice that long, with nothing to do but hang around the house and with Debbie wondering out loud all the time about what we're going to do when our savings run out. To tell the truth, I'm kind of worried myself. Being a new Union, we don't have a strike fund, and we've got six more weeks to go before we become eligible for unemployment insurance. Meanwhile, the bills keep coming in.

The second meeting is to take place this afternoon. All of us have our fingers crossed.

I drew picket duty again this morning. Ike picketed with me, having arranged it with the Organizer to change places with Ben. With my old buddy to talk to, time went by fast.

Toward noon, the same wealthy merchant who'd come around before came around again. After climbing out of his palanquin, he started pacing up and down the way he'd done on his first visit; only this time instead of looking up at the half-finished seventh stage and shaking his head, he kept glancing sideways at Ike and Eli and Zeke and me. Finally he singled me out and came over to where I was standing, shooting the breeze with Ike. He had pink cheeks, with jowls to match, and a big blunt nose. You only had to take one look at his hands to know he'd never done a lick of work in his life.

"You impress me as being a sensible young man," he said. "What's your name?"

"Jake," I said.

"Jake. Well, Jake, I happen to be a wealthy merchant, as you may have guessed. In Frankincense and Myrrh. But I'm here just as an ordinary citizen—a citizen who is doing his level best to try to understand why certain other citizens have put their personal interests above the common interests of the community-as-a-whole and aborted a community project."

"I thought it was a Company project," Ike said, butting in.

"The Company is in the King's employ. The King, *ex officio*, is the very essence of the community. Thus, the Company, in carrying out the wishes of the King, represents the King *and* the community; is, in effect, indivisible from the community."

"Not in my book," I said. "But I can see why it would be in yours. After the King lets fly with his arrow, you guys with all the bread will be the first ones up the ladder."

The wealthy merchant stiffened. "Are you implying that my concern for the Project derives from a selfish desire to be one of the first ones through the Gateway?"

"He's not implying it, he's saying it," Ike said. "You guys just can't wait to grease old Yahweh's palm, can you? You can't wait to tell him you think the King is a kook."

The wealthy merchant's pink cheeks were now a shade darker than his jowls. A purplish cloud had begun to gather on his forehead. "Young man," he said, "you sound positively paganistic. Don't *you* want to get into Heaven?"

"Not if you fat cats get there first," Ike said.

The purplish cloud broke. "Well, you may rest assured you aren't going to!" the wealthy merchant shouted. "Not if I have anything to say about it!" He pointed successively at Eli and Zeke and me. "And neither are you or you or you!" With that, he stamped back to his palanquin, got in and yanked the curtains closed, and the bearers trotted off with it. We stood there laughing.

Tonight at the Hall, the Organizer told us to tighten our belts, that at the bargaining table this afternoon the Company had refused to budge from its original offer of a flat five-percent raise and that he, as our representative, had informed them they could shove it and that despite the Mediator's pleas both sides had walked out.

Afterward, Ike and I stopped in The Fig Leaf for a couple of beers. Ike seemed worried. "Do you think he really has our best interests at heart, Jake?" he asked.

"Of course he does!"

"I suppose you're right. But sometimes I get the feeling that he's using us guys for some purpose of his own."

"What purpose?"

"I don't know. It's just a feeling—that's all."

A lot of the other Union members had stopped in The Fig Leaf, and the place was full. Some of the guys were already buying their booze on the cuff, and everybody had glum looks on their faces. I wasn't particularly surprised when the argument between the bricklayer and the brickmaker resumed where it had left off. This time, nobody broke it up.

It was late when I finally got home. All evening I'd dreaded having to face Debbie with the bad news. But when I looked in the bedroom, she was sound asleep.

At long last the Mediator has got both sides to agree to another meeting. It's to take place tomorrow morning. I think the Organizer should back down a little—settle, say, for a ten-percent raise and forget the fringe benefits. True, it's only been two weeks since we walked off the job, but Debbie and I have already run up a sizable food bill at the Mom & Pop store around the corner, what's left of our savings will just about cover the rent, and I'm smoking Bugler instead of Winstons. And any day now, as Debbie keeps reminding me, we're going to have another mouth to feed. Feeding it doesn't worry me half so much as paying the hospital and doctor bills.

Ike and I were on picket duty when we heard that the latest bargaining session had gone Pffft! Eli was on too, and a bricklayer named Dan. It was clear by this time that the Organizer had no intention of settling for a smaller package, and it was equally as clear that the Company had no intention of coming through with a bigger one.

Eli didn't see it that way. "Hell, Jake, they'll have to come through," he said. "We've got them right by the balls!"

I told him I hoped he was right.

"Look," Dan said. "We've got a visitor."

Four black bearers had appeared, bearing a long black palanquin. They proceeded to set it down directly before the gate. I knew from its length that here was no ordinary wealthy merchant, but I was unprepared for the personage who presently stepped out and stood gazing at the Project with black blazing eyes. Those eyes burned right through Ike and Eli and Dan and me, as though we weren't even there, then swept upward, absorbing the entire Project with a single glance. It dawned on me finally, as I took in the small gold crown nestled in the black ringleted hair, the flared eyebrows, the fierce nostrils and the defiant jaw, that I was looking at the King.

As the four of us stood there staring at him, he raised his eyes still higher, and their blackness seemed to intensify, to throw forth fire. It was the briefest of illusions, for a moment later he turned, climbed back into his palanquin and clapped his hands. We stared after it as the four black bearers bore it away.

"Whew!" Ike said.

I rolled and lit a cigarette to see how bad my hands were shaking. Pretty bad, I saw. I blew out a lungful of smoke. "I wonder what he wanted," I said.

"I don't know. But I'd hate to be in the Organizer's sandals."

"The Organizer can take care of himself."

"I hope so."

We let it go at that.

You've got to give the Mediator credit. Somehow he managed to get the two sides together again.

The Organizer had the minutes of the meeting Xeroxed and distributed them among the members. I have mine before me:

THE MEDIATOR: The Company Representative has informed me that considerable confusion exists among the populace as to the true nature of the Project's purpose, and he would like to clear this little matter up before proceeding further with the negotiations.

THE ORGANIZER: The purpose of the Project has no bearing

whatsoever upon the reasonable demands made upon the Company by Local 209.

THE MEDIATOR: Nevertheless, I feel that in fairness both to the Company and to the King that the confusion should be cleared up.

THE ORGANIZER: Very well. But keep in mind that the typical member of Local 209 is concerned solely with how much his efforts will net him, not with the use to which their end result will be put.

THE COMPANY REPRESENTATIVE: I will be brief. Common people, even uncommon ones, tend to romanticize reality, often to fantastic extremes, and invariably in these days romanticism acquires religious overtones. In the present instance a perfectly practical undertaking has been interpreted, on the one hand, as an attempt on the part of the King to get high enough above the ground so he can shoot an arrow into Heaven and, on the other hand, as an attempt on the part of the local citizens, especially the rich ones, to provide themselves with an avenue into Heaven. The two interpretations have somehow intermingled and become one. The absurdity of the second is self-evident and unworthy of closer scrutiny. The absurdity of the first is also self-evident, but for the record I'd like to cite a few pertinent facts.

According to the best estimates of our astronomers, Heaven is located 1,432 cubits above the world. The Project, if it is completed, will reach a height of 205 cubits. This means that the King's arrow would have to travel 1,227 cubits—straight up. Now, it is a well-known fact that the King is a great hunter—a *mighty* hunter. No one can bend a bow the way he can. But *1,227 cubits? Straight up?*

Thus, the facts alone make it clear that the King has no such intent. His real purpose in building the Project is to provide a haven. A haven to which the people can flee should a second phenomenal rainfall again cause the Twin Rivers to overflow their banks to such an extent that the entire Plain becomes inundated. Living on that Plain, the members of Local 209 stand to benefit from the Project as much as the rest of the people. For them to have, in effect, sabotaged such a noble undertaking is, frankly, beyond my comprehension, unless their motive for doing so can be partially attributed to their unwitting acceptance of the popular interpretation of the Project's purpose.

THE ORGANIZER: If the Project's real purpose is to provide a haven, why weren't they and the rest of the people so informed in the first place?

THE COMPANY REPRESENTATIVE: I cannot, of course, speak for the King. But I should imagine that he considered it so glaringly obvious that there was no need for the dissemination of such information.

THE ORGANIZER: To me, it was never obvious. It still isn't. In the first place, only minimal flooding has occurred since the Inundation; in the second, it's highly unlikely that Yahweh will again choose that particular form of chastisement should future foul-ups on the part of the human race necessitate additional punishment; and in the third, if he does decide on a second Inundation, you can rest assured that it will be of such dimensions that the only thing the Project will be a haven for will be fish. But I'll play the game fair: I'll see to it that the members of Local 209 have access to these minutes; and if, after reading them, they wish to take another strike vote, I won't stand in their way. Meanwhile, the package stays as is.

There was a special meeting tonight at the Union Hall. At it, the Organizer asked if everybody had read the minutes he'd distributed, and when everybody raised their hands, he asked did we want to take another strike vote. There was a big chorus of nays and not a single yea. That shows how Union brothers stick together when the chips are down.

I've got to admit, though, that before I yelled my nay I had a bad moment. I'm still not sure I did right. Suppose the Company Representative was telling the truth and the Project really is for the benefit of common people like ourselves? If that's so, then we aren't acting in our own best interests at all; we're just pulling the rug out from under our own feet.

The Company has pulled out!
Zeke brought us the news while we were on picket duty this morning. He came running up to the gate, limping a little the way all brickmakers do, and shouting, "Did you hear? Did you hear? The Company's gone! They've struck their tents and left!"

I stood there stunned. So did Ike. So did Eli and Dan. Ike got his breath back first. "Where's the Organizer?" he asked Zeke in a sort of whisper.

"He's gone too. We can't find him anywhere."

There was a silence. Then Zeke said, "I've got to go tell the rest of the guys." He looked at us kind of helplessly. "I guess there's not much sense picketing any more."

"No, I guess not," I said.

After he left, none of us said a word for a long time. Then Ike whispered, "It was like I said all along. The Organizer was using us."

"But why?" Dan asked.

Ike shook his head. "I don't know."

"We've got company," Eli announced.

We looked. It was that long black palanquin again. Out of it stepped the King.

This time, he had brought his bow with him. It was slung diagonally across his back. His right hand held an arrow.

Again those black and burning eyes of his seemed to absorb the Project from its bottommost brick to its topmost one. There was a purposefulness about his mien that had been lacking on his previous visit; a fierce, almost an awesome, determination that made him seem larger than life. His black eyebrows were like the wings of a hawk; his lips were set like bitumen. He was wearing a maroon turtleneck with a big N on the front, blue Levis and thick-soled chukka boots.

He strode toward the gate. The four of us were standing right in his path, and we stepped aside when he neared us. If we hadn't, he'd have bowled us over.

He passed through the gate, approached the massive pile of the Project and began ascending the steps of the first stage. Ike and I, coming out of our daze, followed him. Not to try and stop him but to catch him in case he slipped and fell.

When he reached the apron of the second stage, he strode across it and began ascending the second series of steps. We kept right on his heels. It was at this point that I noticed he was mumbling something under his breath. I listened hard, but I couldn't make out what it was.

He surmounted the second stage. The third. Ike and I stayed right behind him. The fourth. The fifth. We were high now. Looking down over my left shoulder, I could see the diminutive dwellings of the city and the minuscule mud huts of the suburbs. Looking down over my right, I could see the Plain, with its myriad fields of millet and barley and its sparkling irrigation ditches. In the distance the easternmost of the Twin Rivers gleamed like gold in the morning sun.

Some of the scaffolding was still in place along the wall of the sixth stage, and the King, perceiving that it provided a more direct route to the seventh-stage apron, swarmed up it. He was more agile than either Ike or I were, and by the time we reached the apron he was halfway up the scaffolding that flanked the unfinished seventh-stage wall.

I became aware of the wind. It was blowing steadily up from the south. I could smell the sea in it. The Project swayed, ever so slightly. But that was all right. The engineers had allowed for the wind. I'd felt it sway lots of times, and I was no stranger to the wind.

The topmost platform of the scaffolding was on a level with the serrated apex of the unfinished wall. Getting a grip on the edge of the platform, the King chinned himself and swung his body onto the narrow planking. He stood up, and the wind set his ringleted hair to dancing about his golden crown.

Ike and I remained on the apron below.

The King shook his fist at the blue and cloudless sky. "I knew all along that fucking Organizer was working for you!" he shouted. "He never fooled me for a second! But he wasted his time, because I'm still gonna do what I said I was gonna do, right from here!" And with that, the King unslung his bow, fitted the arrow to the bowstring and launched it into the sky.

Straight up, it sped, impervious to the wind, seeming to gather momentum with every cubit it traveled. Ike and I no longer breathed. Everything in all creation except that arrow had ceased to exist for us. In our eyes it had become a thunderbolt—a thunderbolt cast heavenward by a madman in a magnificent, if senseless, gesture of defiance.

It neither faltered nor slowed. Any moment now, it seemed, it would pass through the invisible Gateway and disappear. It was high enough: it *had* to. But it didn't. For, all of a sudden, a great hand emerged from the firmament, reached down and seized the tiny shaft. A mighty thumb pressed it between two mighty fingers. There was a distant *snap!*, barely audible above the wind. Then the hand withdrew, and the broken arrow fell back to earth and landed at the King's feet.

He stood there staring down at it.

An aeon went by. There was no sound except the whistling of the wind in the scaffolding. Then a loud sob reached our ears. Another. We turned away and slowly descended the successive stages to the ground. We didn't look back—not once. You might think you'd enjoy seeing a king cry, but you wouldn't. It's like watching a mountain dwindle into an anthill, a city crumble into dust, a kingdom turn into trash.

Well, Local 209 pulled out, just like the Company did. We knew there'd be no more jobs on the Plain for the likes of us. We spread out all over. North and south and east and west. I went south. Right now, I've got a flunky's job in a granary. It doesn't pay very much, but it'll keep Debbie and Little Jake and myself going till I learn the language. Once I learn the language, I'll get back in Construction. There's a big project about to begin just east of here. From what I gather, it's a tomb of some kind, and it's supposed to set a new trend. Building it may take as long as a year, and they're going to need all kinds of skilled labor. I figure that as a bricklayer I can get on easy.

Samuel R. (Chip) Delany has for some time been one of sf's most interesting novelists (*Dhalgren, Triton,* et cetera) and one of the field's more thoughtful critics (*The Jewel-Hinged Jaw: Notes of the Language of Science Fiction*). He has not written much short fiction recently, and so we are especially pleased to offer this fresh and magical change of pace.

Prismatica

by SAMUEL R. DELANY

Hommage à James Thurber

Once there was a poor man named Amos. He had nothing but his bright red hair, fast fingers, quick feet, and quicker wits. One grey evening when the rain rumbled in the clouds, about to fall, he came down the cobbled street toward Mariner's Tavern to play jackstraws with Billy Belay, the sailor with a wooden leg and a mouth full of stories that he chewed around and spit out all evening. Billy Belay would talk and drink and laugh, and sometimes sing. Amos would sit quietly and listen—and always win at jackstraws.

But this evening as Amos came into the tavern, Billy was quiet, and so was everyone else. Even Hidalga, the woman who owned the tavern and took no man's jabbering seriously, was leaning her elbows on the counter and listening with opened mouth.

The only man speaking was tall, thin, and grey. He wore a grey cape, grey gloves, grey boots, and his hair was grey. His voice sounded to Amos like wind over mouse fur, or sand ground into old velvet. The only thing about him not grey was a large black trunk beside him, high as his shoulder. Several rough and grimy sailors with cutlasses sat at his table—they were so dirty they were no color at all!

". . . and so," the soft grey voice went on, "I need someone clever and brave enough to help my nearest and dearest friend and me. It will be well worth someone's while."

"Who is your friend?" asked Amos. Though he had not heard the beginning of the story, the whole tavern seemed far too quiet for a Saturday night.

The grey man turned and raised grey eyebrows. "There is my friend, my nearest and dearest." He pointed to the trunk. From it came a low, muggy sound: *Ulmphf.*

All the mouths that were hanging open about the tavern closed.

"What sort of help does he need?" asked Amos. "A doctor?"

The grey eyes widened, and all the mouths opened once more.

"You are talking of my nearest and dearest friend," said the grey voice, softly.

From across the room Billy Belay tried to make a sign for Amos to be quiet, but the grey man turned around, and the finger Billy had put to his lips went quickly into his mouth as if he were picking his teeth.

"Friendship is a rare thing these days," said Amos. "What sort of help do you and your friend need?"

"The question is: would you be willing to give it?" said the grey man.

"And the answer is: if it is worth my while," said Amos, who really could think very quickly.

"Would it be worth all the pearls you could put in your pockets, all the gold you could carry in one hand, all the diamonds you could lift in the other, and all the emeralds you could haul up from a well in a brass kettle?"

"That is not much for true friendship," said Amos.

"If you saw a man living through the happiest moment of his life, would it be worth it then?"

"Perhaps it would," Amos admitted.

"Then you'll help my friend and me?"

"For all the pearls I can put in my pockets, all the gold I can carry in one hand, all the diamonds I can lift in the other, all the emeralds I can haul up from a well in a brass kettle, and a chance to see a man living through the happiest moment of his life—I'll help you!"

Billy Belay put his head down on the table and began to cry.

Hidalga buried her face in her hands, and everyone else in the tavern turned away and began to look rather grey themselves.

"Then come with me," said the grey man, and the rough sailors with cutlasses rose about him and hoisted the trunk to their grimy shoulders—*Onvbpmf,* came the thick sound from the trunk—and the grey man flung out his cape, grabbed Amos by the hand, and ran out into the street.

In the sky the clouds swirled and bumped each other, trying to upset the rain.

Halfway down the cobbled street the grey man cried, "Halt!"

Everyone halted and put the trunk down on the sidewalk.

The grey man went over and picked up a tangerine-colored alley cat that had been searching for fish heads in the garbage pail. "Open the trunk," he said. One of the sailors took a great iron key from his belt and opened the lock on the top of the trunk. The grey man took out his thin sword of grey steel and pried up the lid ever so slightly. Then he tossed the cat inside.

Immediately he let the lid drop again, and the sailor with the iron key locked the lock on the top of the box. From inside came the mew of a cat that ended with a deep, depressing: *Elmblmpf.*

"I think," said Amos, who thought quickly and was quick to tell what he thought, "that everything is not quite right in there."

"Be quiet and help me," said the thin grey man, "or I shall put *you* in the trunk with my nearest and dearest."

For a moment, Amos was just a little afraid.

II

Then they were on a ship, and all the boards were grey from having gone so long without paint. The grey man took Amos into his cabin and they sat down on opposite sides of a table.

"Now," said the grey man, "here is a map."

"Where did you get it?" asked Amos.

"I stole it from my worse and worst enemy."

"What is it a map of?" Amos asked. He knew you should ask as many questions as possible when there were so many things you didn't know.

"It is a map of many places and many treasures, and I need someone to help me find them."

"Are these treasures the pearls and gold and diamonds and emeralds you told me about?"

"Nonsense," said the grey man. "I have more emeralds and diamonds and gold and pearls than I know what to do with," and he opened a closet door.

Amos stood blinking as jewels by the thousands fell out on the floor, glittering and gleaming, red, green, and yellow.

"Help me push them back in the closet," said the grey man. "They're so bright that if I look at them too long, I get a headache."

So they pushed the jewels back and leaned against the closet door till it closed. Then they returned to the map.

"Then what *are* the treasures?" Amos asked, full of curiosity.

"The treasure is happiness, for me and my nearest and dearest friend."

"How do you intend to find it?"

"In a mirror," said the grey man. "In three mirrors, or rather, one mirror broken in three pieces."

"A broken mirror is bad luck," said Amos. "Who broke it?"

"A wizard so great and old and so terrible that you and I need never worry about him."

"Does this map tell where the pieces are hidden?"

"Exactly," said the grey man. "Look, we are here."

"How can you tell?"

"The map says so," said the grey man. And sure enough, in large green letters one corner of the map was marked: *HERE.*

"Perhaps somewhere nearer than you think, up this one, and two leagues short of over there, the pieces are hidden."

"Your greatest happiness will be to look into this mirror?"

"It will be the greatest happiness of myself and of my nearest and dearest friend."

"Very well," said Amos. "When do we start?"

"When the dawn is foggy and the sun is hidden and the air is grey as grey can be."

"Very well," said Amos a second time. "Until then, I shall walk around and explore your ship."

"It will be tomorrow at four o'clock in the morning," said the grey man. "So don't stay up too late."

"Very well," said Amos a third time.

As Amos was about to leave, the grey man picked up a brilliant red ruby that had fallen from the closet and not been put back. On the side of the trunk that now sat in the corner was a small triangular door that Amos had not seen. The grey man pulled it open, tossed in the ruby, and slammed it quickly: *Orghmflbfe.*

III

Outside, the clouds hung so low the top of the ship's tallest mast threatened to prick one open. The wind tossed about in Amos' red hair and scurried in and out of his rags. Sitting on the railing of the ship was a sailor splicing a rope.

"Good evening," said Amos. "I'm exploring the ship and I have very little time. I have to be up at four o'clock in the morning. So can you tell me what I must be sure to avoid because it would be so silly and uninteresting that I would learn nothing from it?"

The sailor frowned a little while, then said, "There is nothing at all interesting in the ship's brig."

"Thank you very much," said Amos and walked on till he came to another sailor whose feet were awash in soap suds. The sailor was pushing a mop back and forth so hard that Amos decided he was trying to scrub the last bit of color off the grey boards. "Good evening to you too," said Amos. "I'm exploring the ship and I have very little time since I'm to be up at four o'clock in the morning. I was told to avoid the brig. So could you point it out to me? I don't want to wander into it by accident."

The sailor leaned his chin on his mop handle awhile, then said, "If you want to avoid it, don't go down the second hatchway behind the wheelhouse."

"Thank you very much," said Amos and hurried off to the wheelhouse. When he found the second hatchway, he went down very quickly and was just about to go to the barred cell when he saw the grimy sailor with the great iron key—who must be the jailor as well, thought Amos.

"Good evening," Amos said. "How are you?"

"I'm fine, and how is yourself, and what are you doing down here?"

"I'm standing here, trying to be friendly," said Amos. "I was told there was nothing of interest down here. And since it is so dull, I thought I would keep you company."

The sailor fingered his key awhile, then said, "That is kind of you, I suppose."

"Yes, it is," said Amos. "What do they keep here that is so uninteresting everyone tells me to avoid it?"

"This is the ship's brig and we keep prisoners here. What else should we keep?"

"That's a good question," said Amos. "What *do* you keep?"

The jailor fingered his key again, then said, "Nothing of interest at all."

Just then, behind the bars, Amos saw the pile of grubby grey blankets move. A corner fell away and he saw just the edge of something as red as his own bright hair.

"I suppose, then," said Amos, "I've done well to avoid coming here." And he turned around and left.

But that night, as the rain poured over the deck, and the drum-drum-drumming of heavy drops lulled everyone on the ship to sleep, Amos hurried over the slippery boards under the dripping eaves of the wheelhouse to the second hatchway, and went down. The lamps were low, the jailor was huddled asleep in a corner on a piece of grey canvas, but Amos went immediately to the bars and looked through.

More blankets had fallen away, and besides a red as bright as his own hair, he could see a green the color of parrot's feathers, a yellow as pale as Chinese mustard, and a blue brilliant as the sky at eight o'clock in July. Have you ever watched someone asleep under a pile of blankets? You can see the blankets move up and down, up and down with breathing. That's how Amos knew this was a person. "Psssst," he said. "You colorful but uninteresting person, wake up and talk to me."

Then all the blankets fell away, and a man with more colors on him than Amos had ever seen sat up rubbing his eyes. His sleeves were green silk with blue and purple trimming. His cape was crimson with orange design. His shirt was gold with rainbow checks, and one boot was white and the other was black.

"Who are you?" asked the particolored prisoner.

"I am Amos, and I am here to see what makes you so uninteresting that everyone tells me to avoid you and covers you up with blankets."

"I am Jack, the Prince of the Far Rainbow, and I am a prisoner here."

"Neither one of those facts is so incredible compared to some of the strange things in this world," said Amos. "Why are you the Prince of the Far Rainbow, and why are you a prisoner?"

"Ah," said Jack, "the second question is easy to answer, but the first is not so simple. I am a prisoner here because a skinny grey man stole a map from me and put me in the brig so I could not get it back from him. But why am I the Prince of the Far Rainbow? That is exactly the question asked me a year ago today by a wizard so great and so old and so terrible that you and I need never worry about him. I answered him, 'I am Prince because my father is King, and everyone knows I should be.' Then the wizard asked me, 'Why should you be Prince and not one of a dozen others? Are you fit to rule, can you judge fairly, can you resist temptation?' I had no idea what he meant, and again I answered, 'I am Prince because my father is King.' The wizard took a mirror and held it before me. 'What do you see?' he asked. 'I see myself, just as I should, the Prince of the Far Rainbow,' said I. Then the wizard grew furious and struck the mirror into three pieces and cried, 'Not until you look into this mirror whole again will you be Prince of the Far Rainbow, for a woman worthy of a prince is trapped behind the glass, and not till she is free can you rule in your own land.' There was an explosion, and when I woke up, I was without my crown, lying dressed as you see me now in a green meadow. In my pocket was a map that told me where all the pieces were hidden. Only it did not show me how to get back to the Far Rainbow. And still I do not know how to get home."

"I see, I see," said Amos. "How did the skinny grey man steal it from you, and what does he want with it?"

"Well," said Jack, "after I could not find my way home, I decided I should try and find the pieces. So I began to search. The first person I met was the thin grey man, and with him was his large black trunk in which, he said, was his nearest and dearest friend. He said if I would work for him and carry his trunk, he would pay me a great deal of money with which I could buy a ship and continue my search. He told me that he himself would very much like to see a woman worthy of a prince. 'Especially,' he said, 'such a colorful prince as you.' I carried his trunk for many months, and at last he paid me a great deal of money with which I bought a ship. But then the skinny grey man stole my map, stole my ship, and put me here in the brig, and told me that he and his nearest and dearest friend would find the mirror all for themselves."

"What could he want with a woman worthy of a prince?" asked Amos.

"I don't even like to think about it," said Jack. "Once he asked me to unzip the leather flap at the end of the trunk and stick my head in to see how his nearest and dearest friend was getting along. But I would not because I had seen him catch a beautiful blue bird with red feathers round its neck and stick it through the same zipper, and all there was was an uncomfortable sound from the trunk, something like: *Orulmhf*."

"Oh, yes," said Amos. "I know the sound. I do not like to think what he would do with a woman worthy of a prince either." Yet Amos found himself thinking of it anyway. "His lack of friendship for you certainly doesn't speak well of his friendship for his nearest and dearest."

Jack nodded.

"Why doesn't he get the mirror himself, instead of asking me?" Amos wanted to know.

"Did you look at where the pieces were hidden?" asked Jack.

"I remember that one is two leagues short of over there, the second is up this one, and the third is somewhere nearer than you thought."

"That's right," said Jack. "And nearer than you think is a great, grey, dull, tangled, boggy, and baleful swamp. The first piece is at the bottom of a luminous pool in the center. But it is so grey there that the grey man would blend completely in with the scenery and never get out again. Up this one is a mountain so high that the North Wind lives in a cave there. The second piece of the mirror is on the highest peak of that mountain. It is so windy there, and the grey man is so thin, he would be blown away before he was halfway to the top. Two leagues short of over there, where the third piece is, there stretches a garden of violent colors and rich perfume where black butterflies glisten on the rims of pink marble fountains, and bright vines weave in and about. The only thing white in the garden is a silver-white unicorn who guards the last piece of the mirror. Perhaps the grey man could get that piece himself, but he will not want to, I know, for lots of bright colors give him a headache."

"Then it says something for his endurance that he was able to put up with your glittering clothes for so long," said Amos. "Anyway, I don't think it's fair of our grey friend to get your mirror with your map. You should at least have a chance at it. Let me see, the first place we are going is somewhere nearer than you think."

"In the swamp then," said Jack.

"Would you like to come with me," asked Amos, "and get the piece yourself."

"Of course," said Jack. "But how?"

"I have a plan," said Amos, who could think very quickly when he had to. "Simply do as I say." Amos began to whisper through the bars. Behind them the jailor snored on his piece of canvas.

IV

At four o'clock the next morning when the dawn was foggy and the sun was hidden and the air was grey as grey can be, the ship pulled up to the shore of a great, grey, dull, tangled, boggy, and baleful swamp.

"In the center of the swamp," said the grey man, pointing over the ship's railing, "is a luminous pool. At the bottom of the pool is a piece of mirror. Can you be back by lunch?"

"I think so," said Amos. "But that *is* a terribly grey swamp. I might blend into the scenery so completely I might never get out of it again."

"With your red hair?" asked the grey man.

"My red hair," said Amos, "is only on the top of my head. My clothes are ragged and dirty and will probably turn grey in no time with all that mist. Are there any bright-colored clothes on the ship, glittering with gold and gleaming with silk?"

"There is my closet full of jewels," said the grey man. "Wear as many as you want."

"They would weigh me down," said Amos, "and I could not be back for lunch. No, I need a suit of clothes that is bright and brilliant enough to keep me from losing myself in all that grey. For if I *do* lose myself, *you* will never have your mirror."

So the grey man turned to one of his sailors and said, "You know where you can get him such a suit."

As the man started to go, Amos said, "It seems a shame to take someone's clothes away, especially since I might not come back anyway. Give my rags to whoever owns this suit to keep for me until I

come back." Amos jumped out of his rags and handed them to the
sailor who trotted off toward the wheelhouse. Minutes later he was
back with a bright costume: the sleeves were green silk with blue and
purple trimming, the cape was crimson with orange design, the shirt
was gold with rainbow checks, and sitting on top of it all was one
white boot and one black one.

"These are what I need," said Amos, putting on the clothes
quickly, for he was beginning to get chilly standing in his underwear.
Then he climbed over the edge of the boat into the swamp. He was
so bright and colorful that nobody saw the figure in dirty rags run
quickly behind them to the far end of the ship and also climb over
into the swamp. Had the figure been Amos—it was wearing Amos'
rags—the red hair might have attracted some attention, but Jack's
hair, for all his colorful costume, was a very ordinary brown.

The grey man looked after Amos until he disappeared. Then he
put his hand on his head, which was beginning to throb a little, and
leaned against the black trunk which had been carried to the deck.

Glumphvmr, came from the trunk.

"Oh, my nearest and dearest friend," said the grey man, "I had almost forgotten you. Forgive me." He took from his pocket an envelope, and from the envelope he took a large, fluttering moth. "This
flew in my window last night," he said. The wings were pale blue,
with brown bands on the edges, and the undersides were flecked with
spots of gold. He pushed in a long metal flap at the side of the trunk,
very like a mail slot, and slid the moth inside.

Fuffle, came from the trunk, and the grey man smiled.

In the swamp, Amos waited until the prince had found him. "Did
you have any trouble?" Amos asked.

"Not at all," laughed Jack. "They didn't even notice that the jailor
was gone." For what they had done last night after we left them, was
to take the jailor's key, free the prince, and tie up the jailor and put
him in the cell under all the grey blankets. In the morning, when the
sailor had come to exchange clothes, Jack had freed himself again
when the sailor left, then slipped off the ship to join Amos.

"Now let us find your luminous pool," said Amos, "so we can be
back by lunch."

Together they started through the marsh and muck. "You know,"
said Amos, stopping once to look at a grey spider web that spread

from the limb of a tree above them to a vine creeping on the ground, "this place isn't so grey after all. Look closely."

And in each drop of water on each strand of the web, the light was broken up as if through a tiny prism into blues and yellows and reds. As they looked, Jack sighed. "These are the colors of the Far Rainbow," he said.

He said no more, but Amos felt very sorry for him. They went quickly now toward the center of the swamp. "No, it isn't completely grey," said Jack. On a stump beside them a green-grey lizard blinked a red eye at them, a golden hornet buzzed above their heads, and a snake that was grey on top rolled out of their way and showed an orange belly.

"And look at that!" cried Amos.

Ahead through the tall grey tree trunks, silvery light rose in the mist.

"The luminous pool!" cried the prince, and they ran forward.

Sure enough they found themselves on the edge of a round, silvery pool. Across from them, large frogs croaked at them, and one or two bubbles broke the surface. Together Amos and Jack looked into the water.

Perhaps they expected to see the mirror glittering in the weeds and pebbles at the bottom of the pool; perhaps they expected their own reflections. But they saw neither. Instead, the face of a beautiful girl looked up at them from below the surface.

Jack and Amos frowned. The girl laughed, and the water bubbled.

"Who are you?" asked Amos.

And in return from the bubbles they heard, "Who are you?"

"I am Jack, Prince of the Far Rainbow," said Jack, "and this is Amos."

"I am a woman worthy of a prince," said the face in the water, "and my name is Lea."

Now Amos asked, "Why are you worthy of a prince? And how did you get where you are?"

"Ah," said Lea, "the second question is easy to answer, but the first is not so simple. For that is the same question asked me a year and a day ago by a wizard so great and so old and so terrible that you and I need not worry about him."

"What did you say to him?" asked Jack.

"I told him I could speak all the languages of men, that I was brave and strong and beautiful, and could govern beside any man. He said I was proud, and that my pride was good. But then he saw how I looked in mirrors at my own face, and he said that I was vain, and my vanity was bad, and that it would keep me apart from the prince I was worthy of. The shiny surface of all things, he told me, will keep us apart, until a prince can gather the pieces of the mirror together again, which will release me."

"Then I am the prince to save you," said Jack.

"Are you indeed?" asked Lea, smiling. "A piece of the mirror I am trapped in lies at the bottom of this pool. Once I myself dived from a rock into the blue ocean to retrieve the pearl of white fire I wear on my forehead now. That was the deepest dive ever heard of by man or woman, and this pool is ten feet deeper than that. Will you still try?"

"I will try and perhaps die trying," said Jack, "but I can do no more and no less." Then Jack filled his lungs and dove headlong into the pool.

Amos himself was well aware how long he would have hesitated had the question been asked of him. As the seconds passed, he began to fear for Jack's life, and wished he had had a chance to figure some other way to get the mirror out. One minute passed; perhaps they could have tricked the girl into bringing it up herself. Two minutes; they could have tied a string to the leg of a frog and sent him down to do the searching. Three minutes; there was not a bubble on the water, and Amos surprised himself by deciding the only thing to do was to jump in and at least try to save the prince. But there was a splash of water at his feet!

Jack's head emerged, and a moment later his hand holding the large fragment of a broken mirror came into sight.

Amos was so delighted he jumped up and down. The prince swam to shore, and Amos helped him out. Then they leaned the mirror against a tree and rested for a while. "It's well I wore these rags of yours," said Jack, "and not my own clothes, for the weeds would have caught in my cloak and the boots would have pulled me down and I would have never come up. Thank you, Amos."

"It's a very little thing to thank me for," Amos said. "But we had better start back if we want to be at the ship in time for lunch."

So they started back and by noon had nearly reached the ship. Then the prince left the mirror with Amos and darted on ahead to get back to the cell. Then Amos walked out to the boat with the broken glass.

"Well," he called up to the thin grey man who sat on the top of the trunk, waiting, "here is your mirror from the bottom of the luminous pool."

The grey man was so happy he jumped from the trunk, turned a cartwheel, then fell to wheezing and coughing and had to be slapped on the back several times.

"Good for you," he said when Amos had climbed onto the deck and given him the glass. "Now come have lunch with me, but for heaven's sake get out of that circus tent before I get another headache."

So Amos took off the prince's clothes and the sailor took them to the brig and returned with Amos' rags. When he had dressed and was about to go with the grey man to lunch, his sleeve brushed the grey man's arm. The grey man stopped and frowned so deeply his face became almost black. "These clothes are wet and the ones you wore were dry."

"So they are," said Amos. "What do you make of that?"

The grey man scowled and contemplated and cogitated, but could not make anything of it. At last he said, "Never mind. Come to lunch."

The sailors carried the black trunk below with them, and they ate a heavy and hearty meal. The grey man speared all the radishes from the salad on his knife and flipped them into a funnel he had stuck in a round opening in the trunk: *Fulrmp, Melrulf, Ulfmphgrumf!*

V

"When do I go after the next piece?" Amos asked when they had finished eating.

"Tomorrow evening when the sunset is golden and the sky is turquoise and the rocks are stained red in the setting sun," said the grey man. "I shall watch the whole proceedings with sunglasses."

"I think that's a good idea," said Amos. "You won't get such a bad headache."

That night Amos again went to the brig. No one had missed the jailor yet. So there was no guard at all.

"How is our friend doing?" Amos asked the prince, pointing to the bundle of blankets in the corner.

"Well enough," said Jack. "I gave him food and water when they brought me some. I think he's asleep now."

"Good," said Amos. "So one third of your magic mirror has been found. Tomorrow evening I go off for the second piece. Would you like to come with me?"

"I certainly would," said Jack. "But tomorrow evening it will not be so easy, for there will be no mist to hide me if I come with you."

"Then we'll work it so you won't have to hide," said Amos. "If I remember you right, the second piece is on the top of a windy mountain so high the North Wind lives in a cave there."

"That's right," said Jack.

"Very well then, I have a plan." Again Amos began to whisper through the bars, and Jack smiled and nodded.

They sailed all that night and all the next day, and toward evening they pulled in to a rocky shore where just a few hundred yards away a mountain rose high and higher into the clear twilight.

The sailors gathered on the deck of the ship just as the sun began to set, and the grey man put one grey gloved hand on Amos' shoulder and pointed to the mountain with his other. "There, among the windy peaks, is the cave of the North Wind. Even higher, on the highest and windiest peak, is the second fragment of the mirror. It is a long, dangerous, and treacherous climb. Shall I expect you back for breakfast?"

"Certainly," said Amos. "Fried eggs, if you please, once over lightly, and plenty of hot sausages."

"I will tell the cook," said the grey man.

"Good," said Amos. "Oh, but one more thing. You say it is windy there. I shall need a good supply of rope, then, and perhaps you can spare a man to go with me. A rope is not much good if there is a person only on one end. If I have someone with me, I can hold him if he blows off and he can do the same for me." Amos turned to the sailors. "What about that man there? He has a rope and is well muffled against the wind."

"Take whom you like," said the grey man, "so long as you bring back my mirror." The well-muffled sailor with the coil of rope on his shoulder stepped forward with Amos.

Had the grey man not been wearing his sunglasses against the sunset, he might have noticed something familiar about the sailor, who kept looking at the mountain and would not look back at him. But as it was, he suspected nothing.

Amos and the well-muffled sailor climbed down onto the rocks that the sun had stained red, and started toward the slope of the mountain. Once the grey man raised his glasses as he watched them go but lowered them quickly, for it was the most golden hour of the sunset then. The sun sank, and he could not see them anymore. Even so, he stood at the rail a long time till a sound in the darkness roused him from his reverie: *Blmvghm!*

Amos and Jack climbed long and hard through the evening. When darkness fell, at first they thought they would have to stop, but the clear stars made a mist over the jagged rocks, and a little later the moon rose. After that it was much easier going. Shortly the wind began. First a breeze merely tugged at their collars. Then rougher gusts began to nip their fingers. At last buffets of wind flattened them against the rock one moment, then tried to jerk them loose the next. The rope was very useful indeed, and neither one complained. They simply went on climbing, steadily through the hours. Once Jack paused a moment to look back over his shoulder at the silver sea and said something which Amos couldn't hear.

"What did you say?" cried Amos above the howl.

"I said," the prince cried back, "look at the moon!"

Now Amos looked over his shoulder too and saw that the white disk was going slowly down.

They began again, climbing faster than ever, but in another hour the bottom of the moon had already sunk below the edge of the ocean. At last they gained a fair-sized ledge where the wind was not so strong. Above, there seemed no way to go any higher.

Jack gazed out at the moon and sighed. "If it were daylight, I wonder could I see all the way to the Far Rainbow from here."

"You might," said Amos. But though his heart was with Jack, he still felt a good spirit was important to keep up. "But we might see it a lot more clearly from the top of this mountain." But as he said it, the last light of the moon winked out. Now even the stars were gone, and the blackness about them was complete. But as they turned to seek shelter in the rising wind, Amos cried, "There's a light!"

"Where's a light?" cried Jack.

"Glowing behind those rocks," cried Amos.

A faint orange glow outlined the top of a craggy boulder, and they hurried toward it over the crumbly ledge. When they climbed the rock, they saw that the light came from behind another wall of stone further away, and they scrambled toward it, pebbles and bits of ice rolling under their hands. Behind the wall they saw that the light was even stronger above another ridge, and they did their best to climb it without falling who-knows-how-many hundreds of feet to the foot of the mountain. At last they pulled themselves onto the ledge and leaned against the side, panting. Far ahead of them, orange flames flickered brightly and there was light on each face. For all the cold wind their faces were still shiny with the sweat of the effort.

"Come on," said Amos, "just a little way . . ."

And from half a dozen directions they heard: *Come on, just a little way . . . just a little way . . . little way. . . .*

They stared at each other and Jack jumped up. "Why we must be in the cave of . . ."

And echoing back they heard: *. . . must be in the cave of . . . in the cave of . . . cave of . . .*

". . . the North Wind," whispered Amos.

They started forward again toward the fires. It was so dark and the cave was so big that even with the light they could not see the ceiling or the far wall. The fires themselves burned in huge scooped out basins of stone. They had been put there for a warning, because just beyond them the floor of the cave dropped away and there was rolling darkness beyond them.

"I wonder if he's at home," whispered Jack.

Then before them was a rushing and a rumbling and a rolling like thunder, and from the blackness a voice said, "I am the North Wind, and I am very much at home."

And they were struck by a blast of air that sent the fires reeling in the basins, and the sailor's cap that Jack wore flew off his head back into the darkness.

"Are you really the North Wind?" Amos asked.

"Yes, I am really the North Wind," came the thunderous voice. "Now you tell me who you are before I blow you into little pieces and scatter them over the whole wide world."

"I am Amos and this is Jack, Prince of the Far Rainbow," said

Amos. "And we wandered into your cave by accident and meant nothing impolite. But the moon went down, so we had to stop climbing, and we saw your light."

"Where were you climbing to?"

Now Jack said, "To the top of the mountain where there is a piece of a mirror."

"Yes," said the North Wind, "there is a mirror there. A wizard so great and so old and so terrible that neither you nor I need worry about him placed it there a year and two days ago. I blew him there myself in return for a favor he did me a million years past, for it was he who made this cave for me by artful and devious magic."

"We have come to take the mirror back," said Jack.

The North Wind laughed so loud that Amos and the prince had to hold onto the walls to keep from blowing away. "It is so high and so cold up there that you will never reach it," said the Wind. "Even the wizard had to ask my help to put it there."

"Then," called Amos, "you could help us get there too?"

The North Wind was silent a whole minute. Then he asked, "Why should I? The wizard built my cave for me. What have you done to deserve such help?"

"Nothing yet," said Amos. "But we can help you if you help us."

"How can you help me?" asked the Wind.

"Well," said Amos, "like this. You say you are really the North Wind. How can you prove it?"

"How can you prove you are really you?" returned the Wind.

"Easily," said Amos. "I have red hair, I have freckles, I am five feet, seven inches tall, and I have brown eyes. All you need do is go to Hidalga who owns the Mariner's Tavern and ask her who has red hair, is so tall, with such eyes, and she will tell you, 'It is her own darling Amos.' And Hidalga's word should be proof enough for anybody. Now what do you look like?"

"What do I look like?" demanded the North Wind.

"Yes, describe yourself to me."

"I'm big and I'm cold and I'm blustery. . . ."

"That's what you feel like," said Amos. "Not what you look like. I want to know how I would recognize you if I saw you walking quietly down the street toward me when you were off duty."

"I'm freezing and I'm icy and I'm chilling. . . ."

"Again, that's not what you look like; it's what you feel like."

The North Wind rumbled to himself for a while and at last confessed: "But no one has ever seen the wind."

"So I had heard," said Amos. "But haven't you ever looked into a mirror?"

"Alas," sighed the North Wind, "mirrors are always kept inside people's houses where I am never invited. So I never had a chance to look in one. Besides, I have been too busy."

"Well," said Amos, "if you help get us to the top of the mountain, we will let you look into the fragment of the mirror." Then he added, "which is more than your friend the wizard did, apparently." Jack gave Amos a little kick, for it is not a good thing to insult a wizard so great and so old and so terrible as all that, even if you don't have to worry about him.

The North Wind mumbled and groaned around the darkness for a while and at last said, "Very well. Climb on my shoulders and I shall carry you up to the highest peak of this mountain. When I have looked into your mirror, I will carry you down again to where you may descend the rest of the way by yourselves."

Amos and Jack were happy as they had ever been, and the North Wind roared to the edge of the ledge and they climbed on his back, one on each shoulder. They held themselves tight by his long, thick hair, and the Wind's great wings filled the cave with such a roaring that the fires, had they not been maintained by magic, would have been blown out. The sound of the great wing feathers clashing against one another was like steel against bronze.

The North Wind rose up in his cave and sped toward the opening that was so high they could not see the top and so wide they could not see the far wall, and his hair brushed the ceiling, and his toenails scraped the floor, and the tips of his wings sent boulders crashing from either side as he leapt into the black.

They circled so high they cleared the clouds, and once again the stars were like diamonds dusting the velvet night. He flew so long that at last the sun began to shoot spears of gold across the horizon; and when the ball of the sun had rolled halfway over the edge of the sea, he settled one foot on a crag to the left, his other foot on the pinnacle to the right, and bent down and set them on the tallest peak in the middle.

"Now where is the mirror?" asked Amos, looking around.

The dawning sun splashed the snow and ice with silver.

"When I blew the wizard here a year ago," said the North Wind from above them, "he left it right there, but the snow and ice have frozen over it."

Amos and the prince began to brush the snow from a lump on the ground, and beneath the white covering was pure and glittering ice. It was a very large lump, nearly as large as the black trunk of the skinny grey man.

"It must be in the center of this chunk of ice," said Jack. As they stared at the shiny, frozen hunk, something moved inside it, and they saw it was the form of a lovely girl. It was Lea, who had appeared to them in the pool.

She smiled at them and said, "I am glad you have come for the second piece of the mirror, but it is buried in this frozen shard of ice. Once, when I was a girl, I chopped through a chunk of ice to get to an earring my mother had dropped the night before in a winter dance. That block of ice was the coldest and hardest ice any man or woman had ever seen. This block is ten degrees colder. Can you chop through it?"

"I can try," said Jack, "or perhaps die trying. But I can do no more and no less." And he took the small pickax they had used to help them climb the mountain.

"Will you be finished before breakfast time?" asked Amos, glancing at the sun.

"Of course before breakfast," said the prince, and fell to chopping. The ice chips flew around him, and he worked up such a sweat that in all the cold he still had to take off his shirt. He worked so hard that in one hour he had laid open the chunk, and there, sticking out, was the broken fragment of mirror. Tired but smiling, the prince lifted it from the ice and handed it to Amos. Then he went to pick up his shirt and coat.

"All right, North Wind," cried Amos. "Take a look at yourself."

"Stand so that the sun is in your eyes," said the North Wind, towering over Amos, "because I do not want anyone else to see before I have."

So Amos and Jack stood with the sun in their eyes, and the great blustering North Wind squatted down to look at himself in the mirror. He must have been pleased with what he saw, because he gave a long loud laugh that nearly blew them from the peak. Then he leapt a mile into the air, turned over three times, then swooped down upon them, grabbing them up and setting them on his shoulders. Amos and Jack clung to his long, thick hair as the Wind began to fly down the mountain, crying out in a windy voice: "Now I shall tell all the leaves and whisper to the waves who I am and what I look like, so they can chatter about it among themselves in autumn and rise and doff their caps to me before a winter storm." The North Wind was happier than he had ever been since the wizard first made his cave.

It gets light on the top of a mountain well before it does at the foot, and this mountain was so high that when they reached the bottom the sun was nowhere in sight, and they had a good half hour until breakfast time.

"You run and get back in your cell," said Amos, "and when I have given you enough time, I shall return and eat my eggs and sausages."

So the prince ran down the rocks to the shore and snuck onto the ship, and Amos waited for the sun to come up. When it did, he started back.

VI

But, at the boat, all had not gone according to Amos' plan during the night. The grey man, still puzzling over Amos' wet clothes—and at last he began to inquire whom Amos had solicited from the sailors to go with him—had gone to the brig himself.

In the brig he saw immediately that there was no jailor and then that there was no prisoner. Furious, he rushed into the cell and began to tear apart the bundle of blankets in the corner. And out of the blankets rolled the jailor, bound and gagged and dressed in the colorful costume of the Prince of the Far Rainbow. For it was the jailor's clothes that Jack had worn when he had gone with Amos to the mountain.

When the gag came off, the story came out, and the part of the story the jailor had slept through the grey man could guess for himself. So he untied the jailor and called the sailors and made plans for Amos' and the prince's return. The last thing the grey man did was take the beautiful costume back to his cabin where the black trunk was waiting.

When Amos came up to the ship with the mirror under his arm, he called, "Here's your mirror. Where are my eggs and sausages?"

"Sizzling hot and waiting," said the grey man, lifting his sunglasses. "Where is the sailor you took to help you?"

"Alas," said Amos, "he was blown away in the wind." He climbed up the ladder and handed the grey man the mirror. "Now we only have a third to go, if I remember right. When do I start looking for that?"

"This afternoon when the sun is its highest and hottest," said the grey man.

"Don't I get a chance to rest?" asked Amos. "I have been climbing up and down mountains all night."

"You may take a nap," said the grey man. "But come and have breakfast first." The grey man put his arm around Amos' shoulder and took him down to his cabin where the cook brought them a big, steaming platter of sausages and eggs.

"You have done very well," said the grey man pointing to the wall where he had hung the first two pieces of the mirror together. Now they could make out what the shape of the third would be. "And if you get the last one, you will have done very well indeed."

"I can almost feel the weight of those diamonds and emeralds and gold and pearls right now," said Amos.

"Can you really?" asked the grey man. He pulled a piece of green silk from his pocket, went to the black box, and stuffed it into a small square door: *Orlmnb!*

"Where is the third mirror hidden?" asked Amos.

"Two leagues short of over there is a garden of violent colors and rich perfume, where black butterflies glisten on the rims of pink marble fountains, and the only thing white in it is a silver-white unicorn who guards the third piece of the mirror."

"Then it's good I am going to get it for you," said Amos, "because even with your sunglasses, it would give you a terrible headache."

"Curses," said the grey man, "but you're right." He took from his pocket a strip of crimson cloth with orange design, went to the trunk and lowered it through a small round hole in the top. As the last of it dropped from sight, the thing in the box went: *Mlpbgrm!*

"I am very anxious to see you at the happiest moment of your life," said Amos. "But you still haven't told me what you and your nearest and dearest friend expect to find in the mirror."

"Haven't I?" said the grey man. He reached under the table and took out a white leather boot, went to the trunk, lifted the lid, and tossed it in.

Org! This sound was not from the trunk; it was Amos swallowing his last piece of sausage much too fast. He and the grey man looked at one another, and neither said anything. The only sound was from the trunk: *Grublmeumplefrmp . . . hic!*

"Well," said Amos at last, "I think I'll go outside and walk around the deck a bit."

"Nonsense," said the grey man smoothing his grey gloves over his wrists. "If you're going to be up this afternoon, you'd better go to sleep right now."

"Believe me, a little air would make me sleep much better."

"Believe *me*," said the grey man, "I have put a little something in your eggs and sausages that will make you sleep much better than all the air in the world."

Suddenly Amos felt his eyes grow heavy, his head grow light, and he slipped down in his chair.

When Amos woke up, he was lying on the floor of the ship's brig inside the cell, and Jack, in his underwear—for the sailors had jumped on him when he came back in the morning and given the jailor back his clothes—was trying to wake him up.

"What happened to you?" Amos asked, and Jack told him.

"What happened to you?" asked Jack, and Amos told him.

"Then we have been found out and all is lost," said the prince. "For it is noon already, and the sun is at its highest and hottest. The boat has docked two leagues short of over there, and the grey man must be about to go for the third mirror himself."

"May his head split into a thousand pieces," said Amos.

"Pipe down in there," said the jailor. "I'm trying to sleep." And he spread out his piece of grey canvas sail and lay down.

Outside, the water lapped at the ship, and after a moment Jack said, "A river runs by the castle of the Far Rainbow, and when you go down into the garden, you can hear the water against the wall just like that."

"Now don't be sad," said Amos. "We need all our wits about us."

From somewhere there was the sound of knocking.

"Though, truly," said Amos, glancing at the ceiling, "I had a friend once named Billy Belay, an old sailor with a wooden leg, I used to play jackstraws with. When he would go upstairs to his room in the Mariner's Tavern, you could hear him walking overhead just like that."

That knocking came again.

"Only that isn't above us," said Jack. "It's below."

They looked at the floor. Then Jack got down on his hands and knees and looked under the cot. "There's a trap door there," he whispered to Amos, "and somebody's knocking."

"A trap door in the *bottom* of a ship?" asked Amos.

"We won't question it," said Jack, "we'll just open it."

They grabbed the ring and pulled the door back. Through the opening there was only the green surface of the water. Then, below the surface, Lea appeared.

"What are you doing here?" whispered Amos.

"I've come to help you," she said. "You have gotten two thirds of the broken mirror. Now you must get the last piece."

"How did you get here?" asked Jack.

"Only the shiny surface of things keeps us apart," said Lea. "Now if you dive through here, you can swim out from under the boat."

"And once we get out from under the boat," said Amos, "we can climb back in."

"Why should we do that?" asked Jack.

"I have a plan," said Amos.

"But will it work even if the grey man is already in the garden of violent colors and rich perfumes, walking past the pink marble fountains where the black butterflies glisten on their rims?" asked Jack.

"It will work as long as the silver-white unicorn guards the fragment of the mirror," said Amos, "and the grey man doesn't have his hands on it. Now dive."

The prince dove and Amos dove after him.

"Will you pipe down in there," called the jailor without opening his eyes.

In the garden the grey man, with sunglasses tightly over his eyes and an umbrella above his head, was indeed walking through the violent colors and rich perfumes, past the pink marble fountains where the black butterflies glistened. It was hot, he was dripping with perspiration, and his head was in agony.

He had walked a long time, and even through his dark glasses he could make out the green and red blossoms, the purple fruit on the branches, the orange melons on the vines. The most annoying thing of all, however, were the swarms of golden gnats that buzzed about him. He would beat at them with the umbrella, but they came right back again.

After what seemed a long, long time, he saw a flicker of silver-white, and coming closer, he saw it was a unicorn. It stood in the little clearing, blinking. Just behind the unicorn was the last piece of the mirror.

"Well it's about time," said the grey man, and began walking toward it. But as soon as he stepped into the clearing, the unicorn snorted and struck his front feet against the ground, one after the other.

"I'll just get it quickly without any fuss," said the grey man. But when he stepped forward, the unicorn also stepped forward, and the grey man found the sharp point of the unicorn's horn against the grey cloth of his shirt, right where it covered his belly button.

"I'll have to go around it then," said the grey man. But when he moved to the right, the unicorn moved to the right; and when he moved to the left, the unicorn did the same.

From the mirror there was a laugh.

The grey man peered across the unicorn's shoulder, and in the piece of glass he saw not his own reflection but the face of a young woman. "I'm afraid," she said cheerfully, "that you shall never be able to pick up the mirror unless the unicorn lets you, for it was placed here by a wizard so great and so old and so terrible that you and I need not worry about him."

"Then what must I do to make this stubborn animal let me by? Tell me quickly because I am in a hurry and have a headache."

"You must prove yourself worthy," said Lea.

"How do I do that?"

"You must show how clever you are," said Lea. "When I was free of this mirror, my teacher, in order to see how well I had learned my lessons, asked me three questions. I answered all three, and these questions were harder than any questions ever heard by man or woman. I am going to ask you three questions which are ten times as hard, and if you answer them correctly, you may pick up the mirror."

"Ask me," said the grey man.

"First," said Lea, "who is standing just behind your left shoulder?"

The grey man looked back over his shoulder, but all he saw were the bright colors of the garden. "Nobody," he said.

"Second," said Lea, "who is standing just behind your right shoulder?"

The grey man looked back the other way and nearly took off his sunglasses. Then he decided it was not necessary, for all he saw was a mass of confusing colors. "Nobody," he said.

"Third," said Lea, "what are they going to do to you?"

"There is nobody there and they are going to do nothing," said the grey man.

"You have answered all three questions wrong," said Lea, sadly.

Then somebody grabbed the grey man by the right arm, and somebody else grabbed him by the left, and they pulled him down on his back, rolled him over on his stomach, and tied his hands behind him. One picked him up by the shoulders and the other by the feet, and they only paused long enough to get the mirror from the clearing, which the unicorn let them have gladly, for there was no doubt that they could have answered Lea's questions.

For one of the two was Amos, wearing the top half of the costume of the Prince of the Far Rainbow, minus a little green patch from the sleeve and a strip from the crimson cape; he had stood behind some bushes so the grey man could not see his less colorful pants. The other was Prince Jack himself, wearing the bottom of the costume, minus the white leather boot; he had stood behind a low-hanging branch so the grey man had not been able to see him from the waist up.

With the mirror safe—nor did they forget the grey man's umbrella and sunglasses—they carried him back to the ship. Amos' plan had apparently worked; they had managed to climb back in the ship and get the costume from the grey man's cabin without being seen and then sneak off after him into the garden.

But here luck turned against them, for no sooner had they reached the shore again when the sailors descended on them. The jailor had at last woken up and, finding his captives gone, had organized a searching party which set out just as Amos and the prince reached the boat.

"Crisscross, cross, and double cross!" cried the grey man triumphantly as once more Amos and Jack were led to the brig.

The trap door had been nailed firmly shut this time, and even Amos could not think of a plan.

"Cast off for the greyest and gloomiest island on the map," cried the grey man.

"Cast off!" cried the sailors.

"And do not disturb me till we get there," said the skinny grey man. "I have had a bad day today and my head is killing me."

The grey man took the third piece of mirror to his cabin, but he was too ill to fit the fragments together. So he put the last piece on top of the trunk, swallowed several aspirins, and lay down.

VII

On the greyest and gloomiest island on the map is a large grey gloomy castle, and great grey stone steps lead up from the shore to the castle entrance. This was the skinny grey man's gloomy grey home. On the following grey afternoon, the ship pulled up to the bottom of the steps, and the grey man, leading two bound figures, walked up to the door.

Later in the castle hall, Amos and the prince stood bound by the back wall. The grey man chuckled to himself as he hung up the two-thirds completed mirror. The final third was on the table.

"At last it is about to happen," said the grey man. "But first, Amos, you must have your reward for helping me so much."

He led Amos, still tied, to a small door in the wall. "In there is my jewel garden. I have more jewels than any man in the world. Ugh! They give me a headache. Go quickly, take your reward, and when you come back I shall show you a man living through the happiest moment of his life. Then I will put you and your jewels into the trunk with my nearest and dearest friend."

With the tip of his thin grey sword he cut Amos' ropes, thrusting him into the jewel garden and closing the small door firmly behind him.

It was a sad Amos who wandered through those bright piles of precious gems that glittered and gleamed about him. The walls were much too high to climb and they went all the way around. Being a clever man, Amos knew there were some situations in which it was a waste of wit to try and figure a way out. So, sadly, he picked up a small wheelbarrow lying on top of a hill of rubies and began to fill his pockets with pearls. When he had hauled up a cauldron full of gold from the well in the middle of the garden, he put all his reward in the wheelbarrow, went back to the small door and knocked.

The door opened and he was yanked through and bound up again. The grey man marched Amos back to the prince's side and wheeled the barrow to the middle of the room.

"In just a moment," said the thin grey man, "you will see a man living through the happiest moment of his life. But first I must make sure my nearest and dearest friend can see too." He went to the large black trunk, which seemed even blacker and larger, stood it on its side; then with the great iron key he opened it almost halfway so that it was opencd toward the mirror. But from where Amos and Jack were, they could not see into it at all.

The grey man took the last piece of the mirror, went to the wall, and fitted it in place, saying, "The one thing I have always wanted more than anything else, for myself, for my nearest and dearest friend, is a woman worthy of a prince."

Immediately there was thunder, and light shot from the restored glass. The grey man stepped back, and from the mirror stepped the beautiful and worthy Lea.

"Oh, happiness!" laughed the thin grey man. "She is grey too!"

For Lea was cloaked in grey from head to foot. But almost before the words were out, she loosed her grey cloak and it fell about her feet.

"Oh, horrors!" cried the thin grey man, and stepped back again.

Under her cloak she wore a scarlet cape with flaming rubies that glittered in the lightning. Now she loosed her scarlet cape and that too fell to the floor.

"Oh, misery!" screamed the grey man, and stepped back once more.

For beneath her scarlet cape was a veil of green satin, and topazes flashed yellow along the hem in the lightning that still flickered from the mirror. Now she threw the veil back from her shoulders.

"Oh, ultimate depression!" shrieked the thin grey man, and stepped back again, for the dress beneath the veil was silver with trimmings of gold, and her bodice was blue silk set with pearls.

The last step took the thin grey man right into the open trunk. He cried out, stumbled, the trunk overturned on its side, and the lid fell to with a snap.

And there wasn't any sound at all.

"I had rather hoped we might have avoided that," said Lea, as she came over to untie Jack and Amos. "But there is nothing we can do now. I can never thank you enough for gathering the mirror and releasing me."

"Nor can we thank you," said Amos, "for helping us do it."

"Now," said Jack, rubbing his wrists, "I can look at myself again and see why I am Prince of the Far Rainbow."

He and Lea walked to the mirror and looked at their reflections.

"Why," said Jack, "I am a prince because I am worthy to be a prince, and with me is a woman worthy to be a princess."

In the gilded frame now was no longer their reflection, but a rolling land of green and yellow meadows, with red and white houses, and far off a golden castle against a blue sky.

"That's the land of the Far Rainbow!" cried Jack. "We could almost step through into it!" And he began to go forward.

"What about me?" cried Amos. "How do I get home?"

"The same way we do," said Lea. "When we are gone, look into the mirror and you will see your home too."

"And that?" asked Amos, pointing to the trunk.

"What about it?" said Jack.

"Well, what's in it?"

"Look and see," said Lea.

"I'm afraid to," said Amos. "It has said such awful and terrible things."

"You afraid?" laughed Jack. "You, who rescued me three times from the brig, braved the grey swamp and rode the back of the North Wind?"

But Lea asked gently, "What did it say? I have studied the languages of men and perhaps I can help. What did it say?"

"Oh, awful things," said Amos, "like *onvbpmf,* and *elmblmpf,* and *orghmflbfe.*"

"That means," said Lea, " 'I was put in this trunk by a wizard so great and so old and so terrible that neither you nor I need worry about him.' "

"And it said *glumphvmr,* and *fuffle,* and *fulrmp,*" Amos told her.

"That means," said Lea, " 'I was put here to be the nearest and dearest friend to all those grim, grey people who cheat everybody they meet and who can enjoy nothing colorful in the world.' "

"Then it said *orlmnb,* and *mlpbgrm,* and *grublmeumplefrmp—hic!*"

"Loosely translated," said Lea, " 'One's duty is often a difficult thing to do with the cheerfulness, good nature, and diligence that others expect of us; nevertheless . . .' "

"And when the thin grey man fell into the trunk," said Amos, "it didn't make any sound at all."

"Which," said Lea, "can be stated as: 'I've done it.' Roughly speaking."

"Go see what's in the trunk," said Jack. "It's probably not so terrible after all."

"If you say so," said Amos. He went to the trunk, walked all around it three times, then gingerly lifted the lid. He didn't see anything, so he lifted it further. When he still didn't see anything, he opened it all the way. "Why, there's nothing in . . ." he began. But then something caught his eye at the very bottom of the trunk, and he reached in and picked it up.

It was a short, triangular bar of glass.

"A prism!" said Amos. "Isn't that amazing. That's the most amazing thing I ever heard of."

But he was alone in the castle hall. Jack and Lea had already left. Amos ran to the mirror just in time to see them walking away across the green and yellow meadows to the golden castle. Lea leaned her head on Jack's shoulder, and the prince turned to kiss her raven hair, and Amos thought: "Now there are *two* people living through the happiest moment of their lives."

Then the picture changed, and he was looking down a familiar, seaside, cobbled street, wet with rain. A storm had just ended and the clouds were breaking apart. Down the block the sign of the Mariner's Tavern swung in the breeze.

Amos ran to get his wheelbarrow, put the prism on top, and wheeled it to the mirror. Then, just in case, he went back and locked the trunk tightly.

Someone opened the door of the Mariner's Tavern and called inside, "Why is everybody so glum this evening when there's a beautiful rainbow looped across the world?"

"It's Amos!" cried Hidalga, running from behind the counter.

"It *is* Amos!" cried Billy Belay, thumping after her on his wooden leg.

Everyone else in the tavern came running outside too. Sure enough it was Amos, and sure enough a rainbow looped above them to the far horizons.

"Where have you been?" cried Hidalga. "We all thought you were dead."

"You wouldn't believe me if I told you," said Amos, "for you are always saying you take no man's jabbering seriously."

"Any man who can walk out of a tavern one night with nothing and come back in a week with that—" and she pointed to the wheelbarrow full of gold and jewels "—is a man to be taken seriously."

"Then marry me," said Amos, "for I always thought you had uncommonly good sense in matters of whom to believe and whom not to. Your last words have proved you worthy of my opinion."

"I certainly shall," said Hidalga, "for I always thought you an uncommonly clever man. Your return with this wheelbarrow has proved *you* worthy of *my* opinion."

"I thought you were dead too," said Billy Belay, "after you ran out of here with that thin grey man and his big black trunk. He told us terrible stories of the places he intended to go. And you just up and went with him without having heard anything but the reward."

"There are times," said Amos, "when it is better to know only the reward and not the dangers."

"And this was obviously such a time," said Hidalga, "for you are back now and we are to be married."

"Well, come in, then," said Billy, "and play me a game of jackstraws, and you can tell us all about it."

They went back into the tavern, wheeling the barrow before them.

"What is this?" asked Hidalga as they stepped inside. She picked up the glass prism from the top of the barrow.

"That," said Amos, "is the other end of the far rainbow."

"The other end of the rainbow?" asked Hidalga.

"Over there," said Amos pointing back out the door, "is that end. And over there is this end," and he pointed out the front window, "and right here is the other end."

Then he showed her how a white light shining through it would break apart and fill her hands with all the colors she could think of. K15

"Isn't that amazing," said Hidalga. "That's the most amazing thing I ever heard of."

"That's exactly what I said," Amos told her, and they were both very happy, for they were both clever enough to know that when a husband and wife agree, it means a long and happy marriage is ahead.